MW00713193

MARYLANDERS

A Story of the Civil War

By

James P. Zimmerman

Jim Zimmerman
with best wishes
to all who
read

Copyright © 2001 by James P. Zimmerman

ISBN 0-7414-1464-3

Published by:

INFINITY
PUBLISHING.COM

519 West Lancaster Avenue
Haverford, PA 19041-1413
Info@buybooksontheweb.com
www.buybooksontheweb.com
Toll-free (877) BUY BOOK
Local Phone (610) 520-2500
Fax (610) 519-0261

Printed in the United States of America

Printed on Recycled Paper

Published June 2003

MARYLANDERS

A Story of the Civil War

CHAPTER I. 1859

On the day of John Brown's raid, three of Mary Ann's hens laid eggs with double yolks, and that's what she remembered as starting the trouble. Her two boys, nearly grown, were helping her brother Sam with the butchering, so it was just her and Sissy at home, getting on with the evening chores. The 12-year old girl came up from the henhouse, red-faced, eyes popping. "Mama, Mama," she said, "look at the size." She was holding one of the brown whoppers in her free hand. "And I found two more."

"Gracious," Mary Ann said, "Grandma and Mama always said double eggs meant something was gonna happen, something important. I wonder..." She stopped, hearing first the instrument twanging, then the clatter of wagon wheels and harness.

Johnny's voice broke through the sharp October breeze, catching the melody Frankie was strumming on his mouth harp and gaining resonance as the wagon moved up the lane.

"Our cow don't give milk in summer," Johnny sang,
"Sing song kitty, can'tcha ki-me-oh,
So we have to take it from her,
Sing song kitty, can'tcha ki-me-oh."

Lord, she thought, boys musta been around that Rudy Barnes or some of them other mountain boys. Frankie continued playing while Johnny drove the team past the dairy house over to the wash shed.

"Ma," Johnny shouted, "Sam give us some fresh from the butcherin'. You want it in the meat house or should we carry it in the kitchen?"

"What'd he send?"

"Liver, brains, piece of side meat, half dozen feet, brung some cracklins too."

"I'll cook up some of the brains and liver for supper. The rest you best put in the meat house. It's salted down, ain't it?"

"Side meat is, but the feet ain't," Johnny said. He lugged the wooden tub of fresh butchered meat inside.

"What's that racket?" Frankie asked. He'd been unhooking the team's traces and getting ready to lead them to the stable in the towering red barn, but he stopped now and stared down the lane toward the church steeple, which peeked above the knoll below the farmhouse.

That's when Mary Ann heard the boy whooping, even before he got to the hill by the church. "Riding like the devil's after him," she said. "Somethin's happened."

Sissy emerged from the house, having put the eggs in the cupboard, and Johnny followed a few seconds later. All four stood and stared as the horse and rider galloped toward them. "Caleb Matthews," Frankie said.

"What's got him so het up?" Johnny said.

Mary Ann stared at the rider, while a chill October wind whipped about her skirts, bringing tears to her pale gray eyes. The chickens clustered around her, clucking and cackling, their feathers ruffled in the breeze. The team of horses began prancing around, while Frankie held the reins, and one of them whinnied.

"Hush," Frankie said, and pushed open the gate and led the team to their stalls where he began removing harness, watching through the door as Matthews rode up and began shouting.

"Miss Fraley," the boy yelled, trying to be heard over the cackling chickens. "Pa sent me over to tell y'all there's trouble up at Harpers Ferry. Some ol' man from Kansas and

2

a bunch of abolitionists done took over the arsenal up there, and they're gonna set all the niggers free. Johnny, Pa says he's gonna get the guards together, so you best get ready."

"Caleb," Mary Ann said, "what on earth are you talkin' about?"

"It's the truth, ma'am, Mister Holter and Mack Handley was up to Jefferson to get some supplies, and that's where they heard about it. They say it's a feller name of Brown."

"You think it's Osawatomie Brown. He's the one who killed folks in Kansas, just 'cause they had slaves."

"Yes'm, that's the one."

"When's your pa want to get the guards together?"

"He said it's too late today. Assemble the first thing in the morning at the store. Bobby went up to Jefferson to let 'em know. Pa done rode to Frederick to talk to the colonel."

"Don't make no sense, Ma," Johnny said. "What's an abolitionist doin' around here?"

"You know as much as I do," Mary Ann said. "Was there any shootin', Caleb?"

"Mr. Holter, he said they thought there was, but I ain't sure, ma'am. I gotta go now and tell some of the other folks."

"Well, you run on, we still got chores to do."

Francis had gotten the horses stabled and fed and watched the rider gallop down the lane. "I'm goin' with you, Johnny," he said to his brother. "I know I only been to a few drills, but I'm seventeen, that's old enough."

"Reckon Frankie can come along, Mama? Me and Richard will keep him with us, keep him outta trouble."

"I'd rather he didn't, John. Them abolitionists is crazy. There might be shootin'."

"Frankie's a good shot, almost as good as me, better'n most. I'll see he don't get hurt none."

"I don't need nobody to look out for me. I can take care of myself."

Johnny pulled off his brother's cap and roughed up his mop of shaggy brown hair, while Francis laughed and grabbed Johnny's leg and attempted to wrestle him to the ground. Both boys were laughing while Sissy squealed at their antics. Mary Ann shook her head and turned away. "You three stop your foolin' around and get to your chores," she called over her shoulder.

Johnny was the image of his father, dead these past ten years. She had no record of how John had looked, no painting, not even a drawing. Nowadays, there was something called a daguerreotype that could take a man's picture, but still, she could see him in her mind, for her oldest son was like her dead husband, his crooked smile, his slim body, his wily gray eyes. Francis was different, stocky and short, strong in the shoulders and chest, like her father and the clan of Zimmermans that had left the Palatine over a century ago.

At supper, she said to Johnny, "I reckon you'll be seein' Mary Lib."

"Tell her the news," he replied, "unless her pap or that brother of hers done found out."

"He's a brat," Sissy said.

"Well, I can't argue with that, Sis. He's a pain in the behind."

"John, watch your language," Mary Ann said. Sissy blushed and giggled.

Francis wasn't interested in the talk. "Pass over some more or them brains and that sauerkraut," he said.

2

Two miles away from the Fraley farm, Benjamin Horine sat in his parlor alone and ran his fingers through thick white hair. He had just returned from the store and Ed Holter's words rang through his mind. "Damned abolitionist trash," the storekeeper had said, "stirring up the niggers. Something's got to be done."

Had it really come to this so soon, Horine thought. What if they came down here and tried to take away Jeremiah and his family? Why I'd have to fight.

4

Government was doing nothing as usual. Buchanan was as worthless a President as he could remember, even though he'd voted for the man.

"Dinner's ready, dear," his wife said. She had opened the door quietly and looked in with concern. She'd never seen him so disconcerted over something political. It was as bad as he'd been when Queenie, his favorite brood mare, had gotten an infected foot.

The eight children gathered while their father said grace and then sat quietly to their meal. Tillie, the slave woman, stood by while Elsie and Ben served the children and then themselves. It was October and they were having roast duckling from Ben's hunting trip at a cousin's lodge along the Chesapeake. The three oldest boys had accompanied him, but mostly they observed while their father did the shooting.

After the meal, Tillie removed the dishes and served hot chocolate. When she was finished, Elsie closed the doors to the kitchen, and all nine looked attentively at their patriarch. He led them in their usual after-dinner prayers and then held up his hand for them all to stay.

"There is trouble across the land," Horine said. "Holter told me that abolitionists, scum of the earth, have taken over the arsenal at Harpers Ferry."

"Oh dear, I hope not," Elsie said. "Sometimes Mister Holter gets things mixed up."

"No, it's quite accurate, my dear. Hiram sent one of his boys by a while ago. He told Richard to come to a guard rally tomorrow morning."

Richard, his oldest son, nodded. He was quiet, grown to full manhood, shouldering his share of the farm work while studying for the law under the tutelage of a lawyer in nearby Frederick. "A lot of people don't have slaves," he said. "Some even think it's wrong."

Horine nodded. "I know, son, but Maryland's leaders have always been slave holders. We're the people who've made this state, not hill farmers scratching around to raise a few hogs. Slavery is practiced all through history, even in

5

the Bible. The problem is the northern abolitionists. They just won't let the south be, so more and more, it looks like we may have no choice but to secede if we're ever to have peace."

Elsie Horine retired to the kitchen where Tillie was cleaning up after the evening meal. Elsie was a slender woman who had bore her strong-willed husband nine children. All were alive but a baby boy who'd died of croup years earlier. Elsie was from an old Baltimore family, whose branches reached into three states, north and south. She fretted about the slavery problem. Her family was divided over the issue, but there wasn't a secessionist or an abolitionist in either camp, just people who wanted the whole thing put aside so they could continue their lives.

Later in the sitting room, Elsie was joined by her oldest daughter, Rebecca, at thirteen already a striking girl with silky brown hair and crystal eyes. "My goodness, Mama," she said, "Papa surely is riled."

"Your father doesn't like to be told what he can and can't do."

"But nobody could take away Jeremiah or Tillie, could they? They belong to us, and they're so happy here."

"Father thinks the Yankees will pass a law to abolish slavery, so I suppose they'd be set free, though Lord knows what those poor darkies would do with themselves. I just hate to even think about it. Some say it could lead to war."

"Richard says if there's a war, he'll fight for the south, but he wonders about some of his friends."

Elsie listened as the chilly Autumn wind rattled the shutters. "We'll have to pray that it works out somehow, honey," she said.

The three oldest brothers went to the barn to finish their chores after their father finally quit lecturing them about the propriety of slave holding.

"Pop sure has his dander up," Jacob, the seventeen year old, said.

"Don't blame him," Claiborne said. "Imagine some abolitionist comin' down here and stirring up trouble."

"You reckon the guards will be goin' up there?" Jacob said.

"I hope so," Richard said. "Gives me a chance to try out that new bay."

"I should be in the guard," Jacob said. "I'm as good a rider as you."

"You're still a baby," Claib said, "and neither of us can ride as good as Richard."

"Yeah, but you can't see worth spit, Claib. You gotta wear them specs or you'll shoot your own foot off. Raise quite a ruckus if you up and shot ol' Captain Sinn in the butt."

"Yeah, that'd be a Sinn sin," Richard said, "but if you up and winged Brad Johnson or Matthews, there'd be the devil to pay."

Claiborne laughed, pushed Richard backwards, and grabbed Jacob by the waist. In a moment, all three were wrestling and laughing in the straw inside the stable. In the house, the other five, Rebecca and her three younger sisters, Jennifer, Grace, and Betsy, and her three year old brother, Timmy, were already headed for bed.

3

The Horine farm covered two hundred acres of prime rolling farmland a few miles from Frederick, along the road that led southwest through the hamlets of Jefferson and Petersville, and then on to Harpers Ferry where the Shenandoah joined the Potomac. Horine was best known for the quality horses he bred and sold and occasionally raced.

A mile away lay a smaller farm owned by Samuel and Susanna Zimmerman. Sam was Mary Ann Fraley's older brother and her advisor since John Fraley had died suddenly ten years before, leaving her with three small children. Sam stood along the pike as a group of riders gathered, including his neighbor, Hiram Matthews.

"Hey, Hiram," Johnny Fraley called, "we gonna get us some abolitionists." He and Francis had stopped to tell Sam they wouldn't be able to help that morning because the guard was called up.

"Gonna make sure they stay in Virginia," Matthews replied.

"What's our men gettin' into it for?" Sam asked. "That damn fool Brown ain't gonna find no abolitionists around here."

Peck Handley was seated on a heavy farm wagon drawn by a droopy eyed team. "I tell you, Sam," Handley said, "them niggers and them damn abolitionists is got guns from the arsenal and they're gonna raise hell."

"There ain't that many colored in Harpers Ferry," Sam responded, "and Brown ain't got no way to get word out if the Virginia militia's got the town surrounded."

"We'll make sure things are safe on this side of the river," Matthews said. "Shouldn't be too much trouble for these boys." Matthews gestured at the dozen or so men who had gathered nearby at the rally point. They were awaiting the arrival of the bulk of the guard's troops, commanded by Colonel Edward Shriver, and one of the three companies of volunteer firemen, led by Captain John Sinn.

By late morning, the assembly of riders, wagons, and marchers were plodding through Jefferson toward Petersville, joined by more diversely uniformed men as they pushed toward the Potomac and Virginia. They were armed with muskets, some rifled, most smooth bores, and a scattering of shotguns.

The riders moved ahead and when they reached the turn-off to the railroad town of Berlin, Richard Horine shouted, "C'mon, Fraley, race you to the river."

"Yahoo," Johnny yelled and slapped his gray farm horse with his cap. Both galloped off with Fraley in the lead, but it was no race. Horine horses were bred for speed, and Richard's mount soon sprinted ahead, leaving Johnny and his winded workhorse in the dust.

8

"Damn you, Horine," Johnny called, once they were at the river's edge, "you about killed ol' Buck."

Richard grinned. "Get yourself a Horine horse, John, like King here, and you won't keep gettin' whipped."

"You tell your Pa to give me a good price, like maybe ten dollars, and I'll buy one."

"You know my father better than that. He'd skin me if I even suggested such a price."

They waited at the water's edge as other riders rode up-- Frankie, Claiborne, and Shanks Duval, a buddy from a farm near Petersville. A few minutes later their officers arrived and scowled at them. Shriver shook his head and declared, "You boys get back in the ranks so you look like soldiers and not damn fools."

The mischievous riders grinned at each other as they worked their way to the rear of the cavalry and splashed into the river. The infantrymen, many arriving on foot but mostly in wagons, formed their companies and marched upriver to cross on the bridge.

Shriver led his men into the town and found that local militia had surrounded Brown and his small group and kept them contained in the arsenal. Colonel Lee of the regular army had arrived with a contingent of marines and taken charge. With the Colonel's permission, Captain Sinn tried to talk Brown into surrendering, but the hostile abolitionist refused. Shortly afterwards, the marines stormed the arsenal and subdued the insurgents. The Marylanders waited nearby, hoping for action, but never called.

Afterward, Johnny and Richard chatted with a young army lieutenant who'd accompanied Lee from Arlington. "Name's Stuart," the officer said, "James Stuart. Colonel Lee's the best officer in the army."

"How come?" Johnny asked.

"He was a hero in the Mexican War, won a bunch of medals. Man knows his business. You saw how quick he settled this mess."

"Where's he from?" Richard asked.

"He's a Virginian, like me. Virginians make the best soldiers."

"Hah," Johnny said, "what about Andy Jackson? And Winfield Scott, ain't he the top dog? Where's he from?"

"Virginia," Stuart said. "Zack Taylor was a Virginian too."

"Richard," Johnny said, "ain't Maryland had any good soldiers?"

"Yeah, I think some of us fought the British darn good when they burned the White House."

"I'm talkin' about now," Stuart said. "Y'all stick with us Virginians and you'll be in good company."

Johnny watched as Stuart rode away. "Man, ain't he a dandy?"

"Yeah," Richard said, "he's sure full of himself, but with that uniform, he looks like a soldier."

"I don't think I could stand havin' him as my officer."

"I grant you he's not like Matthews, but I could get used to him."

4

On December second, Richard and Johnny rode to Charles Town. The streets were packed, and armed sentries surrounded the jail. Gallows had been built of new timber in the town square, as the huge crowd gathered to witness the hanging. The two young men had to settle for sharing an observation perch with several youngsters in one of the sycamores surrounding the square.

John Brown was led by a troop of twelve armed soldiers, followed by two officers, one of them Captain Thomas Jackson of the Virginia Military Institute, plus a clergyman and Virginia's Governor Wise.

At the steps to the hanging platform, Brown paused and glared at the bystanders, but said nothing.

"That ol' man must be crazy," Johnny said.

Richard nodded. "I hope all this trouble stops here," he said.

10

"I don't reckon," Johnny said. "There's too many other damn fools itching to fight."

The trapdoor dropped and Brown passed into history. The two friends rode homeward together, nursing their thoughts, to where their paths separated.

CHAPTER II. 1860

Mary Ann finished the supper dishes and moved to her rocking chair on the front porch. Lights flickered on across the valley as candles and whale oil lamps were lit. Smoke poured from chimneys, cattle bawled, horses whinnied, chickens fluttered and cackled as they wrestled for roost space. In the woods a whippoorwill called, and a barn owl began to hoot somewhere nearby.

"Ma," Johnny called, interrupting her musings.

"You startled me, John."

"That yellow cow acts like she ready to calve. I put her out in the orchard so she don't go hiding back in the bushes like the last time."

"Is she havin' any trouble?"

"I don't think so. You know me and Horine are going hunting tomorrow, so I'll be using Pa's ol' gun. I got some new powder down at Holter's yesterday. That's when I saw Richard."

"I'm surprised his uppity father let's him come up here. I like Elsie, but Ben Horine is a snob."

"Me and Richard get along."

"Is Francis goin' with you?"

"Nah, him and Eddie are gonna get in the pumpkins at Sam's."

A calico cat ambled onto the porch and leaped into Mary Ann's lap, joined by a gray and white tom who rubbed himself on Johnny's calf. In the yard, the hound napped and periodically scratched itches. "Sam was over for a minute,"

12

she said. "He's all worked up over politics, says if Lincoln gets elected, there might be a war."

"Why's he say that? Because of the slaves?"

"I reckon. Sam says most slave owners think all the Republicans are abolitionists."

"Well, I gotta vote for somebody. Who's Sam like, Douglas?"

"Bell is what he said, though I declare, I hardly ever heard of him."

"The whole thing is crazy. That ol' fool Brown is what got this mess started."

Mary Ann rocked slowly. She'd had bad dreams again, the same as when her husband had died. "I don't want no war," she said.

"Me and Richard is best friends. I sure wouldn't want to have to fight him."

2

Horine looked up from his breakfast coffee as his son entered the dining room. Richard was carrying his rifle, dressed for hunting. "Aren't you going with your brothers?" he asked.

"Jakey and Claib have already left, heading down to the Manor Woods. I saw Fraley at the store yesterday, and he said the woods up beyond his place is full of squirrels, so I'm goin' up there."

Horine frowned. "Fraleys aren't our kind of people," he said.

"Johnny and me have been friends ever since the first grade. He's a lot of fun, and he's a good shot. I like hunting with him."

"You know they don't hold with slavery. Name used to be Froelich, but they changed it because it was too German. If the north elects this man Lincoln, we'll have a fight on our hands. People like them will be on the other side."

Richard sighed. They'd been over this before. "I hope it don't ever come to that, Papa. I'd sure hate to have to fight against Johnny. I'll ask him about it today if I get a chance. See how he feels."

"You do that. Tell me what he says."

It was barely sunrise when Johnny and Richard rode a half mile into the woods behind the Fraley's 105 acre farm. They tied their horses and loaded their rifles. Richard had a light, half stock percussion rifle with an engraved lock. John's rifle was longer and heavier, a flintlock his father had converted to percussion several years before.

They walked quietly about a hundred yards into an oak grove and took positions well apart. Within ten minutes the surrounding forest was filled with sound. John braced his rifle against the tree trunk and took aim. A second later, he fired and a fat gray squirrel tumbled to the ground. The woods resounded with the noise and then quieted, so Richard crept several yards to a new position. A moment later, he also fired, but the only result was a few leaves fluttering downward. John looked at him and grinned. Richard scowled but found a new target as soon as he reloaded, and then he too had success.

By midmorning their pouches were full, and they lounged by a mountain stream. "Folks gettin' all riled up over this election," Johnny said.

"Yeah, my Pa will have a stroke if Lincoln is elected. Are you all for him?"

"Heck no. My uncle said to vote for Bell."

"We'll vote for Breckenridge. Pa can't stand Douglas no more, says he talks out of both sides of his head."

"We don't care for Lincoln, but we hold with the Union."

"People in Frederick really like Breckenridge. Pa and me are goin' to hear him speak next week. Why don't you come along?"

"He sounds too much like a secessionist to us."

"That's the rub, isn't it? If Lincoln wins, Pa says we oughta leave the Union."

14

"Yeah, but if Breckenridge wins, then there'll be more trouble over the slaves and the rest of it."

They sat quietly, staring at the stream and listening to warblers playing in the bushes. "Shucks, Richard," Johnny said, "if things keep goin' this way, you and me will be on opposite sides. That ain't right, I don't want to fight you."

"Me neither, John. That would be stupid."

"What'd happen if Maryland left the Union? Would we be a different country?"

"I reckon. I mean, we've been a bunch of states who got together to help each other out, and now we don't want to do it any more."

"I don't like that. Hell, we'll be quarreling all the time."

"We already are. Some of the northerners say they'll fight to keep us in, whether we want it or not."

"Reckon it's better for us to stay in and work things out."

"Pa says we've been trying to work things out for seventy years, and ain't got nowhere, and it keeps gettin' worse. It may be time to leave."

"I don't want to do it, Richard. This is a good country."

"Not our doing, John, but I reckon I'll go along with whatever Pa decides."

The two friends considered one another and saw the hopelessness of their positions and gave it up. They mounted their horses and rode back to the Fraley farmhouse, each feeling he was caught in a trap.

3

Holter's store stood along the Jefferson Pike near a branch of the Ballenger Creek. It was a modest ramshackle establishment that served as community meeting place as well as general dispenser of staples, canned goods, hardware, nails, farm supplies, tobacco, butchering items, candies, patent medicines, and a selection of wares so varied that the proprietor sometimes forgot their existence. In the front and at the sides stood two saddled horses, three teams hitched to various conveyances, and four lop-eared mules with a wagon load of corn, all awaiting their owners who currently were inside. Several dogs of various shapes, colors, and sizes lounged about, scratching, sniffing, dozing.

Several men sat on wooden benches in back of the store. Peck Handley was holding forth on the day's events. "I tell ya, Holter, it don't make no sense to concern ourselves with secesh. Hell, if them states leave the Union, what's it matter to us. I ain't worried a bit whether they got the niggers as slaves or not. I ain't got none and I don't want none, but if them secesh want 'em, let 'em have 'em, in or out of the Union." Peck leaned over and splashed tobacco juice into the cuspidor.

Squire Henry Fulmer was having none of it. "Peck, you're more full of crap than one of my wife's geese. Dang it, this here is a great country, and if we break it up, why we'll be no better than them people in Europe, quarreling and fighting among ourselves all the time."

Hiram Matthews leaned over to spit and broke in, "Hell's bells, Squire, we're doin' that already--fightin' and quarrelin'-- and it's gettin' worse. Far as I'm concerned, let 'em secede. We don't need 'em."

"What if Maryland secedes? What'll you say then?"

"That ain't so bad neither. All the politicians are crooks anyhow, pickin' our pockets ever' dang chance they get."

"Yeah, that's right," Peck said. "With Maryland outta the Union, why hell, Squire, there'd be only that bunch in the state to rob us, not a bunch here and in Washington too."

Peck and Hiram broke into raucous laughter, amused at their own wit.

The Squire was unconvinced. "You fellas can laugh all you want, but you don't know how serious this is. We'd always be fightin' among ourselves, and before you know it, them foreigners, England and France and the like, would be over here again, messing in our affairs. Don't you think so, Sam?"

Until that point, Sam Zimmerman had avoided the debate, listening with some amusement. "Well," he said, "all you men make good points, but there's other things that worry me. Suppose Maryland secedes and then suppose the federal government, whoever is President, asks the governor to call up the militia and the guards to put down what they call a Maryland rebellion? What're you men gonna do?"

"Could they do that?" Hiram asked.

"I think they could. What about men like you, Hiram? You been in the army. You gonna stand with the country or the state?"

"Dammit, Sam," Peck said, "why'd you have to go and get me all mixed up?"

Ed Holter shrugged. "All I can say, boys, is that somebody better come up with some good ideas quick, or this here country is gonna be in a helluva mess." He turned toward the front of the store when he heard the bell over the door clatter.

"Hell, look who's comin'," Peck muttered.

"Howdy, Mister Horine," Holter addressed his customer, "what can I get you today?"

Ben Horine glanced at the group in the rear of the store. "Um, here's a list from Missus Horine. I'll need some liniment too."

Horine squinted at the group. "Sam," he nodded to his neighbor.

Sam met his stare. "Benjamin. How's the family?"

"Fine, thank you, sir, and yours?"

"Very well, sir, very well."

Horine looked over the group again and nodded. "Gentlemen," he murmured and turned away.

Only Hiram replied, saying, "Mr. Horine."

"Here's your order, Mr. Horine," Holter called.

Horine counted out a dollar and eight cents silently, picked up his supplies and departed without looking back. The atmosphere in the store relaxed.

"I don't think he likes us much," Matthews said.

"Well, I don't like him, that's for damn sure," Peck replied.

17

"First I've seen him for a while," Sam said. "The way he looked at us, I felt like an enemy. If he's secesh, maybe I am his enemy. Maybe we all are."

"Election's the problem," Holter said. "Ain't a one of them candidates I can hold to. I hear Horine and his cronies are pushing for Breckenridge, that's just askin' for trouble."

"Lincoln ain't no better," Peck said. "Hell, all him and them abolitionists want is to free the niggers."

"I ain't sure of that," Sam said. "What I've read of his speeches, he just wants to stop slavery goin' into the territories, but I do believe Bell is a better choice."

"Damn if I can see that, Sam," Hiram said. "We always been Democrats. What's wrong with Douglas?"

"Nothin', except the south don't want him, so he can't win."

"I don't see how none of them can win," Peck said. "North won't go for Breckenridge. South hates Lincoln. No matter what, it's gonna be a mess."

Outside the animals were restless as leaves scraped across the dry October grass. Sam heard his horses rattle their harness. "Time to go," he said. "This conversation riles my innards."

4

Horine and his three oldest sons sat together in the parlor of the brick home built sixty years earlier by his grandfather. A November night wind rattled the shutters and caused the fireplace to sputter and smoke. Richard leaned over and poked at the embers while his father lit his pipe. Claiborne and Jacob whispered to one another across the room. The election was three days past, most of the returns counted, and they knew the worse--Lincoln had won.

"Papa, you always said we can't accept this. What do we do?"

"You're right, Richard, we can be no part of a country run by Lincoln and his ilk. For us, the Union is dead as of now. Maryland must secede, and we must fight to keep her free."

"We're ready to fight," Claib said, wiping his glasses with his handkerchief. "Most of the guards stand with the south."

"It's not that easy, sons," Horine said. "There's a lot of Marylanders who don't want to leave the Union, but they don't like Lincoln any better than we do. We've got to win them over to our way of thinking."

"What will Virginia do?" Richard asked.

"Virginia's the key," Horine said. "I think that if Virginia secedes, Maryland will follow."

"Can't we do something other than sit on our behinds and wait?" Jacob said. "We're ready to take on them northerners now."

Horine smiled. Jacob had always been the most outgoing, the most impetuous of his children. "Keep your shirt on, Jacob. The pot is coming to a boil. I'm meeting with some of our like minded friends in a little while. After that, we'll know better how to proceed. Mark you well, the north will not get away with this outrage."

"Want us to get your horse saddled?" Richard asked.

"Thank you, yes. I'll just make my peace with mother."

Later, beside the barn, the brothers watched their father ride down the farm lane. "I reckon we'll know what's to happen before Spring," Richard said.

"I can hardly wait," Jacob said.

Claiborne nodded and walked away. "What's wrong with him?" Jacob asked.

"It's his eyes," Richard said. "Pa needs help with the horses, and Claib's afraid he'll have to stay."

"Heck, he can shoot as good as you or me."

"That's true, but you know how Pa and Mama are about him. Pa is making plans to supply horses for our army if it comes to war, and that's a big job. He's gonna need help."

"Do you think war's gonna come?"

Richard stared at the crescent moon rising in the east. "Yeah," he said, "it'll come. Country's gettin' riled. There'll

19

be a fight, maybe not for long, but the north won't let the south get away easy. They want our cotton."

"What about your friend, Fraley?"

"I give up on John. His mom was a Zimmerman, and they never have stood with slavery. They came down from Pennsylvania a ways back, and they think like Yankees. Hiram Matthews too."

"To hell with all of them," Jacob said.

Richard frowned but didn't respond. Jacob went off to find Claib, so he strolled out to the pasture behind the barn, next to the cabin where the slave family lived. Three horses looked up and came to the fence where he distributed slices of knobby apples he'd taken from the tree in the backyard. His favorite was a big chestnut named King, but he liked the other two almost as much--Queenie, a heavy boned black mare and her colt, Prince, nearly two years old and already one of the farm's best performers.

"You animals get yourselves ready," Richard said. "We may be doing some traveling pretty soon." The horses munched the apples and flicked their ears. A chilly wind blew a torrent of leaves from the maples, and autumn clouds skittered across the new moon. Night birds flashed overhead in the darkness.

5

In January, five men sat in the shadows by a fireplace in a large Georgian brick home in Frederick. They had met weekly since the November election and their collective frustration had mounted into fury.

A lawyer named Seth Hatcher pounded the table. "Gentlemen," he said, "we agree that Lincoln's election has been a catastrophe for Maryland. I'm convinced that he means to imprison the south so he can keep us in the Union. We must do something to stop him from taking office, and if that fails, the Union must be broken. I've been in touch with Governor Lowe and he agrees wholeheartedly." Enoch Louis Lowe had served as Maryland's governor in an earlier administration. He was an ardent supporter of the south and remained active in the state's political arena.

"Let's get to the point," a man named Varley said. "If we're going to stop Lincoln, what are the possibilities?"

"Kilgour, Horine, and I have been working on this," Hatcher said. "The newspapers say Lincoln will travel cross country by rail, making a number of stops, and eventually getting to Washington by way of Philadelphia and Baltimore. He'll be surrounded by guards, but we think there'll be an opportunity to get him."

"Assassinate him?"

"What else?"

"I guess that's the best choice, but how do we keep our skirts clean?"

"I don't like it," Horine said. "I hate the idea of murder, but nothing else makes any sense if we're to save our way of life without war."

"Won't killing Lincoln set off a war anyhow?"

"Who knows? If it happens, so be it," Kilgour responded. "Let me spell it out. We've got two possibilities. Some of our people are close to two of Lincoln's bodyguards, and we may be able to get one of them to do the job, but that takes a lot of nerve because it might cost the man his life. The more likely opportunity is when Lincoln travels through Baltimore, where he'll have to change trains. Brown here says Baltimore is strongly secessionist and furious at Lincoln, so it will be no trick to get a crowd organized to impede his way through the city. That gives us a chance to plant assassins in the crowd.

The man named Brown added, "I have long felt eliminating Lincoln is our best move, so this is an opportunity where we have the advantage. He's a big man, an easy target. Hamlin is more of a politician, more likely to concede to the south's point of view."

"I think Seward will be running things anyhow," Varley said, "and we can deal with him once Lincoln is out of the way."

CHAPTER III. WAR

On April 14, the day Fort Sumter surrendered, the three older Horine brothers sat with their father in the parlor. Elsie begged her husband to permit her to join them, but as was the custom, she was excluded from man talk.

"Papa," Richard said, "you've taught us to do our duty, and duty requires us to join with those who are forming an army to defend the South, even though Maryland has not seceded. We've prepared ourselves in the Manor Brigade and are ready to fight. Some of our friends have already gone to Virginia."

"Who?"

"Duval and two of his cousins, maybe others."

"They're from Petersville?"

"Near there. They've got farms in the Merryland area."

"I've talked to Captain Johnson and he's ready to leave for Virginia once she secedes, whether Maryland secedes or not. He expects hundreds of men will go with him, but he's still trying to force Hicks to call a legislative session for a vote on secession."

"Can't our supporters do something about Hicks?" Claiborne asked.

"We've tried, but the Governor won't budge. The legislature has to vote on it, and they can't meet unless he calls a special session. The latest rumor is that he's planning to call the session away from Annapolis, maybe here in Frederick. Our people are worried it may be a trick to arrest those who favor secession, but I don't believe that. I voted for Hicks, I still can't believe he's backing Lincoln."

"He wouldn't let federal troops go through the state," Richard said.

"That was encouraging, but he claims the state's neutral, and the Yankees are still getting into Washington somehow. Look, I'm proud of you boys for taking this stand, but there are two things I must require of you. First, wait and see what Virginia does. I expect their legislature to vote in a few days, and if Virginia goes, there's hope we'll gain enough support for Maryland to follow. Then our next move will be obvious. My other concern is that if Maryland does not secede, we must do everything in our power to help the South. It's my plan to make this farm a center for supplying horses, but I can't do it alone, not even with our slave to help. One of you must stay."

"We expected this, Papa," Richard said, "and we've agreed among ourselves that if one must stay, Claib will do it, like you asked. He wants to fight, but there's the problem of his eyes."

"Couldn't you hire someone, Papa, or get another slave?" Claiborne said. "Jeremiah is almost as good as a white man."

"I need help I can depend on. I regret keeping you, son, but you can do as much for the South as your brothers by helping me."

Horine looked at each of the three young men. All were taller than he, handsome and strong. He could not ask for better children, and he was about to send two of them off to what might soon be a war, perhaps even to their deaths. "You honor me, sons," he said. "Perhaps you have the hardest lot of all, Claiborne, helping me here in the midst of many enemies, but sons, many Marylanders share our view, and our cause must prevail."

Moments later their meeting ended and the three brothers walked out of the house onto the front porch and looked across the yard where hundreds of flowers and shrubs were in bloom. The scent of lilacs was strong in the warm air. "Things startin' to move fast," Jacob said.

"Yeah," Richard said, "lotta changes comin'. Hard to know what to expect."

"I'll help Pa for now," Claib said, "but sooner or later, brothers, I'm going to the war."

"I know you will," Richard said. "I sure would if it were me."

"Give me a few months. Jeremiah and a hired man or two can be trained. That's all the help Pa needs. Just be sure there's still a few Yankees left for me to fight."

Inside, excluded from the decisions, her fears ignored, Elsie Horine had gone to her bedroom and wept. There was no one she could turn to for help or comfort. All her family was caught up in the fever of rebellion, and she was powerless to do anything about it.

2

Shortly after midnight on April twentieth, a cloaked rider forded the Potomac south of Point of Rocks, Maryland, riding one sleek thoroughbred and leading another. He rode to a farm on the edge of Leesburg where he met a Virginia militia officer and identified himself.

"Spend the night here," the Virginian said. "Tomorrow we'll see if we can find Colonel Jackson. I'm told he's set up headquarters at Front Royal."

It took the rider, Richard Horine, and his sponsor, all morning to find Thomas Jackson and his hastily formed staff. They were standing around a large dining table in a Front Royal house. Horine was interviewed by two junior officers from the Virginia Military Institute before he met Jackson. They were interested in the likelihood of Maryland seceding and the deployment of Federal troops. Richard had little to offer in either regard.

When taken before Jackson, Richard found him studying maps and reports. After several minutes, Jackson looked up. "You brought a new recruit?" Jackson asked.

"Yessir," Richard's sponsor replied, "Richard Horine. Family is southern in sympathy. He is vouched for by our people in Maryland."

Jackson turned and stared at the tall, slender youth, noting his well cut militia uniform and how confidently he returned the stare. Jackson's blue eyes flashed. "Tell me, young man, what do you want to do here?"

"Fight for the Confederate States, Sir."

"What rank are you expecting?"

"None, just the opportunity to fight." As Richard spoke, the assembled officers began to take an interest in the conversation. Some had been with Jackson at V.M. I., but all had a keen interest in fathoming the temperament of the enigmatic colonel.

"Do you have any training?"

"Yessir, two years in the Maryland Home Guard and a few months with the Manor Brigade."

"Rank?"

"Sergeant, Sir."

"Under whose command?"

"There was Colonel Shriver in the guards, and different people in the Brigade, but mostly in a guard company under Captain Matthews. He had service in Mexico."

One of the staff officers stared at Richard. "Weren't you part of the militia who came up to Harpers Ferry when we put down that wild man Brown?"

"Yessir, I remember meeting you there."

Jackson looked at the officer. "Captain Stuart, do you know this man?"

James Ewell Brown Stuart replied, "Not really, Colonel, but I met him briefly at Harpers Ferry when Colonel Lee was dealing with Brown."

Jackson turned back to Richard. "Tell me, Mr. Horine, will most Marylanders join the South?"

"I'm not sure, Sir. The Maryland militia around Frederick is split, but in the southern and eastern shore counties, I've heard many of the militia units have disbanded to join secessionist forces."

"Interesting," Jackson said, "I would expect Maryland to secede. Did you bring anything in the way of arms?"

"Yessir, a Sharps 1859 New Model carbine and a Colt Dragoon revolver. I also brought an extra horse, and my father plans to send many more to help our cause once he finds the best way to do it."

The assemblage nodded at the recruit's response. "Commendable," Jackson said. "We'll begin Mr. Horine's indoctrination, and then we'll decide how we can put him to use."

After Richard had departed, Jackson looked at his staff and asked, "Well?"

"Seems like a quality young man," one ventured.

Jackson looked at the others.

Stuart spoke, "If Maryland indeed stays in the old Union, this young man and his family could be of service."

"My thoughts also, Captain Stuart. Since I am not one who likes to deal with clandestine affairs, I leave the matter in your hands. We need intelligence and we need horses. See that you work with this family and their friends to procure them. For the time, I suggest that Mr. Horine be assigned to you with the rank of sergeant. We need sergeants." Jackson returned to his maps.

Stuart stepped outside and found Richard waiting nearby with his horses and his sponsor. He took the recruit by the arm. "I see you had some chevrons on your sleeve that've been removed," Stuart said. "You can sew them back on since you're to be one of my sergeants. Now let's take these animals over to the stables and let me see what kind of horseflesh you Marylanders are bringing us."

On his way to the stables, Richard said, "Captain Stuart, a friend of mine joined up around here a short time ago. Name's Duval. Do you know anything about him?"

"Shanks Duval is one of my troopers, him and a couple of others that rode in last week. He'll be around here

26

somewhere so you can say your howdies." Stuart looked over the horses carefully and frowned. "Horine, I didn't realize you had animals of this caliber in Maryland. We'll take all you can provide. Pleasure to have you on board, uh, Sergeant." Stuart was grinning.

"Yo, you ol' rascal," a shrill voice called as they emerged from the stable. It was Duval. "Sorry, Cap'n, but this ol' boy and me done a lot of ridin' together. Gawd, but ain't it a sight to see you here."

Stuart told Duval to show Horine around the camp and returned to Jackson's headquarters.

3

On April twenty second, Benjamin Horine met again with the four men who sought to take Maryland from the Union. The five conspirators were joined by three newcomers at a large stone house outside Cockeysville, several miles west of Baltimore.

Their host, Mortimer Varley, spoke abruptly, "I want to know what happened to our effort to assassinate Lincoln. How did he get through Baltimore? It was our golden opportunity, and we missed. Now he's surrounded by troops."

Both Kilgour and Hatcher began to speak. "One at a time, dammit," Varley growled. "Kilgour, you start."

"We've spent hours trying to sort this out. None of the five of us told anyone. We talked among ourselves and we planned it in considerable detail with the three agents we hired for the job. That's where we think the problem is. One of them shot off his mouth, and somehow our plan got to Lincoln's people. We can't prove it was one of them, all three are ardent secessionists, so we guess it wasn't betrayal, just stupidity."

"I still think we can rely on Kane," Brown said. "I've known him for years, and he's closemouthed and as dedicated to our cause as anyone here, and best of all, nobody on the police force knows he's been part of this scheme."

"I know Kane too, and I agree with you," Varley said. "I propose we do away with the other two." There was a collective gasp. "What do you expect?" Varley demanded. "We sent those men to kill the President. Somehow they leaked information, and Lincoln escaped. They can be traced back to us, and the last time I checked, gentlemen, the penalty for treason is hanging."

"It could never be proven," Horine said.

"Mr. Lincoln," Varley said, "does not seem to be bound by the niceties of the law."

Horine sighed. "I guess Mortimer is right," he said. "We are in jeopardy. Is there any way less severe than execution?"

"I don't like it either, Ben, but I see it as our only choice."

One of the newcomers, Turner from the Eastern Shore, spoke. "Gentlemen, there's a better solution to this. Let me find useful employment for these troublesome fellows in the Confederacy. We need experienced hooligans, and I can get them to Richmond in a few days."

"You're sure you can arrange this?" Hatcher said.

"No problem at all. Just point them out, and my troops will have them in Richmond as part of a squad of irregulars."

"Fine, if you're sure it'll work. What are the activities of these irregulars?"

"Let me state simply that their duty will be among the most dangerous our lads can undertake. These men will not be back soon, if ever."

The group relaxed as the solution to the problem became apparent. "Now," Hatcher said, "let's get on with the business of this meeting. We are pledged to wrest control of this state from Hicks and his no-nothings. Brown, how are things in Baltimore?"

"Splendid. You've heard about the riots when Union troops tried to force their way through our crowds. Our bully boys grabbed some of the Yankees' muskets, chased them, and managed to kill four and wound several others. We had eight citizens dead in the fracas and that fanned still more bad feeling toward the North. I don't expect to see any more Yankee troops marching through Baltimore."

Another newcomer, Merryman, shook his head. "There's still Yankee troops getting into Washington," he said.

"That may be so, but they're not coming through our way."

"I've heard Ben Butler landed in Annapolis with a bunch of New Yorkers," Varley said. "That's how they're getting in."

A third newcomer, wearing the uniform of a Maryland militia officer spoke. "Some of my boys tore up the tracks between Annapolis and Washington. That'll keep Butler busy for a while."

"Maybe, but that's not more than a day's march. We've got to watch out for Butler. I know him from the last convention, and he's one mean son of a bitch. Colonel, are you keeping yourself in the clear?"

"Absolutely. Outside of this room, only my family and a few trusted allies know what I'm doing."

"What's happening on the Eastern Shore," Hatcher asked.

Turner leaned forward. "No need to worry about the Shore. We've got regiments training in Salisbury and Cambridge. There's no state or Union authority left below Easton. For all intents and purposes, our four southern counties have left the Union and joined Virginia in secession. Frankly, I expect to be part of the Confederate army within a week."

"Excellent," Hatcher said. "I wish we all could join you. Merryman, how about southern Maryland?"

Merryman cleared his throat. "There's lots of support and lots of talk, but little has been done to organize military units as yet. Almost everyone favors secession."

"So what's the problem?"

"Two things--our fishermen have been fighting with Virginians for years and they don't trust them. Also, we're so close to Washington, our people are scared they'll be caught and shot or put in prison if we form secessionist units."

"Sounds like a lack of guts to me," Brown muttered.

"Let's not be too critical," Kilgour said. "Colonel, don't you have contacts in the area who might help?"

"I'll look into it. A few names come to mind."

Turner added, "Colonel, let's work together. You need to keep your cover, and I have good connections in both Leonardtown and St. Mary's."

"Fine," Hatcher said. "Our biggest problem is the west. Ben, what's your reading?"

Ben Horine took a deep breath. "Much as I hate to admit it, we've made little progress. Cumberland and Hagerstown seem to be mostly Union, and Frederick the same. We have a number of supporters, but since so many of our men went south, we've been unable to increase our number. Hicks has been devilishly clever in refusing to call a legislative session to vote on secession, and meanwhile doing everything he can to identify who's secessionist. A lot of supporters are scared. We need to try something new if we're going to get anywhere."

"What are you doing yourself, Benjamin?" Varley challenged.

Horine was irritated at being baited. "My oldest son has just left for Virginia. One of his brothers will join him shortly. My second son, Claiborne, has bad eyes, so he's staying home to help me with my plans to supply horses to the South. I don't think anyone in this room has done more than me and my family or is any more dedicated to our cause."

"Hear, hear," Turner applauded.

"I can't imagine anyone having doubts about Benjamin," Hatcher said.

Varley's face reddened and he flicked ashes from his cigar. "Ben," he said, "forgive me, you and your family are a credit and an example for all of us, but it seems we'd better give up on western Maryland for the moment. With the number of troops Lincoln has in Washington and the number of Union lovers in your area, I don't see how we can swing it to our side. What we need is for the Confederacy to give the northern troops a good thrashing."

"It seems to me," Brown said, "that we can help best by messing up their railroads, keeping Baltimore boiling, and generally playing the North for the fools they are."

Horine nodded. "I've been thinking along those same lines. We'll be better off going underground the way things are. Most Marylanders in the west don't want trouble, and right now they think it's more trouble to secede than it is to stay in the Union. If my reading is right, they'll change when it looks like secession has more advantages. I think Governor Lowe feels that way, and he still has lots of support." There was general agreement.

"I'm very nervous about these meetings," Kilgour said. "None of us can afford to be identified as part of a conspiracy."

"I know," Hatcher said. "Let's make this our last meeting of the whole group until Maryland is in the Confederacy."

Varley went to a cabinet and retrieved a bottle of imported brandy. "Gentlemen," he said as he poured drinks for each man, "let's drink to a free Maryland."

4

On April 27, the citizens of Harpers Ferry were roused by the commotion of two hundred horsemen led by Jeb Stuart, followed by nine hundred Virginia infantrymen, the vanguard of Jackson's command. By the time breakfast was over, nearly eight thousand troops had occupied the town, including the railroad station and the bridges crossing the Potomac and Shenandoah. Troops were placed at strategic points overlooking the area, while Jackson set up his command post on the nearby heights.

Richard Horine had been assigned temporarily to Stuart's staff, and that night he was give permission to leave the camp. He slipped across the Potomac at twilight and made his way home. Later that evening, he roused his family, and after the joyous yelps of the five younger children, he shared news and got to the business at hand.

"Jackson is at Harpers Ferry," he told his father, "so now is the time for Jacob to join me. There are no Federals in the area, but we can sure use more horses, Papa."

Horine was delighted, learning that Virginia troops were only a dozen miles away, but his wife was stunned that Jacob was planning to leave. "One is enough," Elsie pleaded. "Don't let Jacob go. Richard, don't take him, he's so young." Tears trickled down her cheeks. The threat of war preyed on her mind. She'd been unable to sleep since Richard left, and when she did nod off, she had frightening nightmares.

Richard and Jacob looked at their father uneasily. They stepped away and hurried to the barn with Claiborne to select the horses.

Horine remained unmoved as his sobbing wife stood with the younger children. "We have our duty," he said. "We must do our part for what we stand for. To do less brings dishonor to this family."

When they had completed their preparations, horses selected, supplies packed, and Jacob in uniform, Horine hugged them both. "Tell Captain Stuart to have an agent contact me so I can establish a reliable link with the military. Tell him I've heard Patterson is assembling a considerable army in Hagerstown to invade the Shenandoah." They repeated their father's instructions and turned to the rest of the family.

Each son kissed Elsie's tear streaked cheeks. "We'll be fine, Mama," they said. "Please don't cry." They mounted their horses, each taking along two additional thoroughbreds.

"Take care of Mama, Claib," Richard called to his brother. "Goodbye, Papa, goodbye, Mama, goodbye children." They turned and began to trot down the lane. The oldest girl, Rebecca, stood with her arms around the younger children, grouped silently by their mother.

The Horines stood in silence as the horses broke into a gallop and the hoofbeats died into the darkness. The only sound remaining was Elsie weeping. Benjamin put his arm around her shoulder, but she pulled away and rushed into the house, followed by her younger children and then her husband.

In the upstairs hallway, Timmy looked up to Rebecca. "I'll miss Jacob so much," he said. "Will he come back?"

Rebecca nodded. "Of course. It's only a short time and they'll both be back."

"Jacob is so much fun."

"I know. We'll all miss him." Fun loving and outgoing, Jacob was the family favorite, always good for a game or a smile or a story.

Only Claiborne remained outside, lingering for several minutes, staring down the silent lane, collecting his thoughts, wishing he could go.

The next morning Richard and Jacob were welcomed by Stuart and his staff. The officers were pleased with the quality of the horses, and Stuart himself took a bay as one of his mounts.

Later, Jackson sat in his tent and squinted at Richard as he related his father's message. "I understand," Jackson said, "the need for such means of warfare--intelligence gathering, spying--all in God's plan, but I prefer the battlefield. Captain Stuart, Sergeant Horine will continue in your command and you are to establish liaison with his father, who seems to be a reliable ally. This arrangement is to continue until Maryland joins Virginia in secession. And young man," Jackson addressed Jacob, "report to Captain Johnson, you are hereby assigned to my brigade."

33

A few days later the Confederate army was reorganized into two Virginia departments, Beauregard in command at Richmond and Joseph Johnston in command of the Shenandoah Valley. Jackson was promoted to Brigadier General serving under Johnston. Stuart's troopers were made a separate cavalry unit with Stuart as Colonel reporting directly to Johnston.

Richard retained the pair of thoroughbreds he had brought with him when he joined the Confederate army. One was King, the five year old chestnut stallion with a white blaze he had ridden in the guard and was his favorite at home. The other was a spirited two year old black stallion named Prince, only recently broken to the saddle. "Take Prince as your second horse," his father had advised. "He's young, but he has wonderful blood lines, and he has the eyes of a hawk." After a few weeks, Richard realized how wise his father was. The young black was rugged, strong willed and hard to discipline, but all in all a marvel, and Richard rode him almost as much as the more mature horse.

On May 8, Bradley Johnson, Frederick lawyer and fervent secessionist, arrived at Harpers Ferry with over eighty Marylanders, primed to join the Confederate army. Johnson had been in touch with Hatcher and Varley, but their lack of progress in extricating the state from the Union had frustrated Johnson beyond endurance, and he left with the full support of the secessionists. Johnson's mentor, ex-Governor Lowe, still held out hopes for secession, but he yielded and also gave the fiery Johnson and his followers his blessings to join the Virginians. Among Johnson's men were troopers from Frederick's Mounted Dragoons and the Manor Mounted Guards. Richard knew some of the newcomers, but the welcome was brief, for armies were in motion and action was at hand.

5

Peck Handley sighed deeply as he lowered himself onto the store bench beside Henry Fulmer. "Well, Squire, our ranks is thinnin' out."

Fulmer, nearly seventy, was know as "Squire" because of his neat attire and courtly ways. "Is Hiram gone?" he asked.

"Yep, rode out yesterday. Him and some of his militia headed for the Potomac. I sure wish I was with 'em, but ever since I started gettin' these damn spells, I can't march no more. Gettin' too old, I reckon."

Ed Holter was working the counter. "Seems to me," he said, "ain't much bein' done."

Peck nodded. "We oughta be doin' a lot more. I hear the second Horine boy is gone."

"Gone south?"

"Nobody's seen him and the ol' man don't say nothin'. I reckon since the Horines hold for slavery, them two boys are in Virginia somewheres, ready to fight for Jeff Davis."

"I been told," Holter said, "that Brad Johnson and a bunch that follow him and Lowe has left."

"Oughta hang him and that dang Lowe and all the rest of 'em," Peck said. "To think I voted for that ol' bastard."

"This is terrible," the Squire said. "Ed, what do you think this country is coming to?"

Holter, a childless widower, shook his head. "I swear I don't know, Squire, but I stand with the Union, come war or perdition, always have, always will. If this puts me against Lowe or Ben Horine and his crowd, well, so be it."

"Who all around here is for secession?" the Squire asked.

"I ain't sure. Lots of folks shut up since the trouble started."

Peck grunted. "I don't trust none of 'em that's got slaves."

"How did Hiram seem when he left?"

"You know Hiram, always ready for a fight. He says his boys can keep up the farm till he gets back, them and his missus."

"Yeah," Holter said, "that there woman is a tiger. Seriously boys, what are we gonna do if Maryland secedes?"

Peck sliced a chunk of tobacco from his plug with his pocket knife. "Get the Federal army up here and jail all them damn secesh, the way Ben Butler done in Baltimore."

"I hope it don't come to that," Squire said. "Seems like our governor doesn't want the state to secede."

"Yeah," Peck said, "but Ben Butler's the one who put things straight. We need more generals like him. Scott's too dang ol' to be any good at a time like this."

"Ain't there nothin' to be done about Horine?" Holter asked.

"Far as I'm concerned," Peck said, "he's a traitor, oughta be hung right along with Lowe and Brad Johnson."

6

Serving with Jackson placed the Horines in the center of Confederate activity. In Harpers Ferry, the Rebels confiscated and sent south several B & O locomotives and a large amount of rolling stock. Jacob was popular with his Virginia comrades, many younger than he, and was made a corporal in his company, part of what was to become the fastest moving infantry on the face of the earth.

Richard found riding with Stuart's troopers an exhilarating experience. The cavalry had a free hand, harassing Federal outposts along the Potomac, and gathering supplies and information from across the river. In Hagerstown, Patterson had Union forces triple Johnston's size but did nothing. General in Chief Scott ordered Patterson to move against the Rebels, but Patterson dithered and delayed, not crossing the Potomac until Johnston ordered a tactical withdrawal from Harpers Ferry.

At Winchester, Richard was designated a squad leader in a company led by a thin, brash lawyer named John Mosby.

Shanks Duval was in the same company. In mid July Jackson learned that Patterson was moving a column of troops toward Berryville. He and Stuart decided to intercept the invaders. Stuart led Richard and over a hundred riders across the countryside to strike the strung out Federal column.

As they rode over the knoll down toward the Berryville Pike, Richard could see the Union soldiers scrambling for cover. An officer was waving his sword and shouting at the disorganized troops. Some ran, some ducked behind trees and the rail fence along the road. Richard pulled King to a halt and drew his Sharps from the scabbard.

Stuart raced to the front of his men, waving his saber. "Fire," he yelled, and a volley of shots rang out, felling several Union men. Some of the bluecoats fired back and two Confederate horses fell. Richard reined up and reloaded. King was trembling at the sound of gunfire and the dying horses. He shook his head and looked back at Richard for reassurance. Nearby, Shanks was having trouble, his mare bucking and balking at the din. "Dismount," Stuart shouted. Richard fired, reloaded, fired again. His horse remained uneasy but refused to panic. Union troops, realizing they outnumbered the cavalry, were finding their nerve and returning a steady fire. More horses fell, and the cavalry had to pull back to better cover, where Stuart ordered his troopers to re-mount and sweep around the enemy.

Duval finally had his horse under control and was dismounted and beginning to fire when Stuart gave his order to ride. "Shit," Duval said as he struggled to mount the mare, "damn horse'll never let me get into the fight."

"Let me see if I can get you a better horse," Richard shouted as he mounted King and joined the charge toward the Union rear.

As the troopers rode around the enemy flank, they heard a piercing yell. Jackson's infantry, a full regiment, was sweeping down the opposite slope, firing as they advanced. Despite a numerical advantage, the Union defense collapsed, the soldiers fleeing back along the road to Charles Town.

The Confederates overran the Union position, capturing wagons and taking twenty prisoners. Exhausted and exuberant, the victors halted to re-group while the wounded were being tended. Richard rode through the infantry lines and hailed his brother. "Chased those Yanks, didn't we, baby brother?"

"Yeah, but I bet you pony riders were glad to see some real soldiers." Jacob laughed and began to stroke King's neck and muzzle.

"You're right about that, but I reckon we could have handled 'em."

Richard dismounted, and the brothers walked to the fence beside the road where the Yanks had tried to rally. They stared at the bodies, boys like themselves lying in pools of blood, frightened eyes staring at the void. A few yards away, one started to groan and cough blood, but he quieted as death closed in. "Not very pretty," Richard muttered. "Hope this mess is soon over."

Jacob turned away, his mouth dry, guts churning. "When you see those boys, I wish it never started."

Jackson decided it was useless to pursue the fleeing enemy. His green troops were disorganized and disorderly, and his immediate goal was already achieved, to frighten the Yankees so badly they would forego any aggressive action.

A few days later, Jackson's troops began to depart, heading for Manassas. Johnston had orders to join Beauregard in the defense of Richmond. A considerable Federal army was moving south and threatening the new Confederate capital. Patterson, who could have pressed the Confederates and forced them to remain in the Shenandoah, was unnerved by the Berryville skirmish, just as Jackson had planned. He disregarded orders and pulled his troops back to Harpers Ferry, never realizing that only a few hundred Rebels remained against his force of over 10,000.

7

Sergeant Hiram Matthews looked down the straggly lines of the men in his company. The lieutenant was away at headquarters, so it was his task to lead the drill this morning.

"Come on, men, dress it up," he shouted. "Gross, suck in your gut. You stick out like a bloated cow."

"I got my stomach sucked in, Sarge. It's this damn uniform that sticks out. It's four sizes too big, and I can't suck it in."

Most of the Marylanders in the militia company had known Matthews for some time and tended to be rowdy. Several chuckled at Gross's remark.

"Let's have some order, men. This is the army and this is war, so dammit, get serious, come to order and dress up them lines."

Matthews' words were interrupted by a loud, ripping sound. "All right, who farted?"

"Sarge," John Fraley yelled, "I think Baumgartner done shit his pants."

The entire company broke into helpless laughter, and Matthews covered his mouth as tears welled in his eyes. When he regained control, he shouted, "Baumgartner, what in hell is your problem?"

"It ain't my fault, Sarge, I got the runs. It's that damn bacon they give us. It's rancid as hell and give me the shits."

"That's right, Sarge," Al Fisher said, "it smelled like a mule's ass. This food here is a bunch of crap."

"Anybody else got the runs?" Matthews asked. Over half the company raised their hands. "Why didn't you say you was sick at report?"

"We didn't have the runs then," Fraley explained.

Two officers rode up. "Sergeant," the captain said, "this is the worse looking company on the drill grounds. What's wrong with these men?"

"Bad food, Sir. Half of 'em is sick. I was gettin' ready to send 'em to the dispensary."

"What did they eat?"

"The bacon was rancid, Sir."

"Why aren't you sick, Sergeant?"

"I didn't eat none. It didn't smell right."

"Lieutenant," the captain said to his fellow officer, "ride over to the commissary and tell them I want an explanation of this. Sergeant," the captain continued.

"Yessir."

"Dismiss your men and keep them confined until we get this matter straightened out."

It was the third week for the Maryland militia in camp near Poolesville. They hated the drilling, the food was nauseous. Only at the firing range could they perform the way they wanted. They were good shots, so their lapses were tolerated. It was July 16, the day they learned McDowell's army was beginning to move south, while they remained in camp.

8

At two in the morning, July 21, McDowell's hastily assembled force was roused outside Centerville to advance toward Confederate forces under Beauregard along the Bull Run stream. It was after three before the troops were in motion, the pace tedious as regiments bunched up in the dark and officers halted to sort out directions.

Nine o'clock found the lead regiments standing near Sudley's Ford, troops awaiting their turn to cross. Groups of soldiers wandered into the fields to relieve themselves and returned carrying handfuls of blackberries. Officers straggled back from the crossing, cursing the delay. Vague orders confused the commanders, and soldiers milled about awaiting orders. Finally, several units crossed and moved downstream.

Two hours later, fighting broke out when Union troops stumbled onto Rebel units downstream near the stone bridge. Heintzelman's brigade attacked, and more Federal regiments moved forward and pressed the assault on surprised and undermanned Confederates.

Also in mid-morning, Jackson's brigade began arriving at the Bull Run area. They had been packed into freight cars and carted down the rail line. They were unloaded onto unfamiliar ground and prodded by their leader to march from the railroad toward the Bull Run fords where Beauregard, unaware the main Federal force was miles upstream, expected the Yankee attack. Once settled into position, Jackson's men waited listlessly in the heat, puzzled by the increasing noise of battle reverberating across the hills somewhere to the west.

The situation was a puzzle to Jacob. Richard and the cavalry had left Winchester earlier, while Jackson's men had sweltered as they marched to the railroad, spent hours on the train, then unloaded and marched to a spot where nothing was happening. Like his comrades, he was tired, thirsty, and baffled. The sounds of battle from the left were getting louder, but they were told to prepare for attack from their front. "This don't make a lick of sense," Jacob told his captain. "There's no Yanks around here."

The officer nodded but said nothing. "We'll miss the whole darn battle," Jacob said.

General Johnston was as troubled as Jacob over the situation. Unwilling to wait longer, he decided that the bulk of Confederate forces were in the wrong place. He told Beauregard the battle was to the left and that's where he was going. Jackson already sensed what was happening, and without prodding from Johnston, led his men toward the growing din of gunfire and the clouds of dust and smoke.

Jacob's company trotted forward with growing excitement. Smoke drifted about them and shells exploded ahead. Dozens of gray-clad troops poured over the hill toward them, frightened, some without muskets. Officers tried to stop them, but the panicked troops kept running.

"What's wrong with you men," Jacob shouted at a fugitive.

"There's thousands of 'em," he answered, "we ain't got no chance."

"They done give up," a comrade said.

"Ain't about to run over us," Jacob said, but his mouth was dry as he heard musket fire over the rise and saw lines of bluecoats approaching.

Jackson sized up the situation, seeing disorganized Confederate units retreating and firing haphazardly. A smattering of troops had gathered on a hill by a clapboard house while officers moved about trying to rally their men.

"Your orders," Jackson told his officers, "are to position your men along the hill below that house. Place them just below the crest. That's where we'll make our stand. Let's get this thing stopped now before it turns into a rout."

They took their positions as Jackson ordered. Federal troops were moving up the hill toward them, and suddenly, Jackson's men rose and fired a volley, driving the Yankees back. More Union soldiers advanced toward their position, but they too were stopped by steady fire. An officer named Bee, shortly before he was killed, exhorted his troops, "There stands Jackson like a stone wall. Rally to the Virginians." The Confederate flight diminished, and the gray lines began to stabilize about Jackson's position and stretching all the way to the Bull Run tree line.

"We stopped 'em," Jacob shouted. He stood and fired a shot. "C'mon, boys, let's give 'em a taste of our guns."

Jackson observed Jacob's enthusiasm. "That's one of the Maryland boys, isn't it?" he asked an aide.

"Yessir, name's Horine."

"Commendable. Might consider him for promotion."

In the hill above Jackson's position, Stuart's cavalry unit moved toward the fray. They had been run up and down the lines for two hours with confused orders from first Beauregard and then Johnston. Desperate for action, Stuart headed toward the clamor of battle. Ahead he saw what he took to be Louisiana Zouaves moving to the rear and ordered his troopers to their aid. A hundred yards from the troops, they began firing at his men, and Stuart realized they were New York Zouaves. "It's Yanks," he shouted. "Hit 'em."

Horine and Duval were in the leading squad of riders. After the hard ride from the Shenandoah, Richard had to rest King and was riding Prince. The New Yorkers fired wildly and two horses fell, but the troopers thundered into the massed Zouaves, firing revolvers and slashing with sabers. The unnerved Yanks broke and scattered from the onslaught. "After 'em," Richard shouted, but Stuart soon waved him and his men off. There were other parts of the battlefield that needed the cavalry's attention.

As the Yankee attack waned, Jackson ordered his men forward. They rose from their positions beyond the crest of the hill and surged ahead, firing and re-loading as they went. A line of bluecoats met them, and the firing intensified. Jacob pushed ahead shouting, "C'mon, c'mon, let's get 'em." He shot down one of the enemy and found himself between two others. He drew his Colt dragoon and fired at one, but the other shot him in the chest point blank and killed him. Jacob fell forward and lay there in the dust and dry grass as the noise of the battle receded across the fields. The Yankees held for a few minutes, but as Johnston poured in more troops to support Jackson's advance, the tide of battle shifted and the Union retreat became a panic. The Confederates won a smashing victory.

Hours later, after the last of the Federals had abandoned the battlefield and fled toward Washington, Stuart's exhausted troopers returned to Johnston's headquarters for further orders. None were issued, so Richard rode off to seek Jackson's brigade. A staff officer directed him to Jackson's position across the stream, but there was no sign of Jacob. He asked several troops and was told, "Some of our boys fell on the hill below that white house yonder," so he rode across the battleground. The wounded were being attended, and a few men were beginning to collect the dead. The smell of death was already evident.

Halfway down the slope, Richard found Jacob's body, laying as he had fallen, his weapon in his hand, facing the enemy.

For an hour, Richard sat by his brother's side, while Prince stood nearby. Why, Richard asked himself, had he brought Jacob to this war? He was only nineteen, tall, cheerful, outgoing, brave, loved by everyone who knew him. Richard could not forgive himself, could not cope with this loss. How could he ever tell Mama and Papa?

As he held Jacob in his arms, Richard became aware of a nearby presence. "Why are you here weeping, Sergeant?" Richard looked up through his tears to see who had intruded on his misery. He was stunned by a pair of piercing blue eyes. It was Jackson, riding about the battleground.

"I'm sorry, General, he's my brother, killed today by the Yankees."

"Yes, I saw your brother, a brave soldier, a fine way to die, doing our Lord's will and our country's work, most commendable. You're from Maryland, I believe?"

Richard stood and saluted. "Yessir. I'm sorry to have you see me weep, but we were so close, and I'll miss him dearly."

"Don't despair when you're doing such good work. Today we have slain the intruder, and this lad was God's instrument in preserving our land. Be joyful that he has crossed the river to a new home in such a noble way." Thomas Jackson, now immortalized as Stonewall, rode on to his headquarters. Jackson had been roaming the battlefield alone, distressed that he was unable to convince his superiors to pursue the beaten Union forces. "Washington could have been ours, O Lord," he whispered, in a bitter voice heard only by his Maker.

9

The Sunday after Bull Run, Mary Ann and her two children attended worship service at the nearby Mt. Nebo Church. The stone and red brick structure was nearly a century old, having been built by German immigrant families who were the principal settlers in the area. Most of the families still lived nearby--Fulmers, Kullers, Summers,

Zimmermans, Derrs, Stones, Hoffmans, Stockmans, Hargetts, Himes, to name a few. There were also scattered English and Scotch families who either had been assimilated into the Lutheran community or attended churches in Frederick. Catholic families had organized a parish a few miles to the south.

The church was located by a dusty country road at the end of the lane to the Fraley farmhouse and outbuildings. It was enclosed with its cemetery by a white washed picket fence. Worshipers came from a one to two mile radius, some walking, some on horseback, whole families in buggies. Horses were tied to fence posts and trees in a large park-like area in front of the entrance. The churchyard was partially filled with a variety of tombstones, separated by a wide grassy path that led to the church doors.

Like most of the women, Mary Ann wore a long cotton dress and a full length petticoat. Her feet were clad in dark cotton hose and high top laced boots. She wore a large bonnet with a veil and carried a parasol to protect herself from the sun. It was a strange thing for a woman whose life was hard work, much of it outdoors, from sunup to sundown, but it was the custom, and she thought little of it, enduring the discomfort, the dust, the chafing of too much apparel.

The preacher spoke of the horrors of the war and the recent Union defeat in Virginia. He and the congregation prayed for peace, knowing full well there would be no peace. They sang hymns from worn hymnals, finishing with Mary Ann's favorite, "A Mighty Fortress Is Our God," written centuries earlier by Martin Luther.

Across the aisle from the Fraleys, George and Beth Stone sat with their four children. The oldest, Mary Elizabeth, was slender and pretty, with light brown hair, brown eyes, and a turned up nose. She was Johnny's girl friend, and she fretted with the Fraleys about what might be happening in the war.

After church, various groups gathered--the women in the church, the men on the steps outside, children romping in the paths. Younger unmarried females gathered in the main path through the churchyard. Francis clustered with other young men by the gate, while Sissy joined her friends.

"Hiram thought it would be a short war," Beth Matthews said, "but after Bull Run, I wonder."

"It worries me so I can't sleep," Mary Ann said. "I keep thinking about our boys out there gettin' shot to pieces by them awful Rebels. Why did it ever happen?"

Mary Elizabeth Stone stood behind her mother and listened to the women gossip. She hadn't heard from Johnny since he left for the war, and she fretted as she heard Mary Ann's troubled voice. Later on, Mary Ann patted the girl on the arm. "Johnny wrote last week," she said. "He said to tell you hello and that he'd write soon as he could."

Mary Lib blushed. "Thank you, Miz Fraley. That makes me feel some better."

Francis listened to the boys talk. Two were ready to enlist. "I don't see how them Rebels ever beat us," Ray Fulmer said. "Bet it'd been different if our boys was there."

"Them Horines and some others from the manor went over to the Rebs," Buck Hargett said. "If Pa don't fuss too much, I'm gonna join up. It makes me mad to think them swell heads whipped us."

Francis walked up the lane alone to the farmhouse. He felt embarrassed, not being able to join the army. He knew in his heart he had to stay home, and yet it bothered him, being old enough to fight and not able to go. Mary Ann and Sissy followed, Sissy picking a wild flower off the bank beside the lane. "It seems so strange, him not being here," she said.

"I know. Let's pray he's back real soon," Mary Ann said, brushing her face to keep her daughter from seeing her tears.

10

Two nights after Bull Run, Benjamin Horine met with two conspirators in the back room of a law office in

Frederick. They had arrived by circuitous routes, concerned over the thousands of Union troops that occupied the town.

"Well, the news is wonderful, Benjamin," Kilgour said. "Have you heard from your sons?"

"Nothing as yet, but both are with Jackson."

"That Jackson is quite a man, turned the tide of the battle, they say, just the kind of leader our boys need, and you, Hatcher, what of your family?"

"Two nephews are with Beauregard, and a third helping to develop the Confederate navy."

"Yes, your tragedy, like mine, is to have daughters, much as we love them, in a time when we need men. We envy you, Benjamin."

"Thank you, I'm very proud, but I fear Mrs. Horine is of a different mind, envying those who have only daughters. What about your sons-in-law?"

"Both from Union families, interested in how rich the war can make them, very disappointing. But enough of this, we have a much improved situation with our army's splendid victory. How can we take advantage of it?"

"My thoughts," Hatcher said, "are to arm our people, particularly our Baltimore supporters. With the Unionists defeated and in disarray, the opportunity may soon present itself to rise and take Maryland into the Confederacy."

"How do you feel about this, Benjamin?" Kilgour asked.

"I'd like to agree, but sentiment here is still pro-Union and Yankee troops are swarming all over the place. Even though Butler is gone, Baltimore is still under the boot-heel of Yankees. Last I heard, they still hold Merryman."

"True enough," Hatcher said, "but we have to be bold and strike while the Washington government is in a panic."

Kilgour stroked his beard. "I understand how you feel, Hatcher, but we don't want to give away our plans until we're sure they'll work. Isn't it likely that Southern troops will soon be in Washington? Let's await their arrival, and then we'll have no trouble taking Maryland from the Union."

Horine nodded. "We want Lowe to return to the Governor's chair once Maryland secedes. In the meantime, I suggest caution until we're sure we can win, but there are plenty of other things we can do."

"What do you mean, Ben?"

"My contacts with Colonel Stuart have been somewhat disappointing. The South has proven it has the best soldiers. Now it needs information about northern troop movements and plans. We can help finish this war quickly with good intelligence."

Hatcher shrugged. "Well, gentlemen, I'll bow to your judgment in this. Perhaps I am a bit rash. Let me move things along by getting in touch with Johns and see if we can get some intelligence from him, now that he's set up in the War Department. Ben, you'll have to find a way to deal with Stuart."

"I'm working on it, and I think I've got a good contact in Lovettsville to help us. Most of Loudoun County is Confederate to the core."

The eight men who had conspired together at the beginning of the war had gone disparate ways. Turner was in charge of a Maryland regiment serving the Confederacy. Merryman had been recruiting for the South when he was apprehended and thrown into jail. Brown, like other Baltimore supporters, was in hiding since Butler began arresting secessionists. Johns had used old army contacts to land a post in the War Department. Mortimer Varley, a veteran politician, was a close confidant of ex-Governor Lowe, one of the most public supporters of secession, but he was forced to keep a low profile to avoid apprehension.

11

Ben Horine was cinching a new saddle on his favorite horse when he heard his slave calling from the front of the barn.

"Massa Horine, Massa Horine," the African called. His voice was a rich baritone.

"In the stables, Jeremiah. What is it?"

"Letter from Marse Richard, Massa."

Ben's pulse quickened. He had not heard from the boys since before Bull Run. The letter was dropped off by a friendly postal employee. Southerners had developed reliable schemes for getting correspondence into the Federal postal system.

Horine ripped open the letter and read:

"Dear Papa,

I have the worse news. Jacob was killed at Manassas. He died a hero's death. He fought with Jackson's brigade and they saved the day for us, so I know Jacob was brave and honorable to the end. I found him on the battlefield where the Yankees shot him in the chest. I buried him beside some of his comrades and saw that he had a nice grave and marker.

I feel so bad that he is gone and I miss him terribly. I pray we win this war so his sacrifice is not in vain. General Jackson commended Jacob and said the Lord would reward him for his sacrifice. Tell Mama and the children that Jacob died for what he and all of us believe in. Papa, please pray for both of us.

Your loving son,
Richard"

As he read the horrid news, his eyes misted and he could barely make out the words-- "honorable, hero's death, commended by General Jackson"--but he was gone, Jacob was dead. Oh God, how am I ever going to tell Elsie?

"Massa Horine, is sumpin' wrong?"

"Yes, Jeremiah, something is terribly wrong." He felt a hundred years old. He put his horse back in its stall and turned to make the longest walk of his life, to tell his wife that their son was dead, the victim of a Yankee bullet at the battle the Confederates called Manassas near a stream called Bull Run.

12

After Bull Run, the militia was incorporated into the First Maryland Regiment, and Hiram Matthews was commissioned a lieutenant.

"Well, I'll be switched," you ol' hoss," Johnny said, "army must be in trouble when they make you an officer."

Matthews chuckled. "Big a surprise to me as you, John, and let me tell you something else that'll get your giblets jumping. We done made you a sergeant. Whadya think of them apples? Al Fisher is another one."

Johnny nearly fell down laughing. "Dang army ain't got the sense of a jackass, makin' me and Fisher sergeants. Why hell, Hiram, I mean Lieutenant, Sir, what're we supposed to do?"

"Well, we figgered since you are two of the baddest soldiers we got, why maybe you'd straighten up and so would the rest of the boys. We got us a new general, name of McClellan, and he don't abide no nonsense from what I heard, so I reckon all of us gotta shape up. This man is supposed to be a demon for drillin'."

"Yeah, I reckon we can do that, but dammit, we come down here to fight, and so far, we ain't took our first shot at them Rebs."

"Once we get into it, we'll see all the fightin' we want."

They settled into the routine of camp life along the Potomac. The food was improved, and living conditions were tolerable.

One evening early in September, several of the company sat around a campfire. Fisher said, "Damn if I ain't tired of bein' stuck here. If we drill another day, I swear my feet will be ground into nubs."

Rudy Barnes tapped his corncob pipe on a rock and began to repack it from a cloth sack of coarse tobacco. "Hell, Al, I druther be drillin' than stuck in front of a bunch of Reb guns and ever'body runnin' away, like that mess they had down at Bull Run."

"Shit, Rudy, just because soldiers can drill don't mean they can fight worth a hoot."

Gross spat into the fire and asked, "When we gonna get some leave to go into town?"

"Hell, Gross, all you want is one of them fancy women we been hearin' about."

"Yeah, and what's wrong with that? I know I ain't the only one what wants one of them whores. Lot of you do."

"Yeah," Johnny said, "if you want a good case of the clap or some of them little lice crawlin' over your privates."

"What I'd like," Fisher drawled, " is some fine, good ol' home cookin', and then go shoot us some Rebs."

Angleberger frowned. "Well," he said, "we ain't gonna get nothin' sittin' around this camp and drillin' all day. I come to fight, not to prance around like some damn trained dog."

Johnny snorted. "When you join the army, that's what you are, a trained damn dog. Arf, arf, arf."

When they stopped laughing, Handley threw his chaw into the dying fire. "You fellers stop worryin' me with all this bull. Things will come when they will. We'll get home cookin' and women and some real fightin' soon enough, ain't that right, Johnny?"

Johnny chuckled and sucked on his pipe. "Sounds about right to me, Mack."

They put out the fire and headed for their cots. Five in the morning would find them roused for mess and more drilling.

13

Whoa, whoa, hold them horses, Sissy," Frankie shouted. "Grandpa, you better help her out."

Grandpa Zimmerman shuffled to the front of the hay wagon and grabbed the unruly team's reins. "Hold on there, boys," the old man said, as he tried to calm the animals.

Overhead, dark clouds were pushing over the mountain ridge that bordered the farm, and the wind was picking up.

Frankie and his Uncle Sam Zimmerman were trying to get the last load of hay into the barn before the storm hit. Lightning flashed, and after a brief pause, thunder rolled across the sky. When she saw the threatening skies, Mary Ann had summoned her brother to help. Sam had left his son, Eddie, at home to finish sacking the wheat they'd flailed out on the barn floor. Grandpa had insisted on coming along.

"Whoa, boys, dammit, whoa," Grandpa yelled as he pulled harder on the reins.

"Frankie," I'm scared," Sissy wailed.

"Hold on, Sis," Frankie shouted, "just a few more piles to go."

The hay had been scythed down a few days earlier and left to dry flat on the ground. In the morning, Frankie had used a short handled fork to gather the dried grass and clover onto piles spaced across the field. As the storm clouds gathered, they worked furiously with long handled pitchforks to load the piles onto the hay wagon. This was their third and final load. Frankie and Sam pitched up the hay, while Sissy in a long gingham dress and sunbonnet was on the wagon with a small fork, attempting to pack and balance the load. Grandpa alternated between pitching hay and helping manage the team of horses.

Two more lightning bolts flashed and the thunder rumbled nearer and louder. The men tossed up the last piles of hay as the wind increased and a few large raindrops splattered nearby.

"It's raining," Sissy cried.

"Let's get movin'," Sam said. "Hang on, Sissy, we're goin' in."

"Frankie," Grandpa called, "give me a hand with these fool horses. They know you." Lightning snapped and more thunder rolled overhead.

"Grandpa, can you get up on the wagon?"

"No, y'all go on. It ain't far to walk, and a little wet will feel good."

Frankie crawled up on the wagon beside Sissy and took the lines. Sam grabbed the horses' reins from Grandpa and they took off at a trot with the old man straggling behind.

A few minutes later they arrived at the bottom of the bridge wall, a ramp of stone and soil built to get wagons into the upper area of the barn where the crops were stored above the stables. "Frankie," Sam said, "you and Sissy jump down."

They scrambled down from the load of hay at the bottom of the bridge wall. The rain was beating down hard, more lightning crackled, and the horses were whinnying and jumping about nervously. "Uncle Sam," Frankie said, "you take the brake. I better lead 'em in."

"Watch that wagon tongue, Frankie. You gotta turn the horses before the hind wheels are in the barn."

"I know. C'mon, boys. Sissy, get outta the way." The girl raced up the grade into the barn.

After rearing their heads and stomping about nervously, the team of horses put their full strength to the task. Frankie backed them up several yards to get a running start, and with a yell, he charged forward, pulling the team with him. Sam raced behind at the edge of the wagon near the brake handle, shouting as loud as Frankie.

The horses hit the bridge wall at full speed with the hayload rocking back and forth and the rain pouring harder. More lightning flashed and thunder roared directly overhead. The horses pawed at the wet earth and struggled up the hill onto the barn's wooden floor as the weight of the wagon slowed them down and they lost momentum. Their front hooves dug into the wood, and then their rear hooves, as they fought to keep moving and avoid falling. Sam yanked on the brake handle when he saw them struggling, but the horses kept their balance and renewed their efforts as the dry barn floor gave them better purchase, so he released the brake quickly and grabbed the nearest wheel to help keep the wagon moving forward. The wagon lurched into the barn, where Frankie jerked the horses to the right to keep from being pushed through the front of the barn into the barnyard below. Sam yanked the brakes on again, and the wagon skidded to a stop.

"Sissy," Frankie shouted, "come take the reins, we gotta get the doors shut. Where's Grandpa?"

"He's here," Sam called. "You aw'right, Pa?"

"Never better. Man, that rain's comin' down." The old man was drenched and gasping for breath.

Frankie grabbed a rope, and he and Sam picked up a wooden ladder and carried it onto the bridge wall in the downpour. The wind was howling so they'd never get the huge doors closed except by tying a rope to the end. This meant placing the ladder against the barn, climbing and tying the rope to the door's cross beam, and then the two of them pulling on the rope to swing the door from the side of the barn against the gale. The greatest hazard would occur when the door had swung far enough to catch the wind. Then it would become almost uncontrollable as the full force of the storm hit it.

Frankie mounted the ladder and quickly had the rope attached on the leeward side. It was a hard pull for the two men to get the door moving, but they managed and were able to ease it closed and get it secured. Then they went through the same process with the other door. When the rope was attached, they tugged at it, but the wind was too strong. There was another crack of lightning, and as the thunder roared overhead, the wind died. "Let's get it," Sam yelled. They pulled with all their strength, and when the ponderous door swung half way, the wind gusted. Frankie caught the door as it began to accelerate out of control, while Sam held onto the rope. "Watch out," Sam cried.

The rope burned its way through Sam's hands, and the uncontrolled door swept Frankie along with it. Before it slammed shut, Frankie pulled himself laterally and leaped onto the cross beam, a four inch square piece of chestnut . The door crashed shut, throwing him off onto the barn floor next to the wagon's wheels. At the same moment, another crash of thunder jarred the barn, causing them to duck their heads. Sam rushed over. "My God, Frankie, are you hurt bad?"

Frankie picked himself up and felt his extremities. "I don't think so. How about you?"

"Just a rope burn. I've had worse. Papa, how you doin'?"

"Don't you fellers fret none about me. Y'all done good."

"Sissy, are you hurt?"

"No, just scared a bit. I never saw such a wind, or the thunder, it's awful."

The storm settled into a steady downpour as the heavy thunderheads moved on across the valley. Frankie inspected the door. "Just a few boards knocked loose. Lucky."

"That was a heckuva ride you took on that there door," Sam said. "I was scared you'd get mashed."

"Me and Johnny used to play on them doors. I took that ride many a time, but never that fast."

"That team of horses done good. I was afraid they'd slip and fall when the bridge wall started getting wet."

"Yeah," Frankie said, "they did good, but they done crapped all over the barn floor." Sissy giggled.

Grandpa laughed. "I mighta done that my ownself if I did what them horses done."

They talked on till the rain slackened and Mary Ann appeared. She took in the scene as the four sat together on the barn floor, grinning, their clothes soaked, hay in from the field, horses munching on some grain. "Thought you loafers might like some fresh water and some of these ginger cookies I just baked," she said.

14

Jacob Horine's death was a catastrophe. Sweet tempered, handsome, full of fun, Jacob was much loved by his parents and all five younger children. They were devastated and Elsie's reaction made the situation agonizing.

Ben was overwhelmed by the vehemence of his wife's fury. "You and your awful Confederacy," she screamed, "you've killed my baby. You never let me have a word. You just sent him away, and he's gone, killed, and for what?" She wept. "For what? For slavery? Is that what this war is all about? Slavery, who cares? I would free every slave and jail every secessionist if I could just have my Jacob back. Oh, oh, my poor baby."

He tried to comfort her, to make her see that it was a Yankee bullet that killed their son and that it was hated Yankee oppression he had died fighting against, but she would accept none of it. "He died for no good reason," she screamed. "The Yankees are people just like us. Some of my cousins are Yankees. You and your friends, people like you, too pig headed to listen or compromise or do anything that would hurt your pride, and now you've killed Jacob. I hope you're satisfied because I'll never forgive you."

She wanted her son's body returned, but that was impossible. Jacob lay in a crudely marked grave on the battlefield in Virginia among his comrades. "I can't even see him again, touch his body, his dear sweet face. Oh Benjamin, why did you do this? How could you inflict such cruelty on your own flesh and blood?"

Ben could do nothing to console his wife. Rebecca tried to help and spent hours with her mother. A female cousin was fetched from Mt. Airy, but neither could comfort the distraught woman. Elsie took to her bed, stayed in her room, ate little, and stared out the window or looked at pictures of the family and wept softly. Doctor Hedges was summoned. "It's melancholia, Ben," the doctor said, "a bad case, and she may or may not come out of it. There's nothing medicine can do. Shame about your boy."

The family held a memorial service in Frederick, performed quietly since the town remained occupied by Federal troops.

A few days later, Claiborne announced he was going south to avenge his brother's death. Ben fretted, but in the end he agreed. Elsie wept silently and turned away from her second son.

"Mama," he pleaded, "I must go. You must understand. Please give me your blessing."

Elsie choked with fear and grief. She wavered, but at last she turned and hugged him. "You'll never come back," she said, "nor will Richard. Thank God Timmy is so young." She sighed. "Go with God. Remember your prayers."

Claib kissed her on the forehead, while tears welled in her eyes and spilled down her pale cheeks. He hugged each of the children and embraced his father. They watched silently as he rode south across the fields until he was out of sight.

It was several weeks since Manassas. Claib made his way through southern Maryland, visiting family friends near Bladensburg, then moving on to contacts in Lower Marlboro and Leonardtown, where he was transported across the Potomac. Two days later, he was inducted into one of the infantry regiments serving in Joe Johnston's Richmond command.

On September 12, Governor Hicks called a meeting of the Maryland legislature in Frederick, choosing the location to avoid the strong Rebel sentiment in Annapolis. To their dismay, when several of the legislators arrived, they were summarily arrested for their secessionist views. Horine and his co-conspirators, Hatcher, Kilgour and Varley, were appalled, powerless to help. Merryman remained in prison, and Brown was under a cloud of suspicion.

A few weeks later, Merryman was released. Then Johns, now entrenched in the War Department, passed along word of a planned Union movement against Leesburg, Virginia, near Ball's Bluff on the Potomac.

15

On September 27, three companies of the First Maryland were posted along several miles of the Potomac's east bank in Frederick County. Confederate raids to damage the railroads, steal horses and supplies, and create other mischief had become a nuisance, so Governor Hicks had demanded protection which Lincoln, mindful of Maryland's tenuous loyalty, was quick to oblige.

A few days after arriving at the new posting, Matthews had Johnny and his squad on picket duty near Berlin. The night was dark and the half moon disappeared and re-emerged among scattered clouds. The river gurgled, higher than normal from recent thunderstorms. Six men were on duty, spaced at fifty yard intervals, while another six rested. Other units were on watch further up and down the river. At their backs were steep hills interrupted only by a gap carved by a small stream.

Shortly after midnight, Johnny was humming a tune and yawning when the moon broke from cloud cover. In the shadows along the far bank he glimpsed movement. His mouth was dry and he clutched his rifle, lifting it to firing position. He wondered what to do, but then he was the sergeant, supposed to be in charge. With sweat beginning to form on his forehead, he whistled at the nearest sentries and pointed at the river. All of them peered into the shadows which began to take form.

"You, down there, halt and be recognized," Johnny called. No reply. "Hey there, you Rebs get back to your own side of the river." Still no answer. "Halt, or we'll open fire."

There were several flashes and loud reports as enemy guns fired at Johnny's voice, the minie balls whining over his head. Johnny cursed and pulled the trigger on his Springfield. Other sentries opened up, as more Reb guns exploded. A quarter of a mile away, Matthews heard the shots and rallied the rest of the company. Soon over a hundred Marylanders were battling with Confederates along the river. Two Reb riders had fallen into the water, their bodies swept along by the current until they lodged on rocks. By the time more men arrived, the Rebs had withdrawn. Night incursions into Frederick County halted.

A week passed without further incident, so the soldiers were given one-day passes on rotation to visit nearby homes. Saturday was Johnny's turn.

Sissy was sitting by the back door peeling potatoes, a task she despised, when she noticed the blue clad figure approaching. Her heart leaped, she dropped her pan, tripped over a cat, caught her balance, and tore across the yard to meet Johnny. Buster the hound had been napping by the back chimney when he caught Johnny's scent and began barking. In the kitchen Mary Ann heard the pan drop, the cat yowl, the dog yapping, and went to the door. "Sissy, where on earth are you going?"

"Ma, it's Johnny."

Then she saw her son and could not contain herself. She ran across the yard after Sissy. Frankie heard the commotion and hurried down from the barn where he'd been tending the cows, and in a moment, the four were crowded together in the front yard.

"We're up outside Berlin," Johnny said, "already had a fight and shot us some Rebs. Me and Pete Angleberger caught a ride to Jefferson and walked the rest of the way, got us a day's leave."

"You mean you have to go back tomorrow."

"'Fraid so, but we might get more leave in a few weeks if we don't get sent back to camp."

"Oh, but it's good to see you."

"Johnny," Sissy said, "I'm knitting you some socks. Come see 'em."

"Got a good crop of hay in," Frankie said, "but we missed you, 'bout killed poor ol' Grandpa."

They ate their noon meal together. Mary Ann boiled potatoes, and fried sausage and apples. "Ain't had no food like this for a while," Johnny said. In the afternoon they hitched up the buggy and went to Holter's store to show off Johnny and to buy something special for supper. Peck Handley and Squire Fulmer were there and allowed as how

59

Johnny looked fit. "Your boy will be home in a few days, Mr. Handley," Johnny said. "He's doin' a fine job."

They talked about Hiram Matthews being a lieutenant and the scrap at Berlin, about McClellan and Bull Run. Pete Angleberger and his folks arrived and joined them, and they were all talking at once. Ed Holter gave each soldier a small sack of brown sugar. Then the Fraleys drove to the Stones so Johnny could see Mary Elizabeth.

After they visited for a while, Johnny said, "Ma, you and Frankie and Sissy better get on home to your chores. I want to talk some more to Mary Lib. I'll be home for supper."

"We'll be on our way," Mary Ann told the Stones, "you two behave yourselves, and Mary Lib, you make sure he leaves in time to eat with us."

"I will, Missus Fraley. C'mon, Johnny, we'll talk with Mom some more, and then we'll take a walk if you'd like."

"You know what I'd like," Johnny said, "find us a place where we can spark a bit."

Mary Elizabeth giggled. They chatted with her mother and two younger sisters and then strolled hand in hand down a grassy path past the vegetable garden and spring house to a clump of lilacs hidden from the house. Her father and brother were working in the barn. She looked up at Johnny and smiled.

"Umm, I missed you, you luscious little darling," Johnny said. "You smell so good, better'n them lilacs."

"Ain't been no lilacs for months."

"I know that, but I remember how they smell." He put his arm around her waist, and she snuggled against him. "You feel so good."

She looked up into his tanned face, and he stared into her clear brown eyes. "Is the war so awful?" she asked.

He kissed her on the lips, briefly. "It ain't so bad. It's just waitin' around for something to happen that riles us. Soldiers want to get it over."

They strolled and talked and kissed again until they heard her mother calling that it was time for Johnny to leave.

60

George Stone had a horse and buggy hitched to carry Johnny to the Fraley farm. Mary Lib rode along and they said little, holding hands an smiling. "Reckon you'll be goin' back to the war tomorrow," Stone said.

"Yessir, they just give us the one day."

"Reckon you heard two of them Horine boys went south. Someone said the younger one got shot, but we don't know if it's true or not."

"I ain't surprised. Richard and me was pretty good friends, but I reckon that's all over."

"Yeah, they're a bunch of dang traitors if you ask me. Makes you sick."

Johnny glanced sideways at Mary Lib, who rolled her eyes and made a face. At the end of the lane, they said goodbye. Johnny gave her a peck on the cheek while her father stared and then turned his buggy for home.

In the morning the Fraleys drove Johnny to Jefferson where he met Pete Angleberger and some Jefferson boys and hitched a ride back to camp. It was Sunday, so they went on to church, arriving late, but happy to share their news about the Marylanders being nearby and Johnny home on leave.

Two weeks later, the regiment was ordered to Poolesville where Union troops were being assembled for a move into Virginia toward Leesburg. General Stone, their commander, sent a large reconnaissance force across the Potomac near Ball's Bluff under Colonel Baker, who also was a U. S. Senator from Illinois. Baker's men marched into an ambush and were severely mauled by a larger Rebel force. The Marylanders, like most of Stone's troops, never got into the battle.

Matthews and his men were horrified by the sights at Ball's Bluff. Baker's panicked troops scrambled down the river bank while enemy sharpshooters took a steady toll, boats floundered or capsized, and little was done to remedy the catastrophe. "It was like," Matthews said, "the Rebs knew exactly what we was gonna do." The defeat angered the troops. It seemed to be caused by the stupidity of the commanders, not the ability of the men.

The soldiers weren't the only ones infuriated. Baker was killed and he was a friend of Lincoln's. Senators and newspapers created such a furor that Winfield Scott was forced to resign as the Commander in Chief, and McClellan, yet to fight a major battle, replaced him.

As winter approached, the Marylanders were moved back to camp outside Washington. There was no movement and no leave, only drill and review. They waited and griped as weeks of cold rain began.

16

Outside Richmond, Richard and Claiborne found one another on Christmas Day and went to an early morning church service. Afterward, they rode King and Prince to have dinner at Aunt Gracie and Uncle Mason Wise's home on a farm between Richmond and Fredericksburg. Aunt Gracie was their father's younger sister. She had married Mason Randolph Wise, a Virginia horse breeder and relative of the Governor. She fussed shamelessly over her nephews and shared their grief at the loss of Jacob. Her three young daughters gazed starry-eyed at the uniformed Horines, and the day became a treasure. They feasted on roast goose with chestnut dressing, an array of side dishes, and mounds of pies and cakes.

Later the Wises entertained guests from surrounding farms for dessert and punch. Richard and Claib's eyes lit up when Marcus Livingstone and his two daughters arrived. Catherine, nineteen, was the eldest, a tall, outgoing, brown haired beauty, and after introductions, she immediately began a light conservation with Richard, who found himself smitten. She was the prettiest, most intelligent woman he'd ever met. Her sister, Letitia, eighteen, a sweet faced brunette with laughing eyes, kept company with Claib, who was having difficulty overcoming his shyness. The time passed quickly as the adults pummeled the young soldiers with questions about the war, the young women standing by the brothers, keeping their glasses filled, and chatting whenever there was an opportunity. But by eight it was time to leave.

"The evening went by so fast," Richard said to Catherine as they waited for a groom to bring the Livingstone carriage. "I hope I can see you again."

"I'd like that," she said, hoping she wasn't being too bold. "Do be careful and get this awful war over soon. If you'd like I'll write you."

"That would be wonderful. Do you think your father would mind?"

"He supports the war, Richard. I think he wishes Lettie and I had been boys, but there's nothing I can do about that. Anyhow, I can tell he admires you and your brother for what you are doing."

"A note from you would be special."

Richard noticed that Letitia and Claib also seemed to be getting along well. A moment later, the brothers shook hands with the Livingstones and the other guests and said their goodbyes.

Grace and Mason Wise waited outside while the groom brought their nephews' horses. I saw you two got along with the Livingstone girls," Mason said. "We're very fond of them. They're nice people."

"Yes," Grace said, "Marcus lost his wife to childbirth years ago, but he's devoted to those girls, and they've turned out wonderful. I'm glad you like them."

On their way back to camp, Claib said, "Those two sure are pretty."

Richard nodded. "Makes you proud, such fine people. You can see what we're fighting for."

The next day, Richard reported to his company commander for assignment. When Claiborne returned to camp, he learned his regiment had orders to report to Ewell's command. They would be leaving to join Jackson's army in the Valley.

CHAPTER IV. THE ROAD TO ANTIETAM

Mary Ann used a kitchen knife to slit the envelope. He was fine, Johnny wrote. His regiment had moved to some place in Virginia, he wasn't sure where, but it looked like the Rebs were retreating. There hadn't been much shooting lately. Say hello to Mary Lib. Mary Ann sighed and placed it on the lamp table with his other letters. As usual, she prayed that the war would soon be over and Johnny home.

She had been barely eighteen when she married John Fraley, the son of a storekeeper in New Market. The Fraleys were relatives on her mother's side, and she and John had met at family get-togethers, and eventually John had come courting and they married. The Fraleys attended the Moravian Reformed Church, while the Zimmermans were Lutheran, and that had been something of a problem, but she kept on going to her church and he to his, and the children were baptized Lutheran.

Her husband's death at such an early age was a calamity, and the decision to sell the store and buy a farm a hard one. Still, Mary Ann knew her sons, they had farming in their blood, so the decision had worked out. They were able to produce crops for both their own use and a little income besides. But Mary Ann relied on Johnny as her rock. If she lost him, it would break her heart, and bad dreams had started again. She was frightened at what they might mean.

While his mother nursed her worries, Frankie was in the barn shoveling out manure from behind the cows and horses. The barnyard was a sloppy mess from winter snows and spring rains. All the animals had survived and there were two new heifer calves. Two days earlier, they had gone to a farm near Frederick and bought four pigs which were now in the pen, eating a mixture of corn, ground barley and kitchen slops.

Frankie missed Johnny, but in a way he knew he was learning to fend for himself without his older brother. Frankie looked like the Zimmermans and naturally took to his grandfather and uncles. Frankie envied Johnny for having a girlfriend and wished he had one too, but he was shy, and the farm took all of his time.

Sissy liked her brothers, even when they teased her, and missed Johnny. Sometimes she liked to help Frankie with the farm work, but she hated housework. She wished she'd been a boy. At thirteen she had her first period, and her mother had to spend a lot of time explaining.

The Saturday after Mary Ann received the letter from Johnny, she and Sissy drove to the store for supplies. There were the usual idlers--Squire Fulmer, Peck Handley, George Stone, Emmert Boyer. "Howdy, Miz Fraley," they greeted, one after the other.

Peck was glad to hear of Johnny's letter and news of the Maryland troops. "My boy don't never send no letters," he lamented. "Course, he only went through the third grade, and he don't write none too good."

"At least we do hear from our boys," Boyer said, "which is more than them as has family fightin' for the Rebs, like the Horines."

"I hear poor Elsie Horine took to her bed when she heard her boy was killed, and she's got two more down there," Mary Ann said.

"That's what I heard too," the Squire said. "We never see Horine no more, and the little Horine children don't have no more friends. It's a darn shame."

"It's worse'n that," Handley growled. "Ben Horine has always been a high handed, strong willed man, and I say now he and his boys is traitors. Who knows what all he's doin' to bring down the Union."

By then Mary Ann had her order filled and paid Ed Holter. "Yes," she said, "it is a shame. Richard Horine and my Johnny used to be friendly, but I reckon they think they have a right to their beliefs."

"The way I see it, Miz Fraley," Holter said, "if it hurts the Union and threatens the lives of boys like your brave Johnny, then maybe they don't have no right to support them Rebels."

"I shore agree with you on that," Handley grumbled. The others nodded.

On the way home, Sissy asked, "Ma, would the Horines hurt Johnny?"

"I don't know, honey, but it worries me now that there's a war on."

2

Claib Horine's company was busy loading wagons and getting their packs organized when an advance party from Jackson's army arrived in Luray. "The General says y'all get ready to move north tomorrow," an officer in the party shouted.

Ewell was prepared. "Have the men get their packs ready," he told his officers. "We'll be movin' fast. I told y'all before, Tom Jackson can be a wild man, and his men move faster than lightnin'."

A half hour later, Jackson's main body of troops started to arrive, a contingent of cavalry first, then infantry, artillery and limbers, caissons, more infantry, supply wagons, a mounted rear guard. The general himself rode alongside his troops near the front, his uniform and beard dusty, a battered cap pulled down over his eyes. He sucked a tattered piece of lemon.

"Pull the wagons on through town," Jackson ordered. "Give the men time to get a drink and then set up camp down the road. Then they can eat their rations. General Ewell," he shouted across the town square, "you and your boys ready to move tomorrow?"

"Whenever you say, General," Ewell shouted as he rode to Jackson's side.

"You'll lead the way on north then, but I don't abide laggards. If your men go too slow, these boys of mine will run right over 'em."

"Don't you worry, General. My boys know how to move." Ewell wanted to ask Jackson where they were headed and what his plans were, but Jackson had already turned away.

Approaching along the road was a drum corps banging a lusty pace. Harness rattled and wheels crunched the dry earth and thumped over ruts as the artillery neared. The air was filling with dust. Officers yelled and drovers cursed as horses shied at the onlookers lining the Luray streets.

"Give those boys some fresh water," Jackson said. "One of you men, fill my canteen and give me a fresh dipperful if you've a mind." Looking back at Ewell, Jackson said, "The Lord has favored us in our work. I expect good things on this journey." Jackson's blue eyes were gleaming. The soldiers called him "Ol' Blue Light" and said the gleam meant fighting ahead.

Ewell nodded and wondered what good things Jackson was talking about. Jackson's army now was 20,000 strong. Ewell nursed a private opinion that Tom Jackson was half cracked in the head, but Ewell's own men looked at both him and Jackson with similar apprehension. Ewell's voice often croaked like a cat with its tail pinched, and his bald head reflected the sun when he removed his worn cavalry hat. The soldiers called him Ol' Baldy and said, "Ain't he sumpin'?"

Claib stood with his company and stared at the oncoming troops. They were the roughest soldiers he had yet seen. Uniforms were ragged, hair and beards filthy and uncut. Rifles were dust coated, and wagons and artillery showed signs of wear and disrepair. Many of the men were barefoot, and of those who were shod, the shoes worn and misshapen.

The formations were orderly, but it was impossible to tell officers from men, but how those men could move. And their weapons, polished under the dust, with rags covering locks and muzzles. The men talked as they marched. They looked at Ewell's well clad troops with good humor. "Howdy boys, fine day for a stroll in the country."

"You girls have such purty uniforms--pity ol' Jack is gonna git 'em messed up."

"Bet them thar boots you boys got is gonna pinch yer poor dainty feets. Why don't y'all give 'em to us'ns so we kin break 'em in fer ya?"

"Ol' Jack'll walk yer legs right down to nubs--hardest damn gen'ral in the army."

They smiled or laughed, got their drinks, lit a pipe or bit off a chew, and moved on. Jackson didn't abide shirkers.

The next day, Claib's company was the fifth to move up the Luray Valley road along the South Fork of the Shenandoah. They maintained the brutal pace, mindful of Jackson's troops at their heels. Each hour they were allowed to rest ten minutes. The furious tempo raised clouds of dust, and many wore handkerchiefs or rags over their mouths and noses. At seven o'clock that evening they halted, ten miles from Front Royal. They ate a cold supper and bedded down. At 6 A. M. they were up and on the road, arriving at Front Royal in the early afternoon, just as the Yanks were finishing their meals. When he learned that most of the Federals were Marylanders, Jackson ordered his own First Maryland regiment to lead the attack. Claib's Virginia regiment was next in line.

The sudden appearance of Jackson's army stunned the Union troops, and they rushed about in a panic trying to organize a defense, but within minutes the outnumbered bluecoats found their situation hopeless. After a flurry of firing, Colonel Kenly, the Union commander, himself a Marylander, led most of his men across the bridge over the South Fork to escape the Rebel onslaught. Union efforts to burn the bridge failed, and Jackson's cavalry galloped across in pursuit of the fleeing troops. Within a half hour, most were encircled and forced to surrender, others had scattered and were being rounded up by the jubilant Confederates. Kenly was wounded and captured.

Also captured were tons of supplies and what remained of the Yankees' noon meals. A group of Jackson's veterans wandered over to Ewell's troops after the battle, chomping biscuits and slices of bacon and drinking hot coffee from dippers. "You boys done purty good," one of Jackson's privates said. "Jest y'all remember, when you march with ol' Gen'ral jack, y'all gits to eat a lot of Yank grub." He chuckled a raspy laugh as he walked on, munching noisily on his booty.

The troops had little time to enjoy their victory before Jackson had them up. "Damn, the crazy bastard is gonna make us move agin," troops griped. "Hell, we just got here."

"That's ol' Jack," others replied. "He's got the Lawd in his bonnet, drivin' him to ketch the devil."

Claib watched as nearly a thousand of his one-time fellow Marylanders, now Jackson's prisoners, were marched to the rear. "Anybody know any of them?" he asked soldiers in the Confederate First Maryland.

No one did. "Don't wanna know any of them bastards," one of the sergeants said.

Claib took a few minutes to talk to some of the captives but learned little. They were still stunned at being caught so easily. Claib returned to his company. Jackson already was on the move.

The next objective was Banks' army, fleeing up the valley from Strasburg toward Winchester, trying to avoid being cut off by Jackson's unexpected move to Luray and then Front Royal. A handful of Union soldiers who escaped from the Front Royal trap warned Banks, who was astonished to find Jackson threatening his rear.

Matthews and his company had been posted on guard duty across the river when Jackson attacked Front Royal. There they witnessed the growing chaos among the

Marylanders as hordes of whooping Rebs streamed upon them from all sides. Matthews tried to lead his men toward the bridge to join the battle, only to be engulfed by hundreds of frightened soldiers fleeing the onrushing graybacks. Realizing the hopelessness of their situation, Matthews ordered his men to retreat and find a position they could hold. He sought Kenly or some other superior officer for orders, but found no one. It was Fraley and Fisher who shocked him to a decision.

"Hiram," Fisher said, "there ain't a damn thing we can do."

"Amen," Johnny shouted, "let's get outta here."

They began to back away when they saw Kenly's effort to form a line along the riverbank collapse and Reb cavalry secure the bridge before it could burn. More enemy troops were approaching to outflank the remaining defenders.

"C'mon, boys," Matthews shouted, "let's skedaddle."

By instinct they ran to the east rather than toward Winchester with most of Kenly's mangled units. Two days later, they straggled across the Potomac to Poolesville and took up positions with militia units where they had been stationed previously to await orders on what to do next.

3

On May 24, forward units of Jackson's army struck Banks' retreating column, but not enough men were able to get to the battle area to stop the Yankee withdrawal. By late afternoon, Union forces took a position on a hill in front of Winchester and set up a defensive line.

Jackson and Ewell sat on their horses and watched their bone tired troops stagger into camp that evening a few miles south of the Yankees. A light rain had begun. "Have them get a good night's sleep," Jackson told his officers. "Tomorrow we take Winchester."

Claib's company cooked supper, using Yank rations and real coffee, but one after another, the men collapsed, against trees, on the ground, oblivious of the steady downpour. Only a few got blankets to protect themselves.

Before dawn they were roused. Two hours later Claib's weariness had vanished and his pulse was thumping. As far as he could see in either direction there were Confederate troops moving into battle formation. Artillery--cannon, limbers, caissons, scores of horses--moved forward, and gunners began the arduous task of getting their weapons set up and aimed. Yankee gunners had already opened fire.

Ewell positioned his men on the right and rode up and down the line, buoyed by a lusty cheer from the troops. Muskets were wiped clean and sparkling, and bayonets flashed. To the left another cheer went up as Jackson rode across the front. Orders barked and traveled down the lines. Their captain shouted at Claib's company, "See that big oak tree behind them Yank lines. Boys, we ain't to stop till we plant our battle flag and have a cool drink under that tree."

The sun was well above the hills to the east. A brisk breeze was blowing, and regimental flags snapped in the wind. The battle lines quieted for a few moments, and then the shouts again, drum rolls, and the long Rebel lines became alive and moved forward as the heavy guns began to blaze.

It was 700 yards to Banks' lines, artillery range. Musket range was 200 to 300 yards, Claib's Sharps a bit longer. Over the first 200 yards the men strode, picking up the pace as they went. Their drums beat more rapidly, and the soldiers began to trot. After another hundred yards, they came to the first fence, a low stone structure on a knoll which they leaped without hesitation. Enemy shells were finding the range, and they were taking hits but running all out, screaming as they went. Overhead they could hear their own shells whizzing, and they could see explosions in the Yank lines.

They were 300 yards from the enemy, still out of rifle range, but running uphill with little cover. Yank rifle fire quickened, still hitting the ground well ahead.

Claib squinted at a second fence, fifty yards ahead, wooden rails, skirmishers firing at him. Some of his mates were down. The company halted and fired a volley at the defenders while other companies circled their flanks. Claib's shot struck a bluecoat and he fell. Flankers cleared the rest. "To the oak tree," the captain ordered. With a loud whoop, the men leaped the rail fence to cover the final 200 yards. They ran, fired, reloaded, yelled, ran again, fired, reloaded, and then raced screaming over the final yardage into the face of enemy fire.

Many of Banks' men fought well, but for others the ferocious Rebel attack was too much, and they broke. Claib and his comrades crashed through crumbling enemy positions and raced to the oak. From there they were able to engage the remaining pockets of Banks' defenders with deadly flanking fire. Several Federals raised their arms in surrender, the rest were driven back. By noon, Banks gave up the battle, ordered retreat, and got his forces through the town and on the road to Harpers Ferry. Local townspeople took up the pursuit, throwing debris and shooting guns at the fleeing troops.

Jackson urged his troops to keep moving, but there were delays as the cavalry gathered scattered prisoners, as officers collected their units, while wounded were tended and sent to the rear, and while exhausted troops, who had just advanced 700 furious yards into the face of death and won, recovered their breath and their nerve.

Claib helped to collect his company and account for casualties, two slain and five wounded, one critically. His first battle, and he stared numbly at the fallen heaps of butternut and blue, all alive a few minutes before. He remembered the thrill when he saw his shot bring down a Yank sharpshooter, but now he saw the body of a boy, younger than him, thin, a stubble of facial hair, his grimy hands clutching his Springfield, eyes glazed in death. They collected the boy's musket, ammunition, and shoes, and left him for the burial details.

He found a comrade dead, only a few feet short of the oak, his body laying across a fallen Yank, his head smashed by a minie, blood and brains congealing on the side of his face. God, he thought, it's awful.

That afternoon they moved on to Berryville and the next day to Harpers Ferry, but Banks kept moving, crossed the Potomac to Williamsport, and found safety from Jackson's determined pursuit.

The Confederate forces returned to cheering crowds in Winchester. They had won a splendid victory, which made the hard marches and battle losses bearable. The spoils were immense. Banks had abandoned vast stores of food and clothing. They feasted on hams, vegetables, and fresh fruit. There were cases of hard drink which officers tried unsuccessfully to suppress, and uniforms and boots, blankets and coats. The shock of death on the battlefield paled, and Claib wrote home, relating the genius of Jackson and the glorious victories the army had won.

Nearby in West Virginia, Fremont had raised an army of 15,000, which he hoped to use in the Shenandoah Valley to trap Jackson in a joint operation with McDowell who was moving toward the valley from the east. His plan was to bring his force through the mountain passes to Strasburg, but the seventy miles of road from Franklin proved treacherous as heavy rains caused the column to flounder in mud. The infantry had to wait for artillery and supply wagons, and when the army finally reached Strasburg, Jackson was gone. Scouts from McDowell's army arrived the next day.

4

In a huge field north of Richmond, clouds of dust whipped about as a crowd of Texans rode in, whooping and waving their hats. Other troopers yelled and waved back, horses shied and bucked at the hubbub, and officers shouted commands to keep the cavalry units from becoming too rowdy.

More riders appeared on the road from Richmond following the Texans--the first of the Virginians, some of Stuart's own, the cream of the Confederate cavalry, over 500 strong, with wagons loaded with supplies and horses pulling several light cannon.

The campground was alive with excitement. With the Virginians rode the Maryland troopers. "Sergeant," the captain shouted to Richard Horine, "get your mounts in line and show 'em the stuff Marylanders are made of."

Horine loved it. "Let's get goin'," he shouted at Shanks Duval, who whooped and rounded up the men. They had ridden with Texans and Virginians for the past few months, and a rich camaraderie had developed. He'd gotten to know many of the troopers personally, and his name had become well known as fresh Horine horses appeared from time to time.

Over the past month a steady stream of cavalry mounts had been forwarded to the Confederate army from Horine's farm. Horine bred and raised some of these himself, but most were funneled into his stables by Southern supporters from the surrounding area. Horine and Jeb Stuart's agents had worked out an effective means for transporting the animals on a route that led across the Potomac into neighboring Loudoun County. Partisans associated with Mosby and his friends were key to the venture, and they moved as many as ten horses a month.

The Maryland squad formed up and paced forward. Twelve beautiful thoroughbreds abreast broke into a trot. The Virginians were not to be outdone, and two companies of skilled riders cantered into place and paraded into the center of the field. John Mosby led one of the companies. Besides being a key collaborator for Horine horse procurement, he had been commander of Richard's company in the Shenandoah.

Yells arose from all directions and a few excited troopers fired their revolvers. Horsemen were parading about the grounds, waving battle flags, shouting and singing, prepared for whatever Jeb Stuart planned, and as it turned out, ready for the largest cavalry raid so far in the war.

A day earlier, Richard had returned dead tired from a patrol and was told to report to his captain. For three months, the troopers had been scouts, couriers, guarding the infantry's flanks, and every other kind of duty except riding with an aggressive, fighting cavalry unit, which is what they wanted most. The snail-like movement of McClellan's ponderous army, the narrowness of the peninsula, and incessant rain and flooding made wide open cavalry action impossible, while the cautious defensive moves of Joe Johnston required the horsemen as the army's eyes and legs.

"This ain't what I come down heah to do," Shanks Duval drawled. "When we gonna see some real fightin'? Hells bells, all I done been fightin' is these damn skeeters."

Richard chuckled at his testy friend's remarks. They had ridden together, along with Granny Coleman, in the Manor Guards, and although Shanks was from a family that his father might have called white trash, he was Richard's best friend in the company

"Maybe now that Joe Johnston's gone, it'll get better with Lee," Richard said.

"I dunno," Shanks said, "some of the boys down here say he's like Johnston, call him Granny Lee."

But with re-organization under Lee, things were changing, changes that the troopers liked.

"We're ordered to a new camp," the captain had said. "General Jeb, bless his heart, is assembling pony soldiers to move against the Yanks. I'm orderin' you Maryland riders in here to ride with us in the Virginia regiment, and I'm putting you in charge, Richard, so all of you'll be gettin' use of your Dad's horses."

Now they were at the assembly point--over a thousand strong, preparing for whatever their dapper commander dished out. Richard had never seen such excitement as he rode about, and despite over a year in uniform and five battles, he was eager for action. "This time we'll whip 'em," he shouted to his men.

"You betcha," Sarge," Shanks shouted back. "We'll whip their ass good."

More officers appeared, and orders cascaded across the field. Units moved into formation, as horsemen pulled reluctant mounts into line. An officer's strong voice roared across the scene, "Troopers, dismount," and the multitude of horsemen dropped to the ground.

A Virginia colonel stepped forward. "Troopers," he shouted, "your commander, General Jeb Stuart." From the command tent, Stuart dashed out, leaped on his chestnut, and waving his plumed hat, rode in front of the assembled cavalrymen. The troopers, officer and enlisted men alike, cheered, waved their hats, and jumped up and down as the youthful general passed. Some had tears streaming down their cheeks.

Stuart rode back to the center of the parade ground and was joined by several officers. Suddenly there was silence as dust swirled in the evening breeze. "Tomorrow," he announced, "the Confederate cavalry rides against the Yankee invader." More cheering. "I know you are the finest cavalry on the face of the earth and that you will do more than your duty. Your officers have my orders. We ride at dawn. Get a good night's sleep, and may God smile upon our endeavor."

A final cheer and the troopers began to disperse. Negro grooms tended to the horses, and tired soldiers began to arrange bedding, cook supper, and speak of their good fortune to ride with Stuart.

Richard found a grassy spot and sat down by a gnarled willow tree. He studied the scene and looked at his brown, callused hands. The Marylanders gathered around him once their horses were fed and bedded down for the night. Not much more than a year since the first battle, he thought, when he and Jacob stood together near Berryville, staring at a handful of dead bodies from the skirmish. They had been revulsed by the grisly reality of death. Now he barely noticed it. Thousands had fallen, their heads and extremities shattered, bodies ripped open in grotesque ways, and he sensed the killing would go on. War was more dreadful than he ever imagined, and he realized as he sat in the twilight, how much he had changed, how nothing appalled him any more. He was a veteran of the carnage. His job was to fight, to kill, to stay alive. Tomorrow they would ride with Stuart, and he expected the war to be exciting again.

They were roused at daybreak. By seven Stuart's men had ridden nearly twenty miles, fording the Chicahominy well to the north of Richmond, their destination still undisclosed. To the Shenandoah with Jackson was what most guessed. They halted and rested while officers reviewed maps and their horses grazed. A group of children gathered and stared.

Then they were on the move again, circling east toward the banks of the Pamunkey before heading southeast to the rear of the Union army's positions, and it was clear--they were going after McClellan. By late afternoon they were in Old Church. A company of Virginians and Marylanders was sent to find what they could about the Union positions to the southwest toward Gaines Mills. Richard had both King and Prince with him, and he rode King while Shanks rode the younger horse.

Three miles out, they surprised a band of Yankee riders who were resting under a grove of chestnut trees. "Rest easy, boys," the Virginia captain said as they surrounded the startled Yanks. "Sergeant, gather up the blue bellies' arms so's they ain't tempted to be heroes."

Richard dismounted and gathered up five Sharps, six sabers, and a Remington revolver from a lieutenant and his five men. "Where in hell did you Johnnies come from?"

"Never you mind, Lieutenant," the captain drawled. "Just give us your papers and tell us where your base is. Then we might not be too hard on y'all."

"You can go to hell."

"Sergeant, get their papers. Some of you boys give him a hand." Quickly they went through the angry Yanks' pockets and saddlebags and came up with their orders and command papers.

"You boys hold these prisoners here a spell, and we'll have a look around," the captain told five of his men. The rest of the troopers rode to the west, back-tracking the Union scouting party, a simple task on the muddy road. On a hill they were able to see portions of the Union lines, and through a telescope, get good detail of enemy numbers and deployment.

When they returned, the captain said, "You Yanks mount up, y'all be ridin' with us. Let's get outta here."

"You damn Rebs gonna be sorry for this," one of the Yanks told Richard.

"You bluebellies better be damn thankful we're good Christian folk and don't shoot y'all for trespassin' on our land," the captain said. "Now shut up and get movin'."

Richard chuckled when he heard the Yanks still swearing under their breath. "You boys best be glad the captain is in a good mood," he told them. "He's meaner'n hell when he's riled."

Stuart was delighted with the scouting party's report. They made camp, held their prisoners for the night, and set out the next morning toward Tunstall's Station on the rail line from the Federal supply base at White House. A raiding party broke off at mid morning and hit Porter's supply area from the rear ten miles south of the point the captives were taken. A group of New Yorkers was unloading wagons when they found hundreds of Reb firearms pointed at them. In a matter minutes, the Yanks lost wagons, horses, supplies, weapons, and trousers, as the whooping Rebs rode back cross country.

Union commanders were aware something was amiss--a scouting party missing, several dozen angry bare-ass New Yorkers--pretty convincing evidence. Porter ordered a force of cavalry to reconnoiter to the east.

By the time the Yanks moved, Stuart was another fifteen miles away, and the Union supply railroad was a shambles. One train was intercepted, its contents taken, and then blown up. Several hundred yards of rails were removed, and the roadbed was blasted.

That night Stuart set up camp five miles north of the Forge Bridge across the Chicahominy. Scouts returned with news that the bridge had been washed out by the floods. Stuart had fifty captured wagons full of Union supplies. He had taken over a hundred prisoners and released most of them at remote areas along the way. He had detailed knowledge of Porter's position and was making headway in locating the remainder of the Union army.

When they arrived at the river, Stuart found that not only was the bridge out but the fords they hoped to use were impassable. In three hours, they improvised their escape, using the Forge Bridge abutments and pillars as a base for long beams and boards stripped from a nearby warehouse. Horses, wagons and artillery crossed, and the makeshift bridge was destroyed before the troopers headed for Charles City Court House and the James River. Along the way, the Confederates were cheered by the locals, and rewarded with baked goods and fruit.

Late on the third day, they hit Harrison's Landing on the James and captured more supplies, then headed northwest back to Richmond on the New Market road. At New Market they were opposed by a belligerent Union regiment, but after a brief skirmish, they pushed by the Yanks who had no artillery support.

A few more hours and they completed the ride around McClellan's army and rode through Confederate lines into Richmond. The daring raid and the massive amount of captured supplies boosted the army's morale and earned Lee's praise. The information gave the new commander what he needed to know to prepare his campaign to drive the Union army away from Richmond.

The following day Richard was summoned to Stuart's headquarters. When he arrived, he found his captain and colonel present. "Horine," the colonel said, "General Stuart has decided it's time to bring you Marylanders together to form a separate company as part of my regiment. You will be the lieutenant. What say you to that?"

Richard burst out laughing, and then stopped self consciously. "I'm stunned, uh, really pleased, Sir. I'll do my best, and I hope you'll find a Maryland company as good as your Virginians."

"Well spoken, Horine," Stuart said, rising from his chair. "You and your boys did fine in our little run around the Yanks, and we want to give you some recognition. I've known you since we first met at Harpers Ferry, and I appreciate the horses your family has sent us."

"Th-thank you, Sir," Richard stammered. "Thank you." He saluted and left walking on air.

A few miles from Richmond, days later, the Horine brothers re-united. Richard had gotten a few hours away from his regiment and rode King to where Ewell's men were positioned. He found Claib sitting with his squad by a graveyard near a village on the New Market road. Only a few weeks after eluding the Union trap at Winchester, and then winning two more major battles, Jackson was called to the Peninsula to help Lee drive McClellan's army back to the James River.

"Godamighty but it's good to see you, little brother."

"You too, Richard. Well, would you look at this. You got promoted."

"Yep, a gen-u-wine lieutenant in the cavalry, courtesy of General Jeb himself. Claib, I'd give anything to get you to join us. Isn't there some way to get you transferred to Stuart?"

"I've tried, Richard, but I don't think Jackson will ever approve it."

"Let's try again. I'll talk to my colonel. We could really use you."

"Sure, I'll push from my side. Were you on the ride around the Yanks?"

"You bet I was."

"I'd give anything to have been with you."

Richard described the adventure in detail. "How is it with Ewell?" he asked.

"Since I got transferred to Ewell, we've been part of Jackson's army. I never believed men could move as far or as fast as we do. It's hard soldierin', but brother, it's exciting." Claib described the Valley campaign from Luray to Front Royal to Winchester, the battles at Strasburg, New Market, and the last two at Cross Keys and Port Republic, the supplies and men captured, the cheers of the womenfolk, the growing pride of the troops.

When Richard asked about Jackson's action in the recent campaign, Claib shook his head. "I don't know what went wrong, but we only got into real fightin' one day. Ol' Jack didn't seem to have his heart in it. We got lost and when we finally found our way, it was dark and the fighting was over. Then we ran into bridges that were washed out so we couldn't get to the position Lee had ordered, and after that, I swear, ol' Jack just sat down under a tree and went to sleep. I don't know what Lee thought."

"That's funny, but I heard about the same thing around camp. They say Lee was fuming."

"Have you heard anything from home?"

"Not for a month or so," Richard said. "How about you?"

"Longer than that, maybe two months. We just did not get mail in the valley, not the way we moved."

"Papa doesn't say much. Mama's still not over losing Jacob, so I reckon things aren't too good. Most of the people have sided with the bluebellies and won't have nothing to do with Mama and the children."

The brothers sat and stared down the road. They were homesick, and it seemed the home they were sick for might never be the same. Claib broke the silence, "I'd sure like to see 'em and the old place sometime soon. I guess, in a way, I'm like Mama. I'm not over losing Jakie either."

"I know," Richard said. "I'd give anything to have him back. I wanted him in the cavalry with me, but it was the same problem as with you. Once he got with Jackson, he was stuck. I'm not sure he even wanted to change. He was fascinated with Jackson."

"I'm the same way," Claib said. "Jackson has us do things I didn't think were possible. He acts like he's crazy some of the time, but he outsmarts the Yanks at every turn."

"Well," Richard said, "let's pray it's soon over, now that the Yanks are whipped down here."

"I hope so too, but they sure fought us hard enough. If only they'd give it up and let us be."

"Yeah, but who knows? I'm proud to be a Confederate, no matter what happens."

"Me too. I can't stand the northern bluebellies. We fought a bunch of Yank Marylanders at Front Royal and they were the sorriest lot you ever saw. They didn't fight very good and had no idea what they were fightin' for, just save the Union and bunk like that. They don't care about states rights or freedom or anything we believe in."

"Well it's a darn shame Maryland hasn't seceded. Must drive Papa wild."

"Maybe Lee will move that way and get something done."

"When we came down here from the Valley, we were near Uncle Mace and Aunt Gracie's place. I sure wish we coulda stopped."

"I reckon it's not our aunt and uncle you were thinking about."

"Well, it would sure be nice to see those Livingstone girls again."

"I got a letter from Catherine and wrote her back. She said she would like me to write."

"How'd you know where to send it."

"I didn't. I sent it to Aunt Gracie and asked her to pass it on, and I got an answer last week."

"Do you think I could do the same thing with Letitia?"

"I think it'd be a darn shame if you didn't. Cathy wrote that she passed on her sister's regards to you and they wondered how you were."

"Cathy, huh?"

"That's how she signed her letter."

"You rascal. I'm gonna do it. Give me Aunt Gracie's address."

The brothers shook hands and embraced before parting. They were bloodied by the months of raw, bitter battle, now old hands at the business of waging war. Their once stylish uniforms were worn and soiled, and their firearms showed the marks of heavy use. As he started to ride back to his camp, Richard glanced back. Don't be foolish, little brother, he thought, it would kill us if we lost you too. One last glance as he rounded a bend, Claib was still waving.

Ten days later, the cavalry moved north. McClellan was withdrawing from Richmond. Pope's army in northern Virginia was becoming a nasty threat, and Lee decided he must stamp it out.

5

"Mama, I hate squashing potato bugs. They're nasty and makin' my hand all green."

"It's got to be done, honey," Mary Ann replied. "Would you rather hoe these here beans?"

"No, I don't wanna do none of it. I'd rather help Frankie."

Mary Ann paused and rested on her hoe in the boiling sun, while she mopped the sweat from her face and neck with a worn red handkerchief. "I want you to help Frankie this afternoon, honey. He's got to get the rest of the wheat in before it's so dry the grain all shatters out in the field."

"Why can't Grandpa and Uncle Sam help?"

"Grandpa is too sick to help any more. His dropsy is worse and his rheumatism has kicked up so bad he can hardly walk. With Vernon leavin' to work at the foundry, Sam can hardly keep up with his own work, much less help us." Vernon had been Sam's hired man.

Sissy shook two mature striped bugs into her hand and beheaded each, making a face as she performed the execution. "I don't know why God made potato bugs," she said.

"Same reason he made ticks and skeeters and varmints, I reckon, testing our faith."

Mary Ann squinted at the sun, nearly midday, time to fix dinner. The garden lay in a large plot by the log farmhouse and supplied a substantial portion of the food they would need for the year. When Johnny was still home, the garden had been Frankie's job, but now the farm took all his time. There were rows of potatoes and sweet corn, cabbages for sauerkraut, pumpkin vines just beginning to bloom, the pumpkins for canning and pies, pole beans and snap beans, nearly ready for picking, canning, and drying. There were red beets, carrots and turnips. Cucumbers were pickled as was watermelon rind, and Mary Ann made and bottled a sweet relish of corn and chopped vegetables.

"Sissy," Mary Ann said, "you finish up here. I gotta go start dinner." Noon was their heaviest meal. She was fixing a stew with a hen they'd found killed by a weasel the night before. The meat was still fresh, since the weasel had done little more than cut the chicken's neck and drain its blood. Frankie had set a trap in hopes of catching the varmint. The chicken was simmering in a black iron pot over the wood stove, and she added peas, green onions and a few of last year's potatoes, which were soft but still edible. She had thought of making coffee, but was just too tired from the work and nagging worry. They had not heard from Johnny for weeks.

Sissy came in, and without a word, began to wash her hands.

"Did you finish, honey?"

"Yes, and I can't get this green slime off my hands. It's all under my fingernails. I hate it."

"It won't kill you. Ring the dinner bell for Frankie."

Sissy threw the dirty water out the back door, dried her hands, and sulked out into the yard where the cast iron bell hung from a pole. She pulled the rope back and forth, and the bell clanged its familiar loud ding-dong, echoing across the valley. Buster began barking.

A few minutes later, Frankie came in and began to wash in the same tin basin Sissy had used, ladling water from a wooden bucket. He scrubbed his face and hands with home made lye soap and used a worn cotton towel to dry himself. He had let his whiskers grow into a thin beard and took considerable time trying to clear it of wheat chaff and dust.

"How you doin' with the wheat, son?" Mary Ann asked.

"I still got a small patch left to scythe. I guess we can get most of it in this afternoon if Sissy helps."

"I'm tired out from killin' them nasty potato bugs," Sissy complained.

"Potato bugs is fun," Frankie said.

"You ain't a girl, and girls shouldn't have to squash bugs."

"No letter from Johnny, I reckon?" Frankie said.

"Ain't had a chance to check on the mail. I'm scared Lee is moving on Washington, and he'll be back to fightin' again."

"Maybe Pope's army will stop him," Frankie said. "This ol' hen ain't none too bad."

"I wish this dumb war was over," Sissy said. "I don't like eatin' chicken killed by some awful ol' weasel."

They were quiet for a while, eating and thinking their private thoughts. Keeping up the farm work had gotten more and more difficult. During the winter they had coped, getting wheat ground into flour at the nearby mill and making their own cornmeal with a hand grinder. In November they had butchered three hogs and the meat had been cured. This had seen them through, along with the chickens, eggs, milk, home churned butter, and the fruits and vegetables Mary Ann stored in various ways.

The spring work was hard. One of the four horses came up lame, and another was suffering from old age and a bad eye. The war had taken many of the state's best horses, and they could not find affordable replacements. Then Grandpa

Zimmerman had gotten ill and could no longer provide the help and good humor that they enjoyed. Frankie did his best, and Mary Ann and Sissy did all they could to help, but work piled up.

After they had eaten, Mary Ann said, "Next year, Frankie, we won't plant all the fields. It's too much."

Frankie scowled. "Aw, Mama," he said, "I'll get it done. We gotta have all the fields." He walked to the door. "You comin', Sissy?"

Sissy grabbed her sunbonnet and followed her brother to the wheat field.

6

At the store, several men crowded around Oscar Fisher. Peck Handley and Squire Fulmer were there, so were Boyer, Gross, and George Stone. Cletus Barnes had ridden down from his mountain home for his weekly visit.

"See what Oscar's boy says here," Peck exclaimed. "Read it again, Oscar, read that part when them boys was down near Poolesville."

Fisher adjusted his spectacles and stammered, "Just hold your horses a minute, Peck, yeah, now, here it is. He says, 'Papa, see if you can find out how to stop the Horines from sending horses to the Rebs.' Now here's the part, 'Three of us, Hiram Matthews, John Fraley and me, seen a bunch of Reb cavalry down near Poolesville, leading what surely was Horine horses. What we want to know is how does old man Horine get word to the Rebs, and where do all them horses come from. Hiram told our commander, but we don't know if he has time to do something about it. Can you and your friends please check on this and see if it can be stopped?'" Fisher hesitated for a moment. "Albert goes on about other things, but this business of Horine and them horses, why that's awful."

There was a general buzz of agreement. "The ol' sonuvabitch oughta be hung," Boyer said.

Clete Barnes threw his hat on the floor. "Dang right. I been fer that all along. I niver did like the ol' buzzard, and now he's gittin' our boys kilt."

George Stone agreed. "One of my girls is sweet on the Fraley boy, and she tells me from his letter that he's dang put out about it, just like Oscar's boy says."

Peck spit accurately into the cuspidor. "Whadya think, Squire?"

"Well, it sounds bad, gentlemen, I'll grant you that, but I'd just as soon leave the hanging to the army and the courts. One thing I do wonder about, Mr. Fisher. How could our men tell a Horine horse from any other horse?"

The men looked at one another. "Well sir," Fisher said as he scratched his head, "I reckon Horine has always dealt in a certain kinda horse, mostly thoroughbreds. I dunno, how would they know that, Peck?"

"I think our fellers seen Rebs with horses like Horine always kept and figgered it out."

"Figgered it out right too, if you is to ask me," Gross snapped. "Me and my youngest boy go by the Horine place ever' day, and we done seen men and horses always comin' and goin'."

The Squire said, "Shouldn't we ask the sheriff to look into this? Men like Hiram Matthews and Oscar's boy and John Fraley are pretty dependable."

Ed Holter agreed. "That's what I'm thinking too, Squire. If we try to do something among ourselves, we may alert the Rebs, but if we get the authorities involved, maybe we can get to the bottom of it."

"Well," Boyer growled, "you fellers do what you think best, some of us think we got a rat in our midst, and something's gotta be done to stomp on it. Too many good people around here got boys fightin' for the Union." Three of the men nodded and got up to leave.

Fulmer and Holter talked with Oscar Fisher afterwards. "By golly," Fisher said, "I didn't mean to stir up no bees' nest. I was just bein' neighborly, showin' Peck the letter, seein' as how his boy and mine are out there together."

Holter shook his head. "It don't make no difference, Oscar. Some of them men have been hot about Horine for a long time, ever since the war started and his boys went south."

"I hope they don't do anything dumb," the Squire said. "I'll talk to the commander of the Home Brigade in Frederick and see what he says. I don't like Horine no better than any of the rest of you fellows."

7

They had ridden most of the day in the rain and were soaked. Their horses were tired and needed to be rested and fed. "Where in the devil is Jeb takin' us, Richard?" Granny Coleman asked.

"Dang if I ain't about drownded," Shanks Duval said.

Richard Horine nudged King along, riding his more experienced horse, while one of Stuart's staff officers, whose mount had come up lame, was riding Prince. "We're tryin' to get behind the Yank lines is all I know, Granny," Richard said.

"Never find them in this rain," Granny complained.

A few minutes later, they entered the town of Warrenton, and townspeople soon came out to greet them. "What can we do for you boys?" one of the ladies asked.

"Grain for the horses would be appreciated, ma'am," Richard said. Stuart and his aides talked with the town fathers, collecting information about Federal deployment, so Richard led his men off the street to a small livery stable where their horses were fed, and the ladies appeared with platters of ham, fresh baked bread, hard boiled eggs, and fruit. The respite was welcome but short lived, for Richard was summoned by Fitz Lee who explained their assignment.

"Boys," Richard said when he returned, "it's the railroad, station's about five miles from here, and we're gonna raise hell." In a few minutes they were on their way.

After dark, Fitz Lee's men were in position and began to move toward the unsuspecting enemy. The Marylanders were part of the contingent moving on the depot when a rolling thunderstorm swept into the area. Unable to see, they had to dismount, but the downpour hid their movement. They had the depot surrounded before an alarm was raised and a startled but determined band of defenders began to resist. Heavy musket fire erupted in the rain.

Rooney Lee led the attack. When the rain slackened, he shouted, "Let's charge 'em."

With a whoop, the regiment remounted and raced through the ranks of the stunned defenders. Several were captured, and the remainder fled into the darkness. Efforts by Stuart's other units to burn the railroad bridge failed as heavy rainfall began anew. Nonetheless, they captured several hundred Union soldiers and hauled away a huge amount of supplies, including General John Pope's dress uniform.

8

A few days later on an embankment near the Manassas battlefield and a half mile from the Groveton crossroads, Claib and a comrade played a game of checkers on a captured Yankee checker board. A group of soldiers gathered around watching the action and making comments.

"If you fellas is so dang smart, then y'all play him," the soldier growled as Claib completed a double jump. "I'm hongry, give me another can of them Yank peaches."

Ewell's men had been resting along this concealed ridge for over a day, feasting on spoils collected from their raid on a Union supply depot only a few miles away, after an incredible march through rugged terrain that got them behind Union lines. Now Jackson had hidden them away, and they were gettin' much needed rest and nourishment. All along the abandoned railroad embankment and the surrounding forested ridge, 20,000 troops were having a picnic--eating, smoking, gossiping, playing games, and waiting for whatever ol' Jack had for them next.

After the brothers separated outside Charles City Court House, Claib had again requested transfer to the Maryland cavalry, but as feared, his request never got past his captain. "Horine, y'all the best of my sergeants, and I need you, what with the General about to hit them blue bellies again."

So Claib had marched north with Ewell. On August seventh they had their first battle of the new campaign and defeated Banks' corps at Cedar Mountain. Then they had circled around the Yank lines and captured their main supply depot. Jackson's veterans felt they were close to invincible, and although many still felt he was somewhat tetched in the head, they held a grim respect for the military genius of General Tom Jackson.

"Holy shee-it," a soldier exclaimed from the edge of the woods where Claib and the rest of Ewell's men were lounging. "You fellers ain't gonna believe this."

"Ain't gonna believe what?" Claib shouted.

"A whole damn Yank army is marchin' down the road out yonder, and ol' Jack is out there reviewin' 'em."

"What?" Several of the soldiers arose and trotted to the soldier's vantage point.

"If that ain't the damndest thing you ever seen," another exclaimed. "Sarge," he yelled at Claiborne, "get your ass over here and look at this."

Claiborne scrambled to his feet. "Captain, best you come over here too."

In a few more seconds, most of the regiment was staring in amazement as their commander, Stonewall Jackson, paraded on his horse, Little Sorrel, up and down in front of the wooded embankment in full view of a Yank division, without getting any attention from the column only a quarter mile away. "The thing of it is," the captain said, "ol' Jack looks like some dumb ol' sumbitch wanderin' around lost out there."

"With that ol' cadet cap pulled down over his eyes and dirty ol' coat he always wears, I can see why the Yanks don't pay him no mind," Claib said. "He don't look no more like a general than any of us."

"Look at that little Fancy strut," a soldier shouted. Fancy was the troops' name for Jackson's small, homely horse. Claib's captain shook his head in wonder.

Several horsemen skidded down the bank to join their commander. "Look, there's ol' Goggle Eyes," someone said, referring to Ewell.

"Hell, there's Hill," the captain said. "Them Yanks still ain't givin' 'em no never mind. Boys, be lookin' to your weapons. I don't think ol' Jack is gonna let them Yanks march by much longer."

For a mile along the ridge, men were moving. Muskets and ammo boxes were gathered, canteens filled, newly captured shoes and boots pulled onto callused feet, flags and drums collected, and units assembled, veterans prepared to fight.

Regiment by regiment they moved to the edge and watched as their high command conferred. When the officers turned and rode back toward them, they knew what was coming, and a moment later, as their officers shouted and waved their sabers, the troops cut loose, yelling and charging down the bank and through the trees.

Once more the battle lines formed. Startled Union regiments groped their way into fighting formation. Confederate artillery was shoved into place and began to boom. Units dressed up their lines, battle flags moved to the front, and the drum roll of attack echoed across the valley.

The Confederates trotted forward with a piercing scream until they were in musket range and opened a deadly fire. They expected the Yanks to buckle and run. The enemy was mostly green farm boys from Wisconsin, conspicuous in their black parade hats, but they stood, took their punishment, and delivered the same to the Rebs. Hundreds fell to a fusillade of rifle and cannon fire.

The Yanks brought up reinforcements, and Claib found his regiment being pushed back by superior numbers and heavy gunfire. Ewell himself came forward leading more infantry, to increase the pressure on the advancing Yanks. Someone shouted, "It's General Ewell," and a loud cheer resounded, followed by a hail of Yank gunfire aimed at the area of the cheer. "For God's sake," the captain shouted, "don't do that again." More men fell as shells exploded, but Confederate artillery was effective, and the Yank advance halted. The fierce battle near the Groveton crossroads and around Brawner's farm raged for two hours with neither side giving quarter.

Jackson lost over a thousand men dead and wounded, and the Union as many, until darkness halted the carnage. Then the Rebels moved back to the position from where they had advanced a few hours before.

Ewell did not return with them. When the fighting died down, his men found him unconscious from loss of blood. His knee was shattered, and in the fury of the battle, his wound went unnoticed. The surgeons saved his life, but he lost his leg.

At the camp, the soldiers threw themselves down exhausted. "Helluva fight," Claib told his captain.

"Those Yanks fought harder'n I ever expected, but I think ol' Jack got what he wanted."

"What's that?"

"He wants the Yanks to come after us. He figures nobody can push this army outta this position, no matter how many troops they throw at us, and their casualties will be dreadful."

Claib looked about the camp at the weary men. They had just learned that Ewell was carried off the field in grave condition. "We're gonna miss Dick Ewell," he said. Then he pondered. "I wonder where Marse Robert and Longstreet are?"

At that moment, Claib's brother knew exactly the whereabouts of Lee and Longstreet. The cavalry had been screening the army's movement as Lee brought up the bulk of his troops from the Peninsula, leaving Richmond lightly defended and duping McClellan as to his intent. Now Longstreet's corps was moving toward Jackson's right, hoping to arrive in time for an opportunity to attack the Union flank when Pope struck at Jackson. The Maryland troopers were part of the cavalry units on Longstreet's extreme right, creating confusion for Union reinforcements from the Army of the Potomac.

"Bring your men around," Fitz Lee's orders were relayed to Richard.

"Company, follow me," Richard ordered. He was riding Prince, while Shanks had King, having lost another mount a few days earlier.

9

As Jackson's corps moved back to their defensive positions, Pope was ecstatic for he now knew his enemy's location. He sent forward most of his forces in an effort to destroy the army that had plagued the Union in northern Virginia since the beginning of the war. Jesse Reno commanded the Second Division of the Ninth Army Corps. His First Brigade, under the command of Colonel James Nagle, included the Second Maryland Regiment. Matthew's company, after fleeing the debacle at Front Royal, had remained posted along the Potomac during most of June. The First Maryland no longer existed as an effective fighting force since being overwhelmed at Front Royal, and it would have to be re-organized later. Matthews' company was sent to join the Second Maryland a few days before the battle at Groveton.

August 29, the day after Groveton, opened just as Claib's captain predicted. Pope took Jackson's bait and ordered an all out attack. First, Sigel, who had replaced Fremont, mounted a spirited assault on the embankment, gaining some ground before being pushed back by Confederate counter strokes. While Sigel's survivors held on in the brush at the base of the embankment, Hooker's corps smashed into Hill's position and nearly overran the Confederates before Jackson sent reinforcements to repel the Union forces. Pope poured in more troops, and by mid afternoon, Jackson's lines were struggling to hold on.

At four in the afternoon, Reno ordered Nagle's brigade to attack the center of Jackson's position. The Marylanders formed on the right, a New Hampshire regiment on the left, with the 48th Pennsylvania in a second line about fifty paces behind. Matthews and his men peered into the heavy woods several hundred yards ahead where remnants of regiments that had made earlier assaults were holding on behind trees and rocks, hidden by swales and ditches. Numbers of dead and wounded littered the ground, and steady cannonading and musketry fire blanketed the area.

"What a bloody mess," Al Fisher said.

"What's in those woods?" Johnny asked. "Have the Rebs got some kind of fort? Why don't our artillery blow 'em outta there?"

"Can't see nothin'," Fisher said.

Matthews sucked on a sore tooth. "I heard the colonel say there's dirt bank the bastards are hidin' behind."

A shell exploded a few dozen yards away. Far behind them, three Union napoleons belched their reply. Nagle stepped to the front where two men held the regimental colors. Drummers began a rhythmic cadence, and the line began to move. "Dang if I don't wish we was caught along with Kenly's men," Fisher grumbled.

"What, and miss this nice little frolic General Pope has got set up for us?" Johnny said.

"Step lively, boys," Matthews ordered. "Gotta get to cover of yonder trees." A half dozen rifle shots whistled into their lines. Two men fell. Gross and Baumgartner were cursing.

Johnny began to sing:
"Way down yonder in Beaver Creek,
All the gals have great big feet,

Sing son, kitty, can'tcha ki-me-oh."

A shell crashed behind them, scattering a few Pennsylvanians. "Fraley, well you shut up?" Fisher yelled. A minie kicked up dirt at Fisher's feet.

"If you sing," Johnny shouted, "Rebs won't shoot atcha'."

"We'll hang Jeff Davis from a sour apple tree," Fisher croaked. They'd entered the woods, and a bullet clipped a branch above Fisher's head. "You're full of crap, Johnny."

"Froggy went a-courtin', and he did ride," Johnny sang, as the regiment fired an erratic volley at the unseen enemy. A minie hit the tree beside him. Another nipped his pants leg. "You damn Rebs had better hide," he improvised, as he squeezed off another shot.

A soldier named Hargett fell beside Johnny, struck in the leg. "Got me, John," he said. Johnny crouched and started to loosen the soldier's belt to make a tourniquet.

"C'mon, John," Matthews called, "keep movin'. Orderlies will look to the wounded."

"Sorry," John said, "gotta go."

"I'll manage," Hargett said as continued working on the tourniquet.

Now they could see the enemy position through the brush and the smoke. The Rebs were raising up over the bank and firing, and then ducking back. The Marylanders positioned themselves behind trees and began a steady fire. Nagle moved behind the Maryland and New Hampshire positions, prodding his men forward. After a minute, he shouted, "Let's go get 'em, boys, run them bastards off that bank."

The two regiments split, Maryland to the right, New Hampshire to the left, permitting the Pennsylvanians to move forward and fill the center. As Rebel fire sharpened, Nagle and his regimental officers ordered the brigade to charge. Firing and shouting wildly, the soldiers scrambled up the embankment. When they reached the crest, they found themselves able to fire down upon the Rebels who had sought cover in the old railroad cut. The Confederates were stunned by their predicament and many were shot while others either surrendered or scrambled out of the trap and ran for their lives. Pockets of Rebels continued to fire from nearby positions, causing Nagle's men to scatter and seek cover.

Matthews tried to gather his disorganized company so they could advance further. Several of his men were missing and others were in the process of moving a handful of prisoners to the rear. "Where's Fraley?" he asked Fisher who was still firing at the fleeing enemy.

"Don't know, probably singing to them prisoners."

"Fraley," Matthews shouted.

"Over here," Johnny replied, "got my hands full, dammit. Give me a hand." Fifty yards away, a cluster of Rebels had taken cover behind several fallen logs and had Fraley and a half dozen of his comrades pinned down in the railroad cut.

"Sing to 'em, John," Fisher called.

"Stop it, Al," Matthews said. "C'mon, let's get the rest of the company and roust the bastards outta there."

It took the Marylanders a few minutes to collect themselves and move around the defenders. As soon as the graycoats found themselves threatened by flanking fire, they skedaddled. "You boys can come out now if you ain't shot," Matthews called.

A half dozen soldiers climbed out of the pit, led by Johnny. "Oh, the ol' gray mare," he sang, "she ain't what she used to be."

"I think she shit on the single tree," Fisher said.

"Many long years ago," Johnny sang.

"Let's move, men," Nagle ordered.

The brigade surged forward into the forest after Jackson's fleeing troops. Matthews' entire company, those still able to fight, was singing, "The ol' gray mare, she ain't what she used to be, ain't what she used to be, ain't what she used to be, many long years ago." Al Fisher continued to add irreverent comments to the company's amusement as they moved through the woods. It was then that a heavy burst of gunfire from reinforcements, Brad Johnson's brigade rushing forward to seal the breech, stopped Nagle's men and drove them back. Jackson sent more troops and the Rebels began a robust counter attack.

First, the New Hampshire troops on the left began to fall back as Confederates smashed their flanks. Their collapse exposed the Pennsylvanians' and they were forced to give way, and the Marylanders found their forward position untenable. In a matter of minutes, the entire brigade was falling back, pursued by superior numbers of the enemy.

Matthews' company crashed through the woods, leaping over bodies, trying to help the wounded. Nagle was trying to get his troops to form a line to stop the Confederate onslaught. Matthews found his men strewn among remnants of other commands and could not locate anyone from his own command. A West Virginia Captain was trying to stop the retreat and get a battle line formed.

"Stop," Matthews shouted to his men, "form up here with these boys."

The Marylanders turned and fell to the ground. Johnny loaded his Springfield and peered into the woods. A ragged line of Confederates was moving toward them. Someone shouted, "Fire," and he fired. They reloaded and fired again. The gray line staggered and slowed. On the next volley, the Rebels stopped, fired a volley, and then dissolved back among the trees.

Matthews led his men back to the hill where they had started their attack and found Nagle with what remained of his command. The disconsolate soldiers collapsed and listened as the firing began to intensify again. They were still in the same position a few hours later when night fell.

10

Claib's unit and the Stonewall Brigade had lost nearly half their men in the bitter fighting near Groveton, and the troops were held out of the brutal battles of the next day, but on the afternoon of the thirtieth, Porter launched an attack with thousands of fresh troops, and the brigade's weary veterans, now barely 500 strong, were sent forward as the last resort to meet the attack. Claib watched as the massed lines of blue swept into the Confederate line, and another hand-to-hand battle for survival began.

When Brad Johnson's brigade began to collapse under the pressure from Porter's division, the Stonewalls were sent to stop the rout. Hundreds dropped on both sides. The Stonewall Brigade's Colonel Baylor was killed, as was the Fourth Virginia's captain when he took the colors and led a counter charge. Jackson saw that his old brigade was about to be overrun and ordered Claib's company to the front from where Early had positioned them. Next he sent for artillery fire, and Lee initiated an intense barrage that battered the Union flank, pinning hundreds of bluecoats around the unfinished railroad bank.

The troops held, although driven back from the embankment, and Jackson's flank was in contact with Longstreet's corps.

After holding on for an hour, the Union position was being decimated by artillery fire, and Porter had his men retreat from the death trap as best they could. The Union defenders clustered in the center away from the bombardment, weakening Pope's left flank. Stuart reported to Lee that the Yankees had committed their last reserves, and Longstreet struck.

Hood's Texans rolled into the Union flank. A small contingent of Federals tried to meet this threat, and fierce fighting broke out along the hills south of the Warrenville Pike. Thousands dropped, as the desperate Union army struggled to save itself. Soon Matthews and his men were thrown into the cauldron trying to slow the devastating Rebel attack.

As the Union defense fell back and night approached, Jackson brought his troops forward and began to advance, catching Pope's army in the jaws of a vicious pincer. Claib was among the thousands ordered to pursue the panicked enemy army, but Jackson's men were exhausted from three day's of hard fighting, so fresher troops had to take the lead. Time elapsed, and most of the Yanks reached the safety of Centerville.

A despondent band of Marylanders marched along a dirt road in the pitch dark, trying to keep contact with their comrades. "I tell you, Hi," Johnny said, "I don't think this feller, Pope, has the sense of a jackass."

"Shit, John," Fisher said, "don't you go insultin' no mule."

"We'll git 'em next time, dammit," Matthews said.

CHAPTER V. ANTIETAM

On September 4, Lee invaded Maryland. Stuart was the first to cross the Potomac, his Marylanders among the troopers taking the lead. Near Point of Rocks they were fired upon by Federal troops, but as more riders crossed, the Yankees fled.

Jackson's infantry followed on Stuart's heels. They drove off scattered resistance near Poolesville and the Monacacy railroad crossing and moved on to Buckeystown where they stopped for the night. Stuart set up camp near Urbana and then sent men on to scout Frederick.

Richard was given permission to separate from Stuart and visit his father and gather information. Stuart had quarreled with many of the Marylanders and assigned them to unpopular scouting duties. With his picked squad of six troopers Richard waited until after midnight before riding across country lanes to the Horine farm some two miles from their camp.

A mile from home, Richard and his men rode quietly by a ramshackle log house sitting in an oak grove where the Gross family lived. Bill Gross was outside relieving himself, having drunk a considerable amount of hard cider during the evening, when he saw the riders and recognized their gray uniforms. He hurried back into his house and got his shoes, hat, clothing, and his muzzle loading shotgun.

A few minutes later, the riders cut across fields to the Horine home, tied their horses quietly by the backyard, and waited as Richard tapped on the back door. Presently a light appeared in the kitchen and there was movement of window curtains. "Papa," Richard whispered, "put out the light and open the door."

Horine did as told and embraced his son. "My God," he said, "it's been so long." He hesitated when he saw movement in the shadows.

"Our men, Papa, Marylanders come along to help. We need horses."

"Come in, all of you. Let me get Mother."

"We can't linger, Papa. Our whole army is on the way."

"Your whole army? Lee's in Maryland?"

"Jackson is in camp below Buckeystown. Lee and the rest of the army not far behind. Stuart's already in Frederick. And Papa, Claib is with Jackson. If there's any way for him to get home, I know he will, but he's infantry, and Jackson is a hard man."

"But he's all right?"

"Right as rain. I saw him two days ago."

"Thank God. So Lee really did win there in Manassas?"

"Yeah. We whipped Pope so bad, he's still runnin'."

Richard introduced his troopers, and they told Horine where they were from--Shanks and Granny from nearby, two others from Annapolis, and one each from Easton and Taneytown.

"Papa, we need all the horses you can give us, and we need to know where we can get more around here, riding and work horses, mules too. We need supplies, everything, food, shoes, wagons, hay and grain for the animals, harness and leather for repairs."

A frail woman in a long housecoat appeared at the kitchen door. She squinted into the room lit only by moonlight. "Ben, who are these people?"

"Mother, it's Richard. He's come home to visit us."

"Richard?"

"Mama, it's me. I've come to see you." Richard went to her, put his arms around her shoulders, and kissed her on the cheek.

"Oh Richard, you're alive. Dear God, you're alive." She was trembling as she grasped her son's arm. "But Richard, you did a terrible thing. You took Jacob away to be killed, and then you took Claiborne away too, and we've heard nothing for months. Is he dead?"

"No, Mama, I saw Claib just a few days ago. He's a sergeant with General Jackson and he's doin' fine." He looked into his mother's eyes. Tears streamed down her cheeks. "Mama, don't cry. Jacob fought for what he believed in. He died a hero. General Jackson said so."

"But he's dead. I never even got to see his body, to touch his dear sweet face one last time, he was just gone, and for nothing, oh, I hate this war. I hate men like your General Jackson, who sends my sons out to kill or be killed." She lapsed into quiet sobbing and pulled away from Richard and left the room.

"I'll see to her, Richard," Horine said. "She'll be fine. I just have to make sure she gets back to her bed." He stopped and looked back. "Boys, there's pie and fruit in the pantry, help yourselves."

Richard guided his men into the pantry and passed around the food. "Sorry about my mom," he said. "She's always been so nice, but my brother being killed really upset her."

"I lost a brother, too," one of the troopers said, " and I reckon my mom's the same way. It's hard on the womenfolk."

When he returned, Horine sighed. "She's been like this for over a year. The doctor says it's a sickness, and I haven't been able to do a thing for her. Sometimes days go by and she never says a word. Sometimes she just sits in her bedroom and rocks. It's hard on the younger children. The two older girls help out, and our colored girl, Tillie, does the cooking and the housework. But God, I wish she'd get over it." He looked up. "Sorry to put you boys through my problems, we got a war to win. Before we go out, Richard, let me bring the children down."

"Oh, please do, Papa. I miss them."

One by one, they filed in. Betsy, at seven the youngest, barely remembered her brother and hung back. Timmy, nine, and Grace, eleven, ran to Richard with squeals of delight. The older girls, Jennifer, thirteen, and Rebecca, just sixteen, waited their turns, hugging Richard and smiling shyly at the troopers. At last, Betsy overcame her reticence and she too ran into Richard's arms. They talked a few minutes, and then Horine sent them back to bed.

Horine led the troopers through the darkness to the barn. "I've got to light a lantern, Richard," he said. "Six more horses came in last week, so I've got ten you can take, everything but my brood mares and their foals."

"Won't you need to keep a stud?"

"Not unless you say I should. My mares are not in heat, and I can find a stud when I need to."

"You better keep your best one, Papa." Richard checked and saw the troopers were finishing putting bridles on the horses. "We gotta take these horses and go, Papa. I can't say when I'll be back, but by late tomorrow there'll be Confederate soldiers all over. Quick, tell me where we can get more horses and supplies.

Horine rattled off names and locations. Richard knew most of the names already, so he embraced his father again, and after the troopers said their goodbyes, they rode off into the night.

A few hundred yards away, hidden behind a fence row, Gross whispered to Peck Handley when Horine lit his lantern by the barn, "See there, Peck, what did I tell you. Them is Rebs, and they're taking a bunch of horses right off Horine's place. What we gonna do? Should I take a shot at 'em?"

"No, hell no. You'll git us both killed. Let's foller 'em and see which way they go."

It was over two miles down the Manor road to the Rebel camp outside Buckeystown. Handley and Gross trailed the Confederate riders easily, but the unexpected appearance in the moonlight of sentries, tents, wagons, campfires, and other evidence of a large encampment sent them scurrying to cover.

"Didja see that, Peck, that must be the whole gahdamn Reb army."

Peck's eyes were equally wide and his heart thumped. "Hell, we heard there was Rebs around here, but not that many. Too many to be raiders. We gotta tell people about this. I'm gonna ride into town."

2

Handley and Gross spread the word, but the ride to Frederick was wasted. The town already was in the hands of Jeb Stuart's cavalry.

For Hiram Matthews' wife, the warning was too late. Confederates rode in and emptied the Matthews stables and meathouse, leaving only on old horse and a small supply of pork. "You stinkin' Rebs," she shouted, "my husband will fix you."

"Yes, ma'am," a sergeant replied, "y'all should take a look at what Yanks done down our way." The soldiers were restrained somewhat by Lee's orders that Maryland citizens be treated as friends, since they were being coerced to remain in the Union. Lucy Matthews was given a handful of Confederate currency which she considered worthless. She was thankful for one thing--Hiram's favorite mare, Maude, was still at her brother's on the other side of Frederick.

The Zimmerman and Stone families got word early enough to hide their horses and hide some of their meat and canned goods. Caleb Matthews was sent to warn the Fraleys. "What's wrong, child?" Mary Ann said, " don't tell me Osawatomie Brown is up at Harpers Ferry again."

"No ma'am. It's Rebs. They're stealin' horses, done got ours. Ma says to tell you to hide ever'thing you can."

"Good Lord, help us." Mary Ann scanned the valley and made out groups of riders. "Frankie, Sissy," she shouted, "come here quick."

They came running, Sissy from the kitchen, Frankie from the barn, recognizing the desperation in their mother's voice. "Listen," Mary Ann said, "there's Rebs comin', and we gotta hide as much stuff as we can."

"Rebs, where?" Sissy asked. She looked at Caleb who pointed at the pike. Sissy gaped at the riders who could be seen in groups around the Derr and Zimmerman farms.

"Gotta go," Caleb said. "Y'all git them horses hid."

Frankie watched the gray riders' progress as they rounded up animals and loaded wagons. "I'll bridle the horses," he said. "Sissy, you'll have to lead 'em back to the big ditch. Stay with 'em in that deep spot covered by honeysuckle. Don't come out till Ma or me come and getcha."

Mary Ann went with her children to the barn. "I'll turn out the cows and the chickens and shoo them away," Frankie said. "Mebbe they'll hide themselves. What about the pigs?"

"Let them out too. I been thinkin', Sissy, you just take the good team. The other two are too much for you to handle. If the Rebs take 'em, it ain't no big loss."

Canned goods were hid underneath the attic floor. Cured meat was placed in rafters above the wash house. A few items were left, so the Rebs would think that's all they had. They had just finished when they heard the horses on the hill below the church.

Six soldiers with a wagon rode up and looked around while Mary Ann and Frankie stood staring at them. "What do you men want?" Mary Ann demanded.

"We need food and horseflesh, ma'am," a sergeant replied, "and we'll pay."

"U. S. Currency?"

"Why, no ma'am, we're Confederates, and we pay with good Confederate money."

"There ain't no such thing as good Reb money."

"Don't tell me y'all has Union leanings. Maryland is a southern state, and we thought y'all would be on our side, standing with the Confederacy."

"How do you know we ain't?"

"Well, y'all won't take our money."

"Why should we take it when we can't buy nothin' with it."

"Like it or not, ma'am, we're gonna take us some food and some horses. Go ahead, boys."

The marauders emptied the meathouse and the pantry. "Not much here, Sarge," a soldier complained.

"You folks ain't hidin' stuff on us, are you?"

"We got barely enough to live on, what with a few chickens and two mangy horses."

The sergeant stared at Frankie. "This here fella looks pretty well fed. How come you ain't in the army, boy?"

"Ma is a widow, and I got to stay and look after her and the farm. Otherwise, how could she get along?"

The sergeant stared at them some more and grumbled. "Git some of them chickens that's runnin' loose," he ordered.

His men were able to grab eight of the flying, squawking birds and stuff them into a sack. One of the Rebs yelled, "Shit, these ol' hens will be tough as a mule's ass."

"Dammit," the sergeant said, "we're wastin' time. C'mon, boys, let's move on, leave those two nags. The captain would kick my butt if I brung back them two sorry critters."

A few seconds later they were gone. "Should I get Sissy?" Frankie asked.

"No, wait to see if they come back."

Later, Frankie got his sister, but they left the horses tied in the huge ditch. Then they began rounding up the hogs, cattle, and chickens. Afterwards, Mary Ann hugged Sissy. "You done real good, honey. I'm proud of you."

"I was skeered, Mama, but I saw you and Frankie was gonna stand up to them Rebs, so I wanted to be like you."

Mary Ann stared out their front window across the valley. "I wonder where Johnny is."

3

When Richard returned to Stuart's camp near Urbana, he learned his commander had plans for more than fighting. Several of the officers had renewed acquaintances with a group of charming young women and made plans to hold a dance in an empty school building.

After reporting to Stuart on the results of his visit to his father, Richard received his orders. "We're to post sentries and guard the perimeter," he told his men.

"Dang," Shanks said, "I wonder what we did to git in Jeb's doghouse. We'll be out thar fightin' skeeters while them Virginians are in thar enjoyin' themselves."

"Don't seem right," Granny said.

"Reckon somebody has to do it," Richard said. "Our commander has always been partial to his Virginians and the ladies."

They were posted a few hundred yards from the school, hearing the music echoing through the nearby woods, and grousing about their bad luck, while Stuart and his Virginians swirled about the floor with the local charmers, when several dozen Yankee riders made an appearance. Horine's men set up a firing line and sent word to Stuart that help was needed. More Union riders heard the shots and joined the skirmish. There was a brisk exchange of gunfire and several men were wounded before the bluecoats withdrew.

"Nice work, Horine," Stuart said. "What're your casualties?"

"Eight men down, Sir, no help for one of them."

Stuart rode back to the building and cajoled the frightened young women to remain. The band began to play and a few couples began to dance. This lasted only a few minutes before the casualties were carried in. The shocked females quickly changed roles and began to care for the wounded, some even ripping cloth from their ballroom gowns to bind the wounds.

In the morning Lee ordered Stuart to move on toward Pennsylvania, and Jackson, whose men had enjoyed their first day's rest in weeks, moved into Frederick. There was a brief skirmish with a small Union force that had gathered after Stuart's appearance, but the defenders were quickly dispersed.

Claiborne's request for leave to visit his family was denied. He missed the eccentric Dick Ewell and found his replacement, Lawton, a hard man to like, but he stepped smartly as his regiment marched down Market Street into the heart of Frederick and then turned west onto Patrick.

"Hey, Sarge," one of the soldiers yelled, "I thought you said a lot of folks here was on our side."

The town was silent, windows shuttered and stores closed. A few children gawked at the invaders, and only an occasional supporter would work up enough nerve to make an appearance. They were, Claib realized, an unappealing bunch, many shoeless, uniforms ragged and dirty, unshaven, smelly, some infested with lice.

"I guess many of them are scared to show their support," Claib said. "I sure expected more of a welcome than this."

A commotion developed ahead on Patrick Street, and an officer rode ahead. "What's goin' on here?" he asked.

Several men pointed to a small house sitting back from the street beside a creek. "Sir," a soldier responded, "some ol' biddy put out a Yank flag yonder, and we tol' her to take that damn rag down. She give us some sass, so me and some of the boys want to shoot it down, but she won't git outta the way."

An ancient crone leaned out the upstairs window and croaked, "You Rebs let my flag be. Don't you be shooting your guns this way."

The officer chuckled. "Let her be, boys. That flag won't do us no harm, and if you shoot over there, she might fall out of the window and bust something, and you boys would feel real bad."

The soldiers laughed. "Aw'right, Granny," one yelled. "Keep your dang flag. We already got more Yank flags than we knows what to do with." The drums picked up again, as a regimental band played a lusty version of "Maryland, My Maryland."

Jackson and Stuart halted west of the town while the rest of the Confederates made camp five miles south near the Monacacy River and the B & O railroad. The troops got more rest and added to their supplies while Lee planned his campaign.

That afternoon, Richard cajoled Claib's major to permit a family visit and then got permission from his own colonel to return home. There he helped his father hitch two mares to the family carriage. They convinced their confused and reluctant mother to join them in a visit to Claiborne where his regiment was camped. Elsie Horine harbored forebodings that Claib was dead, and only Richard's heartfelt promises got her to agree to the trip. The excited children all were allowed to accompany them, Rebecca and Jennifer riding on King, Timmy with Richard on Prince, and the two younger girls squeezed in with their parents.

They drove to a grassy knoll a mile below the heights named for Braddock after the French and Indian War, and there the Horines and their two soldier sons were reunited. Benjamin pumped Claib's hand and hugged him warmly. The four girls, pretty in their best dresses, fussed over him shamelessly, his new mustache and beard, his scarred eyeglasses, his sergeant's stripes. Timmy wanted to know about the war, the guns, the battles, and pelted the brothers with questions.

Elsie watched mutely for a while, and then with a sigh, she wrapped her arms around Claiborne. Her head barely came to his chest. "You've grown still taller, and you've changed. You're too thin. They must not feed you. And your clothes are so ragged."

"I'm fine, Mama, really fine. Don't worry, I get enough to eat."

"Your uniform needs cleaning and your shoes are all worn."

"I know, Mama, but they work us pretty hard, chasing Yankees."

"Can't you come home, darling? Please, won't you come home? I miss you so much. We've lost Jacob, and Richard is more than enough to give the army."

Claib hugged his mother again. "The war oughta be over soon, Mama. We got the Yanks on the run, and they'll soon let us be. Don't you think so, Richard?"

"That's right, it won't be much longer, Mama."

"I couldn't bear to lose you, too."

"Nothin' bad will happen, Mama. I promise."

The nine talked for nearly an hour. Horine had brought fried chicken, biscuits, hard boiled eggs, so they could have a picnic, and for a while, Elsie seemed her self.

Finally, it had to end. "I've got to get back," Claib said, "or that major will have us court martialed. You children mind your Papa, and take good care of Mama."

She kissed her son as in the old days and waved as he ran back to his camp. She was still waving as they rode away, Richard in the lead, Claib turning and standing in the field in the dusk, waving back. "I'll never see him again," she said, stifling a sob and staring rigidly ahead.

Benjamin tried to reassure her, but she said nothing more on the ride home, and when she got to the house, she ignored Richard, got down from the carriage, and rushed inside.

Richard hugged each of the children and his father. "I don't know what will happen, I'll be back when I can." With a final salute, he galloped down the farm lane and disappeared as the night closed in.

4

Outside Washington, the Marylanders, still a part of Reno's division, were posted on a defense line to protect the nation's capital from attack. Nothing was happening. After the disaster at Bull Run, they expected to be attacked, but Lee's army had vanished.

Matthews gave part of his men overnight leave to go to Washington, while the others remained in camp awaiting their turn. Fisher, Fraley, and others walked across the Potomac bridge, gawked at the White House, the Capitol with its unfinished dome, the officers and ladies, ate and drank at some of the saloons, and returned.

"The place smells worse than our pigpen," Johnny said.

"Streets ain't nothin' but mudholes," Fisher added. "Why don't Abe Lincoln do sumpin' about the mess?"

"Some of them women didn't look none too bad," Remsberg observed.

The next night, Baumgartner, Handley, Gross, and Liston were part of the second group. "Whoopee," Gross yelled, "gonna see some of them fancy women."

"You boys better watch what you're messin' with," Matthews warned.

Deaf ears, they were hell bent to wet their whistles. It didn't take long. They sauntered down Pennsylvania Avenue and found the side streets where the saloons were. They sampled the beer, stared at the people, and moved on.

"Howdy, boys," a woman in a shiny red dress called. They stopped, tongue tied. "You fellas look like you're lonely. Would you like a little female company?"

"Uh, er," Gross stammered, "we was, uh, lookin' around."

Liston was red faced. "Yes'm," he said, "uh, we just got leave and was lookin' over the town and all."

"Well, honey, y'all look like big boys. I bet my girls could show you some things you'd like."

"Uh, yes ma'am," Gross said. "Do you, uh, that is, are you, uh?"

"Gross, hush up," Handley said, "you sound like a dang fool. What we want, lady, is to wet our whistles, if you know what I mean. Is that what you do?"

"That's right. You boys can get in bed with one of our nice looking girls, and they'll show you a real good time, and it's only five dollars."

Liston blurted out, "Some of the boys from New York said it only cost them two."

"Well now, if you boys want to screw one of them cheap whores down the street, that's your business. We got nothin' but high class girls like you might want to marry."

"Count me in," Baumgartner said.

"Me too," said Handley.

"Yeah, me," said Gross, finally without stammering.

"Not me, boys," Liston said. "I'll see y'all later."

The next morning some very unhappy soldiers found they had the crabs, tiny pubic lice transmitted from the prostitutes. Liston laughed at them until a few days later when he had a horrifying burning sensation every time he urinated, and realized he had the clap, gonorrhea, from one of the two dollar tarts.

"I tried to tell you dumb farts," Matthews scolded, "but no, you had to get your poontang. Now you know what it really costs."

The treatment for the crabs and the clap was worse than the disease itself as far as the soldiers were concerned. It was even more distressing when they were ordered on the march two days later.

Reno himself rode through the camp announcing their orders. They were marching north and were to be fast about it. "If we hurry," Fisher said, "we'll get quicker to where we can sit around on our butts some more."

"Look at it this way, Al," Johnny said. "We can sing together on the march."

Tents and supplies were loaded into wagons, horses fed, watered, harnessed, and hitched up. Packs were assembled and canteens filed. They were veterans, preparations orderly and fast.

There was a bit of ceremony before they left. McClellan and his staff rode by, savoring the troops' cheers. "Boys who served with him seem to like the little fart," Al whispered to John, "though I be danged if I can see why."

"After Pope," Johnny said, "I reckon any change has to be for the better."

Three columns moved from Washington into Maryland. Franklin followed the Potomac and crossed at Point of Rocks, taking almost the same route as Lee to Buckeystown. Sumner and Hooker moved directly northwest through Gaithersburg toward Frederick, while the third column under Burnside marched north to New Market on the Frederick-Baltimore pike. It was September 7 when the march began.

For Marylanders the road led through familiar terrain, Silver Spring, Rockville, Gaithersburg, Germantown, Hyattstown, and on to Urbana.

"Corn looks good," Johnny remarked to Matthews. They passed field after field of tall green stalks in neat rows, tassels waving in the September breeze. Ears were well formed, with green silk darkening to maturity.

"Yeah," Hiram said, "I miss the farm this time of year, when the crops are gittin' in the barn."

"This, and Spring," Johnny said, "when things are startin' to green up."

The troops stirred billowing dust clouds. Nearby fields were void of horses and cattle, the animals either taken by the Rebs or hidden by farmers who knew livestock was fair game when armies were about. Old men and women of all ages sat in buggies or stood by fences as the soldiers tramped past. Some waved, others watched, a few offered fresh water and fruit.

Children trotted alongside the troops and ogled their weapons. Officers shooed them away.

"The farms here sure look good," Fisher said, "not like those sorry places we seen in Virginny."

As the day passed, the heat got intense, and the troops were rested every hour, so they could take a drink and wipe the dust from their faces and weapons. Horses sweated and smelled. Riders were constantly searching the area for forage and water for the animals. "War is hell on horses," Matthews said.

"I wonder what horses feel," Johnny said. "They sure scream when they get hit, just like a man."

Matthews pondered the question and lit his corncob pipe. "I always figgered they felt like us. I reckon they get scared like a man. They sure shit themselves often enough."

Fisher spit tobacco juice into the dust. "I ain't shit my pants yet, but I know some of the boys has, they was so bad scared. I seen 'em cleanin' themselves."

"Well," Matthews said, "if you got the runs and get in a tight spot, like we did there in Manassas, it can't be helped. It's just gonna leak on you."

"Hiram, is there any way to get us time to visit home?" Johnny asked.

"I'm gonna do my best. Come on, boys, the colonel's signaling, time to hit the road."

Like a massive animal, the Union column rose and began to move. On September 11 they were only five miles from Frederick. Scouts had kept contact between the three columns and had repeatedly met Reb scouts with resulting skirmishes near Poolesville, Barnesville, and around Sugarloaf Mountain. But they did not find Lee's army.

As evening neared, Johnny and Al began to sing, and soon dozens of voices joined the chorus:
"We'll hang Jeff Davis from a sour apple tree,
A sour apple tree, a sour apple tree,
We'll hang Jeff Davis from a sour apple tree
As we go marchin' on."

5

On September 9 Lee issued orders. Jackson, Walker and McLaws were to move by different routes to envelop and capture the large Federal base at Harpers Ferry. Longstreet and Stuart were to march to Hagerstown in preparation for an advance into Pennsylvania once Harpers Ferry was captured. Splitting his army was a bold plan, but Lee was confident the Union forces were leaderless and confused, giving him the opportunity to move on Harrisburg, and from there, with the control of key railroads, he could advance on either Philadelphia or Baltimore.

After the Horine brothers parted, Jackson's army moved first toward Hagerstown, then left the National Pike to ford the Potomac at Williamsport. The weather was pleasant and the troops in a jubilant mood, restored by three days' rest and decent food for a change.

"Hey, Sarge," one of Claib's men called, "why don't ol' Jack let us run. We might git to where we're goin' before I wear through these Yank boots."

"Your trouble is you'd rather fight than march."

"You're right on that, Sarge, it's a heap more fun shootin' Yanks than it is chasin' 'em."

"I thought the folks around here would be a heap more friendly than this. My Pa and my brother and our whole family is secesh. I was certain most Marylanders are, but they sure don't show it."

"Horine," their lieutenant said, " it seems to me these folks ain't like real southerners. Most of 'em don't have slaves."

"But hell," a soldier said, "most of us got no slaves nor do we want any. We're fightin' to keep the Yanks away from our states and let us alone. Pardon me, Sarge, but these is some strange folk if this is supposed to be part of the south. They're just a bunch of damned Yanks, if you ask me."

Richard made one last stop at his home before riding north with Stuart. He was accompanied by a Confederate major from Loudoun County who was to be the contact between Stuart and Horine's group of sympathizers.

"Mister Horine," the major said, "if the Yankees move into this area in force, we need to know it quick. If you learn anything, contact the scouts we've posted along the west bank of the Potomac from Berlin to Harpers Ferry. They'll be looking for you. Can you reach that area unseen?"

"Don't worry, I'll get there."

"Papa, don't take any chances."

"Yes," the major said, "you're too valuable to our cause. Don't give yourself away."

In Hagerstown, Longstreet and his staff spent the day trying to purchase supplies from balky merchants who were unwilling to accept Confederate currency, despite assurances it would be useful while the town was occupied. In the end, Longstreet gave up arguing and ordered his men to take what they needed, whether the merchants accepted their scrip or not.

On the evening of September 13, Jackson's troops arrived at the western approaches to Harpers Ferry. They had driven a small Federal force out of Martinsburg and chased them into the besieged town. McLaws had occupied the heights on the opposite side of the Potomac, while Walker had moved onto Loudoun Heights above the Shenandoah, blocking the last Union escape route.

"Reckon we'll go for 'em tomorrow, Sarge?" one of Claib's men asked.

"Not likely on Sunday, unless they come after us first. Jackson never attacks on the Lord's Day."

So the army rested, feasting on fruit from local orchards and staring at Sunday School cards their eccentric commander had taken from a Martinsburg church and passed out to his troops. "Keep close to your Lord, boys," Jackson said as he handed one to every soldier he could find.

6

On Thursday, September 11, a group of men met in the back of Holter's store. George Stone started the palaver with a statement, "All of us done had enough of them Rebs. They stole our horses, took our meat, even took most of our wagons. Poor Lucy Matthews was about cleaned out. Gross here's been watchin' Horine, and he's seen Rebs in and outta there again since him and Peck seen that whole bunch gittin' horses the other night."

"That's right, by God, and I ain't a gonna put up with it no more," Peck Handley said.

"They're there all right," Gross said. "I seen two of 'em last night. One of 'em was that oldest boy."

Stone continued, "What I'm saying, by golly, is that it's time to put an end to it."

Ed Holter tried to calm them down. "Boys," he said, "do we know if there's any others besides Horine? It won't do no good if we stop him and somebody else takes his place."

"I ain't gonna wait, Ed," Handley said. "We know we got us a traitor, and the way things is around here, we got to take care of it ourselves."

"That ain't real smart," Squire Fulmer said. "You'll let the rest of the spies get away."

"I don't see it that way, Squire. We gotta deal with the rat we know, and if there's others, by God, we'll deal with them when the time comes."

A commotion outside interrupted Handley, and Holter stepped outside. "Fellas," he shouted, "you better break this up. There's a whole passel of Rebs marchin' this way."

"Let's git the hell outta here," Peck said. In a moment the room was empty.

From their farm, Mary Ann and her children watched McLaws' troops moving up the Jefferson Pike. Groups of horsemen were fanning out in all directions, and one group galloped past the church by the farm entrance. "Goin' to Middletown," Frankie said.

"They're sure in a hurry, not lookin' to steal anything this time."

An hour passed and still the troops came. There were shots to the west where Rebs tangled with a Yank patrol. Artillery rumbled along the rutted road. They could hear the drivers cursing the horses. Another group rode up to the church, unpacked a spyglass, surveyed the valley, and then moved on.

As the last units passed, dust swirled in their wake. "There was thousands," Mary Ann said.

"Why are they goin' back to Virginia?" Frankie pondered.

Later the same day, McClellan's advance units reached Frederick. Sumner and Hooker were approaching on the Washington road. Later, Burnside would reach New Market. Franklin's men were already moving into fields near Buckeystown.

That evening Matthews and his men settled into camp outside the village of New Market. In the morning, he begged his colonel to give them a brief leave to visit their homes, but hours passed and no answer.

"What would happen if we snuck home anyhow?" Johnny asked.

"Probably get ourselves shot," Matthews replied.

"Damn if I ain't likely to risk it," Al Fisher said, and others nodded in agreement. The torment of home a few miles away was tearing them up.

Late in the afternoon, General Nagle, newly promoted, appeared and conferred with Matthews. "Boys," Matthews said, after Nagle departed, "we got special orders. Our company is assigned for two days to scout the area west of Frederick around the Jefferson Pike."

There was a loud shout, but Matthews continued, "So get your gear ready to move, and if any of you don't follow my orders and do as you're told, why by golly, I'll put you in the stockade, or worse."

They made a rapid march to Holter's store where Matthews dismissed part of the company so they could visit their families for the night. The remainder marched on to Jefferson where they also would be given leave to go home. Matthews called to Ed Holter, "Tell my wife I'll be back soon as these men are dismissed."

When Matthews and his thirty infantrymen entered Jefferson, they startled a half dozen Confederate cavalrymen who were lounging under an elm tree. Matthews shouted at the Rebs to surrender, but they grabbed their mounts and sped away, chased by Yank bullets. As the Rebs fled toward Petersville, they were met by scouts from Franklin's corps, moving up from Buckeystown. There was more firing, but the Rebs turned north to the safety of McLaws' lines. Matthews brought his men to attention and then dismissed them to the cries and cheers of the townspeople.

Lucy Matthews waited and worried. Holter had ridden to the farm and told her Hiram was coming home, but the minutes dragged. "Ma, he's comin'," Bobby yelled, and the boys were racing down the lane, and she was too, unable to contain herself.

Hiram scooped up the younger boy, Caleb, and then reached for her and Bobby. After giving Bobby a hug and a handshake, he held her and they kissed. They said nothing for over a minute, while the boys examined the contents of the saddle bag.

"Can you stay?" she whispered.

"For tonight, then back to work. Maybe another night."

"You can't imagine how I've worried."

"I know. The war goes on and on, longer than I ever dreamed. Bobby, can you and Caleb put my horse away?"

"Sure, Pa." He took off the saddlebag and reached inside, producing candy for the boys, which they'd already discovered, and a Rebel battle flag he'd saved from Virginia.

"It'll be the only horse in the stable," Lucy said. "I'm so sorry."

"What happened?"

"The Rebs came before we had a chance to hide anything. Some of the neighbors were able to save things, but they got all our horses and most of our meat. They left me with worthless Confederate money. Your folks and mine were spared so they can help us out."

"Those bastards. Did you see who got Maud?"

"Oh dear, I forgot to tell you, Maud was down at your brothers for shoeing. They didn't get her."

Hiram grinned broadly. "They didn't take Maude. That makes the rest of it a lot easier to take. Let's forget all this bad news and enjoy what's good. For starters, here's my back pay, over three hundred dollars, and here's something else." He reached back into the saddlebag and brought out a silver brooch. Lucy eyes widened. "Got this in Washington and thought it would look real nice on that blue dress of yours." They kissed again.

"It's so beautiful."

"I knew you'd like it. Honey, I'm famished. What's left to eat."

"How about fried chicken, roastin' ears, string beans, fresh biscuits, mashed potatoes, and peach cobbler?"

"I must be in heaven. Maybe the Rebs got me after all."

A mile and a half away, Johnny Fraley was at the back door when Buster's barking brought Frankie out of the barn. The brothers waved and met by the barnyard gate. "If you ain't a sight, my God, Johnny, where'd you come from?"

"Our whole army is around Frederick. Our general sent Matthews and our company over here to see if there's any Rebs around. Where's Ma and Sissy?"

"Out at the henhouse, last I knew," Frankie said. "Ma," he yelled.

"What is it?" Mary Ann shouted back.

"We got company."

Mary Ann stepped out and blinked into the sunlight at her two sons. "My Lord," she said. "Sissy, come out here, it's Johnny."

Together again, the Fraleys were frantic, all talking at once, excited and happy. Mary Ann described the Rebs they'd seen and how they'd fooled the marauders and hid the horses. Johnny recounted the march from Washington, the Bull Run battle, the boys who'd died or been wounded. Then Mary Ann hurried to the kitchen to prepare supper.

Johnny looked at the farm. "Plenty of corn, ready to cut. Wish I could help out."

"Me too," Frankie said, "but you got the war. I wish I was with you. Is it real bad?"

"So many boys get themselves shot up and blowed all apart, grape shot from the cannon, explosive shells, I don't like to think about it, it's gahdawful."

They stood together, looking at the barn, the fields, the valley below, the mountains in back. "This is a nice place," Johnny said. "I didn't know till I went away to the war."

"Johnny, will you soon be home for good?" Sissy asked.

"I hope so, Sis, if we can catch Lee and beat him, but we ain't been up to it so far. Need better generals." He stared at his sister. "You've grown. You'll soon be having a beau."

"No, I won't, you and Frankie are my beaus."

After eating, Johnny hitched up the team and went calling on Mary Elizabeth. It was a mile ride to the Stone's small farm, nestled along a country lane south of Holter's store. Their clapboard house sat next to an apple orchard.

Mary Elizabeth was standing on the front porch. News of the soldiers' arrival had reached the Stone family, and she had been waiting with a pounding heart, when she heard him coming and waved. She trembled when Johnny handed her a bouquet of strawflowers, goldenrod, and a few early mums Mary Ann had gathered for him. They embraced shyly, and Johnny kissed her on the cheek. "Gee, you're gettin' purtier all the time, you sweet thing," he said. "Let's go somewhere where we can do some sparkin'."

Mary Elizabeth blushed. She knew her two younger sisters would be peeking from behind the parlor curtains. Her mischievous brother was helping her father. "I've missed you," she whispered, "I'm so afraid something will happen to you."

"It's scary, but I, uh, we all try to be careful. We need to catch those Rebs and lick 'em for good and end this dang war."

"Do you have to go right back?"

"Yep, probably tomorrow or the next day."

Mary Elizabeth held his hand and looked at his face. He was deeply tanned, and his pale gray eyes had a dash of fire in them. His beard, grown since enlisting, was light brown and he looked years older, but he had the same pleasant, somewhat crooked smile she loved. He was thinner and his hands were rough, but different--soldier hands, not farmer hands. The calluses for guns and shovels weren't the same as those for pitchforks and reins.

Johnny smiled at Mary Elizabeth. Her brown eyes were soft and sparkling, the traces of tears showing. Her figure was fuller under the long gingham dress, and she had tied her dark hair with a red ribbon. Her upturned nose was as cute as ever, and her pale lips covered white teeth in contrast to Johnny's, which were tobacco stained. She smelled of apples and clover, a warm, rich farm girl's smell which he loved. He couldn't wait to give her a hug.

"Promise you'll come back for good, soon," she said.

Johnny put his arm loosely around her waist. "Course I will, you know I'll come back to you. You're my onliest girl."

"I like you to say that," she said with a smile, "over and over, I like you to say that."

Her mother appeared at the door. "Now, Mary Lib, you've had him to yourself long enough. John, you come on in the house so we can get a look at you."

Obediently, Johnny climbed the front steps and entered the Stone parlor. "My goodness, don't you look the picture in that uniform. Look at him, girls, ain't he handsome?"

The sisters were tongue tied, now that the object of their curiosity stood before them. The best they could do was murmur, "Hi, Johnny."

"They'll find their tongues after you're gone," Mother Stone said with a chuckle.

She gave them lemonade and cookies and left them alone in the parlor, the sisters shooed off to the kitchen. Mary Elizabeth and Johnny talked on and on about nothing in particular, happy to enjoy each other's company and the sound of each other's voice.

They walked to the barn and greeted her father, George Stone, and her 12-year old brother, Cornelius, who were pitching down hay for the livestock's evening feed, the pasture having dried up in the late summer heat. Stone shook Johnny's hand and passed on his suspicions of the Horines, and Cornelius admired Johnny's uniform and lamented he was too young to be a soldier.

They strolled about the yard and orchard until Johnny had to go. "Ma sent Sissy to fetch Uncle Sam and Aunt Susie and Grandpa, so I've gotta get home. I'll try to come over tomorrow." They kissed goodbye, and this time she kissed back harder than she ever had before, and the feel of her lips and her body pressing hard left Johnny woozy. He got into the buggy in a daze, snapped the reins and waved, singing a mountain folk song at the top of his voice. She watched the dust clouds whirl and then settle for several minutes. Long after he was gone, the ballad he sang echoed in her mind:

"Down in the valley, valley so low,
Hang your head over, hear the wind blow.
Hear the wind blow, love, hear the wind blow.
Hang your head over, hear the wind blow.
Roses love sunshine, violets love dew,
Angels in Heaven know I love you.
Know I love you, dear, know I love you.
Angels in Heaven know I love you."

7

Sam and Susie did their best to rejoice in Johnny's homecoming. They embraced him and smiled and said how fit he looked, but they couldn't quite be happy, for Grandpa wasn't able to come. They said he seemed better sometimes, but underneath, everyone realized their beloved, funny, crotchedy grandfather was failing. Their oldest son, Eddie, came with them. He was growing up and helping with the farm work.

"With Papa sick and all," Sam said, "Eddie's had to do a man's work, and he's been a big help."

They spoke of the boys lost, killed, dead with the fever, wounded, missing. "We never knew what happened to some of 'em," Johnny explained. "The fight was such a mess, they were just gone, and no one knew where."

When supper was finished, Susie and Sam prepared to visit their neighbor and friend, Hiram Matthews. "Do you think I could ride over and see Grandpa?" Johnny asked.

"Well, sure," Sam said, glancing at Susie for guidance, "only..."

"His mind ain't clear, Johnny" Susie said, "he might not know you."

"Well, I'd like to see him, if it won't do no harm."

"No, no, it would do him good to see you," Susie said.

Sam and Susie left in their buggy, joined by Mary Ann and Frankie, so Johnny went to the barn to saddle a horse. Sissy had decided to go with him.

They rode double to the Jefferson pike and turned west a quarter of a mile to the Zimmerman homestead, where they were welcomed by two dogs and the two Zimmerman daughters left to tend their grandfather. Jennie and Anna, both in their teens, were delighted to see Johnny, but ignored Sissy.

Johnny chatted with his infatuated cousins and then they went to the parlor where Grandpa was seated in a large wooden chair padded by a number of pillows. Johnny lit a candle, and the old man blinked and muttered, "Who's that? What time is it? Is that you, Mama?"

"It's me, Grandpa, Johnny Fraley. Me and my sister, your grandchildren, we come to visit you."

"Huh? Come to visit, you say, I'm kinda tired. Where's Mama?" His wife, Charlotte, who he always had called Mama, had been dead seven years.

Jennie, the oldest daughter, whispered, "Sometimes he thinks Grandma is still alive." Then louder, "It's John Fraley, Grandpa, he's a soldier, he's home from the war."

The old man reached forward, his hand groping for his cane, and then leaned back in his chair. "You don't say. Johnny, is that you?"

"Sure is, Grandpa. How you feelin'?"

"Not too bad. How long you been gone, Johnny? Here, let me look at you." He leaned forward. "Sure, you got on a uniform. You girls, go tell Mama that Johnny's here."

"Mama's gone away," Jennie said.

"Johnny, sometimes my head ain't too clear. Gettin' old, I reckon. C'mere, let me touch you." Johnny took his grandfather's hand. Grandpa looked up at him and stroked his sleeve and fingered the material. "Them stripes, you're a sergeant, ain'tcha?"

"That's right, Grandpa. Do you feel like talkin'? I don't want to tire you, I just wanted to see you since I got home for a while. It's been a long time."

"Yes, it's been a spell. Johnny, I can't help no more on your mama's farm. I'm too tired and weak, but don't you fret none, that brother of your'n, he can work real good, he'll get the work done." He sighed and slumped back in the chair. "I'm pooped, can't talk no more. I reckon I'll see you again sometime soon, Johnny. We'll get together when I'm feelin' better." His eyes closed and he began to breathe deeply.

"Is he all right?" Sissy asked

"That's what he does," Jennie said, "just lays back and nods off to sleep. I'm surprised he knew you. That's the most he's talked in a while."

"Me and Sissy always liked him a lot, didn't we?" Johnny said. Sissy nodded.

On the way home, Sissy said, "Funny how Grandpa said you'd get together when he was feelin' better."

"I know," Johnny said, "his mind was wanderin', I reckon."

The next day the troops assembled at Holter's store. Families and friends came with them in buggies and wagons and on horseback. Matthews found it impossible to get his men in any semblance of order. People crowded around him asking questions, shaking his hand, admiring his uniform, examining his saber and sidearm. The rest of the company was pouring in from Jefferson with still more buggies and riders. His orders were to march up the mountain to Braddock Heights and scout for enemy positions in the Middletown area. It would take only a few hours, so he had delayed until the afternoon to conduct the reconnaissance. The troops from Jefferson reported that much of Franklin's corps was situated on a line from Buckeystown to the Potomac.

Matthews was just getting the company into formation when a rider galloped in from Frederick. He saluted and handed over a message to Matthews, who read and re-read it, and then called for quiet. "I have new orders," he shouted, "we're to re-join our regiment in Middletown. It appears we've located Lee's army. Unfortunately, this means we won't be back to our homes tonight."

The crowd groaned. Then Matthews continued, "There will be a fifteen minute break here so everyone can say their goodbyes, and then we'll be headin' out."

They broke into family clusters--Johnny with his mother, Frankie and Sissy, and with Mary Elizabeth and her parents. Other groups were the Matthews, Fishers, Anglebergers, Derrs, Handleys, Grosses, Barnes, Listons, Baumgartners, Remsbergs, and more. Ten new soldiers, from Frederick and Middletown, had joined their ranks. The adventurers into Washington brothels were healed, pubic lice gone, Liston urinating without cringing.

Tears and farewells, no one wanted to let go, but Matthews finally got the column moving. Family members followed for a while as the troops moved up the Mt. Nebo Road, past the church, past the entrance to the Fraley farm where Johnny's family stood, tears running down Mary Ann's cheeks. Mary Elizabeth had not followed. She had kissed Johnny hard on the mouth again and turned away, feeling her heart was about to break.

They marched up the steep dirt road, past more farms and wooded hillsides, to the top of the Catoctin Mountain. Before them lay the Middletown Valley and South Mountain, and beyond that, Boonsboro, Sharpsburg, and the Antietam Creek. They found Nagle's brigade waiting on the National Road at the base of the mountain a half mile from Middletown.

The entire brigade moved out, drums thumping listlessly. The hot September sun boiled down, and dust rose in tiny puffs from every footstep. The people of Middletown had seen thousands of soldiers pass before them, so there was little welcome, except for the families whose boys were with the Maryland troops.

They passed a barn that had been burned, the ruins still smoking. Two dead horses lay by the road covered with flies and maggots. Buzzards hovered overhead, waiting for the troops to pass. A wagon with a broken axle lay on its side in a field. A cavalry platoon raced by kicking up more clouds of unwelcome dust. "You dandies stay away from us," Fisher yelled.

When they arrived at their campsite, a field outside Middletown, they shook dust from their hair and clothes, checked their weapons, and awaited orders. They would be joined by thousands of troops that night and the next day.

8

On September 13, General George McClellan and five of his staff rode down Church Street, tied their horses and climbed the steps of Winchester Hall. McClellan was meeting with Frederick civic and business leaders to negotiate the purchase of supplies for his army.

The reception for the Union troops had been friendly. Units of various commands had marched down Patrick Street, and crowds of people had turned out. The enthusiasm was unexpected and in sharp contrast to the sparse welcome given the ragged Confederates. Most Frederick citizens had made up their minds, they were for the Union, and the Union troops decided this was the best town they'd seen in the whole darn war.

Mayor Cole introduced his group to McClellan, and many were effusive in praise of the Union army, its appearance, discipline and conduct, in contrast to the dirty, rowdy, profane Rebs. Among those assembled was a Frederick lawyer named Hatcher.

As McClellan began the meeting, a singular event was occurring at Franklin's encampment near Buckeystown. Two soldiers, a sergeant and a private, were looking for a latrine site in an adjoining field where they studied signs of prior occupancy.

"Sarge, them filthy Rebs was here for sure."

"Yeah, I better tell the captain. We sure don't want to camp where those bastards were."

The private leaned over and picked up an object.

"What you got there?"

"I'll be danged. It's cigars them fool Rebs dropped."

The sergeant studied the packet, three slim cigars wrapped in some paper and tied with a string. He handed one of the smokes to his companion and bit off the end of the one he held. The paper held his interest because it looked like something important, the handwriting neat and legible. He lit his stogie and began reading.

"Whatcha lookin' at, Sarge?"

"Shit, this here is a Reb order. Doggone, it's signed by Bobby Lee himself."

"Lemme see." The private stared at the paper, but his reading was too poor to make out most of the words. "Hell, what are you gonna do?"

"I better get this to somebody. Let's go over to the command tent."

The two trotted to Franklin's headquarters with their find. There it was passed on to a colonel who immediately recognized Lee's handwriting as genuine. Wasting no time, he mounted a horse and galloped off to Frederick to find Franklin and McClellan.

The group at Winchester Hall was still conferring when the colonel burst into the meeting, and after apologizing, closeted with the Union command. McClellan heard the story and wondered if it might be a trick, but the colonel had been a West Point classmate of Lee's adjutant and was certain the handwriting was genuine. They all knew Lee's signature, affixed to the orders to his armies. McClellan read it twice, and as the facts of the matter became clear in his mind, he exclaimed with hushed excitement that Lee had split his army and given his exact plans and dispositions. This gave Union forces an opening to destroy the Confederates. With mounting excitement, the officers studied the document. "By God," McClellan exclaimed, slamming his fist into the palm of his hand, "we've got him."

The Frederick men observed the growing excitement among the Union officers with considerable curiosity. Finally, McClellan remembered where he was and turned to the group and spoke. "Gentlemen, I cannot give you any details, but since we're among friends, I will tell you that with this paper I believe we have the key to defeat the Rebel invader."

"That is indeed good news," the mayor said.

McClellan laid the paper on the table and quickly finished their business discussion. His hosts could not help but eye the document covertly, particularly Hatcher. The meeting was soon over, McClellan pocketed the paper, and the military men rushed out. The businessmen lingered, except Hatcher, who made his way down back stairs, climbed on his horse, and proceeded to the Horine farm. He was stopped twice by Union patrols, but was permitted to continue on his way.

By twilight, Hatcher was tapping n the Horine door. Tillie answered. "I need to see your master," he said.

"He's out at the barn, suh," she said. "You want I should get him."

"No, I'll find him."

"Seth," Horine exclaimed when he saw his friend, "what are you doing here. We agreed not to be seen together."

"It can't be helped, Benjamin. The worst possible thing has happened. Somehow McClellan has gotten a copy of Lee's plans and thinks he can destroy the Confederate army."

"Oh my God, how did you find that out?"

Seth described the afternoon events. "Incredible," Horine said. "I'll have to get word to Stuart."

"Can you manage? There's patrols everywhere."

"I've got a way I can use once it's dark. You get on home. People are watching me all the time."

Horine explained to his family that he was going to Frederick for supplies and might stay overnight. He saddled his horse and followed the Ballenger Creek from the back of his farm south toward the Monacacy. When he neared the B & O railroad, he dismounted and walked for a half mile until he was sure he was clear of the sentries patrolling the area. Then he remounted and followed the rails toward Point of Rocks.

Here was the most danger from Union patrols. However, the river was low and he was able to ford it without being spotted. He made his way to Lovettsville where he located one of Stuart's agents. Together they rode along the river until they met two Confederate troopers.

From that point, the group re-crossed the Potomac and galloped to Rohersville where they awakened their exhausted commander and convinced him of the potential calamity of the lost orders. Soon Stuart was on his way to Lee's headquarters twelve miles away at Hagerstown.

9

Sunday, September 14 was another clear, hot day with dust clouds marking the movement of tens of thousands of soldiers on both sides of the Potomac.

To the west of Harpers Ferry, Claiborne Horine was wearing newly earned lieutenant's bars while his men waited with the rest of Jackson's troops for word to attack the besieged town.

At Turner's Gap on South Mountain, Stuart's troopers were sent to hold the rugged terrain against an oncoming column of Yank cavalry and infantry. Stuart was bleary eyed from lack of sleep, having spent most of the night seeking Lee and convincing him of the emergency and then assembling troopers to make the stand. Already there was the rattle of muskets as a forward unit made contact with the enemy.

A few miles away, Matthews and his men were part of Reno's division assigned to move over South Mountain. They were aware that what was happening was important. Fisher summarized their feelings, "Let's whip 'em and get this dang war over with," he said.

"How about a song?" Johnny said.

"Mebbe a hymn," Fisher replied.

"You know any?"

"I might if somebody else gets it started."

"Yankee doodle went to town riding on a pony."

"That ain't no hymn." A minie ball hit a rock above them and whistled away.

"Stuck a feather in his cap, and called it macaroni."

"What the hell is macaroni?"

More rifle fire from above. Several hundred of Stuart's troopers had strong positions on the ridge, blocking the Union advance.

"Yankee doodle, keep it up, Yankee doodle dandy," Johnny continued. More gunfire.

"John," Matthews shouted, "time to shut up. We got some Rebs don't like your singin'."

Johnny squeezed off a shot, and the regiment maintained a steady volley at the enemy moving more troops into position on the mountain above.

10

Mary Ann and her children attended church along with most of the people who had watched their boys march off the previous day. They prayed for Johnny's safety, but there was battle in the air, and the premonition of danger and death.

Ben Horine returned home at six in the morning. He was escorted to a crossing below Berlin, and from there he had slipped back to the railroad and worked his way to the farm. He was exhausted but exhilarated that he and Seth may have saved Lee's army.

By late afternoon Reno's troops were attacking the thin Rebel line on a wide front. More Union regiments moved onto the hillside and took the initiative so Reno and his commanders could give their men a chance to rest, but as the sun dipped lower, all the troops were ordered to the front in an effort to drive the Rebs from the mountain. They were driving ahead, making progress, when more Confederates appeared and the battle became fierce. Artillery began to blast the Rebel line and the Rebs withdrew further below the crest, out of range from artillery. Reno called up two reserve brigades and launched an attack on Longstreet's infantry which now occupied the Rebel front.

Richard Horine was part of the cavalry that was ordered forward to stem this vigorous Yankee attack. The Confederate lines were bending to the superior enemy force when a furious counter-attack led by Hood's Texans, newly arrived from Hagerstown, smashed the Union advance, killing hundreds, including General Reno. Once again, Union forces re-grouped and renewed their advance. By twilight, Longstreet had enough and withdrew his tired soldiers to Boonsboro. His men had done the job Lee had assigned them. They had delayed the Union advance for a day, giving Lee time to collect most of his scattered units and move them back to the Potomac crossings so they could not be separated and destroyed piecemeal.

That same day, Franklin's troops attacked McLaws at Crampton's Gap near the Potomac. By dark, the Yanks had the victory, but it was an empty one since it did nothing to relieve Harpers Ferry. McLaws still held his artillery position on Maryland Heights poised to support Jackson's attack from the opposite side.

Early Monday morning came the attack. Jackson, Walker and McLaws began a bombardment at daybreak with brutal effect. By eight it was the infantry's turn. They moved forward, drums beating, pace quickening. Suddenly, before they could fire another shot, it was over, a white flag fluttering ahead of them. "Well I'll be damned, ain't that something," Claib exclaimed.

11

No sooner had Jackson completed the capture of Harpers Ferry than he received an urgent message from Lee to bring his forces to Sharpsburg. McClellan was moving forward with overwhelming numbers, and Lee had only Longstreet's corps, Stuart's cavalry, and a few extra brigades to meet this superior force.

For Jackson, this order presented a huge problem. He had 12,000 captured Yankees on his hands, and had to leave A. P. Hill and his division behind in order to disarm and parole the prisoners. McLaws was unable to leave his position until Franklin moved, but Walker's smaller unit was able to move back to Maryland with Jackson.

Claib's men were desperately unhappy with the order to rush back to Maryland and demanded an explanation.

"My guess is that Marse Robert has found us some more Yanks to lick," Claib said.

"I reckon you're right," Claib's new sergeant, Jeremy Taylor, said, "but by golly, MacLaw's fightin' Yanks over yonder, we done captured a whole army, and now more turn up back where Lee is. How many damn Yanks do we have to lick before they quit?"

"Long as they keep tryin' to hold us in their damn Union, we'll have to keep stompin' 'em."

By evening Jackson had most of his foot cavalry on the road, marching fifteen miles and fording the river. By early Tuesday they were in position next to Longstreet in the woods and fields outside Sharpsburg.

Stuart was positioned on Jackson's left. Richard's regiment patrolled the Potomac north of Lee's main force, where they were constantly pressed by Pleasanton's riders, and there were repeated skirmishes among the opposing troopers. It was clear the Yanks were looking for Lee's flank and hoping to get into the army's rear and disrupt supply lines.

By late Tuesday afternoon McClellan had his army over South Mountain and in camp around Keedysville and along the Hagerstown pike. On the right, Hooker moved his men forward to positions in the woods northwest of the Antietam Creek in preparation for an attack the next morning. That evening Meade's division ran into an enemy skirmish line, and a brisk fire fight erupted which flared for a half hour until artillery support drove away the troublesome Rebs.

To Hooker's left, beyond Meade, were Mansfield and Sumner's corps, and beyond them, Burnside. In their camp, the Marylanders heard the rattle and roar of Meade's guns and knew the next day would be another bloody one. "Looks like one bitch of a fight comin' up," Matthews told his men.

They pitched their tents and ate cold suppers. Fires were not permitted. Most of the men limited themselves to chewing dry coffee and eating whatever was left of the food from home. They were thankful that casualties on South Mountain had been limited to a half dozen wounded.

It was hard to sleep. Some played cards, others sat and smoked. Sitting by themselves, Johnny sang old mountain ballads while Liston played his mouth harp. A few soldiers walked about, passing time with sentries, kibitzing the games, watching the officers for clues to what might happen.

"How do you think it'll go?" Johnny asked Fisher.

"I dunno. We're in our own state, makes a difference."

Baumgartner and Gross sat down with them. "Guess this'll be the big 'un," Baumgartner said.

"'Fraid so," Johnny said.

"You fellers ain't scared of them Rebs, are you?" Fisher chided.

"I ain't scared of them, it's their guns I'm scared of."

"Hell, we'll have John here sing to you."

"Well, boys," Johnny said, "if it gets as hot as it did in Virginia, maybe we oughta be scared." He leaned back against a chestnut tree and carefully cleaned his musket, piece by piece until it gleamed in the moonlight. Then he took out his bayonet and began to hone it one more time.

12

After the soldiers left and the church service was over, Mary Ann stood outside with friends. She chatted with Lucy Matthews and the Fishers, the Derrs and Remsbergs. Frankie, embarrassed at being home when so many were at war, walked up the farm lane alone.

"Armies all over," Kate Fisher said, "it's just too horrible."

"I reckon the fight will be up around Harpers Ferry," Oscar Fisher said. "I can't understand why they sent our boys over to Middletown."

Mary Ann listened to the talk intently, there was worry on every face. A battle was looming, but no one knew where or when, and seven dead from their community already.

Afterward, Mary Ann and Sissy trudged up the lane bordered by ripening corn on one side and a weedy stubble field on the other, the wheat harvested two months before. Goldenrod and Black Eyed Susans bloomed on the banks. The day was hazy hot, filled with busy insects and lazy swirls of dust.

The mountains beyond the farm showed a bit of autumn color, which Mary Ann noted. "Fall will soon be here," she said.

Sissy didn't respond. Instead she said, "I wish Johnny woulda stayed for Sunday."

"He couldn't."

"I know."

The house was still cool, shaded by tall maples. They climbed the stairs slowly to their rooms. Mary Ann felt tired and old. It took forever to remove her Sunday clothes and get into her work dress. She sat and stared out the window, close to tears.

They ate a silent Sunday dinner of cold sliced pork shoulder, boiled potatoes, squash, and apple cobbler. "It's so quiet after he leaves," Frankie said.

Mary Ann cleaned the kitchen and sat in the living room, alternately dozing and reading the Bible. Her children had wandered off somewhere outside. Then she roused herself to finish her chores. She lowered a bucket into the well back of the house and carried water to the chickens. Then she went to the corncrib and shelled a small pail of corn which she scattered on the ground for the cackling, fluttering birds that crowded around her. She gathered ten eggs, noting a decrease and thinking it was time to boil another old hen. Her flock had declined, mostly because of the chickens the Rebs had stolen.

Across the mountain she heard a rumble and looked up. The sky was clear, but there were more roars. With a chill, she realized it was cannon fire, from the direction of Middletown. The fighting had begun. Sissy heard it too and ran out into the yard. Frankie was the last to hear it, but soon he came out of the barn and stood listening to the explosions in the evening air.

Mary Ann went back to her kitchen, rinsed her face and sat in her rocker and prayed. The noise dwindled when the wind shifted, so Frankie and Sissy went back to their chores.

Lucy Matthews heard the cannon also. Hiram thought a major battle was shaping up, but the roar of artillery gave her a numb feeling. He said little about the battles, but once he had observed that the worst of the carnage was caused by grape shot and canister from massed artillery.

The next day was quiet. Farmers were working to get their corn cut and shocked. It was a dirty, tiring job. Frankie would count in twelve rows from the edge and tie several stalks of corn into a buck which was the support for building a fodder shock. Then, using a short handled corn chopper, a two foot wooden handle with a sharp blade set at a forty five degree angle attached to the end, he would chop an armful of stalks and place them upright against the buck. Once that was accomplished, he would chop and gather four rows of fodder on each side and stack them evenly around the buck to form the shock. Then the shock was tied with twine, and he would proceed to do the same thing again.

A cornfield of fifteen acres produced about three hundred shocks of fodder, and Frankie could cut about forty shocks in eight hours if he worked steadily. The corn leaves cut his cheeks and neck like knives as they dried, and he had to contend with prickly nettles, thistles and cockle burrs that grew wild in the field.

Tuesday arrived, and a Union calamity became apparent as paroled Federal soldiers tramped down the Jefferson pike. They told a story of being surrounded and pounded into submission by the Rebs at Harpers Ferry. They had surrendered their weapons, been given paroles, and were on their way home.

The appearance of these blue vagabonds caused Mary Ann to send Frankie on horseback across the fields to the Zimmerman farm. "It ain't our boys," Sam told Frankie. "Most of these troops been in Harpers Ferry for months, and they say they got hit by Jackson's whole army. That's where those Rebs were goin' that marched by here a few days ago."

Ed Holter and Peck Handley talked to the parolees, many from the Maryland home guards. "Why'd you give up?" Peck asked. "There's Union armies all over the place."

"Damned if we saw any of 'em," a Frederick guardsman replied. "All we saw was a hunnerd Reb cannon and Jackson's whole army comin' at us."

"Dammit," Handley swore, "why are we always behind the Rebs? It must be spies who tell 'em what we're doin'."

Frankie related to his mother that Sam had said the parolees were from the Harpers Ferry garrison and then returned to his work.

That night Mary Ann awoke with a severe start. She'd had her death dream again, a horrid sensation of trying to grasp someone, then that ghostly figure became Johnny, and as she reached for his hand, he drifted away and was lost in the darkness. When she looked for him, all she found was a death's head, and her mind was frozen with fear.

She was trembling so bad she had to sit up. She tiptoed down the stairs to the kitchen for a drink from the water bucket, and sat and rocked for some time. Finally, she went back to bed and slept, dreaming not at all. She awoke refreshed, calm, at peace. She felt the hand of God had touched her heart.

Near Sharpsburg the next morning, the Union camps came to life. Ten thousand men on the right drew into battle formation, and by six, Hooker had them on the move toward the Confederate left.

The troops advanced through the drizzle into woods and across farmland toward a cornfield. Behind them the dawn was smothered by the morning mist. Ahead they saw the glint of muskets among the green stalks of fodder. Hooker ordered a halt and called for artillery fire. While they waited, there were flashes from the cornfield. Soldiers standing in the front fell backwards as bullets hit about them.

Shells soared and exploded in the cornfield, tearing up chunks of turf and blowing men and cornstalks alike into the air. Rifled Parrots threw explosive shells into the Rebel flanks, while the Union troops waited, knowing their turn soon would come.

In the center, Ricketts began to edge his troops forward, seeking the Rebel line. On his right, Doubleday moved through a grove of trees, and on the left, Meade's brigades entered the cornfield, stepping over the torn bodies and limbs of dead soldiers. Soon they were halted by heavy fire from the Rebels as Jackson sent troops to meet their advance.

Artillery fire from both sides began to sweep across the clustered troops in the cornfield. The additional Rebel infantry forced Rickett's men to retreat, while Meade's men still pushed ahead. Hooker rode forward and surveyed the field while aides were relaying orders to his regiments. Rickett's men were pressing forward again as Union artillery stemmed the Rebel thrust. On the right, Doubleday was still unable to move forward because of heavy artillery fire.

"Abner can't get his division out of those damn woods," Hooker shouted, "because of their artillery back toward the river on our right." He sent a messenger to the nearby batteries to re-direct their fire toward the offending cannons. He sent a messenger to McClellan, requesting more artillery and urging that Mansfield corps join the assault.

Meanwhile, Meade was surveying the woods beyond the pike and saw that more enemy troops were preparing to attack. Before Hooker could react, Hood's Texans burst from the woods and sent the Union troops reeling backward. Mansfield's re-inforcements a few minutes later saved the Union position. Hooker's corps suffered catastrophic losses, and Hooker himself was wounded while rallying his men to stop the Texans. Mansfield was severely wounded, and died shortly afterwards.

13

On the opposite side of the Hagerstown Pike, Claib sat beside a beech tree, exhausted by the indescribable events of the previous two hours. His division, now under Lawton, had camped in the woods after an all night march following the easy victory at Harpers Ferry. The men had food from captured Union supplies and caught up on their rest despite a skirmish the previous evening.

When the Yanks opened the attack that morning on the cornfield, Jackson had sent the Stonewall Brigade forward, but with disastrous results as heavy artillery fire and superior numbers routed them. Lawton was sent forward with the rest of his men to stop the Yanks, and a ferocious battle erupted as both sides poured in troops. Claib found himself unable to hold his company in position as one man after another was downed by enemy fire. They were forced out of the cornfield and back to the woods where they had started. They were taking Yanks down with them, but their casualties were appalling.

Jackson ordered Hood forward to save the situation, and the Texans had burst from the woods and sent the Yanks reeling. Claib was able to get his remaining men into formation and join the attack. They smashed their way back through the ruined cornfield, stumbling over piles of bodies, until Union reinforcements and artillery fire blunted their assault. Finally, both sides fell back, too exhausted to fight further.

To his right, Claib could see more Union troops moving forward, and Confederates moving to meet them. He looked about. Of his forty man company, only seven were with him. "Are any more alive and able to fight?" he asked Jeremy.

"A few over yonder, but ain't many. We sure got blowed to pieces today."

Claib sighed and stood up. "Let's get ourselves in line. We ain't many, but we still got our weapons."

Richard was less than a mile away from his brother. Stuart's men were positioned between the North Woods by the Pike and the loop of the Potomac. Richard had spent the morning assisting a contingent of horse artillery attempting to keep Doubleday's division from joining the Union attack.

Fitz Lee kept Pelham's artillery moving and firing to give the impression of a larger force than existed. It was hard, grueling work, and Richard and most of his men were assigned to help the artillerymen. Richard had both his horses working the guns since two teams from the horse artillery were lost. He would hitch his pair to a cavalry field gun with another team and rush to a new position. As the battle raged in the cornfield, Stuart had them concentrate on the North Woods until Hooker identified the problem and ordered Union batteries to target the cavalry guns.

Suddenly, Richard's position was bracketed by heavy incoming fire. He was hitching his team to get his guns to a safer spot when a shell burst in front of him. King was hit and pitched forward in his traces. Prince whinnied and reared as King fell and pulled him off balance, while the other two horses struggled to get free. Richard had felt tugs at his uniform and examined himself for wounds as his men rushed to his side.

"Let's get out of here," Horine ordered. "Shanks, you and Granny send the men back to where Fitz Lee is posted. Then the two of you help me untangle this mess."

"You're hit, Richard," Shanks said.

"Ain't nothing. Get movin'."

Granny already had sent the troopers running back to better cover, while Shanks helped Richard unhitch the traces of the wounded King and free the artillery piece. Another shell burst near them, further panicking the other three horses.

"Let's get that gun outta here," Richard shouted. Granny and Shanks got the team re-hitched to the cannon and looked at Richard. "Go on, boys, I'll be with you in a minute."

Another shell burst nearby. Richard stroked the neck and muzzle of his frightened black horse and got him calmed. Then he knelt by King who lay on his side, blood flowing from several severe wounds. He stroked the horse's head and mane. They big chestnut's eyes were glazing over, and he had stopped kicking.

Richard pulled his Dragoon revolver from his holster. "God, I hate to do this," he murmured, "you've been such a great horse." He bent over and kissed the horse on the muzzle and stroked his head one last time. Shells were exploding nearby. "Gotta go, boy. God be with you." King's eyes became clear for a moment, and he raised his head slightly and looked at Richard. Then they glazed over once more, and he lay back and closed them.

Tears rolled down Richard's cheeks as he cocked the revolver. "Goodbye, old friend," he said. He placed the end of the barrel behind the horse's ear and pulled the trigger.

Prince jumped at the explosion. Richard arose, holstered the Dragoon, and again quieted the young black. "Just you and me now, boy," he said. He pulled himself into the saddle and galloped off to join his men. He hardly noticed the deep bloody lacerations on his left arm and thigh.

14

Johnny awoke with a start that Wednesday morning. He had slept sitting against a chestnut tree, and his body was stiff. Matthews stood over him, chuckling. "Time to get the company up," he said.

"I'm wetter'n tadpole," Johnny complained. He wiped the moisture from his Springfield. A fine drizzle was soaking the camp. "Shoulda had sense to get under my blanket, but I couldn't sleep and didn't feel like laying down."

"Nobody slept much, so don't fret yourself."

Slowly the company came to life. Most were already awake. There was little talk, as the troops kept their thoughts to themselves. They were wet and unhappy, uncertain of what was to come. They ate a cold breakfast of dried beef and hardtack.

Already nearby artillery batteries announced Hooker's attack over three miles away. Riders rushed back and forth from McClellan's headquarters to their right. The battlefield noise grew steadily, making talk difficult.

After Hooker and Mansfield's attack failed, Sumner led 20,000 men across the Antietam to hit the Confederate center. The drizzle ended and murky sunlight seeped through the mist. Sumner's troops were slaughtered as they marched into Rebs concealed in a sunken road, but other Union forces outflanked the Reb position and hundreds of the graycoats were killed.

Smoke drifted among the Marylanders, and the thunder of artillery and the rattle of muskets grew closer. Nagle's brigade was ordered forward to join the battle, and they marched toward the lower bridge on the Antietam Creek. A shell exploded near the lead troops, wounding several. Two more hit behind them. Union batteries on a nearby rise were firing toward Rebel lines.

Word came down from Burnside that the stone bridge was to be taken. They watched as the lead regiment attempted the crossing, only to be driven back, leaving dozens of men lying on the approaches. Rebels on the opposite hill held a commanding position to sweep the bridge with gunfire.

Johnny was quiet as the regiment moved forward to await their turn. This was as bad as anything in Virginia. Some of the boys said prayers. Others swore. Someone cried, "I'm gonna die in this damn place."

Another attack was driven back, leaving more bodies. Matthews' men moved past a farmhouse and over a small ridge into a cornfield where they halted in a low gulch at the field's edge.

"It's our turn, boys," Matthews said. "Give us a song, John."

"Not that, Hiram," Fisher said, but others shouted, "Go on, Johnny."

Johnny began singing as they broke into the open and rushed up the bottom road along the creek toward the bridge. Other companies were coming up from other directions.

"I got an ol' hoss," he sang.

"Back in the stable.

I druther be there

If I was able."

Johnny started to make up another verse, singing,

"Had an ol' dog," when a volley of enemy musket fire swept their ranks. Two men in front of him fell. From a knoll above the stream, hundreds of Rebel muskets began spitting fire. More men went down, and those remaining tried to find cover and return the fire. Johnny fired and reloaded but could see no target, the Rebs were too well concealed.

"Keep firing," Matthews shouted. Johnny reloaded and fired again, but more of his comrades fell.

Matthews saw their position was hopeless. "C'mon, boys, let's get outta this. Colonel," he shouted down the line, "we can't hold."

The officer hesitated when he too was hit. Two minies nipped Matthews' uniform, and he dove to the ground behind a low bank. "Get your asses back to cover," he ordered.

Johnny fired again and arose to move back to where Matthews had taken cover, when a bullet hit him in the left shoulder. He dropped his rifle and grabbed his shoulder with his right hand. It burned, and as he turned, he was struck in the right thigh, jerking him back, so that he faced the Reb line. He groaned and started to pitch to the right when a third shot hit his abdomen, doubling him over. Oh God, he thought, I'm gut shot, I'm dead. He slumped to his knees.

Mercifully a fourth Rebel shot smashed into Johnny's skull as he knelt on the grass by the Antietam Creek, knocking him backwards and killing him instantly. His last view was the misty sky overhead with the bright sun burning its way through the clouds.

Fisher saw Johnny fall and rose to get him. Matthews pulled him back to the ground. "He's gone, Al, keep down, or you'll be with him." Minies thudded into the ground in front of them, and the company crept back out of the withering fire. As they withdrew, still more troops were sent forward to attack the bridge.

Once they had escaped the carnage, Matthews assembled his company. They were numb, horrified at the slaughter of friends. Johnny and the Derr boy were dead. Liston, Gross, Handley, and Barnes were badly wounded.

Matthews went in search of Nagle. With his colonel dead, he had no orders. "I've no orders either," Nagle said. I can't find Burnside. We'll just have to wait."

"What can I do?"

"Bring your men back here, and collect any others you can find. Let's see what's left of the brigade."

In the afternoon, fresh units smashed through the fierce Confederate defense and moved toward Sharpsburg. Nagle's men were ordered to follow up the advance, but before they could cross the Antietam, A. P. Hill's men arrived from Harpers Ferry and stopped the Union assault. As darkness fell, the day's violent action came to a close. The Marylanders settled into a defensive line and lit a campfire. They huddled together, listening to the screams and moans of the wounded, the noise of the ambulances, and the curses of stretcher bearers stumbling about in the dark.

15

On Wednesday afternoon Mary Ann knew Johnny was dead. Her dreams of the previous nights, the signs in the misty sky, a quiet voice inside her head--all told her. She couldn't cry, she just faced the reality that somehow she knew he was gone, so she sat in her kitchen and pondered what to do.

She would have to find him. She made up her mind to bring him home, back to the farm he loved and the people who loved him. She would go to the battlefield.

She called in Sissy and Frankie. "I'm goin' over to Middletown," she said, "in case Johnny or some of the boys need help."

Frankie stared at her like she'd taken leave of her senses. "Some of the people around here have already gone," she explained. "I saw Peck Handley on horseback and some buggies on Mt. Nebo road, headin' that way."

"I better go with you," Frankie said.

"No, I thought it all out. It may be some time before I get back, and I want you to keep workin' on the corn and tend the animals. Sissy, I want you to take care of the chickens and fix your brother's meals for him."

"Ma, this don't make no sense," Frankie said.

"Yes it does, Frankie. Now don't argue no more. If your brother needs me, I'll be nearby, and if he don't, then

145

there'll be others. I know somethin' about nursing and can help."

By mid-afternoon Mary Ann had hitched up the one horse buggy and was driving down the lane.

She decided to take a short cut she knew across the mountain, following a small trail that led from Mt. Nebo toward the ridge. It was seldom used, although a few cabins were located in the surrounding woodland. The stillness was broken only by bird calls and an occasional small animal scampering across the leaves. Along the way, two barefoot, long haired Barnes children stopped their play and stared at her and waved as she drove by. She smiled and waved back. In about fifteen minutes she reached the ridge and drove down a narrow path that cut through scrub pine, milkweed, and pokeberry. Weeds brushed the sides of the buggy, and gnats irritated both her and her horse. The lane widened as she passed two houses built overlooking the Middletown Valley below. Another mile, and she reached the National Road and began the steep descent.

She met a constant flow of military traffic. Wagons lumbered along, carrying supplies to the battlefield, and horses galloped in various directions. Ambulances filled with wounded moved toward Frederick. A group of Union soldiers sat by the road under a shade tree, awaiting orders. Another group herded a disgruntled bunch of Rebel prisoners. Occasionally she could hear muffled sounds of battle on the other side of South Mountain.

Middletown was in turmoil. Home guards mingled with Union troops on guard duty. Hundreds of citizens milled about looking for news of the battle. A field hospital on the outskirts was filled with wounded from the battle at South Mountain, and several ambulances had stopped because all the hospitals were overflowing. Family members mingled with volunteers, surgeons and the wounded.

Mary Ann asked an ambulance driver for news of the battle. "It's an awful fight, ma'am," he said, "the worst ever, and still goin' on."

Sentries were stopping all civilian traffic beyond Middletown, and a Union officer cursed people pressing him to go forward and threatened to have them arrested.

Mary Ann found Peck Handley, but he had no news. "Miz Fraley," he said, "this ain't no place for you. You better go back home. If I get any news, I'll let you know."

Mary Ann thanked him and led her horse down a side street and rested. When darkness came, she saw her chance. While sentries were occupied with a jam-up of ambulances and wagons, she took her horse's reins and slipped by the sentry point on a side lane in the shadows. Stepping lively, she was soon out of sight. She climbed back into the buggy and started the steep ascent of South Mountain. All she met were ambulances, but the smell of death permeated the air. In the pale moonlight, she could make out the gray forms of dead, decaying bodies, men killed three days before.

Soon the shooting stopped, the night quieted, and she was descending toward Boonsboro. Sometime around midnight she found a grassy spot near a church, spread a blanket and quilt on the ground, and went to sleep.

Early in the morning, she awoke, drank water from a nearby well, watered her horse, and ate the biscuits and fruit she had packed. She led her horse into Boonsboro and mingled with a group of local people preparing to go to the battlefield. There were volunteers preparing to help the burial details, a group of clergymen, reporters, and several local women taking fruit and baked goods to the soldiers. Unlike Middletown, the sentries asked no questions but waved them on down the road toward Keedysville.

Mary Ann lifted a basket of peaches onto the back of her buggy and moved with the group. When she got near the battlefield, she got directions to the Maryland camp. There she found Matthews and his men cooking breakfast over a campfire.

When she pulled up in her buggy, Matthews and Fisher were speechless. "Hello, Hiram," she said, "I've come for Johnny. Here, help me with these peaches."

"Miss Fraley," Matthews sputtered, "what are you doin' here?"

"Johnny's dead, ain't he?"

"How did you know?"

"Never mind, I know, and I come to take him home. Are you gonna help me with these here peaches or do I have to lift them myself? Your men should enjoy some fresh fruit after what they been through."

Matthews and Fisher bumped into each other rushing to grab the basket. "Miss Mary," Matthews said as he again tried to get his composure, "this here battle ain't over yet. This is no fittin' place for a lady like you."

"Hiram Matthews, I've driven all night to get here and take my son home, so I'm not gonna go back now. I don't see no battle goin' on, and I don't hear no guns, so why don't you just tell me where I can find Johnny and I'll be on my way."

"Ma'am," Fisher said, "Johnny was shot up real bad. Last night we got him and laid him out for the burial parties. It don't seem right for a lady to have to look at him that way."

"Are you men gonna help me, or do I have to go look for him on my own?"

Matthews and Fisher looked at one another and shook their heads. "You win, Miss Mary," Matthews said. He climbed up on the buggy. "I'll help you."

They wheeled toward the lower bridge where the Marylanders had fought. Ambulances were still gathering the wounded. Burial details had begun their work. Already there was the odor of decaying flesh.

The horse stepped nervously up the trail along the creek. Buzzards and crows circled the area, trying to get at the dead horses. It's down here," Matthews said, "where we fought, lost a bunch of men in a few minutes. I think he's right over yonder."

"You hold the horse," Mary Ann said, "I'll find him."

A group of Negro men were digging graves nearby and stopped to stare at her as she stepped across the bodies. Their jaws dropped as they watched the thin little woman examining the rows of corpses.

Two of the men came toward her. "Missus," one said, "what y'all doin'?"

"I've come for my son."

"She's with me," Matthews called. "He should be right around here."

"Yes," she whispered, "here he is." Tears streamed down her cheeks as she knelt beside him. "Look what they did to him," she sobbed. Johnny's face was turning black where the bullet had struck his skull. Blood had dried into dark stains on his uniform. Flies buzzed about his eyes and mouth. His eyes were wide open, staring at nothingness.

Gently she closed his eyes and brushed the flies away. She took a handkerchief from her dress pocket, moistened it with warm water from his canteen, and wiped his face. She went back to the buggy and got the blanket and quilt to wrap him in. Matthews went with her, and they lifted him onto the textiles. His body was stiff, so they attempted to straighten his legs which had doubled under him.

"Let me he'p," the large black man said. He jerked the legs violently and they straightened with a snap. Mary Ann gasped. "They ain't broke, Missus, that just be the way we has to do it."

They got his arms folded and finished wrapping him. "He smells bad," Mary Ann said. "I'll have to get him buried right away."

They lifted him onto the back of the buggy and tied him securely.

"Missus," another one of the burial crew called, "you can take some more of 'em if you wants to. We's got more'n enough."

"Why don't you hush up," his companion scolded.

They drove back to the camp in silence and Matthews got down, while the soldiers stood and stared. "Thank you so much, Hiram," she said. "God bless you all." Tears were still streaking her cheeks, but she snapped the reins and started on the road back to Keedysville.

As the horse and buggy began to move, Matthews snapped to attention and saluted. By the time she got to the road, every man in the company stood at attention, saluting Mary Ann and her son.

A mile past Boonsboro, she pulled off the road to rest her horse before approaching South Mountain. She led him to a stream to drink while she got water for herself from a spring. The horse grazed on the grass while she rested. The clatter of vehicles was constant, but the guns were silent.

Then she began Johnny's final journey. They crawled up the mountain, the horse straining with the added load. From the crest they eased down into Middletown Valley. The sentries halted her, but waved her on through when they detected her burden. In Middletown the crowds had thinned out. A group of residents was beginning to clean up debris.

The horse had increasing difficulty with the climb to the Braddock Heights, so Mary Ann got down from the buggy and led him. She skipped the shortcut and followed the National Road toward Frederick. A mile out, she cut across Butterfly Lane to the Jefferson pike, three miles from home.

She stopped at Holter's store and explained to the dumfounded storekeeper that she had Johnny with her and needed help. "Do you have any ice left?" she asked. Holter went to his icehouse and retrieved two blocks from storage in straw deep underground. He agreed to contact the church sexton and the minister for an immediate funeral. He loaded the ice into the front of the buggy, and she headed home.

She parked the buggy in front of her house, found her children, and spoke to them in the kitchen. "There ain't no way to give bad news except to say it, my loves. Johnny's dead. He was killed yesterday in an awful fight over at Sharpsburg."

Sissy and Frankie were shocked. "Ma," Frankie said, "how can you be sure?"

"I brought him home. I been to the battlefield with Hiram Matthews. We found Johnny lying there, and I fetched him back home with me."

"Can we see him?" Sissy asked, trying not to sob.

"Honey, he's been all shot up. His body is, uh, corrupted. Do you know what that means?"

"I guess, like when an animal is dead a while and smells awful."

"That's right. I want to bring him up on the porch till his grave is opened. I want to pack him with ice I got from Mr. Holter. Frankie, do you think you can bear to help me carry him?"

Frankie's mind was numb. "Them damn Rebs killed him."

"Honey, there's thousands of boys over there, Reb and Union alike, all dead. It must be what hell looks like. Do you think you can help?" she repeated.

"Huh? Oh sure, Mom, I can help."

They carried him to the porch, unwrapped his body, and began to chip the ice and pack it around him. "God, he looks awful," Frankie said.

"It doesn't even look like Johnny," Sissy said.

"He was killed fightin' for us. He was a brave soldier," Mary Ann said. "Now we have to be brave and remember him as he was, the boy we loved."

The ice started to work. The bloating of the body ceased and the odor became less noticeable. Tenderly Mary Ann cleaned up his uniform and rinsed his face, taking care to add ice as it began to melt.

By the corner of the house, Buster and three cats sat and watched. "Even the animals look like they know what's happened," Frankie said.

Later, Sam and Susie Zimmerman drove up the lane to tell them the grave was open and to deliver a rough pine coffin which Sam had constructed after being contacted by Holter. Susie embraced first Mary Ann and then Sissy and

Frankie while Sam stared at Johnny's body, trying to hold back his tears.

Sam and Frankie lifted the corpse off the blanket into coffin and loaded the coffin onto the wagon. Then they drove down the lane to the church where several people, contacted by Holter, were waiting along with the minister.

A mound of dirt showed where the grave had been opened.

The group gathered around Mary Ann, offering sympathy. Many were sobbing. The Stones were there, but Mary Elizabeth was too distraught to attend. A few chose to view the body, and then Sam nailed the lid on the coffin.

The minister began to read from the King James Bible as the men lowered the coffin into the grave. He recited the 23rd Psalm which Mary Ann loved and knew by heart. She closed her eyes and whispered the words as he finished, "Surely goodness and mercy shall follow me all the days of my life, and I will dwell in the house of the Lord forever."

There followed a brief sermon noting, "For as man is born of woman, so shall he die. Today we mourn the death of a son, a brother, a friend, as so many have lost the ones they love. We cannot reason why this loss, there is no reason, only the will of a great and almighty God. Lord, we pray that this brutal and horrible war may end." He concluded, "John Fraley, we consign your body to the earth and your soul to the Father. May God grant you eternal rest, in the name of the Father, the Son, and the Holy Ghost."

The sun had set, and the whippoorwills were already calling when the group parted. The ride back up the lane was the saddest of all. Johnny was gone, and the reality of his death was upon them. Frankie sat and stared, heartbroken. Sissy cried her heart out.

CHAPTER VI. BEYOND ANTIETAM

Mary Elizabeth wanted to perish with Johnny when her mother told her he was dead. She rushed to her room and flopped on her bed, sobbing in anguish. She wouldn't talk to her sisters, and nothing her mother said consoled her. She had cared for Johnny more than she let herself realize, and her whole life, all her dreams, came crashing down when he was killed.

Beth told her husband, "I don't know what's to become of that child. She won't talk. She won't eat. I can't get her out of that bedroom. She cries constantly."

"It's a darn shame," Stone said, "so many boys killed, we're raisin' a bunch of ol' maids."

"She's makin' herself sick."

"What can we do? She'll just have to get over it."

A half mile away in a closed shed, four men met. Three of them, Peck Handley, Bill Gross, and Clete Barnes, had sons at Antietam. It had taken days for Handley to find his son on a cot in the Lutheran Church in Frederick and missing a leg. Josh Barnes was nearly dead, shot down by the Confederates' murderous fire near the stone bridge. Gross' son was wounded by a shell fragment that ripped away part of his cheek and lacerated his neck. The fourth man, Boyer, was a close friend and long-time Rebel hater. They had decided to take matters into their own hands.

They drifted out of the shed one by one. Cletus Barnes headed back toward Mt. Nebo road and saw a horse and buggy approaching. He pulled his mule up and waited. "Howdy, Missus Fraley," he greeted.

"Hello, Mr. Barnes," Mary Ann said. "How is your boy, Joshua, doing? I heard he was shot real bad."

"Yessum, he's in turrible pain, still in one of the churches in town, but we feel so bad you done lost your boy. Joshua liked young John a lot. They allus sang songs together. It ain't right, them Rebs comin' up here and shootin' our boys."

Mary Ann rode on, thinking what a strange man, with his battered felt hat, his black coat and riding britches, and scuffed boots. The Barnes family had lived in the mountains above the Fraley farm for over a century. They were among the first settlers in the region.

In a few minutes, Mary Ann pulled her buggy to a stop in front of the Stone home. George Stone was in the back, splitting firewood which his son was stacking. The younger girls were in the orchard picking up apples. Beth Stone met her on the porch and they embraced. "You poor dear, lost your oldest boy, and still you come visit."

"I got to thinkin' about Mary Elizabeth, Beth. She and Johnny were gettin' close, and now he's gone. It musta hurt her bad."

"You don't know how bad, Mary Ann, she's just broken hearted. I reckon in her heart she expected to marry Johnny, although to tell the truth, I don't know if they ever talked about it."

"Johnny never said, but he sure was fond of her."

"Well, there was no better company than your Johnny. Lordy, but I think about him all the time, and a person can't help but remember him singing some song or the other whenever he was around."

Beth sent Mary Ann on to her daughter's room, where she sat down quietly on the bed. The girl was lying on her stomach with her face buried in a stained pillow. After a few seconds she raised up to see who had entered. She jumped up and stared. "Missus Fraley, I'm sorry, I thought it was Mama or one of my sisters."

"Don't fret, honey. I just come to sit with you a spell."

"Mama said you brought Johnny, uh, Johnny's body, back all by yourself. I'm sorry I didn't come to the funeral. I just couldn't."

"Never you mind, I understand. You wouldn't have wanted to see him anyways, honey, he was shot up so bad. I just wanted him back home with those of us that cared for him."

"Yes ma'am, that was good of you." She sat up and started to sob, falling into Mary Ann's embrace. "It's awful," she wailed, "I, we'll never see him again."

Mary Ann stroked her back and hair. "We can always remember him, that's all we can do, and pray he's in the arms of the Lord, honey. But life has to get on, and we can't weep forever. You remember that. Johnny was so fond of you, he wrote about you in all his letters, and I would have been proud to have you as his wife, but it can't be, and he would want you get on with livin'. Do you see than?"

"I guess, that's what Mama says too, but it's so hard."

"Of course, it's hard, but it's how life is."

They talked for a while and then walked down the steps together. They held each other for a moment, and Beth joined them, and the three women clung to each other before Mary Ann departed. They watched her buggy as it disappeared around the bend down the lane. "Mama," Mary Lib said, "I guess you better give me something to do. If Missus Fraley can keep goin' after losin' Johnny, I'll try to be like her." She choked back another sob, and then her mother led her outside.

The two women soon were picking pole beans in the garden, while George Stone paused at his wood chopping, and the other children stopped doing their chores, and all of them stared.

2

Five nights after the battle, Ben Horine was awakened by shouts and heavy thumping on his kitchen door.

"Massa Horine," Jeremiah shouted, "Massa, wake up, wake up, oh Lordy, the barn's on fire."

Horine came to his senses and rushed to the window. Flames were coming from at least two parts of the building, and horses were whinnying in panic. "Jeremiah," he shouted, "get the horses out."

The Negro slave ran back to the barn while Horine slipped on trousers and shoes and raced outside. When he got to the barnyard, he found Jeremiah had forced open a door. Flames were visible inside. "We must get the horses out," he screamed.

"I'se tried, but they's too skeered, they won't come out."

Together they tried to enter through a second door, but the heat was already intense. The horses had broken their halters and crowded into the back stalls. The two men pushed through the smoke and heat and attempted to shove the animals outside, but Jeremiah was knocked backwards by a panicked horse, and Horine was nearly overcome by the heat. Hay in the next stable had caught fire. They kept shouting, trying to get the horses to move, but were defeated by the growing flames.

The two men fled the barn to save themselves. Flaming fragments of straw and wood showered the area, and the fire lit up the night sky. Jeremiah's head was slashed and bleeding. His face and arms were singed, and the backs of his arms blistered. He collapsed across the barnyard where his wife fetched a bucket of well water and began washing his wounds. Their three children sat in the darkness and watched the growing fire with awe.

After coughing and strangling for minutes, Horine was able to catch his breath and sit up, weeping as sounds from the horses died and parts of the barn floor collapsed. Elsie and the five children stared at the disaster in numb disbelief.

"All dem beautiful horses bein' burnt up," Jeremiah said. "Dem three mares and de babies, and two more soon to be mamas."

Ben Horine continued to gasp for air. His chest hurt and his throat was raw. He started toward the barn again, but the heat drove him back. He stepped backward and lost his balance. His children rushed forward to help him.

Elsie Horine stared at the fire and then at her fallen husband. "It's God's will, Ben," she declared, "for sending our sons to die in an unjust war." She turned and went back to the house.

A few minutes later, Horine roused himself, and Rebecca, Tillie, and Jeremiah helped him stand. The fire had burned through the beams and the roof was beginning to collapse. "Guess I had a spell," he said. "Thank you, Jeremiah, for trying to save the horses. What an awful loss."

"Yassuh," Jeremiah said, "it's truly turrible. How you s'pose that fire got started?"

"Papa, are you feeling better?" Rebecca asked.

"Yes, I'll be fine. Where's Mother?"

"She went back in the house, Papa. She was upset, you know how she gets, her mind's not right."

"Yes, I understand. Thank you, children. I want you all to go back in, tend to your mother, and go to bed. You'll get sick out here in the night air."

"We're worried about you, Papa," Rebecca said.

"Don't fret, I'm fine now, just shocked at losing our horses and our barn. Now back in the house, all of you."

The burning barn was visible from Frederick to Jefferson. Even though it was after midnight, the unusual light from the flames roused many people. Whole families watched from porches or windows for several hours, wondering where the fire was. Some figured out it was Horines and were sympathetic. They're secesh, others said, and it serves them right, damn traitors. A few were satisfied that they had gotten some measure of revenge.

Two men came to help as the fire burned itself out--King, a long time friend and southern sympathizer, and a cousin of Elsie's, who offered to help although he was a Union man.

Afterwards in their two room cabin, Tillie scolded Jeremiah as she doctored his injuries. "You do too much for dat ol' man. You coulda died in dat fire. What gonna happen to me and de chillun if you gone? Sell us away, I 'speck, chilluns to one place, me to 'nother."

"I loved dem horses, raised 'em, trained 'em. I hated to see dem burn like dat." Tears ran down his cheeks. "I don't know what to do. Wish I could see my pap."

"Your pap 'n mom done gone, like mine, sent south, sold with my brothers, be field niggers, reckon dey already dead."

"Pap talk how his pappy recollect comin' here from Africa, how he was born free down dere. Mebbe we be free sometime."

Tillie sighed. It was so confusing. She had been bought by the Horines from a Frederick family to be the wife of Jeremiah, who was a wedding gift from relatives in Virginia. Her family was sold soon afterwards, she didn't know where, and Jeremiah learned inadvertently by hearing the Horines talking, that his entire family also was sold as Virginians cut back on their numbers of slaves, and as deep south planters increased their demand for slave labor. It was common talk among blacks that those sold down south were lost forever.

The children were asleep, so they went outside and sat in front of the cabin, watching the smoldering ruins. "We got to stay together, Mister," Tillie said. "If'n Massa Abraham's army win dis war, we be free."

"I know, but what we do then? I gotta work good so ol' Massa here think I a good nigger."

"You right, but I skeered you be killed."

Jeremiah lit his corncob pipe. He looked at the stars in the early morning sky. "I be keerful," he said.

3

In Baltimore, two days later, four men discussed the burning of the Horine barn. Mortimer Varley, career politician and former state senator, observed, "These problems with Horine are getting out of hand. People in Frederick County thinks he's a Confederate agent."

Merryman agreed. "Ben's done a lot of good for the cause, his ride may have saved Lee, but he's too visible, with two sons fighting for the South and a steady flow of horses from his farm to our army."

"Well, the barn burning has stopped that."

Brown, a Baltimorean, drew on his cigar and coughed. "I don't see what we can do about it," he said.

"I propose," Varley said, "that we tell him to stop all activities and stay away from us. Otherwise, he's liable to get all of us arrested."

"Do you agree with that?" Brown asked Merryman.

"The best thing would be for Ben to take his family south. They've got relatives in Virginia."

"I don't think Ben would agree to that," Seth Hatcher said.

"He may have no choice."

Brown reflected for a moment. "What did you tell him, Seth, when he came to your office?"

"I told him not to come again and to lay low, not get involved with anything for a while."

"My opinion," Varley said, "is that this war is far from over. The Federals claim a victory at Sharpsburg, but it seems to me it was about even, and from reports, Lee is still in the vicinity. Ben's a valuable man, so maybe he should do just what you told him, Seth--lay low for a time."

"Ben wants to know who set that fire."

"I understand that, but we can't have him doing anything to find out, at least not until the Confederate army occupies this area again."

"What about Ben's contact with Stuart?"

"Too dangerous, we'll have to give that up, at least for now."

"Hear anything from Johns?" Brown asked, switching to a different area of intrigue.

"Not much. The War Department is convinced Lincoln will replace McClellan, probably put Halleck back in the field, although there's rumors about both Hooker and Burnside taking over. Some of McClellan's generals, starting with Porter, are said to be on the way out."

"Sounds like they're tearin' themselves apart," Brown said, "all to our advantage."

"So what's our next move?" Merryman asked.

Varley shrugged. "We'll tell Ben not to contact us for a while and to curtail all his activities. We'll have to get word to Stuart, and we'll keep promoting the anti-war protests. More than anything, we need to get our man elected in November."

4

Two weeks after the battle at Sharpsburg, Lee was back in Virginia, and McClellan had yet to move his army across the Potomac. Bodies and wreckage still littered the battleground, and the stench made the soldiers' lives almost unbearable.

Nagle had pulled together the shattered remnants of his brigade, and Matthews had tracked down his missing men and found that two more--Getzendanner and Miller--were among the wounded. The loss of so many officers led to promotions. Matthews was now a captain, and Fisher promoted to lieutenant.

Francis Fraley could not accept his brother's death and was determined to avenge it. He vowed to himself to take Johnny's place, but first, he had to convince his mother. In the evening when his work was done, he'd go to the hayloft and play his mouth harp, wishing Johnny was there to sing with him. Sometimes Eddie Zimmerman and Bobby

Matthews would visit, but it wasn't the same without Johnny's jokes and his songs and his fun.

Sissy cried every time she thought of Johnny. She had finished seven grades and was begin instructed by Mary Ann on how to be a farm woman. She helped to cook and with the housework. There was water to be drawn from the well for drinking, cooking, cleaning, and bathing. Lye soap had to be made. The garden needed to be tended, and vegetables dried or canned for the winter. In the fall, there were black walnuts to be gathered, their hulls removed, shells cracked, and the tiny nutmeats removed. Frankie would go hunting for squirrels and rabbits, and the catch had to be skinned and cleaned. A fire was started each morning. Pots had to be scrubbed. The yard had to be tended, and there was always sewing and needlework. Sissy had made her first sampler when she was seven and was becoming an adept seamstress.

The farm work was endless. Frankie worked hard, and Sam and Eddie helped when they could, but still Mary Ann and Sissy had to pitch in. The cows had to be milked in the morning and evening. There was butter to be churned and cheese to be made. Cows, horses, hogs, chickens, dogs and cats must be fed and tended. Woodchucks, rats, hawks, weasels, skunks, possums, raccoons, mice, crows, foxes, and other varmints had to be stopped from taking the farm crops and animals. Manure had to be cleaned from the stables and barnyard, and fresh straw bedding provided. Fences had to be mended, and tools and equipment repaired. The work was endless, and the days drifted from season to season with no break.

Frankie argued over and over with his mother on his need to replace Johnny. Each time tears would swim in her eyes and she would reply, "You and Sissy are all I have. If I lose you, what are Sissy and me to do? You'll be gone, and we won't be able to tend the farm, and we'll lose everything. I don't know what'll become of us." Frankie could not cope with his mother's tears, and he drifted deeper into despair.

In early October a singular event occurred. Grandpa roused himself, and with surprisingly clear mind and speech, requested that the Zimmerman family be gathered together. He wanted to talk to them.

It took most of the day to locate all his children and grandchildren plus his living siblings and their families. Most of the men were working the fields, while others were in the woods hunting. Two were in Frederick trying to buy livestock to replace animals lost to the armies. But before twilight, buggies and riders were coming up the lane from the Jefferson pike to the home place where George Zimmerman and his dead wife, Charlotte, had raised their family, and where Sam and Susie now lived with their children and cared for Grandpa George.

The old man sat on the front porch in his large wooden rocker, wrapped in a quilt against the chilly evening air, watching the arrivals and greeting each by name. When the last had arrived, Sam and Susie helped him into the parlor and seated him on a black horsehair parlor chair. His legs were swollen and weak, his arthritic joints gnarled and painful.

"Ever'one gather round," he said. "My voice ain't strong." The family wedged themselves into the parlor. Men squatted in the doorways so those behind could see. Children and young people sat on the stairs.

"I wanted you here to tell you what I feel. Our family's been livin' hereabouts for over a hundred years, ever since my great grandpappy come down here from up in Pennsylvania. It's been a hard life but a good life, and now this war has messed things up." There were nods around the room.

"Y'all know I ain't got much longer." Murmurs of concern. "Don't fret none. I done lived longer'n most, and I'm ready whenever my Maker wants me. We all go sometime, and I do miss my sweet Charlotte. Most time, it seems like she's still here.

"This here Civil War's done hurt us bad. We lost young Johnny Fraley and that just makes me sick. Johnny's a fine boy, good farmer, and it's broke Mary Ann's heart, lost her man when he was young and now her oldest son. Willie's boy, Ike, he got shot up down in Virginny, and he's still mendin'. And all of you got robbed by them Rebs comin' through here a few weeks back.

"Now young Eddie here and Mary Ann's other boy, Francis, and probably some more of you young bucks wanna go off to fight them Rebs, but I say we done give enough." His voice rose. "We gotta keep this family together, and we can't if our young men keep marchin' off and gettin' themselves killed. You boys have gotta stay home and tend to our farms. Now that's about all I gotta say cause I'm gettin' tuckered out."

Grandpa slumped in his chair for a moment and the group stirred, but then he sat up and shook his fist. "Losin' Johnny is more than enough for us to give. Keep the family together. Don't let 'em take no more of our boys, but you young fellers, if you gotta fight, do it here. Join up with the home brigades, like that militia we had before the war. That's what y'all can do." He lay back again and closed his eyes. In a moment he was asleep.

The family moved out of the parlor into the dining room and began to talk. "What Grandpa said makes sense," one of Mary Ann's brothers said, and after a lot of discussion, there was general agreement.

On the way home, Frankie asked, "How did Grandpa know I want to go fight?"

"I swear I don't know," Mary Ann said. "I never told him. Sometimes when people get ol' and dyin' like Grandpa, they just know things. How do you feel about what he said?"

"I ain't sure, Mama, signing up with the guard wouldn't be the same as the real army, but I reckon if some of the other boys do it, I will too."

Sissy shivered in the chilly air as the horse trotted up Mt. Nebo Road. "I think Grandpa is right. I already lost one brother."

The next day they learned Grandpa had died in his sleep. Sissy remembered when she and Johnny had visited him, back before Antietam, and he had told Johnny they would be getting together real soon.

5

Like a wounded predator, Lee's army waited in the Shenandoah and gathered its strength, while the Army of the Potomac idled in camp.

The Confederate cavalry was active every day, watching for Union activity, while the generals argued over strategy. Jackson wanted to strike into Maryland, believing the Federal leadership was paralyzed, but Lee needed more time, so he could gather supplies, wagons, horses, so badly needed. Instead, Lee authorized Stuart to strike northward to capture and bring back some of these items.

It was like the peninsula, Richard decided, when he received the orders. His men, tired of the routine, were excited. It was to be a cavalry raid, not the exhausting, deadly fighting of Sharpsburg, but the incursion, rapid movement, deep into enemy territory.

Over a thousand riders stirred the autumn dust, Stuart wearing a new plume on his vaunted hat. Richard had captured a northern saber for the event, and Shanks was wearing new sergeant's stripes. Both Richard and Prince were healed from battle wounds, and his troopers were fresh and recovered from the carnage of September.

They galloped from Winchester past Martinsburg and crossed the Potomac between Hancock and Williamsport. At Waynesboro they gathered wagons and draft horses, and in Chambersburg they cleaned out the hardware and grocery stores, loading merchandise on the 200 wagons they'd accumulated along the way. Alarmed Pennsylvanians telegraphed ahead and tried to organize opposition, but no one knew where the rapidly moving Rebels were or would strike next.

Near Mercersburg Richard and his troopers rode into a prosperous farm with two large red barns and a three story stone house. "Who be ye?" the gray bearded farmer asked.

"Troopers of the Confederacy," Richard replied. "We want your horses and the contents of your meathouse."

"Why do ye bother us? We have no part in the war. We care not to have ye in the Union, and we care not whether ye keep Negro slaves or no."

"You're part of the North which is trying to deprive us of our freedom. Your soldiers kill our men and destroy our property. We're taking your animals and goods to replace what we've lost."

"Ye be stealing according to the Good Book, and no good will come to ye. Leave our animals and let us be. We are not your enemy."

"Sorry, but I have my orders." He waved to his men. "Let's get this job done."

That was how the raid went. By the time they returned to their lines, they had collected 2,000 horses and 300 wagon loads of supplies. Only a few troopers were wounded, none killed. Even the dour Jackson praised the raid.

Stuart's raid touched a nerve with the Army of the Potomac. McClellan began to move men into Virginia, and winter was at hand. Lee would have to wait till Spring before he could move north again.

In November Burnside replaced McClellan, creating a tremendous furor as most officers and many enlisted men objected to the change.

Al Fisher was one of the soldiers who didn't object. "I don't understand what the fuss is about," he said. "Little Mac had us sit on our butts for a month after we whipped the Rebs at Antietam."

Matthews wasn't so sure. He had no great love for McClellan, but he had no confidence in Burnside. "Damn generals ain't near as good as the men," he grumbled.

Burnside re-organized the army and the Marylanders became part of a corps under Hooker. They were marched past Manassas to the Rappahannock, where they waited for pontoons to build a bridge to cross to Fredericksburg. The wait stretched too long, allowing Lee to move his men to the heights overlooking the town.

Finally, the town was occupied, and Burnside prepared to attack Lee's positions. He ordered his army forward to attack an entrenched, experienced enemy holding the high ground.

Initially the assault seemed promising when Union troops made headway against Jackson's flank at the far end of the battle line. Claib and his company were part of a counter attack that drove Meade's division away from the breech his men had made in the Rebel line. Since no troops were sent to take advantage of Meade's initial success, the Rebel line was secured.

Next, Sumner's corps was sent against the Confederate line along Marye's Heights. Union losses were horrendous, and after a half-hearted effort to support the attack, Hooker pulled his men back, including his Marylanders, seeing no sense to more useless slaughter.

Matthews was bitter over the battle, even though his men suffered only two wounded. "This army deserves better generals. That was the worse planned damn attack I ever seen. Al, you and me coulda done a helluva sight better."

6

In Baltimore Mort Varley sought out Merryman the day after the November election. "A disaster," he said, "we lost Baltimore and all the western counties. What went wrong?"

"Everything," Merryman said. "All the Yank soldiers voted for the Union ticket, while our soldiers couldn't vote at all. They simply outsmarted us."

"Well," Varley growled, "I hate to keep fighting this war underground, but it appears we have no choice. I've been in touch with Vallandigham, and he says there's strong sentiment against the war in New York and Ohio. Even people who've supported the Union are tired of the killing. That seems to be our best hope."

"Ben Horine," Merryman said, "is the only one of us who's stuck his neck out. He's lost a boy, saved Lee at Sharpsburg, and had his barn burned and horses killed. We're supposed to be his friends, and he can't even be seen with us."

"It don't seem fair, but what else can we do?"

"I don't know. The colonel is too nervous to help. We should be doing more."

"I agree, this has gone far enough. I'll get in touch with Brown and see if we can get the group back together."

"What about Kilgour?"

"What difference does it make, now that the election is over? He'll be there."

7

Squire Fulmer read the paper while Peck Handley and Emmert Boyer looked over his shoulder. "Says here that Burnside is still at Fredericksburg and may attack again."

"What's wrong with that man?" Boyer asked. "Why's he keep sending our soldiers up a hill where the Rebs has all the advantage?"

Ed Holter was measuring out sugar from a barrel. "Seems to me we need better generals. We ain't got that kinda trouble in the west."

"You're right about that, Ed," the Squire said. "Says in here both Grant and Rosecrans are doin' well."

"Any news about our boys in Virginia?" Handley asked."

"Nothin' so far. Reckon we'll hear soon enough."

Bill Gross entered the store, stomping his feet and blowing on his hands.

"Cold enough for you?" Handley asked.

"Too damn cold."

"Anything happenin' at the Horines?" Boyer asked.

"Nothin', no horses, no riders, barn's still smokin'. How you doin', Peck?"

"Fair, I reckon. The missus can't get over our boy losin' his leg. We rode over to the battlefield last Sunday, and it's still a mess. Dead horses layin' around, bodies half buried, mostly just bones now. It's hard to believe how many boys went down in that one day."

"It's a shame," Gross said. "Our boy is about healed up, but he still looks like hell."

Boyer re-lit his pipe and Peck cut a fresh chew of tobacco. Holter went down the cellar steps to fetch some nails for a customer. Gross sat down and spit into the cuspidor. "I think," he said, "we can forget Horine. Them Reb raiders that was over in the manor a few weeks ago, I talked to a feller who claims they was put up at the King place."

The winter of 1862-63 was bitter. For the Fraley farm, sitting high on the ridge of the Catoctin range, it was especially bad. A week before Christmas, snow began falling, and by the New Year, the lane was drifted shut and winds had piled drifts against the barn and sheds.

Frankie had been unable to get much of the corn husked and in the corn crib since he had joined the Home Brigade. Sissy got sick the week before Christmas, and this dragged on as she developed bronchitis that spread into pneumonia. Mary Ann found it impossible to cope with all her chores and tending Sissy. Frankie had to dig paths through the drifts and take over care of the chickens. Three of the hens froze, so he brought the rest of the flock into the cellar and kept them warm with hot coals in an iron kettle.

The horses and cows took most of Frankie's time. He had to carry water to them from the well since they couldn't get to the creek. They stayed in the stables and keeping them clean was impossible. He had to shovel out manure every day into the barnyard, where the filth piled up. One of the older cows and a lame horse died from the cold and it took him hours to hitch a team, clear a path, and haul the carcasses into the field.

At supper that night, Mary Ann said, "I swear, Frankie, the Good Lord must be lookin' somewhere else, the way things are. Sissy ain't a bit better."

They lived on cured pork, sausage, dried and canned vegetables and fruits, and potatoes they'd stored in the cellar, covered so the chickens couldn't peck at them. As the hens stopped laying, Mary Ann would chop off their heads, dress and stew them. Sissy liked the broth, and the meat, tough as it was, was a welcome change from salt pork.

By the end of January, Frankie was running short of grain. Part of the corn crop was still in the field, so he rigged up a sledge of timber, anchored a double tree to it and hitched up his team. With this contraption, he was able to load a few shocks of corn, drag them into the barn, and husk out the ears. They used the corn for cornmeal for themselves, grain for the livestock, and fodder for roughage for the animals and a crude source of bedding.

Keeping the house warm was a major problem. The wind whipped around the logs, finding any spot where the chinking had loosened or cracked. The wood shingles on the roof lifted in the winter winds and snow sifted into the attic and down the attic steps.

Windows and shutters rattled in each storm and snow found its way into the rooms along the sills. Mary Ann covered them with old blankets and quilts, but she hated the darkness. The oil lamps and candles flickered and smoked in the drafts, and though she struggled to keep a fire in each of the three fireplaces, the flames died and smoldered when winds howled down the chimneys and kept them from drawing properly. Sissy complained constantly of the smoke and the drafts. She alternated between too cold and too hot. Mary Ann piled quilts on her, but the girl remained restless and feverish.

Frankie had to spend time every day splitting firewood. He had felled several chestnut and oak trees during the summer and cut them into log size, but had not had time to cut and split them to fit the fireplaces.

Each night Mary Ann and Frankie would go to bed exhausted, only to lie awake listening to Sissy's relentless dry hacking cough. Mary Ann finally put Sissy and her bed in the parlor and set an open kettle of water by the fireplace.

The steaming water moistened the air and gave the girl some relief from the dry throat and nasal passages that plagued her.

After the snows came, Mary Ann and Frankie twice tried to go to church, but the first time, they were there only with the pastor and one other family. The second time, not even the pastor showed up as the roads drifted shut. They were alone in a freezing, lonely building. They stopped by Johnny's grave, hidden under the snow. "We ain't forgot you, son," Mary Ann said, "but it's hard without you and your Dad. We're doin' our best, but we want you to remember us and talk to the Lord and ask him to help Sissy get well." On the short walk back to the farm, Frankie twice had to help his mother through deep drifts.

One day late in February the wind stopped blowing and the sun broke through the bitter gray skies. Water dripped from the eaves, and the trees groaned and cracked as ice and snow dropped from the branches. A rider worked his way up the lane, the first visitor in weeks. It was Eddie Zimmerman. They brought him in the house, wheezing and shaking and blowing on cold hands.

"What on earth brings you out?" Mary Ann asked.

"Rebs," Eddie replied, "just got word. Raiders come across the Potomac below Point of Rocks. We think they're headed for the Manor, and the guards are being assembled. Papa said I should get Frankie, but first I'm to help lay in enough wood and food for a few days."

The boys hurried to their chores while Mary Ann fretted about what might happen to her son.

Frankie got himself ready with painstaking effort. He put on two pairs of wool socks and long woolen underwear, wool shirt, heavy wool uniform trousers tucked into leather boots, and a heavy blue overcoat, wool muffler wrapped around his neck and ears, and finally a wool cap with ear flaps. He packed two day's rations, a blanket, a belt with his scabbard and bayonet, and a canteen. Finally he got his regulation Springfield percussion rifled musket and a pouch of ammunition.

Mary Ann kissed her son on the cheek and thanked Eddie for his help. She watched them mount up on Eddie's horse and called, "You be careful."

"We will, Mama, don't fret none."

When she got back into the house, Sissy was sitting by the window watching the riders go down the lane. "Honey, you shouldn't be up."

"I know, but I'm feelin' some better."

8

The King farm lay south of the Monacacy near the Frederick-Montgomery County line. At the end of 1862, Stuart and Lee approved John Mosby's request for an independent partisan command in Loudoun County, Virginia, directly across the Potomac from Frederick County. When Mosby sought assistance for his forays against the Union troops in Maryland, the King family promised food, water, forage, and fresh horses if needed.

The Kings' helpfulness was observed by Union supporters, so when Mosby's men crossed the Potomac, a spotter got word to the telegraph station in Berlin, and Frederick was notified. Within a few hours, the Potomac Home Brigade, including Cole's Cavalry, began assembling.

The Rebels moved through Adamstown, collecting horses, wagons and supplies from irate farmers and merchants. Two freight cars were emptied, but considerable time elapsed while wagons were loaded. It was nearly twilight before the raiders completed their work and headed toward the Kings.

This allowed enough time for the Marylanders to get into position along the road from Adamstown to the King farm. Nearly five hundred infantry awaited Mosby's horsemen and wagons lumbering over the frozen ruts of the country lane.

Lick Liston, wounded at Antietam, had recovered and joined the guard. He was sergeant in Frankie's company and he cautioned his men, "Keep down and keep quiet till they're mostly past us. Any of you farts shoot before I tell you, I'll bust your ass."

The entire Reb line was in front of them when the Marylanders raised from their positions and opened fire. Chaos erupted as horses and riders scrambled for cover. After the initial shock, the well armed and experienced Virginians began an effective counter fire that pinned the guard down behind their defenses. Neither side could get decent shots in the growing darkness.

It was then that the cavalry struck. Cole had followed the road from Frederick to Buckeystown and then cut over to the railroad and followed it toward Adamstown. Local people told him the direction the Rebs had taken, so he was able to hit the enemy's rear and catch them in a trap between his cavalry and the Home Brigade infantry.

The veteran Rebs were outnumbered, but they fought hard and held their ground, using wagons and dead horses for cover until darkness saved them. Abandoning their captured wagons and supplies, they rode out of the trap and raced back to the Potomac, leaving four dead. The Marylanders were exuberant, having chased the enemy and recovered most of the captured loot. They made camp for the night and celebrated. Cole decided it was too dark to follow the invaders.

The next morning Frankie returned home, proud of the victory. Mary Ann wiped her eyes with relief, and Frankie's excited description of the skirmish made Sissy feel better than she had any time since she became ill.

9

Outside Warrenton, in early Spring, Claiborne and Richard squatted together by a stream and watched Prince drink from the clear water racing across the stones. "How many of Dad's horses are left?" Claib asked.

Richard observed his brother. He looked thin and tired, his beard scraggly and his hair down to his shoulders. His uniform and coat were ragged and dirty, his shoes badly worn. "Prince and four more, far as I know," Richard replied. "There may be others I lost track of. Most of them were killed at Sharpsburg and Fredericksburg. Four in our regiment died this winter. Thank God I still have Prince. He's a wonderful horse. I miss King, but this black gets better all the time." He stroked the stallion's flank.

"When I think of them cowardly bastards burning our barn and all our horses, it makes me sick."

"I know. Papa wrote he's not sure who did it." Richard tugged his mustache. He was still able to shave the rest of his face and keep his hair trimmed. His uniform and boots were in good repair, the result of being on the move and able to make purchases in Richmond.

"I bet he's got suspicions. Papa always has a good idea of what's going on."

Richard arose and gathered the horse's reins. "Easy, boy, that's enough. Don't overdo it."

"He sure looks fit. How do you keep him fed?"

"It isn't easy. I've spent all my money to buy grain and hay for Prince and my men's animals. Sure can't depend on the army for anything."

"Thank God that winter's about over. I've never been so cold. Half my company don't have decent shoes. We musta burned every piece of wood within ten miles tryin' to keep warm. We've even had to burn turds."

"Have you got any money left?"

"Not much. How about you?"

"None. I'll try to see Uncle Mace, see if he can get a bank draft out of Maryland."

Claib stood and stretched. "Wonder what the Yanks' latest commander, Hooker, will do."

"If he's no better than Burnside, maybe we can finish up the war this summer. I sure wish I could get you transferred to my unit."

"It's no use. I've tried and tried, and now I'm used to the infantry, and my men depend on me. So many of our officers have been killed, Richard, I couldn't bear to leave."

He looked at the sky. "Weather looks bad, better get back to camp."

"It looks like we'll be camped nearby, so I'll come by whenever I can. When I get over to Uncle Mace's place, I'm gonna try to see Cathy Livingstone. Do you want me to say anything to Lettie?"

Claib smiled and nodded. "I wish you would. She and her pa came to see me when we set up camp in November and invited me to their house, but I couldn't go. She writes me every week. I try to write her too, but there ain't much paper here in the wilderness. Find out if she got my letters and explain why I can't write more."

It was April and the armies soon would be on the move again. New recruits poured into the Confederate camp. Lee's army was the strongest it had ever been, yet the Union army a dozen miles away was nearly double its size.

Claib rode double with his brother back to their camp. They said their goodbyes and Claib strode back to his company. Gaunt men were sitting around campfires and smoking pipes or whittling, their wood shavings for starting the next day's fire. Tent flaps slapped about in a stiff breeze, and the soldiers clutched blankets or tattered coats about themselves.

"New 'uns comin' in," Jeremy informed Claib.

"More recruits? God knows we need 'em. Green?"

"Nope, most of 'em have fought before. Can't say how much, but they know how to load a musket."

"When we gonna get some shoes, Cap'n?" a soldier asked.

"The colonel says any day now. We sure need 'em."

"We need another good fight with them Yanks," Jeremy said. "They're better quartermasters than them damn fools in Richmond."

"Any mail?"

"No, still ain't none."

"It's been weeks."

The soldiers sat and stared at the fire. A chilly breeze was whistling through the camp. Evening was coming, a few raindrops splattered, and they began scrounging around, gathering provisions for another wretched evening meal.

10

On the afternoon of May 2, Claiborne and his company were near exhaustion. They had marched across dusty narrow lanes all day to the southwest from Fredericksburg at a pace that was excessive even for Jackson. Now they had circled back and were being pressed forward into thick underbrush and briers which tore their already tattered uniforms and scratched their faces and bodies. Men winced as unprotected feet stepped on rocks and snags that no amount of calluses could protect.

The sun had settled almost to the horizon and still they pushed on. Finally, a halt was called, and the men flopped down and opened canteens. The colonel called his officers together. "Men," he said, "General Jack says the enemy is only a half mile ahead through the woods. He says they don't know we're here, and if we hit 'em right smartly, we'll smash the whole right side of the Yank army."

The exhausted officers stared at the colonel in disbelief. How could they have marched across the enemy's front all day and not have been recognized. "I have no idea," the colonel said, "sometimes the Yanks ain't none too bright."

"Boys," Claib told his troops a few minutes later, "it looks like we got the Yank army just up ahead. They don't know we're here, and it's only a half mile to their position. We'll go fast, and we'll go quiet till we get there. Then we give 'em our yell and chase the bastards right out of Virginia."

Like a flood the Confederates rolled through the woods, smashing vines and brush, oblivious to the thorns and snags. Ahead, Howard's division cooked their suppers, amused at the rabbits and deer that scampered out of the woods from the west. "Wonder what's spookin' them varmints?" a soldier asked.

Jackson's men were near the enemy position, so the officers halted the advance briefly. "Check your weapons," Claib ordered. "Fix bayonets. Dress up the line. Keep in touch with your left and right. Let's go." They began walking, then trotting. As they broke into the clearing where the enemy was camped, they were running and screaming the Rebel yell.

The sudden appearance of Rebel soldiers and the shrill Rebel yell paralyzed the Union troops. Many fled, others grabbed their weapons and tried to resist, but they were quickly overrun by the jubilant, rampaging Confederates.

Claib fired his Sharps, reloaded, fired again. Ahead a bewildered group of Yankees raised their arms to surrender. He shouted at them to drop their weapons and assigned two of his men to take them to the rear where prisoners were being herded together.

A rider stormed up behind him shouting, "Don't stop, press on, men, drive them, drive them." It was Jackson, screaming, waving his cap, urging his men forward.

And they did just that, driving the Yanks out of the woods and into fields as thousands of Confederate troops burst into the open, shouting and firing at the fleeing bluecoats. A battery had set up on the hill to their right as Stuart sent his horse artillery into the fray. Claib prodded his men to stay in battle order, while his colonel rode up and down the field shouting at his men, "Keep moving boys, we got 'em on the run, keep movin'."

Artillery and rifle fire routed the remainder of Howard's men who had tried to form a battle line. Hundreds of Yanks were captured, and Jackson's men crossed more fields to attack positions set up by Slocum and Couch who sent part of their brigades to the rescue when they saw Howard's position dissolve.

Jackson continued galloping along the front, urging his troops, faster, faster. More artillery moved to the front as Lee sent fresh units to join the rout. Hooker was bewildered, unable to muster artillery support or direct fresh units to help his beleaguered men. Stuart sent his troopers to hit the flanks of the new defense line the Union was attempting to establish. Richard was part of the cavalry that hit the Yank's flank, and this second line also began to collapse. Confederates swarmed over the Union center, and more panicked bluecoats fled to the rear.

The victorious Reb attack slowed to a walk when night fell, and Jackson's men lost momentum in the thick forested area called the Wilderness. Officers were separated from their troops, men lost their units, and there was confusion as the army re-grouped and caught its breath.

The next hour brought unexpected tragedy. As Union forces withdrew into the Wilderness, Jackson and his staff rode forward trying to find passable roads on which to continue the pursuit. On the way back to his lines, some of Jackson's soldiers mistook their general and his staff for the enemy, and Jackson was wounded by his own men's gunfire.

Word of Jackson's wound drifted through the Confederate lines. A. P. Hill took command and rode the lines, reassuring the men that their commander was hit in the arm and would recover. Claib and his men listened numbly, and prayed that Hill was right.

The smashing of his flank had dazed Hooker. When Lee followed up his victory the next day, he found the Union positions empty. The unnerved Hooker had pulled his men back to safety and given up this latest march on Richmond.

11

Matthews' men never got into combat at Chancellorsville. When Hooker had taken command from Burnside in January, the re-organization placed them under Reynolds, and Sumner was retired. At Chancellorsville, Hooker failed to protect his flank and then failed to get half his army into the battle. "Fisher," Matthews said, "if we ever got our whole army into a fight with Lee, this war would be over."

The Army of the Potomac was an unhappy, subdued force as once more it retreated toward Washington. Hooker had done a good job of revitalizing the army after Fredericksburg, and they had marched south confident that all they needed was a leader who would fight Lee with intelligence and vigor, and Joe Hooker looked and acted the part. Instead, he led them to another disaster and retreat. Many were talking about quitting and going home. "We oughta be plantin' corn and cuttin' hay instead of wastin' time with generals who can't fight," Fisher argued. Then they learned Jackson had died from complications of his wound, and they knew how much this would hurt the Rebs, so they decided to stick it out, at least for a while longer.

"What we need," Matthews said, "is for John to sing us a song."

"Much as I used to bellyache about his singin'," Al said, "I gotta say I miss it, I miss him, he was fun."

The center of action shifted northward. At Brandy Station on June 9, Stuart's troopers were attacked by Yank cavalry. Over ten thousand riders from each side participated in the largest cavalry battle of the war. Richard and Prince were part of Stuart's counter attack, the black horse sweeping across the battleground like a scourge, and the Maryland troopers were part of the force that blunted the Union assault and at last drove the Yankees back.

To the west, Confederates pushed up the valley to menace Milroy in Winchester. Jackson's corps led the way, its fallen leader replaced by his former top lieutenant. Ewell was back, one trouser leg empty, but the rest of him full of fight, often riding at the head of his column in a buggy.

"Never expected to see him back," Claib said. "We lost ol' Jack, but Dick Ewell knows how to fight."

Milroy marched his men out from Winchester to meet the threat and was trounced by the fast moving Rebels. Ewell hit his flanks, blasted his front with artillery, and then drove his troops through the town into the countryside. Milroy withdrew to Romney in the West Virginia mountains.

When Hooker heard of Milroy's retreat, he ordered additional units, including the Maryland regiment, to Harpers Ferry.

Ol' Baldy Ewell could have cared less about any of this. He was in the vanguard of Lee's army, heading north, now reinforced by Longstreet's corps which had returned from fighting in the Carolinas.

Ewell crossed the Potomac at Williamsport, and marched through Maryland into Pennsylvania toward Chambersburg. Hill, Longstreet and the remainder of Lee's army followed, and all were north of the Mason-Dixon by the end of June.

Claib's men enjoyed the march. They were in the midst of fertile farmlands with fat cattle and hogs, chickens and eggs, gardens and orchards. The north fed them well.

On a fifty mile front, the Confederates moved forward, brushing off militia and home guards, moving through towns and countryside, taking the battle to their adversaries, seeking a triumph that would end the war. Stuart cut away from Lee's main body and crossed the Potomac into Maryland, heading toward Frederick.

Rumors flew across the north as three infantry columns and a separate cavalry contingent were reported. Hooker responded and got his army up and marching through Maryland. The state braced for the worse and received a series of shocks. At Poolesville, Point of Rocks, Middletown, along the Catoctin Creek, and in Frederick, the Home Guard and advance Union army units skirmished with Rebel invaders.

The action became confused when Stuart crossed the Potomac and found the bulk of Hooker's army had just completed the same crossing. Stuart was forced to move east, away from Lee and seek an alternate rout to Pennsylvania from what had been planned.

Several miles north near Burkittsville, a Potomac Home Brigade unit on patrol bumped into a scouting party from Longstreet's corps. A nasty gun fight began until the appearance of another Rebel patrol convinced the home boys to scurry away into the nearby hills. A similar action occurred in Middletown where some of Longstreet's men were procuring supplies before moving through the mountain passes toward Hagerstown and Greencastle.

The hardest fighting in Maryland occurred outside Frederick when a contingent of Rebs on a supply search ran into a large home guard force positioned west of the town. Frankie was one of several guards posted around a barn near the Jefferson pike. The experienced Rebs tried to outflank the Marylanders, but Liston and other veterans kept their heads and moved their men to meet the threat.

Frankie's company burrowed behind a stone fence and an overturned wagon and kept the Rebs busy with steady gunfire. The exasperated Confederates pulled back to the National Pike and sent for more troops and artillery.

"Why'd they stop shootin'?" Frankie asked.

"I ain't sure," Liston said, "but I'm a-feared they sent back for artillery. If they did, we're up shit crick."

Liston explained his fears to their captain. "Dammit, Lick," the officer said, "I ain't gonna roll over and let them bastards walk into Frederick. We've had enough of that stuff."

"Let's get 'em while they're waitin'," Liston said.

"Too many of 'em. They'll blow hell out of us. We need help, so the colonel sent a rider down the road to see if he can find some. We heard Hooker was movin' his whole army this way."

An hour later, help arrived from an unexpected source. A train of flatcars from Harpers Ferry backed into the B & O station with Matthews and three companies. Townspeople hastened to tell the new arrivals that the guards were being attacked to the west of town. Hiram was provided transport from the locals in the form of wagons and carriages, but most important, the new arrivals had a dozen horses and two napoleons. Matthews loaded one company into the vehicles and ordered the rest to the battle area double time. In fifteen minutes, he was on the scene to direct the action. When the artillerymen pulled up with their two field guns, the Rebs decided they had enough and fled.

CHAPTER VII. GETTYSBURG

Mary Ann tried to concentrate on the peas she was shelling, but her hands kept shaking. Three times the past two days soldiers were moving along the Jefferson pike. Then she'd heard shots, a lot of them, from Frederick where the home guards were posted. She and Sissy were trying to care for the farm without Frankie, but it was the busiest time of the year, with crops to get in and weeds to hoe.

She wiped her hands on her thread-bare apron. She'd spent hours with a sick horse, and it was supper time and they still hadn't eaten. "Let's get some food in our bellies," she said to Sissy. "I'll fix the rest of the sausage and boil up some greens. You get down a jar of apple butter, and slice up some bread. Lordy, I'm a mess, and this dress is about soaked." She poured a basin of water and washed her arms and hands, then stirred up the fire and started heating a kettle of water for the greens before going upstairs to change. Later, after finishing their meal, she heard a buggy coming.

"Looks like Sam's buggy," Mary Ann said. "I hope something hasn't happened." She rushed outside.

"Our boys beat back the Rebs in Frederick, Sis," Sam said. "Frankie ain't hurt, neither is Eddie."

"Well, thank God, we were so worried with all that shootin' this afternoon."

"We heard it too. There was Rebs on the pike, so we hid the horses. I knew you'd be worried, so that's why I went into town and checked. Anything I can do?"

"No, you go on. You got enough of your own work with Eddie away. Sissy and I will manage. Thanks so much for comin' by."

They watched him drive down the lane and then Mary Ann said, "Sissy, gather the eggs and give the chickens some water and grain. I gotta check that sick horse and I still got two cows to milk. I swear we'll never get the work done."

"What's wrong with ol' Star?" Sissy asked.

"I guess it's the epizootic, but I don't think anybody knows what causes it or what to do about it. They seem to say that's what ails any horse that looks poorly."

The next day Frankie returned for a few hours. The Army of the Potomac was arriving at Frederick so the guards could relax. Frankie was full of the previous day's battle. "We held 'em till Hiram and his men got there from Harpers Ferry. We shot some of 'em and only two of our boys was wounded. Hooker's already in town, and you know what, he's put up at Prospect Hall, only a couple of miles from here. Ain't that sumpin', Union headquarters right down the road."

Mary Ann smiled and nodded, but she thought, I won't be happy until they're all gone for good.

2

Twenty miles to the south, Richard Horine and his troopers were bearing down on a group of Yank wagons trying to escape back to Rockville. They had spotted the wagons near Gaithersburg, and the Yanks, rather than give themselves up sensibly, had decided to flee. The mule teams were running all out while Union soldiers lay in back of the wagons firing at the pursuing Confederates.

A minie ball whizzed by Richard's ear and another felled a horse of one of his men. "Crazy bastards," he muttered. "Shanks," he yelled, "take your men and cut across the field and try to cut them off."

A few minutes later the Yanks were trapped. Duval and his men shot the lead mules in the first wagon, and the entire column bunched up in a melee of howling mules, sprawled and profane drivers, and overturned wagons. Wagon wheels were spinning wildly and bags of grain had spilled across the road. Three Yanks were killed and several more injured. The troopers rounded up the rest and began to untangle the mules and wagons. It was an hour before they got the column turned around and began moving back toward Gaithersburg.

When they passed through the town, Stuart surveyed their haul and found they had captured 200 wagons loaded with valuable supplies. His plans were to meet Lee in Harrisburg, but he needed to find the fastest route. Union troops were reported to be moving into the area in large numbers, but he hoped he had time to move through Frederick and proceed north into Pennsylvania. He summoned Horine to scout the possibilities.

"The enemy may be moving into Maryland faster than we expected," Stuart told Richard, "and I need to get our men and these supplies to Marse Robert as soon as possible. Our best route is through Frederick. I know we promised not to contact your father, but this is urgent. Take your company and scout the area. Talk to your father and see what he knows."

"Get our men together," Richard told Shanks and Granny, "we got work to do."

3

It was Sunday morning and a family of five picked their way along the Ballenger Creek toward Frederick. After a half mile they came to the Manor road and followed it to the Buckeystown pike, and from there they walked the last half mile into the edge of town where the road became Market Street. Another fifteen minutes would bring them to their destination.

Jeremiah led the procession followed by his oldest son, Nathan, now ten, then Asa, seven, and finally, his wife, Tillie, holding their four year old daughter, Leah, by the hand. They were dressed in their best clothes, the males in cotton shirts and denim trousers that Tillie had sewn, the females in long calico dresses, also hand made. Most of the cloth had come from hand-me-downs from the Horines, but they would be quite presentable at the church where they were headed.

As they walked, Jeremiah asked the children questions about the Bible. None of the family could read, but Jeremiah and Tillie listened and learned, determined to improve themselves. The Emancipation Proclamation issued by the President after Antietam had not freed them since it pertained only to the states in rebellion, but they felt things were changing. Horine was not a bad master, and they had their cabin and enough food. Tillie had a garden, and Jeremiah raised one pig of his own which he tended along with the Horine's swine.

"Nathan, do you remember the Commandments?" Jeremiah asked his son.

"Yes, Papa," the boy rattled them off.

"Asa, what did Jesus say was the most important Commandment?"

"He say, love God."

"Right, and what else?"

"He say, love neighbors."

"Real good, son."

They continued in this manner until they entered the town. There they walked down the street, looking straight ahead, careful not to offend whites taking a Sunday stroll on the sidewalk. Union soldiers on patrol stared at them as they passed. A white youngster taunted, "Where you niggers goin'? Betcha goin' to the nigger church," but they ignored him. A few more blocks brought them to the area where many of their people lived and where their church was located. Here were people like them, many feeling for the first time the hope of freedom. The congregation was nearly 50-50 slave and free, but that made no difference. The preacher put it simply, "As long as one of our people is a slave, all of us are slaves."

Ben ' Horine sat alone on his front porch and contemplated his unhappy lot. He was lonely, shut off from the cabal, and a pariah among his neighbors. He was still sick over the loss of his horses and barn, but felt powerless. Most of all, he missed his sons and the love of his wife. Elsie seemed a little better. She spent more time out of her room, sewing, gardening and teaching their children, but the strain, the hostility was still there. He wanted her back, as she used to be, when she loved him.

It was hard for the children. He had to send the older two to a private school in town, and a sympathetic tutor came to the house twice a week for the younger ones. Elsie was helping with their education and so was Rebecca. He tried to spend some time with them also, particularly Timmy, who pined for his older brothers.

From time to time Horine thought of giving Jeremiah and his family their freedom, but he couldn't bring himself to take the step. He was afraid they would leave, and he couldn't face that. For all his inferior status, Jeremiah was a good worker and a good companion.

Horine wracked his brain trying to think of a way to get Maryland out of the Union. From the beginning it had been clear that if Maryland seceded, Washington would fall and the Confederacy would be safe. Maryland was the key. If Lee could smash the Union army once and for all, then Maryland would be ripe for secession. He wished he could see Richard and Claiborne and talk this over. He anticipated that Lee's chances were excellent since his victory at Chancellorsville, but Jackson's death cast a pall on these expectations.

4

Peck Handley and Squire Fulmer were the only people in the store when they heard the trio ride up. They walked to the front and shouted greetings when they saw who the visitors were. "My Gawd," Peck said, "you're a sight for these ol' eyes. Who's that with you?"

"Al Fisher and one of my Jefferson boys," Hiram Matthews replied, slapping his hat against his trouser to knock off the dust.

"How long you been here?" the Squire asked.

"Got home yesterday."

"Why didn't you let us know?"

"Had to see my wife and get refreshed." They all chuckled.

"How long you gonna be around?" Holter asked.

"Ordered back tomorrow. It appears Hooker has quit, some sort of huff over us and Harpers Ferry and whether he's to defend it or not since our recall."

"Who's takin' his place, McClellan again?"

"That's the surprise. I expected Reynolds. He's in line, but the man that brought me my orders said the scuttlebutt aroun' camp is that it's to be Meade."

"Who?"

"George Meade. He's had a command ever since the war started and he fought in Mexico. His men call him a mean ol' goggle eyed snappin' turtle."

"Seems to me Lincoln does an awful lot of general changing," Holter said.

"Too much," Matthews agreed, "but from what I hear, Meade's strong enough. He's fought in a lot of places and fought well, and his men say he's ornery, but they stand by him and that's important. He don't lose his nerve, like some of 'em. We lost a lot of men because of bad generals."

The new commander was far from happy over his situation. He thought Reynolds should have had the appointment, so he met with him and told him so. Reynolds explained that he could not handle the politics that went with the job. Reynolds' corps had moved into camp near Jefferson. Those who survived the war would long remember their pleasant stay.

Next Meade saw Hooker and made arrangements for the turnover of command. He reviewed Hooker's plans and met with each corps commander besides Reynolds--Hancock, Howard, Sickels, Sedgwick, Slocum, and Sykes. Rebel troops were reported in various locations in southern and central Pennsylvania, and it was the army's job to move north to meet this threat. The next day Meade had the army in motion. By nightfall they were in camps spread from Thurmont to Westminister.

5

When the Union army departed Frederick, the Home Brigade was recalled. Most were ordered to join Meade's army as it sought the Rebels, but Frankie's company was inexperienced and placed on guard duty around Frederick. Before leaving home, the guards pooled their manpower and finished as much farm work as they could. On the Fraley farm, forty scythes and five wagons made quick work of the grain harvest, leaving Mary Ann more relieved than she'd been in months. She fed the men as best she could, but most had brought food with them. She and Sissy carried water and provided biscuits and fruit.

Matthews' regiment also remained on guard duty outside Frederick. Stuart was reported somewhere to the south of the town, and they were on the alert for his troopers. "That dandy little bastard ain't gonna sneak in here on me," Matthews declared, "if I have to walk the damn picket line myself."

When Richard led his company to scout Union strength, he ran into a hornets' nest of Yanks around Buckeystown. Meade's troops were just beginning to move toward Pennsylvania and many were still posted with Matthews. Troops along the Adamstown-Buckeystown road opened fire from a wooded area on the Reb cavalrymen and sent for help. Cole's riders and a full infantry battalion were hurried from Frederick to meet the threat, and additional guard units were summoned.

With Union troops converging from several directions, Richard withdrew his men back toward Montgomery County and analyzed the situation. From his men's reports, there seemed to be enemy everywhere.

"Shanks," Richard said, "take our men back to Buckeystown and try to draw the Yanks away. I know this country better than anybody, so I'm going to slip through to see my father once it gets dark. You've got to keep the Yanks busy. I'll meet you at Hyattstown tomorrow morning."

Shortly after dark, riding alone, Richard arrived at the Ballenger Creek and dismounted. He tied Prince to a gnarled willow hidden among a heavy growth of brush. From there he trotted along the stream on foot until he reached the edge of the farm. He scooted over the fence and hightailed it to the farm buildings. The surroundings were calm, so he entered the kitchen where he found Rebecca. In a moment he was surrounded by the rest of his family. "You've all grown," he said to his siblings.

"Wow," Timmy said, "you're a captain."

Ben Horine hugged his son. "You're the best thing I've seen for a long time."

Elsie also hugged him and asked about Claib.

"He's fine, Mama, saw him a few days ago. I can't stay. I've been ordered to find how many Yanks there are around here. Papa, do you have any information that will help us?"

"I wish I did, son. All I know is that there have been Union troops marching through here for days."

"Going to Frederick?"

"I believe so, but whether or not they're still there, I can't tell you."

"We've been skirmishing all afternoon, but the soldiers seemed to be home guard, not regular army."

"I've seen a lot of both."

"I guess I better scout the area some more."

Elsie grasped her son. "Are you sure Claiborne is well? He looked so bad last Fall."

"He sends his love, Mama. Like I said, I saw him after Chancellorsville before we left Virginia."

"Where is he now?"

"I don't know. Somewhere with our army in Pennsylvania, I think."

"I worry about him so."

From outside they heard a noise. "Riders comin'," Richard whispered. "I've got to get away."

Earlier some of the home guard had spotted Richard among the Rebel cavalry near Buckeystown. When the Rebs retreated and then attacked again, both Liston and Frankie noticed Horine did not seem to be with the enemy riders. They raced off to tell Matthews who was nearby commanding their combined units.

"I betcha that Reb Horine is headed home," Liston shouted, and Matthews wasted no time responding. "You boys, over here," he shouted at a group of Cole's cavalry, "Let's get movin', and see if we can bag us a Reb officer."

It was these riders that Richard heard as he ran up the stairs. "You'll be trapped," his father called.

"No, I won't. Get Mama and the children back to their rooms like nothin' has happened. Don't worry about me."

"Hurry," Horine said. "You older children, back to your school work. You little ones, into bed. I'll go to the door. Mother, can you handle this?"

"Yes, yes," Elsie said, her voice quavering. "Don't let them catch him."

Richard rushed to the bedroom he had shared with Claib and Jacob and slipped out of the window onto a narrow dark roof, carefully closing the window behind him. Riders had surrounded the house. From the roof he swung himself up onto the limb of a huge oak tree and worked his way to the tree's trunk where he shinnied up to a higher branch.

Someone was banging on the front door. Riders were milling around throughout the area. Several were rummaging through the outbuildings and around the ruins of the barn. Jeremiah and his family had stepped outside their

189

cabin to view the commotion. Someone said, "No sign of that black horse around here."

Yanks were talking to Ben Horine, demanding to search the house. After an argument, he let them inside.

When the Yanks completed their search of the wash house, Richard edged out on another branch of the tree and eased himself down on the wash house roof, just as he and his brothers had often done before the war. He lay face down on the roof listening. The Yanks seemed to have given up their search outside the house and were concentrating on the interior.

No one seemed to be nearby. He dropped to the ground on the far side of the wash house and crouched and listened, then raced quietly off in the dark, crossed fences effortlessly, and retrieved Prince. He led the horse for about a quarter mile until he was sure they were out of the Yanks' hearing. Then he rode swiftly back to join Stuart and his men at Hyattstown.

His report was a disappointment. Stuart decided he had no choice but to bypass Frederick and travel toward Harrisburg on a route to the east of the vast, sprawling Union army.

6

On June 30 Meade had his army positioned along Pipe Creek near Maryland's Pennsylvania border. A well armed cavalry unit under Buford was sent forward in an effort to locate the Confederates. Fifteen miles north the riders reached a major intersection of roads in a town called Gettysburg.

To the east, Lee was fretting that he had not heard from Stuart. He was receiving reports that the Union army was moving toward him, but he doubted their accuracy.

In Frederick, Seth Hatcher waited until most of Meade's army had departed and then drove to Hagerstown with this information. A fellow sympathizer was contacted who took Seth's report to Chambersburg where Lee was currently headquartered.   The   Confederate   commander   was increasingly concerned. A spy commissioned by Longstreet had brought in similar intelligence.

Lee decided to bring his scattered army back together. He immediately ordered Hill and Longstreet, who were nearby in Cashtown and Chambersburg, to move toward Ewell, whose forces were further east in Carlisle and York, and he ordered Ewell to withdraw toward the rest of the army. The roads these forces would take all converged on Gettysburg.

Claib and his men were in camp near Carlisle when they received their orders. They had met little opposition, militia who would fire a few shots and then skedaddle, and unhappy citizens who resisted having their animals and crops taken. "Sounds like Marse Robert has found us some Yanks," Claib told his men as they pulled down the tent poles and shouldered their packs.

On July first, A. P. Hill's units were approaching Gettysburg. One of his brigadiers, Henry Heth, heard there were shoes in the town and he wanted to be the first to get them. Instead, Heth's lead regiment found Buford's cavalry blocking the way. Heth studied the situation and decided to attack. He didn't realize that Buford's men were more like mounted infantry and that they were armed with Spencer repeating rifles.

"What are they shooting with?" Heth asked when the Yanks beat back his first attack.

"They got those new little carbines," an officer replied. "They load 'em up and keep shootin'."

Heth rode back and reported the situation to Hill who was ailing. "I don't care what they're shootin' with," Hill said. "I'll send up some help so we can drive 'em out of there and get on into the town."

At the beginning when he saw Rebel infantry, Buford sent word back to Reynolds, whose corps was the nearest to the area. Reynolds rode ahead of his column, and when he heard gunfire, he spurred his horse and found Buford. Seeing the Rebs were massing troops for another attack, he ordered his lead regiments forward double time and sent word to Meade that a battle was developing at Gettysburg.

The fighting escalated rapidly as troops poured in from both sides. There were heavy losses in both armies as the Union stopped repeated attacks. Reynolds was riding about the field, marshaling his forces, when a Confederate sharpshooter killed him. The much admired general was dead when he hit the ground.

A few miles from the town, Ewell's men were marching quick time, ol' Jack time they called it, when the sounds of battle reached them. Ewell ordered them forward, but they needed no urging. That's why they'd come north.

Ewell's corps streamed into the outskirts of Gettysburg and crashed into the flanks of Union troops trying to hold on in face of repeated assaults from Hill's divisions. With a shout, Ewell's men attacked the unprepared Yanks and shattered their line, forcing bewildered troops to fall back through Gettysburg. Fighting was fierce as both Ewell and Hill pressed their troops forward. Yanks fought back among the houses and yards and on into the countryside, finding cover wherever they could.

Claib and his men were in the thick of it, but the sudden collapse of the Union line and the enemy's stubborn defense through the town created confusion among Ewell's men. More Union troops were moving to the battle site and setting up positions on the hills outside the town. Ewell surveyed the situation once the town was occupied and ordered his artillery forward along a front which now stretched for a half mile along the outskirts of Gettysburg.

At the far end of the Union line, Doubleday's men had been driven back by the steady increase in Confederate numbers. Doubleday had replaced the fallen Reynolds, but he and Howard were unable to hold their line. The latest Rebel arrival was Jubal Early with several thousand more troops from the east, and the situation for the Yanks was desperate. Howard and Doubleday's men scrambled back to Cemetery Hill and Culp's Hill after the rout. They were digging in for the next attack when General Winfield Scott

Hancock arrived to take command with fresh troops to help secure the defensive line.

For a mile along the hills and on an adjoining ridge, sweating troops dug in. Officers gathered stragglers and prodded their exhausted, frightened soldiers back into line. A few Reb shells were hitting about them. Some Rebel troops moved toward the Union right, threatening Culp's Hill, but Hancock ordered new arrivals into position to block that threat, and the Rebs did not press further.

Across the way a tired but elated Claib Horine watched the bluecoats massing on the hills before the gathering Confederate lines. He fingered Lettie's last letter, wrinkled and sweaty in his tunic pocket, received before they left Virginia. She said she missed him, told him to get the war over soon. He read it every day, and it gave him new resolve. "Those Yanks think they're safe," he said. "There ain't a position this side of hell this army can't take. We'll do it tomorrow and get this war over with."

7

George Meade paced up and down his tent trying to decide what to do. Finally he addressed one of his staff, "Warren, go up to Gettysburg and find Hancock and see what's goin' on. While you're doing that, I'll get Sickles and Slocum's corps moving up the road. I don't want this army separated any longer, and if we're to fight Bobby Lee in Gettysburg, let's be getting on with it."

G. K. Warren found Hancock working his men into position along Cemetery Hill and the adjoining ridge and juggling units to cover Culp's Hill. Hundreds of wounded and confused soldiers straggled about the area and along the roads. Artillery was being pressed forward, and regiments milled about, trying to find positions to take advantage of the terrain.

Hancock and Warren conferred under a clump of trees. "Over yonder," Hancock said, pointing at Cemetery Hill, "Doubleday has a good position with what remains of

Reynolds' corps. They had awful losses. Howard is next to him, and I've got my men lined up along this ridge, with one brigade over there to help Howard cover that other knob, the one called Culp's Hill.

"When I got here, I thought sure Lee would hit us again, but it's been two hours and nothing's happened other than artillery and sharpshooter fire. We're holding, but we need the rest of the army. You look for yourself, this is good ground, a good place to fight."

"I agree, it's excellent ground. Where should Slocum and Sickles be positioned?"

"I'd say at each end of our line. We need to be much stronger on Culp's Hill and down toward those two knobs to the south. They're called, I'm told, Little and Big Round Top."

Warren stared at the hills. "We better make sure we keep the Rebs off them. What's Lee's position?"

"He's got a large concentration along the town facing Cemetery Hill, and the rest seem to be assembling across the way on the ridge that runs down by the Lutheran Seminary. You can see the buildings through the trees from here."

"It'll soon be dark. I better hustle back and tell George to get the whole army up here tonight."

"What about Sedgwick? He's pretty far east."

"George sent for him. He should be here tomorrow."

The next morning Meade, Warren and Hancock studied a map of the area along with two local citizens recruited to help them understand the terrain.

"Did we get everybody in line finally?" Hancock asked.

"Everyone but Sedgwick, and he'll be up soon," Meade replied. "Funny thing, some of his men bumped into Reb cavalry way east of here. I can't understand what Stuart's up to. Do you think maybe he's separated and trying to find Lee."

"Never heard of Lee not having his cavalry at hand when there's a battle," Warren said.

"That's just it," Meade said, "Lee ain't so stupid as to let his cavalry ride off and get lost. He must have something up his sleeve."

"Tell you one thing," Warren said, "a few days ago, there was a report from Frederick about Reb cavalry down around Buckeystown and another report that the Rebs captured a bunch of our supply wagons around Gaithersburg. Could be that we moved into Maryland faster than Lee and Stuart expected, so that Stuart lost contact and had to go east to get around us."

"These Maryland reports pretty reliable?"

"Should be."

"That does make some sense, George," Hancock said. "You look at the map, if Stuart crossed here," he pointed at the Poolesville area, "he'd expect to move on toward Pennsylvania through Frederick and Thurmont, but when we beat him there, he had to cut east to get around us."

"What do you think, Warren?" Meade asked.

"Seems logical that could be what happened. I say let's stop worrying about Stuart and concentrate on Lee. We're all infantry and know cavalry's a side show anyhow."

The generals all laughed. "You know I agree with you," Meade said, "but don't let Pleasanton or Buford hear you or you'll have another battle on your hands."

"Buford's different," Hancock said, "his men get down off their butts and stand and fight."

"You're right, and he did well yesterday. Let's get busy," Meade said. "I don't know where the Rebs will hit us, but I know they'll be coming. Warren, you cover the left. Make sure Sickles knows what he's doing. Hancock, the right and center are yours. I had Newton replace Doubleday who don't seem to know any more about what he's doing here than he did at Antietam. The preacher," Meade added, referring to Howard, "has his hands full trying to get his Germans ready to fight. He filed a complaint because I placed you over him and he says he has seniority, but that doesn't bother me one bit. Good thing Slocum's down there too. He's solid. That's it. Let's get crackin'."

Hancock moved off to the Union's far right. Men were cooking breakfast, digging latrines, throwing up earthworks, sighting in cannon. Many were writing letters or pinning carefully written names and instructions to their uniforms. Everyone was drinking coffee. Few gave the general a glance as he passed by.

He stopped at Newton's tent, but Newton was down the line and a harassed major grumbled, "Sorry, General, but this corps is a mess. We lost over a third of our men yesterday, got the living shit kicked out of us. Our Iron Brigade got hit by ten times their number and has hardly anybody left."

Hancock moved on to Slocum's position, which spread from Cemetery Hill to a half circle at the top of Culp's. He found the general with a small group of officers surveying the terrain below. When Hancock arrived, Slocum put down his field glasses. "Rebs must be up to something," he said, "but I can't make it out. This hill has gullies and rocks in amongst the trees. Ewell can work his men in there and we won't see them till they're close."

Hancock peered down the hill and realized Slocum was right. "Meade's talking to some local people who know the area. Maybe one of them can help."

"Send them up here," Slocum said, "if any of them know this hill." He picked up his glasses again while Hancock mounted his horse to ride back to headquarters.

After hearing Slocum's problem, Meade asked the local men if they knew Culp's Hill.

A lean farmer named Pettibone nodded. "I hunted that hill many of time, always got a rabbit or two. The Culps give up tryin' to farm it years ago."

Hancock hoisted the man double on the back of his horse and rode to Slocum's tent, but the general had moved down the hill. Already a skirmish line was working its way downward.

"I allus come on the hill from below," Pettibone explained to the generals.

"What's it like down there?" Slocum demanded.

Pettibone scratched his head. "I gotta think on it a minute, it's been a while."

"How big a while. These places can change in a hurry."

"Last fall I was around here. I got me two rabbits up a big gully. There's a good sized spring that's named for a feller called Spangler."

Slocum was losing patience. "I got some of my best soldiers out there right now. I don't want them shot up for no reason. Can a lot of the Rebs hide themselves close to the top?"

"I understand, Sir. See, you come outta town and down the dirt road at the bottom. Then you cross a crick and then there's a bunch of woods, still not too steep but purty thick and a lotta briers. From there you have to work your way up a few narrow paths, game trails mostly, and a few gullies that're growed shut. It's all tough goin'."

Slocum stroked his chin. "That's what I need to know," he said. "I'll halt the skirmishers and have them dig in where they're at. Greene and his New Yorkers can build earthworks here near the crest, so I can hold the rest of my men as reserves for wherever they're needed. That make sense to you, Hancock?"

"Very good sense."

"Will you tell Meade?"

"Right. Anything else you need."

"Just eyes that can see through trees and rocks, and I don't think we have any of those."

By noon the New Yorkers were dug in. They could hear heavy fighting far to their left. It was late afternoon when Hancock returned. "We need your reserves," he told Slocum. "They're attacking full force on our left." Slocum gave the orders for the reserve brigades to join the fierce battle developing in the Peach Orchard, hoping that Greene could hold his position unaided.

Soon after the reserves departed, Ewell sent Johnson's division forward toward the crest of Culp's Hill. With numbers now in their favor, the Confederates overran the Union skirmish line and soon were moving against Greene's entrenched New Yorkers near the top of the ridge.

Artillery on both sides was firing, with the Union having the advantage of higher elevation. The heavily wooded slope made canister of little value. For a while, Reb shells soared in from the rear, smashing trees and brush about the Union position, but the Union guns soon silenced the barrage. Slocum rushed back to the front when he heard the increase in gunfire.

"Looks like a full blown attack," Greene said.

"Can't let them get this ground," Slocum said, "they'll flank our whole army." Slocum rode away to find help when he heard the sounds of another battle erupting. Early was attacking Cemetery Hill at the same time Johnson was moving up Culp's.

8

"Damn these brierses," a private swore.

"Not so bad as Chancellorsville," Claib told his company, which was part of General "Maryland" Steuart's command. Nearly five thousand of Johnson's troops were working their way through thickets and gullies up Culp's Hill. "Not far to the top, boys. Let's just get through this brush and drive 'em."

A quarter of a mile away Matthews and his company had been ordered into position on Cemetery Hill. Hiram was peering down the slope, studying enemy movement. The regiment had marched north from Frederick and arrived that morning. Already there appeared to be Rebs moving toward them. Heavy firing on Culp's Hill had joined the thunder to the left where Longstreet's corps was attacking on Little Round Top and in the Peach Orchard.

A rider galloped behind them to the command tent. "That's Hancock," Matthews said, "he'll put some fire under Newton's ass. Reckon we'll be in it purty soon."

Thirty miles north Richard Horine's company trudged wearily into Carlisle with the rest of Stuart's men. It was early morning. From an informant near York, they learned Lee's army had been there but had departed and headed west. For a week Stuart's troopers fought their way through Maryland and Pennsylvania. In one of the battles, Stuart himself had narrowly escaped. Still they had not found their army. They had 200 wagons loaded with captured Union supplies, but that was unimportant. Lee's forces were deep in enemy territory and cavalry was indispensable. Even Stuart was glum and baffled.

Meade poured in reserves to meet the Rebel attack. Sickles had blundered into the Rebels' hands by moving his men too far forward and exposing his flanks. Longstreet sent his divisions forward in an effort to crush the Union left and gain the high ground. Earlier he had conferred with Lee and expressed his doubts about this action. "General Lee," Longstreet had said, "I suggest that we move to the right, past the Union flank toward Washington, force them to come at us. If they don't, we can drive right on to the capitol."

Lee studied the fields that separated the armies, weighing the odds. "Yes," he said, "that's a good plan, and I have considered it, but the enemy is there," he pointed at Cemetery Ridge, "in front of us, and I propose to strike those people and whip them."

Longstreet lowered his head and said no more. Lee's blood was up, and there was no changing his mind. So Longstreet proceeded to prepare for the attack, which presently was driving the Union lines backward in the Peach Orchard and on Little Round Top.

9

Three shells burst above them, one, two, three, in cadence, and clouds of leaves, bark and wood showered on

Claib's company. "Move up, boys," he shouted. Their colonel trotted up beside him, hunched over and sweating.

"Where's the rest of our brigade?" Claib asked.

"Tryin' to catch up, and havin' rough goin'. Can you see the Yank position yet?"

"No sir, but we sure in hell can hear 'em." A shot hit the tree a few inches above their heads.

"Hold here till Jube gets his boys into action on our right." The officer worked his way down the hill. A cascade of canister hit the trees overhead, sending bits of wood and metal scything through the area. A few men were hit, while others hugged the ground.

"Move into that swale ahead," Claib yelled. "Keep down." The troops rose and ran to the shallow ravine which cut laterally along the hill to their right. Less than a hundred yards ahead Yank skirmishers rose from cover and fired, dropping two men.

"Jeremy," Claib called to one of his sergeants, "take a dozen men and work around to the left, see if you can get a clear shot at that position. The rest of you, follow me." Claib moved twenty men behind cover of boulders and scrub brush on the right. Others were still pinned down and unable to advance.

To Claib's right, a regiment moved into position beside them, having finally pushed stubborn Yank skirmishers out of the way. Now several Confederate units began to pour fire toward the Union entrenchments. The remaining skirmishers were scrambling to escape up the slope. Johnson's division began pressing forward toward the crest of Culp's Hill.

Moments later as Matthews predicted, Newton's corps was ordered to attack the Confederate force moving up Cemetery Hill. The Marylanders set up a skirmish line, but concentrated fire of Early's men forced them to withdraw and take cover to meet the enemy advance. Officers ordered them to dig in, and they used bayonets and spades to throw up mounds of dirt. Artillery shells began to explode nearby, and Reb fire was growing in intensity.

Two union batteries were moved forward and the napoleons loaded with canister. The Rebs were two hundred yards away.

10

Three riders raced through Carlisle to the town square where Stuart was resting. "Found 'em," one yelled.

"Our army?" Stuart demanded.

"Marse Robert's fightin' at Gettysburg, Sir," one of Stuart's troopers replied. "Here's one of his scouts." The riders dismounted and saluted.

"Report," Stuart said. Several officers had gathered around him.

"Gettysburg, Sir," the scout from Lee's staff reported. "Big battle yesterday, 'nother one today, against Meade and the whole Yank army."

"Meade?"

"Yessir, Meade done replaced Hooker and brung the bluebelly army up here. Marse Robert sent us out to find you and we run into these men you sent to find us."

"Get word to General Lee that we're on our way."

"Already done that, Sir. Marse Robert, he say, you see the cavalry, you tell 'em where we are and tell 'em to tear back here fast as you can ride. My other rider, he went back soon as we learn y'all in Carlisle."

Stuart squinted at the sky. "Part of the day already gone," he said, "but we'll be there this evening. You go tell General Lee we'll be there and ready to fight." He turned back to his men. "Let's get ready to move. Officers, get your men saddled and ready to ride."

Richard Horine was stunned, sick to his stomach, the biggest battle of the war, and they'd missed the first two days.

An hour earlier, Claib's unit had moved further up Culp's Hill. Some of Johnson's men reached the entrenchments that Greene and his New Yorkers had built earlier, and it became a toe-to-toe infantry battle. Sweat soaked Claib and his men's uniforms and dirt caked their faces and arms as they edged forward. Minies splat and whizzed about them, and the smoke and dust was so thick they could barely make out the flashes of the enemy gun muzzles.

A gray horseman rode up on their right--General Steuart, the brigade commander. "Keep pushing them," he shouted, "break that line." He prodded lagging troops forward to join the attack. The regiment's colonel stepped forward, waving his saber, and the men began to push their way further into the enemy trenches.

The view from Hiram Matthews' position had been clear in the late afternoon, but it became murkier in the twilight as the fighting escalated. Shells were exploding along the front, throwing up dust and debris. They were firing constantly and the acrid smoke surrounded them. The enemy was approaching, but they could not make them out.

Howard sent a brigade forward to help the defenders and ordered an attack. He raised his hat with his one remaining arm and sent his brigade and Newton's corps forward.

They came out of their earthworks and worked their way to where their skirmishers had taken cover. Now they could make out the enemy and see the flash of their guns. Sweating and swearing, they opened fire. A battery moved forward and fired canister over their heads. "Keep pouring it on," their colonel shouted.

Early saw the threat and rushed a brigade to his right. Behind the cover of ditches and fences, the Confederates stopped Howard and Newton's troops. On Culp's the desperate fighting continued as Johnson's men tried to overrun the New Yorkers' trenches, but Slocum was able to recall some of his reserves to prevent the breakthrough. As night fell, the two sides fell back, too exhausted to fight further.

11

Midnight in Meade's tent, Warren and Hancock stood together. "If I was George, I'd court martial the stupid bastard," Warren muttered.

"He lost a leg. Maybe that's punishment enough. Besides, there's always the politics in this army. He's got friends. But you're right, that fool move into the orchard damn near cost us our army."

Meade strode and looked around. "Everyone's here but Slocum. Sickles is back at the hospital. Maybe after losing a leg, he'll think twice next time before disobeying an order. There's still fighting on the right. That's what's keeping Slocum. Give me your reports. General Sykes, you start off."

Sykes related the desperate battles fought in the Devils's Den and on Little Round Top. "The Maine boys saved our flank on Round Top, and if it hadn't been for Warren and Hancock moving men over there to cover our flank, we'd be in deep trouble. I never saw men fight the way those Minnesota boys did in the Peach Orchard."

Hancock nodded. "They're about wiped out, the whole regiment dead or wounded."

"Those Texans of Hood's fought like demons."

There was a clatter outside and Slocum appeared, his uniform sweaty and smeared.

"We held," Slocum said. "I thought it was over, but just after dark they came at us again, got men all the way in amongst our guns till my men beat them off."

"Are they off Culp now?" Meade asked.

"God no," Slocum said. "They've backed down a ways and set up for the night, aiming to have another go at us in the morning."

"Can you hold?" Meade asked.

"Yes, but we'll be tested again."

For over an hour the generals reviewed the day and discussed what the enemy might do. In the end, Meade had his say. "Bobby Lee has hit us on both flanks and we've held.   All that's left is the middle and that's where he'll strike us tomorrow.   Mark my words."

When the shells hit in front of their line the next morning, Matthews awoke with a scream.   He had collapsed at three in the morning after helping two wounded members of his company trapped in a nasty fight that had started after dark.

Fisher's reaction was worse.   He lurched and stood bolt upright, ignoring enemy shots that whizzed around his head.   His men pulled him down into the trench, but he was fighting them and swearing in confusion and anger.   Matthews had come to his senses and crawled to Fisher's side.   "Dammit, Al, snap out of it.   Wake up, you crazy bastard."   Matthews shook his friend and shouted into his face as the Rebel infantry fire intensified.

Fisher's mind finally cleared.   "What the hell?   They comin' again?"

"Yeah, and it's still dark.   Dang Rebs never sleep. C'mon, Marylanders, up and at 'em."   Along the lines on Cemetery Hill, men groaned and swore.   Shells continued to crash about them, and a direct hit killed two soldiers and wounded several more.   Union batteries had started returning the fire and the racket intensified.

Dawn was breaking on the horizon.   Flashes of musket fire showed enemy infantry closing in, no skirmish line, this was a full infantry attack.

Hancock had spent the night on Cemetery Ridge with his corps when he heard the growing crescendo of the attack. He had his horse brought forward and rode to his right, seeking Newton but unable to find him.   Riding on, he located Howard and asked what was happening.

"Newton's under heavy attack," Howard said.   "I've already sent one brigade to his support."

Hancock rode back across the hill and finally found Newton who was stunned at the unexpectedly savage assault. Hancock ordered another reserve brigade brought forward to help hold the Union position.

The Marylanders were under heavy pressure when Fisher glanced up the hill and shouted, "There's General Hancock. We'll get help." They stepped up their firing as the sky brightened and the men from Howard's corps moved up to join the defense. Their combined fire power stopped the Reb advance and forced Early's men to take cover in the trees to the Marylanders' right.

12

Before dawn one of Maryland Steuart's staff moved quietly among the brigade's troops. "General says to get ready," he said in a hoarse whisper. "Ol' Baldy wants us to attack in a quarter hour."

"Oh shit," Sergeant Jeremy Taylor said.

"Movin' out in fifteen minutes, boys," Claib said as he moved about, rousing his sleeping company.

"Hell, Cap'n, we can't even see."

"Neither can the Yanks."

"Cold rations again," Jeremy said.

"Look lively, men," Claib said, "make sure your cartridge boxes are full." He wiped his glasses, surprised they were still intact. Their colonel had already stepped out front. They would attack when what remained of their artillery began firing.

During the previous evening, Johnson's men had been unable to break the Union line at the crest of Culp's Hill, but they had occupied some of the Yanks' trenches and were positioned to renew their attack. Union reserves had returned from the battle in the Peach Orchard after midnight, and there had been sporadic fighting when they found their former positions occupied by the enemy. Now Johnson's men waited in the dark, sipping from canteens and munching hardtack. Some coughed and blew their noses. Most urinated in the brush. A loud fart brought a round of snickers. "Is that our signal to go?" someone asked. More laughter. Then the artillery began to fire, and they began their advance, working their way blindly along the ridge where they had fought to a standstill a few hours before.

At first the going was easy. They could make out the enemy position in the eerie light of shell explosions, but soon the Yanks were alerted and awake, and their gunfire increased. Claib and his men had to hunker down and wait for a break. Most of Johnson's men were pinned down along the hillside, while artillery fire intensified. Yank gunners were more effective as the sky brightened.

Claib's colonel crept up beside him and shouted over the din, "We need to move to the left. Their position can be flanked, and if we move right smartly, we can bust through." The Confederates lost no time as Steuart's brigade rose and charged ahead, screaming and driving the Yanks back. They overran the Union lines and began to fan out into the Union rear.

13

Slocum was standing by a battery of his artillery when he saw the break. "Turn those guns," he ordered. "Give them grape." The sweating, struggling artillerymen maneuvered their guns quickly, but musket fire killed two before they could load the cannon. Slocum called for more artillery support. Another man fell, but a reserve company saw the problem and came to the rescue.

"We're ready, Sir," a sergeant said, "but we may hit some of our own if we shoot down there."

"Can't be helped. Commence firing."

The first cannon roared, felling dozens of men in the milling mass where the line was breeched. Then a second and a third. More troops took positions around the batteries and began firing at the advancing Rebs, and reinforcements raced forward to bolster each side of the salient. More Rebs poured into the breech, but they too were greeted by infantry fire and grape shot. Reb artillery found the range and one of Slocum's cannon was smashed.

Both sides poured in troops as the bitter battle continued. A regiment from Newton's corps was sent from Cemetery Hill after Early's assault was repelled, but still Johnson's men pressed forward, intent on completing the break in the line. Another Union cannon was destroyed, but the artillerymen, seeing the desperation of the battle, positioned additional guns further back on the hill to bear on the Rebel attackers.

Behind the cover of dead horses, broken gun carriages, earthworks, felled trees, and stacked bodies, the fighting went on for nearly an hour. The dead piled up, and the wounded struggled to escape the deadly cauldron. Johnson threw the last of his forces into the effort, but the Rebs could not complete their breakthrough. When Ewell attempted to bring reinforcements from Early's command, Howard and Newton's corps put so much pressure on Early's position, he was forced to pull back to save his flank.

Mid-morning and the battle was over. Exhausted Rebs withdrew to positions down Culp's Hill. The Federals regained their original lines and exhausted troops dug in to guard against further attack.

Claib took stock of his company. Ten casualties and two missing. We had them, he thought, and still they threw us back. Why weren't we given more help? Where was the attack on the center? General Steuart wept openly. "My boys, my poor boys," he said. "So many lost. So many dead."

In the First Maryland, Matthews was examining his stomach, bared where a Reb minie had creased the skin, making a deep, four inch laceration. "Never felt a damn thing," he said, "and that' the God's truth."

Fisher was looking at his cap and feeling the burn on his scalp. "Guess I'm too hard headed for 'em to hurt me," he observed.

Two more Marylanders were dead in Matthew's company, and at least five seriously wounded. Ewell's attacks on Culp's and Cemetery Hill had failed. Lee's last effort would now be directed at the center, against Cemetery Ridge.

14

Stuart's cavalry had rumbled into the Confederate lines the previous evening. Lee anticipated Stuart's arrival, but his reception was cold. Even two hundred wagons loaded with needed supplies could not atone for two days' absence during this crucial battle.

Pickett's infantry division was moving to the front, uniforms trim and clean, muskets and bayonets flashing in the sun looming at the horizon. By mid-morning battle plans were completed, and by eleven, Stuart's men were on the move.

Around noon, Richard and a dozen other officers sat on their mounts with Stuart in a grove of trees on a ridge three miles east of Gettysburg. Stuart was smarting from Lee's scolding and determined to redeem himself. They were inspecting Yank lines with their binoculars. "I don't see any cavalry," Stuart said, "but plenty of infantry around those supply wagons."

Richard could see little. Their orders were to cut across the enemy rear to block their escape route once Longstreet and Hill had smashed the Yanks' center. They had circled the Yank right behind Ewell along the edge of Gettysburg and were now in a reasonable position to carry out their mission.

Prince snorted and swished his tail to brush away a plague of green flies. "Easy boy," Richard whispered. At a skirmish near the Maryland line, two more Horine horses had been wounded and destroyed. Many of their current mounts had been captured in the north.

They rested in the noonday heat, quiet except for the stomping and swishing of the horses and the rustle of leaves from an occasional stirring of air. The minutes passed slowly as they munched on pieces of ham and dry cornbread and sipped from canteens. Then there was thunder as the crash of Confederate artillery opened Lee's attack. "That's it," Stuart shouted, "let's ride."

The cavalry units rode into formation and began to cross the Union rear when Yank cavalry appeared in the distance. At the same time, infantry began to move toward them from the Union supply area. Stuart sent part of his men to face the infantry while he and most of his troopers confronted the Yank riders.

Richard had his men dismount and form a skirmish line along with three other companies, and they drove back the Union soldiers up the York road. The enemy retreated into a rocky, wooded area and began to fire from cover. Horse artillery set up a battery nearby and began to shell the Yanks.

From the south, more Yank cavalry appeared. Richard was ordered to terminate the skirmish withYank infantry so his men could help meet the new wave of enemy horsemen. Charging forward, the Confederates were soon immersed in a cloud of dust and smoke. Riders milled about firing and slashing at one another, trying to distinguish friend from foe. "Fall back," Stuart ordered, and his men began to ride out of the confused melee. "Dismount and form a firing line." Quickly they found strong positions among fences and trees, leading their horses and covering for one another.

Dozens of horses and riders fell, and as the dust settled, Richard saw the Yanks had the same idea and many were dismounting and finding cover. Stuart had led most of his men out of the maelstrom, and the remaining units escaped through a gap in the Union line to rejoin the main force.

Both sides held their ground. After skirmishing for several minutes, Stuart ordered most of his men to re-mount while Richard's company and two others were to hold the line with steady gunfire. Then raising his plumed hat, Stuart led a charge between the Union cavalry and infantry. Seconds later, Richard and his men jumped on their horses and followed. The move was spectacular as the Rebs broke into the Union rear. They set up another line of defense while the enemy cavalry was re-organizing across the fields.

Stuart looked at his watch. "Our attack began an hour ago. We should see retreating troops any minute."

Yank cavalry was working toward them once more and heavy firing began as the two sides faced one another. Time passed with no evidence of a rout. Pressure from Union forces increased. A large contingent of enemy troopers under Custer attacked the Confederate line, and more fierce fighting ensued. With no sign of a breakthrough, Stuart could hold his position no longer. He ordered his disappointed troopers to withdraw.

Richard and his men were stunned, but they responded to the order and fought their way clear of the Union attackers. More troopers died or were captured, but two miles later, they were able to halt and re-group. Firing from the battleground had died down. A bullet had cost Richard the heel of his boot and creased Prince. Two jagged holes marked where minies had clipped his uniform. Shanks and Granny rode to his side, sweating and exhausted, but unhurt.

Along Seminary Ridge, Lee stood rigidly as Hill and Pickett's survivors stumbled back from their attack. Thousands of their comrades lay along the approaches and at the top of Cemetery Ridge, but the Union center remained intact. Longstreet could not bear to watch. Pickett cried in frustration. Hill remained stoic. Trimble was wounded. Lee consoled his returning men. "No one has ever been braver," he said. In the end, choking with remorse, he turned away. "Too bad," he said. "Oh, too, too bad."

Ewell's troops withdrew to the bottom of Culp's Hill. Twice they had nearly broken the Union line, and they were ready to try again, but the failure of the attack on the center made further action futile. Claib swore in frustration as they retraced their steps over ground they had gained in two days of ferocious fighting.

The next day, the Army of Northern Virginia collected its wounded, packed its wagons, and waited for a Union counter attack, but Meade held his position. The following day, the Confederate army began a march back to the Potomac.

Matthews and Fisher counted their casualties, five dead, including the fun-loving Freddie Baumgartner, one of their original enlistees. Only four remained of the boys who had enlisted before the first Bull Run battle--the two of them, Pete Angleberger and Claude Franklin Kuller.

CHAPTER VIII. AFTER GETTYSBURG

The battle was over, Lee's army had departed, but the bodies remained and the wounded cried for attention. A heavy thunderstorm washed away much of the blood, but the summer heat soon returned, corrupting the remains of men and animals which lay in grotesque patterns over miles of battleground. Army burial details and grim, stunned citizens began the endless tasks of identification and grave digging, while surgeons, orderlies, nuns, and volunteers did what they could for the wounded.

The strung out Confederates struggled toward the Potomac. Meade might have pursued aggressively, but he judged his army too exhausted and sent only cavalry in pursuit, hoping perhaps to keep Lee from crossing into Virginia until the Union army was ready to move. The river was in flood, forcing the Confederates to remain in Maryland, but Meade continued to linger.

The day after the army began its withdrawal, Richard started searching for his brother. Ewell's wing was struggling across congested roads and fighting off Union bushwackers who managed to capture a number of supply wagons. On the third day, Stuart made camp and Richard rode back to Johnson's division.

Northeast of Hagerstown, the brothers found one another and embraced, relieved to find themselves alive and unhurt. They rode down a quiet country lane where Richard shared his rations with Claib, and they purchased fresh berries and biscuits from a farmer's wife.

"We had 'em whipped on Culp's Hill," Claib said. "It took Longstreet too long to attack the center, and by the time he finally got started, we were exhausted. A few hours earlier, we'd been able to break through."

"Not having us there for the whole three days was a terrible blunder. I don't know what Marse Robert and Jeb were thinkin' to let us ride off from the main army and get separated. Still, if there had been a break through, we had the Yanks' retreat well covered and could have turned it into a rout, just like Chancellorsville."

"It's a shame. We sure missed ol' Jack. Much as we used to despise him sometimes, he knew how to fight."

"I know. We were so close to winning, and now look at us, tails between our legs, goin' back to Virginia. When we were passing through Maryland, I saw the folks. They worry about you."

"How'd you get home?"

"Stuart sent me to find a way north through Frederick. I no sooner got home than there were bluebellies swarming all over the place. The folks seemed fine, but I spent most of my time tryin' not to be caught."

"How'd you get away?"

"Remember how we used to sneak out of our room at night when we wanted to have some fun?"

"The oak tree."

"Yep, that's how I got away, off the back porch roof up into the tree and then swing down to the wash house."

"You hear anything from Virginia? I haven't heard from Lettie since before Chancellorsville, but heck, nobody's got any mail."

"I had a letter from Cathy just before we left Virginia. She said she and Lettie were fine and missed both of us."

"I sure am fond of Lettie, she's so nice."

"Same with me. Reckon we're in love, huh?'

"Golly, with the war and everything that's happened, I hate to even think about love and all that stuff, but if we get out of this mess in one piece, I reckon you're about right."

They filled their canteens from a nearby well, and then Richard swung his brother up on Prince's back and carried him to where his company was camped in a chestnut grove near a village called Leitersburg.

Richard rode back to his unit where he found a message from Stuart awaiting him. Yank cavalry had been spotted moving toward Hagerstown, threatening one of Lee's wagon trains. The brigade was ordered to strike the enemy before they could reach either the wagons or the Potomac crossings.

2

Below Thurmont, Matthews looked across the landscape and observed, "Beginning to look like home." The sun was beating down on the exhausted troops, and they trudged along in no particular order, the horror of Gettysburg still clouding their minds.

"Mebbe them Rebs will give up," Angleberger said, "and we can all go home for good."

No one spoke for a while, but then Fisher, unusually serious, replied, "I wish that was true, Petey, I surely do, but they ain't gonna give up. They done lost as many good men as we have, and the damn war's gone on for three years. We gotta go back down there to Virginia and beat them Rebs to hell right in their own backyard."

They plodded on for a while longer, and then Matthews, at the top of a knoll, said, "Look yonder, see the steeples. That's Frederick."

Pete Angleberger began to sing a number John Fraley had entertained them with in earlier battles. In a moment, most of the company was singing:
"The ol' gray mare, she ain't what she usta be,
Ain't what she usta be, ain't what she usta be,
The ol' gray mare, she ain't what she usta be,
Many long years ago."

3

After the skirmish with Stuart's troopers two weeks before, the Home Brigade was assigned to guarding the roads and railways carrying supplies to Meade's army. Raiders had damaged bridges and railroads, which had to be repaired to avoid horrendous logistical problems. When battle casualties began pouring into Frederick, the guards were re-assigned to setting up cots, and gathering medical supplies and food for the emergency wards in the city's churches.

As the crisis eased, they were given leave to tend their neglected farms. Frankie found his mother and sister exhausted. The hay hadn't been cut. Only part of the corn had been planted. Two young cattle had broken through a fence and disappeared into the woods. Stables were a mess. "Sometimes, Mama," Frankie said, "I think it's easier in the army."

From his front porch, Ben Horine could follow the clouds of dust marking the march of Meade's army back toward the south. The Gettysburg defeat was heartbreaking, and there was no word from his sons. He and Jeremiah had started to rebuild the barn, but with so much else to do, it was slow going. He yearned to see his fellow conspirators, but they had forbid any contact.

Jeremiah and Tillie also watched the dust raised by the Union troops moving from Frederick toward Virginia. Tillie said nothing, but her husband saw how her eyes brightened as she stared at the columns of the victorious Yankees.

"Woman," Jeremiah said, "dem bluecoats done come back, run dem Rebs off. I reckon it like our Reverend say in church Sunday, freedom comin'." He savored the words. "Freedom comin', if Marse Abraham's army win da war, and it look like dey will."

"What you s'pose Marse Benjamin gwine do when we free?" Tillie asked. "What we gonna do if he say, you free, now you go away, git off my place."

"Dunno," Jeremiah replied. "Best we wait and see. Marse Ben and Miss Elsie, dey treat us good 'nuff, but I wanna work for mah ownself, for us, have a piece of land, horse or a mule, chillun go to school, live like white folks."

"Lordy," Tillie said, a tear streaking her cheek, "dat would be nice."

At Holter's store over a dozen people lined up by the pike to watch a brigade of Union soldiers march by. Squire Fulmer was not among them, the old gentlemen felled by pleurisy. Peck Handley and some of the regulars were there along with several occasional customers. They waved at the troops, and Holter sat our pails of cool water with tin cups.

They asked various passing regiments if they knew the whereabouts of the Marylanders. Finally there was an answer. "Saw Captain Matthews in Frederick," a mounted officer said. "They've been told to stay there for further orders. Matthews thought they might be placed on duty along the Monacacy since Stuart is on the loose again."

The following Sunday, Mary Ann and Sissy went to church alone. Frankie had guard duty along the B & O railroad line near Adamstown. Two of the families had lost sons at Gettysburg and Mary Ann consoled them. "So many of our young men gone," she said, "killed in this awful war."

After most of the congregation had departed, Mary Ann and Sissy stood by Johnny's grave. "Seems like he's been gone forever," she said, "but it's less than a year."

Tears rolled down Sissy's cheeks. "I miss him," she said. "I keep dreamin' he's alive and walkin' up the lane to see us."

4

After leaving Claib, Richard and his men galloped toward the Potomac where Yankee cavalry was threatening their supply train. In the early afternoon, they arrived outside Hagerstown where an undersized Confederate regiment was battling Pleasanton's Union cavalry brigade.

They struck the Union flank and pushed the Yanks back into the hills, but there the enemy formed a strong defensive position among boulders and rail fences southwest of Hagerstown.

"This is no fit place for horses," Rooney Lee told Richard, "let's get our men on foot and drive 'em out of there."

Once dismounted, they raced forward, yelling and firing their carbines. The Yanks unlimbered a six pounder, but the troopers outflanked it and forced the Union riders further back. More of Stuart's men rode into the battle, and after two hours of skirmishing, the Yanks withdrew and the threat to the supply train eased.

For five days, Stuart's men skirmished with Union troops attempting to break through and attack Lee's army. All the Potomac bridges had been destroyed, and Lee's engineers were building pontoon bridges but were hindered by heavy flooding. The Yankees were trying to destroy the pontoons before they could be completed.

From the Antietam Creek to Boonsboro to Funkstown and as far north as Leitersburg the struggle continued. Richard and his weary men were constantly on the move, fighting, falling back, re-grouping and attacking once more. Horses were lost and men rode double until new mounts could be captured or found in an area already depleted by two major campaigns.

"What' taking so long?" Richard asked Rooney Lee.

"The river's so high the engineers can't get the pontoons in place. You've never seen such a mess as Williamsport, Horine. The whole town is a hospital. Our poor wounded lads are starving. Ewell lost nearly all his supplies to the Yanks, and we've eaten everything we can find around here. Thousands of our men sick and wounded and not a damn thing we can do but wait for the river to go down."

Claib was among those trying to care for the sick and wounded. He scrounged for food for his dozen invalids. Ewell was said to be sick and despondent. Early had his men build breastworks and then he holed up in a shack. Johnson came around daily to visit the men and keep their spirits up, although he had little tangible to offer them. Longstreet stayed with Lee. Pickett rode about the area like a wild man, embittered at the destruction of his division. Finally, on July 13, the bridge was completed and the Army of Northern Virginia crossed to safety.

5

A pair of whippoorwills exchanged calls with quickening urgency in the woods bordering the farm. Evenings were shorter and Mary Ann rocked quietly on the porch, chores and kitchen work finished. She wiped her face with her apron and pushed her thin, gray hair back from her forehead with a sigh. Sissy was in the back, feeding the cats and Buster, probably playing with them a while.

Frankie strode in from the barn where he had put the milk cows out to pasture and given the horses their rations of grain for the night. It was late in September and he had been chopping corn for a week, so the early crop was finished.

"No rain for weeks," Frankie said. "Pasture's dried up and the rest of the corn is so parched it ain't worth cuttin'. Planted it too late."

"Too bad, son, but it couldn't be helped. You had your duty."

"The first planting is pretty good, so we won't starve. I looked at the sweet corn, but it's done."

Sissy and the dog romped around the corner of the house, and Frankie braced himself as Buster jumped against him.

"I got three ticks off him," Sissy said.

"Fool dog always full of ticks."

Mary Ann smiled. "Reminds me how Johnny used to write when he was in Virginia. Weren't no Reb soldiers to fight, but they had to fight Reb wood ticks ever night."

Lights were twinkling on across the valley. Down the lane they could hear a horse trotting and snorting by the church. "Somebody's takin' a ride," Frankie said.

"Nice night for it," Mary Ann said. The whippoorwills continued their calls. Night birds flashed through the sky. Three cats joined them, two parking themselves on Sissy's lap, the third cleaning itself by Mary Ann's rocker. "Cat, why don't you go catch some of them rats out in the barn?" Mary Ann asked.

"He had one today," Sissy said.

The hound jumped up suddenly and bounced across the yard, barking in the shadows.

"Somebody's comin'," Frankie said.

Mary Ann squinted into the dusk. "That's Sam's rig."

They all arose and greeted Sam and Susie as they pulled up in their one horse buggy. "Land sakes, it's good to see you," Mary Ann said.

"Nice night for a spin," Sam said, "so here we are."

"Seems like everybody's so busy with the war," Mary Ann said, "we don't visit no more."

"I know," Susie said, "hardly have a chance with so much to do. Speaking of the war, Hiram got his new orders."

"Back with Meade?" Frankie asked.

"Nope, goin' over to the other side of Harpers Ferry, guardin' the railroad."

"Bet he don't like that," Frankie said.

"Not much. He said he could do as much good staying home and farmin'."

"How much longer can it last?" Mary Ann said.

"God only knows, Sis, but the Rebs still got a lot of fight left in 'em, and Lee is about as slick a general as there is. Could be another two or three years."

"Oh Lord, I hope not."

"So do I, but our army has never been able to beat Lee in his home state."

In mid-October a train with several flatcars rolled into Grafton on the B & O line. The forward cars carried West Virginia veterans, most of whom had fought through the new state's early campaigns and who were happy to be free of the guard and rear echelon duty they'd had since Gettysburg.

Behind them was a Maryland battalion and their newly promoted major, Hiram Matthews. The rest of the train consisted of boxcars carrying supplies and two Napoleons.

The West Virginians were ordered to march immediately down the Buckhannon Valley and join General William Averell's command. Averell was gathering a small army to drive out the only significant Rebel force still active in the state. The Marylanders were to patrol the rail line from Grafton east to prevent further damage by guerillas.

Matthews was not a happy commander of his small force. "I guess we're stuck," he said to Fisher. "Seems like we're wastin' time fartin' around here."

Cold winds already were sweeping into the mountains, and the Marylanders would have to patrol through the cold and the snow where bushwhackers had the advantage. "Our best bet is to ride the rails," Matthews told his men. "When we get a report of raiders, then we can think about infantry action. For now, we'll fix up these barracks so they're livable, and get a fire going so we can have decent food."

CHAPTER IX. 1864

By November, the bitter cold promised a winter even worse than the previous year. Early snow swept across the farm, killing the autumn flowers, forming ribbons of ice that shimmered over the creek, and sending shivers down Mary Ann's spine.

As the winter progressed, the guards disbanded. Roads were impassable and trains could not get through the snow that drifted on the rail lines. Only Cole's cavalry remained active around Frederick. After Mosby's raiders ventured into Maryland in January, Cole and his men pursued and defeated the Virginians in a confused battle outside Harpers Ferry, but the harsh weather prevented either side from continuing the action and Cole returned home.

As the bitter cold continued, Mary Ann gave up on her chickens and slaughtered them one by one until all were gone. Two of their cows died, and they butchered a third when it appeared she might not survive till Spring. Frankie worked constantly to save the remaining livestock. He kept clearing space in front of the barn so the animals could move about from the stables to the wagon shed next to the corn crib.

They ground their own flour and corn meal because they couldn't get through to the mill. Heating the house was a never ending struggle. Frankie had to split and carry in firewood by the armful several times a day. The upstairs was so cold, they closed it off and Sissy and Mary Ann shared a bed in the parlor. Frankie set up a cot and slept in the kitchen which was also occupied by Buster and the cats.

One Sunday afternoon Sam appeared, driving a one horse sleigh. He glided through the fields, avoiding drifts, and the runners squealed and squeaked as he raced along.

"You all managing?" he asked his sister as he warmed his hands by the kitchen stove.

"Barely," Mary Ann said, "but Lordy, Sam, we ain't never had such weather as these two winters."

"We sure ain't. I remember Pap talkin' about some bad winters when he was a boy, but nothin' like this since you and me was hatched." He shook out his coat. "I guess you heard the news."

"What news?"

"They brung Hiram home. He was shot in the chest over in West Virginia. He was in a hospital in Cumberland and started mending, so they put him on a train to Frederick and some of the troops posted there fetched him on out to his house."

"I thought a chest wound would kill a man."

"Me too. I was over to see him yesterday, and he's as full of vinegar as ever. Said he went through all them big fights, Antietam and Gettysburg and the like, and then gets shot by some Reb bushwhacker in the hills over there. Said the shot hit him in the side and tore up his ribs, but he was padded real good with a heavy coat and it bounced on out without goin' clean through. He figures he was plumb lucky, and I gotta agree with him."

"What's he say about the rest of our boys?"

"Says they're all sick of guard duty and winter, want to get back to real fightin'. Hiram's been made a major and that Fisher boy's a captain."

Mary Ann sighed. "I reckon Johnny woulda been an officer by now."

"Sure he would. He was a dang fine soldier."

"Will Hiram stay home or go back to the war?"

"Go back. Couldn't keep him home."

Sissy and Frankie had appeared and were listening to the conversation. "It don't seem right," Sissy said. "If you get shot once, you shouldn't have to fight no more."

"Sis," Frankie said, "most of the soldiers that been fightin' for a while have been hit at least once."

"Hiram's boy, Bob, wants to join up," Sam said, "but Hiram and his Missus want no part of that. The younger boy, Caleb, is too little to do much farmin'."

"That boy gets Catherine all worked up," Mary Ann said.

"I know. She says one in the family is enough."

"At least, Hiram's still alive. It seems like the war will never end."

They talked on for a half hour before Sam began donning his boots and winter wraps. He removed the blanket from his horse and tossed it in the back of the sleigh. "Well, folks, I'm glad to see you ain't froze stiff. Send Frankie over if you need anything."

As he sped away, Sissy watched with envy. "Wish we had a rig like that," she said. Mary Ann hugged her and they went inside while Frankie returned to splitting firewood. He had it in his mind to get Bobby Matthews to join him and Eddie in the Home Brigade. Bobby was younger, but they'd hunted together, and he knew Bobby was a good shot, learned it from his Pa.

2

In the Spring, Ulysses S. Grant came east to command all Union armies. When the roads became passable, the Army of the Potomac moved south toward Fredericksburg and that tangled piece of Virginia known as the Wilderness. The western army, led by Sherman, was advancing into Georgia, and Grant had ordered Sigel to advance down the Shenandoah Valley.

Matthews and his men were back in action as part of a battalion in Crook's division along the Virginia-West Virginia border. Their orders were to join Sigel, and with the combined forces, capture Roanoke, and subsequently, stop the flow of food and forage to Lee's army.

On May 4 Grant and Lee were closing in on one another in the Wilderness. Claib's company of Maryland and Virginia veterans camped the first night near the Chancellorsville battleground. Campfires threw eerie shadows across the brush and fallen timbers. Spring rains had washed out shallow graves, exposing the bones of fallen comrades. It was unnerving and sinister.

"This is awful," Jeremy said. "Those poor dead boys weren't buried proper, and we shouldn't have to camp at a place like this. It ain't fittin' to die fightin' and then be washed outta the earth like that."

Claib nodded. "I hate lookin' at 'em, Jeremy," he said. "The burial details got too busy and didn't do their job right." He stared into the darkness beyond the shadows and listened to the wind whispering in the forest. "Maybe they're the lucky ones."

In the morning they moved into the tangled brush and rough terrain they remembered from the year before. Their wing, Ewell's corps, came under attack by a Union corps under Sedgwick. Artillery began to thunder, and musket flashes in the brush and smoke marked the enemy position. They heard intense gunfire from the right and then the shadowy forms of enemy soldiers began to materialize through the smoke and dust. A runner appeared and told Claib, "Colonel says to move back. Yanks are forcing Hill's lines."

"Time to withdraw, men," Claib shouted, and the company joined others in retreat to a knoll where a narrow game trail cut diagonally across the forest. They could see only a few dozen feet into the brush, but they could feel the presence of thousands of comrades about them.

Suddenly, a hail of shells, most falling short or showering torn branches upon them. "Damn Yanks firin' blind," Claib shouted. "Dig in, they'll be comin'."

Minie balls whizzed wasp-like into their position. Hordes of blue emerged from the brush and smoke. "Fire," officers ordered. More bark and twigs fell from surrounding trees. Dozens of men were hit, but they hunkered down and kept up a ferocious return fire. Dozens of bluecoats dropped in front of them, before they pulled back.

"Forward," the Colonel shouted. Their own artillery was active, shells whipping above and crashing in the forest ahead. They had gone a few hundred yards when the Yanks arose from cover and stopped their advance in its tracks.

Once more they hugged the ground, smoke burning their eyes, finding it impossible to see the enemy. More of their comrades were moving forward on their left, seeking the Union flank. Heavy gunfire broke out from that direction. "Let's go," the Colonel ordered, and with a yell, the regiment charged ahead, pushing the Yanks further back.

But after a few hundred more yards, dreadful gunfire again stopped them. Fresh Union troops nearly broke through their line and they were forced to retreat to where their assault had originated, exhausted by the hours of confused battle. Brush fires were spreading and the wounded screamed for help as flames moved toward them.

They ate a cold supper of kush and settled down to spend the night in their works. Lee rode by, sitting erect on Traveler, inspecting their positions while on his way to confer with Ewell. "I'd go to hell and fight the ol' devil hisself for that man," Jeremy said. There were many nodding heads.

The second day opened with the Union striking the Confederates all along the line. Two Yankee corps launched an all-out assault on Ewell, and only a fierce counter-attack by Longstreet saved their left side from being overrun. Lee himself was so concerned he rode to the front as it was crumbling and would not leave until hundreds of Rebel voices screamed, "Lee to the rear."

At the end of the two days in the Wilderness, the Confederate army had 10,000 casualties. Longstreet was carried from the field with a gaping wound. They had smashed the Union attack at every point and claimed a victory, but the enemy did not quit or retreat. As night fell, Lee moved his men to a stronger defensive position to await the Union army's next move, but in the morning, nothing happened. Patrols and skirmishers reported the Yank lines seemed to have emptied.

It took a while for the cavalry to find the enemy. Despite crippling losses, the Union army was pressing forward to their left, attempting to gain tactical advantage by turning Lee's right flank.

Lee seemed baffled as he listened to the report. "Are you sure?" he asked Stuart.

"Yes, General Lee," Stuart said. "Colonel Horine spotted the movement and I verified it myself. We could see them along the Orange Plank Road--we counted five corps. Anything else, Horine?"

"No Sir, General. All that's left in the Wilderness is a rear guard."

Lee stepped back and peered at maps on his camp table, discerning the meaning of this unexpected move. "I believe," he said, "that it's not Meade we're fighting any more. This has the feel of a new commander. General Grant is running their campaign." Lee stroked his beard and meditated for a few moments. "Well," he said to Stuart, "keep your eyes on them. I best be getting this army moving down the road to give General Grant the fight he seems to be looking for."

The armies met again in the fields around Spotsylvania County Courthouse, southwest of Fredericksburg. They smashed into one another, veteran infantry units fighting to the limits of human endurance and nerve--no sparring, no fancy maneuvers, simply artillery and musketry, charge and counter-charge, with enormous losses on both sides. An entire Confederate division was decimated, but Union losses were greater. Sedgwick, one of Grant's three best field commanders, was killed. Lee kept his men in front of the northern troops, shifting, entrenching, shifting again, determined not to give any advantage.

Richard's regiment was tested constantly by the demands of constant warfare. Often his unit had to function as infantry, adapting methods to protect infantry flanks, but then harassing enemy movement, utilizing the horse artillery, keeping the Yanks at bay and avoiding entrapment. They no longer had the advantage enjoyed early in the war. Then Sheridan with a force of over 10,000 mounted a raid southward toward Richmond. Stuart countered by shadowing the Union flanks with his smaller force, seeking an opening.

At Yellow Tavern, north of Richmond, the cavalry units fought furiously across the fields and along the roads, clashing with carbines, pistols, sabers, and even lances. The battle was a draw, but Sheridan's troopers were undeterred. They reached the outskirts of the Confederate capitol before being driven off by entrenched defenders. Sheridan led his men on to a base on the Peninsula where they were rested and re-fitted before returning to Grant's lines.

On the last day of the running battles, J. E. B. Stuart was mortally wounded in the fighting near Yellow Tavern. He lingered several hours before dying, apologizing to his distraught men.

The Confederate cavalry returned to Spotsylvania in mourning. Richard could not stop weeping, he had idolized Stuart.

Lee also grieved. "I cannot bear to think of him gone," Lee said to the assembled cavalry officers. "I have lost my right arm," meaning Jackson, "and now I have lost my eyes. I loved him as if he were my own son."

Wade Hampton and Fitz Lee would replace Stuart, dividing his command.

On the Spotsylvania battle line, Claib and his weary troops hung on in face of waves of attacking bluecoats. God, Claib thought, don't they ever run out of men. We've been beating and killing bluecoats for three years and still they come. Two more of his men had died in a brief orchard clash. Three others were wounded and one had disappeared.

When the battle waned, Claib collapsed against a tree and two other officers slumped down beside him. Exhausted soldiers lay on the ground among corpses. Too tired to eat or drink, they fell asleep where they dropped.

When he awoke, Claib looked about the area and realized they were near the Wise and Livingstone homes. He had seen Lettie in February, and they had held hands and spoke of their fondness for one another, but he soon had to return to duty. He reached inside his tunic and fingered her letter, and thought how much he cared for her. So much to live for, but the war had changed, and he wondered if he would see her again. Union attacks were relentless, pushing Lee's army hard. Hopes for victory were fading, and they fought on only because it was their duty, to Lee and to each other.

A rude shake prodded Claib from his reverie. "Orders to move to yonder knoll and dig some works," Jeremy said.

Claib struggled to his feet but lost his balance. His loyal sergeant steadied him. "Thanks," he said, "I'm just tired. Let's see if we can get our boys movin'."

3

The Spotsylvania battles lasted two weeks. Grant kept edging his army to the left, seeking Lee's flank, while Lee kept pace, always finding a way to fend off the Union advance--their troops in lockstep, a death waltz toward an uncertain end.

Each day since the Wilderness, the armies fought and men died, but Grant pressed onward, launching a massive assault on a bulging section of Lee's line. Grant's generals took too long to get their units in place, and the Confederates were given enough time to prepare. Claib and his men worked furiously at the salient as the danger mounted.

The Federal attack exploded in the dark shortly before dawn. Masses of infantry swarmed forward behind a hellish hail of exploding shells and canister. Thousands of men fell in a matter of minutes at the Bloody Angle, holding a position the Confederates called the mule shoe.

My God, Claib thought, as men died around him, no one can live through this. They killed two attackers for each man they lost, but the weight of Union numbers was too much. A man beside Claib lurched from the parapet when he was struck, hurtling into Claib and sending his glasses flying to the bottom of the trench. Claib stooped to retrieve his spectacles when a falling musket smashed them to pieces.

Claib arose and peered forward over the log breastworks, trying to gauge the situation. Enemy soldiers swarmed toward him. He fired his Sharps into the oncoming mass, but then he recognized the dreadful reality. Moments later, a hail of Union bullets blew his life away. His body fell to the bottom of the trench among dozens of comrades, the last of the Marylanders who had fought together and stood with Ewell since the glorious Valley days.

Lee had ordered a second line of defense behind the first, where Claib had died, and that saved the Confederate position, but thousands of his men were dead and wounded. Yank losses again were far worse, but Grant held his ground and brought up re-inforcements. A few days later the Union army disengaged again to move around Lee's right, toward Richmond and Cold Harbor.

4

Matthews was with Crook in West Virginia when he heard Hunter had burned the Virginia Military Institute. "What is wrong with that man?" he said to Fisher. "Don't he see that'll infuriate the Rebs, and they'll be lookin' for revenge? Wish Crook was in command instead of that fool."

A few days later Phil Sheridan was sent by Grant into the Valley where Breckenridge had defeated Hunter's forces after the V. M. I. destruction. Sheridan took command and defeated the Rebs, allowing Hunter to occupy Lynchburg, but after Sheridan returned to the Army of the Potomac, Lee sent Jubal Early with 10,000 men to deal with Hunter. Early defeated the Union soldiers and Hunter withdrew up the Kanawha Valley into West Virginia.

Crook was livid. Hunter had left the Shenandoah Valley open to Early and his troops, and Crook predicted the Rebs soon would be moving north.

Hunter was unimpressed. "Early," he said, "will be recalled to help defend Richmond and then we can continue our work. Besides, where can he get supplies?"

Matthews shook his head in disbelief when he heard this. "If Lee can move his whole army north, then Jube Early can damn sure move his division the same way."

By June 28, with supply wagons filled from friendly farms, Early was advancing north, heading toward the Potomac and Maryland.

5

In April the drifts had finally begun melting on the Fraley farm. The dull gray snow hardened around the edges at night, but would slush when the sun hit it each morning, sending streams of water down the lane and into new gullies washed out across the fields. The soil was too wet to plow, but enough spears of green grass were appearing to feed the remaining cows and horses. Mary Ann bought two biddy hens and four dozen eggs to begin a new flock. Frankie spaded a portion of the muddy garden plot so they could plant a few early vegetables.

Bobby Matthews had joined the Home Guard, so he and Eddie and Frankie were frequent companions. They were ordered to part time duty in March to assist in the patrol of the railroad lines and rivers. Mosby's raiders harassed the Union camps south of Harpers Ferry, but Cole's cavalry, grown considerably stronger, was a deterrent.

In May, Frankie finally got the fields plowed and most of the planting completed. The weather had not damaged the wheat, but the clover and timothy hay crop was disappointing. The weather remained chilly and the daffodils and bluebells missed blooming for Easter, the first time Mary Ann remembered that happening.

In June, Mosby's raids became more frequent. Cole's Cavalry crossed the Potomac to attack Mosby, and they fought a pitched battle outside Charles Town, but the Virginians forced the Marylanders back into Frederick County. Home guards were assembled to support Cole's men, and set up defensive positions along the B & O railway. Mosby veered south where his men were able to outflank the guards.

Finding themselves outmaneuvered, the Marylanders scrambled up the ridges near the river and found positions among trees and rocks that were impenetrable by cavalry. Meanwhile, Cole's riders had fled to Frederick, where they gathered support and re-grouped. The two sides skirmished for several miles from outside Frederick to the Jefferson and Adamstown areas before the Rebs broke off the action and returned to Virginia.

A week later, Mosby struck again, this time to the south through Poolesville, along the base of Sugarloaf Mountain, and then north toward Buckeystown, seeking to sever the rail line. The Virginians caught the guards posted at the station by surprise, took four prisoners, and began tearing up railroad tracks.

Alerted by a telegram, several hundred guards assembled outside Frederick and hurried toward Buckeystown. A small contingent of Federal troops guarding the Jug Bridge over the Monacacy joined them, and a detachment from the Harpers Ferry garrison boarded a train and began to steam down the rail line. Two hours after entering Buckeystown, Mosby found himself under attack. First, the guards moved in and set up a firing line which halted the rail dismantling. Then the Union troops arrived from Harpers Ferry with a six pounder and joined the attack, and the Virginians withdrew.

The guard members were pleased at their success, but they were riled at the ease with which Mosby's men got into their backyard. "Gotta be them Kings and some of them other Rebel lovers," Liston said.

"How about Horine?" Frankie asked.

"I don't think so. Gross and Handley keep an eye on him and there ain't nothin' goin' on aroun' his place."

Six days later they forgot about Mosby. Jubal Early had crossed the Potomac and occupied Hagerstown. He levied a ransom on the city in retribution for Hunter's destruction in the Shenandoah. Early collected $20,000, but it was a mistake. He had ordered a $200,000 levy, but one of his staff omitted a zero from the written demand.

Frederick was in tumult. Cole and most of his cavalry had been sent to West Virginia, so local forces were depleted. Fortunately, Clendenin's Eighth Illinois cavalry was on guard near the Potomac. Scouts spotted Early's approach north of Middletown and sounded the alarm.

On July 8 Early's troops reached the outskirts. His artillery fired a few shots across the city's rooftops, doing little damage, but terrorizing several distinguished citizens who were blithely observing the invaders from the tower of the new courthouse. Clendenin's troopers and units of the Home Brigade began to set up a defense line to the west of Frederick, but gave it up when large numbers of Confederate infantry appeared.

From his headquarters in Baltimore, General Lew Wallace learned of the danger and assembled available Union soldiers to mount a defense. A division under Ricketts was sent north by Grant and joined Wallace south of Frederick. They formed a six mile front so they could react to whichever direction Early took. The Potomac Home Brigade was added to Wallace's ragtag force, which numbered about 6,000.

Early's scouts soon identified the Union position, and Jube prepared to strike before more opposition appeared. The Home Brigade was positioned next to Wallace's men along the Monacacy, while Ricketts guarded the Union left and held a few companies in reserve to help wherever necessary.

Liston told his guards, "Boys, this ain't gonna be like fightin' them raiders. This here is reg'lar Reb army and they're tougher'n a mule's behind. You gotta fire fast and keep your nerve when you see 'em comin'. Don't waste your shots, wait till they're in range."

"We ain't got no cannons," Eddie Zimmerman griped.

"Yes we do. Both Wallace and Ricketts brung 'em. Now don't none of you make us look bad by skedaddlin'. We all git skeered, but we gotta keep our nerve."

They edged to the river bank and dug in behind willows and brush. Frankie's mouth was dry, and he was sick to his stomach. His bowels felt like they wanted to move, but he'd already done that job in the bushes. Bobby Matthews whispered, "You reckon they'll come this way?"

"Reckon they'll go any way they want to."

"Why don't the guv'ment send us some help?"

"They sent Ricketts. Maybe they ain't got no more to send."

"Don't make no sense. All our army down in Virginia and none up here to stop the Rebs from marchin' into Washington."

"Mebbe more help is on the way. We gotta hold off them Rebs till the help gets here."

To their right, firing commenced. Artillery shells hit Wallace's center, directly in front of the bridge. Reb cavalry rode across their front, out of range, heading downriver. Behind them, Clendenin's men mounted their horses and gave chase.

Gunfire on the right continued. Liston squinted across the river. "Cap'n," he called, "company comin'."

"I see 'em, Lick," the old man replied. He sent an aide to Wallace to request artillery support.

The Marylanders stared at a contingent of Rebs that marched into position about 300 yards away. The enemy moved three 12-pound napoleons into position and began to sight them in. "They're pointin' them guns right at us," Bobby Matthews exclaimed.

"Sightin' 'em in," Liston explained.

One of the guns belched and a shell hit above them on the hillside, doing no damage. The gunners continued with their work. One after another the cannon fired. The fifth explosion hit nearby and two guardsmen yowled with pain. "Damn," Bobby Matthews said, "I can't stand this. I'm gettin' outta here."

"You stay right where you are, Bobby," Frankie said. "Your pa would never forgive you if you run." Two Union shells burst near the Reb position and several of the guards cheered. For several minutes the Rebs continued the bombardment. There were several direct hits, so the guards dug in deeper. Downstream they could hear the sound of a spirited cavalry battle. On their right, there was a growing rattle of infantry fire.

Across the river, a Reb officer stepped in front of his men. Battle flags moved to the front of the regiments and the gray line started to advance. Several of the guards fired their weapons but the shots kicked up dust well in front of their targets. Liston grumbled. "Let me take a crack at 'em," he said. He sighted through the trees, checked the wind, estimated his elevation, and squeezed off a shot. The Reb officer grabbed his leg and fell. The guards cheered.

Their joy was short lived. The Reb lines split, some finding cover and firing on the Union line while the rest worked their way toward the defenders' flanks. The guards came under heavy musket fire from several directions, and the men hugged the ground as minie balls zipped and splattered among them. While the Rebs were re-loading, Liston ordered his men to fire. Only half the guards had the nerve to raise up and fire their muskets.

"What's wrong with those men?" the captain shouted to Liston.

Liston grabbed a musket from a frightened boy and fired it at the Confederates. A graycoat grabbed his side, but the Rebs kept firing steadily, and two more guards were hit. Liston ducked his head when a Reb minie plucked at his sleeve. "Dammit, boys, shoot them guns."

Frankie, Eddie and Bobby raised together and fired, and several others squeezed off shots. Two arose and began to run, but the captain and Liston caught them and sent them back. "Get back in there and fight," the captain shouted, "we don't abide no cowards."

The Confederates did not attempt to cross the river. Their artillery and musketry had Wallace's men pinned down along the Monacacy while their cavalry and a large contingent of infantry worked around the Union flanks.

By mid-afternoon the Union position had become untenable. Early's cavalry had driven across the river to their rear and Reb infantry had turned Rickett's flank. Wallace's men realized they were trapped and began to abandon their lines. Clendenin's troopers and some of Wallace's men attempted to hold on but they were outmatched, and Wallace ordered a retreat. The Home Brigade was isolated and their officers began to seek some means to avoid capture.

The guards worked their way along the river until they found an unprotected ford. A mile down river, they slipped across and raced toward the woods along the Ballenger Creek when they ran into Confederates moving back toward the city. Several hundred Reb cavalry and infantry chased the Marylanders into an overgrown field of scrub locust and blackberry briers that bordered the creek, and where there was enough cover for the guards to make a stand. Their first volley slowed the pursuers, and as more of their men came to the line, subsequent volleys discouraged the Rebels. "Let 'em go," a Reb officer shouted. "They can't do us no harm."

With the enemy shattered, Early returned to Frederick to collect the $200,000 levy he demanded to save the city from being burned. Local banks lent the money to the town fathers, and Jube prepared for his army's march on Washington.

6

Five days after the battles around Spotsylvania Courthouse, Richard Horine rode into Ewell's lines near the Pamunkey river to see how his brother was faring. He'd taken a detour to see Cathy and told Lettie he would check on Claib and extend her regards. Both sisters and their father were showing wear from the war. Union cavalry had taken most of their horses and two of their slaves had vanished. Decent food was scarce since both armies had helped themselves to the Livingstone stores.

Richard asked where Claib's regiment was posted and was told that Ewell's men were on the lines facing the Union army a mile or so north. He forded the river and rode Prince toward the sound of sporadic gunfire. He followed a line of empty supply wagons to Ewell's headquarters, a few hundred yards from the front, but the commander was away, conferring with Lee.

A major who Richard knew appeared and asked what he wanted. "Gave my men a few hours rest and came over here to see my brother" he replied. "Where's his regiment posted?"

"Horine, I hate to be the one to tell you, but those men were at the mule shoe. They were wiped out."

"Oh, God. All killed?"

"They were in the front ranks in the breastworks. They killed three or four Yanks for every one of them, but Grant kept pouring in men and overran our position. Lee had to order those men to hold those trenches while we constructed a backup line, and the bodies piled up on top of one another. There must have been five hundred men in that death pit. If your brother was there, all I can say is he died a brave man, a hero. Without the sacrifice of those soldiers, our lines would have been broken. We likely would have lost our whole army."

Richard dismounted and sank to the ground. "Guess I better sit for a spell," he said.

"It was worse than anything we saw at Sharpsburg or Gettysburg or in the Wilderness, men stacked up like cordwood."

"My poor, brave brother, they finally got him. I wish it had been me, so I didn't have to tell Mama and Papa."

"That's the worst of it, having to tell the home folks they lost their baby boy."

"No, they lost their baby boy at First Manassas. Claib was the second. I'm the oldest. I'm so sick of this killin'. Damn the Yanks. Damn them. They killed Stuart and now my brother."

Richard sat in silence, remembering how it had been when he and his brothers were together on their farm in Maryland. They had so many plans, Jacob with his good looks and sharp wit, and Claib who was the strongest and maybe the smartest. They'd teased him about his glasses, but he was good natured and teased them right back. God, Richard thought, how I'll miss him. I always looked forward to seeing him. He was so strong, so confident, I thought he'd live forever. Another thought crossed his mind that made him feel even worse--he'd have to tell Lettie.

"I have to get back to my men," Richard said after a few minutes. "Can you tell me where he was buried?"

"There's several hundred, all his regiment I reckon, plus a lot more, buried together in the mule shoe. There's a post and a marker with the regiments' names. You shouldn't have any trouble finding it, if you ever have the chance. The Yanks are holding that area now."

Richard mounted Prince and started down the lane at a slow walk, his body slumped in sorrow. After a few seconds, he raised his head, brushed the tears from his eyes, looked back briefly, returned the major's salute, snapped the reins, and galloped away toward the sun in the western sky.

Moments later, Ewell and two of his staff returned from Lee's headquarters. "Who was that colonel that just left?" Ewell asked.

"Cavalryman by the name of Horine, lookin' for his brother. They're Marylanders. Turns out his brother was one of our men that was killed at the mule shoe in that mad Yank attack."

"Horine, Horine--unusual name. I think I remember the boy that was killed, too bad. I thought that colonel looked familiar when he saluted me. Help me down, will you, Major?"

7

Two locomotives hitched in tandem ground their way into Union Station and hissed to a stop. Several officers leaped down from the train and began shouting orders. Hiram Matthews stepped out from the forward car and strode back along the loaded flatcars as his regiment started to scramble down to the pavement.

"Are you Colonel Matthews?" a young lieutenant demanded. "General Augur wants you to report to him immediately."

Matthews ignored the young officer. "Al," he called to Fisher, "any more sick?"

"Just a few cases of the army shits," Fisher replied.

"I need you to help the battery boys get those napoleons down. Augur's got one of his pups down here yappin' at my heels."

"Sure. Should we get 'em movin'?"

"Damn right. We ain't gonna fart around here waitin' for orders. Early was in Rockville yesterday, so you can bet your sweet ass that sonofabitch will be in Washington today."

"Colonel Matthews," the lieutenant scolded, "General Augur was very clear that you are to report to him as soon as you arrive."

Matthews turned and glared. "Look, Sonny, my boys been ridin' these damn flat cars for over a day. Our commander is George Crook, and he got orders from Grant to send us up here and help General Horatio Wright drive off a mean bastard named Jube Early and his army. We've fought Jube before so we know what we're doin'. Now I'm movin' my men and our guns on out toward Silver Spring, and you tell your general we'll meet him there. Tell him if he's got other orders for us, he better clear 'em with General Sam Grant. Now go away and let me get on with this damn war." He turned and stalked back to where his men were assembling. "Let's go, boys," he shouted.

Fisher was laughing, and he told his top sergeant, Pete Angleberger, "Did you see the look on the face of that little shitass?"

The regiment had already started to move. Horses were hitched to artillery and supply wagons were loaded from the freight cars. Company by company, they formed ranks and hastened toward the outskirts of the Capitol.

Matthews and a dozen of his officers and staff mounted horses and rode ahead, toward the sound of sporadic gunfire. They found Union lines thinly held on a two mile perimeter, anchored by breastworks in front of Fort Stevens. Early's men had reached Silver Springs a few hours before, and the morning sky was illuminated by fires. A brigadier who had just arrived from Virginia met Matthews and confessed his difficulty in dealing with Augur's orders on one hand and Early's plans on the other.

"Looks like he's fired Silver Springs," Matthews said. "I wouldn't put anything past that miserable son of a gun. What outfit you with?"

"Wright's corps."

"Wright's a damn good man from all I've heard. All this is Hunter's fault. He backed away from Early down in Virginia, and let him loose to march right up to our homes in Maryland, and that's what got us in this mess. We've fought Early before, and he's tougher than a mule's rear end, but we beat him before and I reckon we can do it again."

"Where'd you fight him?"

"Gettysburg, and down at Second Bull Run. He may have been agin us at Antietam, but we got beat up so bad there, I don't know who was on the other side."

"Well, I'm glad you're here. I sent word back to Wright to get the rest of our men up here quick." He glanced down the road. "Looks like your men."

Matthews hustled off to supervise his regiment. Maryland and West Virginia troops moved smartly into position. Companies set up firing lines and scooped out shallow trenches or threw up barricades. The veterans replaced nervous clerks and reserves who had been hustled into duty when Early's advance panicked Washington and who were greatly relieved at being sent to the rear.

Dawn appeared and they saw plumes of smoke swirling on the horizon. Matthews mounted the breastworks and inspected the front with field glasses. "There they are, Al," he said, "formin' up about a mile out."

"Get ready," Fisher called down the line, "they'll be comin'."

As if on signal, a Reb shell burst in front of them. "Jube's wake up call," Matthews said. "Don't want none of the boys takin' a nap."

More of Wright's corps moved into position on their left. Matthews rode over to investigate. "Still more of us on the way," a bearded colonel said, "but it'll take an hour for them to get here."

"We should have enough men to hold the line for that long. Is Grant comin'?"

"Not that I heard. He's got his hands full with Lee."

Matthews turned his horse and trotted back to his command where he found General Augur, his adjutant, and the brigadier waiting for him.

"Colonel Matthews, how nice to see you," Augur said. "I expected you at my headquarters, but my messenger said you were too busy."

Matthews saluted. His horse lurched as two Reb shells exploded nearby. Augur's horse pranced nervously.

"Yessir," Matthews said, "I was ordered out here to the line without delay, so I decided it best to report here, like I'm doin', Sir."

Another shell burst, very close. This sent Augur's horse into a spasm of bucking and twisting that took the general a full minute to bring under control. "Should I return the fire?" Matthews asked. "I've been having my gunners hold up till the enemy was closer."

Augur got his horse settled when two more shells hit nearby and the beast began snorting and stomping about once again. "Use your own judgment," Augur shouted, "I've got work to do." He yanked on the horse's reins and galloped away.

The brigadier remained, grinning slightly. "Matthews," he said, "I reckon those Reb gunners did you a favor."

Matthews chuckled. "Prob'bly did, Sir," he said. He saluted and rode back to his regiment. "What's goin' on?" he asked Fisher.

"Looks like they're ready to move on us."

A Reb skirmish line advanced toward them while sharpshooters ran forward and took cover where they could lace the Union line with steady fire. "Bastards are good shots," Fisher shouted, "keep your heads down."

Matthews edged his way to the front and peered over a mound. "Bullshit," he swore, "I ain't waitin' no more. You company commanders, get your best shots up here and shoot me some of them damn Rebs. Angleberger, go tell the gunners to start plunkin' some shells on 'em. I want 'em to know we ain't nobody to be messed with." A cheer went up from the ranks.

Within minutes Early's skirmish line was in trouble. Wright's men continuing arriving and began adding to the Union firepower. Bullets kicked up dust and debris about the Rebs and several were hit. Union artillery began using canister as the graycoats neared, and the skirmishers soon had enough and withdrew to their main force. "That'll show ol' Jube he ain't got a bunch of green home guards to fight today," Matthews muttered to Fisher.

From behind Matthews an imposing, high pitched voice spoke, "Some mighty fine shootin' there, Colonel. Where you fellows from?"

Matthews turned to see who was dumb enough to walk into the battle zone, and for once in his life, he and everyone around him were speechless. Standing there was a tall, commanding presence--top hat, cape, beard, clear eyes set deep in his ponderous head. He had strolled over from a carriage driven by another civilian.

"Mister President," Matthews sputtered, "you can't be here."

"I understand," Abraham Lincoln replied, "but here I am. Wanted to see for myself what those Rebels look like. Only you boys drove them off before I could get a good view. Can I borrow your field glasses?"

Matthews handed him his binoculars and stood aside as the enormous gaunt man scanned the Confederate lines. Artillery and rifle fire continued. A shell burst twenty yards away, a minie ball clipped a tree branch and whined overhead. "Mister Lincoln," Matthews said, "I insist you take cover. Your safety is my responsibility, and Sir, those Rebs over there can see you. They've got glasses too." Two of Wright's officers joined in warning Lincoln.

"Well, Colonel, this is pretty special for me. It's the first chance I've had to see our enemy up close."

"Please, Sir, no disrespect, but I want you out of here so we can fight our battle. I can't let you get shot here in my command, even if I have to wrestle you down and carry you back to cover myself." Reb bullets hit nearby and a soldier clutched his arm and swore. Matthews stepped in front of Lincoln and faced him.

Lincoln stared at Matthews with a twinkle in his eye. "You're Marylanders, aren't you," he said, "tryin' to drive those Rebels out of your home state. Well, Colonel, since you seem pretty determined to get me away for her, I guess I'll mosey over and see if I can find General Wright."

The President glanced back and waved before climbing into his carriage. Matthews continued staring, but then thought better of it and saluted. "Well, Hayes," Lincoln said to his secretary, "let's move on back to the rear. These boys seem to want to fight this battle without me in the way."

Hayes snapped the reins and sent the team trotting away. "That was crazy, Sir. You could have been killed." Perspiration ran down the young man's face and neck.

Lincoln slapped his knee and chuckled. "I like that fellow," he said, "rough as a cob, telling his President he'd wrestle him down if he had to."

Fisher and Angleberger stared at Matthews in amazement. "I heard you," Fisher said. "You told the President to get outta here."

"What else could I say? I like ol' Abe, but I can't have his skinny ass blown off here on my battle line."

The story was repeated up and down the Union line. Angleberger said, "Ol' Hi would tell the divil hisself to git his ass back to hell if he showed up here."

For the next two hours they held off the Rebs. Early tried a flanking movement to the left but met strong resistance from Wright's growing force. By afternoon he gave up the effort and moved northwest toward the Potomac. The Union defenders were unable to organize an effective pursuit, and Early slipped across the river back into Virginia.

8

"I am very angry," Seth Hatcher sputtered, "at the way I was treated by General Early."

"What exactly happened?" Varley asked.

"I went to him and asked that Frederick be spared since so many of us support the Confederate cause. He refused to believe me and wondered why he should even listen to me. The man even threatened to put me under arrest. I pointed out our long standing relationship with Stuart, and he said

Stuart was dead and that meant nothing to him. I pointed out that one of our men got word to Lee at Sharpsburg about the orders found by the Yankees. He grunted. I told him that I myself had gotten word to Lee that Union troops were in Frederick and headed for Pennsylvania before the battle at Gettysburg, and he yawned. He said that was nonsense, that Longstreet was the one who found that out. I told him of the horses Ben Horine sent south, and of his sons, and how we'd fomented anti-war activity in Baltimore, and he ignored it all and dismissed me. He is the most obtuse, ignorant man I have ever met."

The three conspirators, Hatcher, Varley, and Kilgour, were meeting in an upstairs room in Hatcher's offices three days after the Battle of the Monacacy. Varley leaned back and sighed. "Well Early's a fool," he said, "and there's nothing we can do about it. He got his $200,000 in tribute and the South has the undying hatred of most of our people. What can we do now?"

"We've got to cut off their head," Kilgour said. "We must get rid of Lincoln. Without him, the war ends."

"Very well. How do we go about getting rid of him?"

Kilgour leaned forward. "Leave it to Merryman and me. We're in touch with people in Prince Georges County who feel like we do. They are close to the White House and can get the job done."

"That seems to be our best chance," Varley said. "What about Johns?"

"He's all for it," Kilgour said. "He knows these people, and he knows enough about Washington to be helpful. He and Rhodes will take care of it. All we need to do is contribute the money."

"Should we contact any of the others?" Hatcher asked.

"Who's left?" Varley asked. "We heard Turner was killed in the Wilderness. People are still watching Horine, and now they're watching the Kings too. We better keep this to ourselves. The fewer who know, the better, so Kilgour, it's your game.

After the battle and their narrow escape, the guards scattered. Some had gone into hiding while Early's troops occupied Frederick. The rest camped at various places about the area awaiting orders.

The Ballenger and Jefferson company made camp in a field across from Holter's store. As word of their location spread, family and well-wishers flooded the area with food, conversation and curiosity. Their captain was ill and had returned to his home near Jefferson, so Liston took command and tried to retain some semblance of order. "Folks," he shouted to the visitors, "you gotta clear outta here. We got beat purty bad down by the Monacacy and them Rebs may come back. We'll be gettin' orders soon and movin' out. Now go on home."

Mary Ann had brought Frankie a basket of food. "I'm so relieved you ain't hurt, but I feel so sad about the ones who was," she said. "Come home soon as you can." She waved as she climbed into her buggy. The crowd hesitated and milled about for a while, but soon they dispersed while Liston looked over new orders which had been delivered by a rider from Frederick.

Frankie sat with his friends and waited. After the battle and their narrow escape, they had hid in the woods near Adamstown, exhausted and scared. Three of the men were wounded, and two had been left on the battlefield. They had lost all contact with Wallace. Frankie wasn't sure he ever wanted to fight a battle like that again.

The orders Liston received were simple enough, they were to return to lookout duty along the railway. There the days passed easily, and Early's army never reappeared, so after a week of inaction, the men in Frankie's unit were released to return to their farms.

A few days later Squire Fulmer returned to the store to sit a spell. He was pale and thin, but his voice was strong and his spirits good. "I wish I coulda been here when the guards were assembled," he said. "It seems to me they did us a good service, slowed down Early so Lincoln had time to get help up from Virginia. Early had 'em outnumbered, but they held him off just long enough."

"That's the way I see it," Holter said.

"That Liston boy knows what he's doin'," Handley said. "You can tell he got trained by Hiram."

Oscar Fisher pulled up in his farm wagon and rushed up the steps into the store. "Fellows," he said, "I got sumpin' to read for you. It's a letter from my boy, he's a captain now, and the whole regiment got sent down to Washington to stop Early. Now listen to this."

Fisher put on his glasses and squinted at the rough lined pages which he took from his shirt pocket.

"Dear Mom and Pop," he read

"The army sent our regiment up here to fight off Jubal Early. We rode the railroad most of the way from West Virginia and got here just in time.

As you know, Hiram is colonel for the whole regiment now and we're all sure glad of it. We were into a big fight with the Rebs out toward Silver Spring when who shows up but Abe Lincoln himself.

Nobody knowed what to do. The shells and minie balls was hitting all over the place and here's our President talking to Hi like it's just a regular old summer day. He borrowed Hi's field glasses and was looking things over while the bullets was whizzing. So what does Hi do? He tells old Abe to get his behind out of there or he's going to rassle him down and drag him away his ownself. Lincoln ain't bothered at all. He just says he wanted to get a good look at them Rebs since he ain't never been close to them before. Old Hi don't budge an inch and he hustled Lincoln right out of there.

I asked Hi why he did it and he said he didn't want the President to get his skinny behind blowed off on his battle line. All of us boys still are talking about it.

I'm well. Hope you are too. Say hello to our friends. I don't know how long we'll stay here.

246

They clapped and laughed and made Fisher read it again. "Just like Hiram to do somethin' like that," Holter said.

"That's why he's such a good soldier," Boyer said. "He don't take nothin' from nobody."

"Lordy, but I wish I coulda been there," Handley said. "I wish my boy hadn't been shot and coulda seen it. Imagine tellin' ol' Abe to git his skinny tail away from his battle line."

Each newcomer to the store heard about the episode. Oscar Fisher and Peck Handley rode to the Matthews farm and showed the letter to Hiram's family. Lucy Matthews shook her head in wonder. "That's Hiram," she said. "He's as bossy with Mister Lincoln as he is with everybody else."

Bobby Matthews was thrilled by the story. It took all the sting out of the defeat at the Monacacy.

10

A few weeks after Spotsylvania, Richard was able to get a letter out of Richmond to his family. It would take weeks to arrive through a circuitous route.

In late July, Ben Horine received the well worn envelope. The hopes of Early's invasion had been dashed by reports he was back in the Shenandoah Valley. The frame of a new barn now rose above the old stone foundation, and the barn floor was started. Jeremiah was tending two new colts, and Elsie and the children were working in the garden. A mounted postman delivered the letter, glared at Horine, and turned away without a word. Feelings were still running high because of Early's levy on the town.

Ben opened the letter and his hands began to shake as he learned of Claiborne's death. Tears trickled down his cheeks as he thought of his three older sons, now only one left. He clutched the letter to his chest and leaned against a chestnut tree along the farm lane. His head throbbed, his chest tightened. He felt as if a huge weight was pressing down on him. Claiborne, oh Claiborne, my son, not you too. He tried to call out, but his voice failed and he sighed heavily. He slid to the ground, his head spinning, his body a mass of pain that became numb as he lapsed into unconsciousness.

Rebecca saw her father slumped on the ground when she went to find him for the noon meal. She ran to the house, and Elsie came with her to see what was wrong. "Must have had one of his fainting spells," Elsie said, but when she saw him, she knew it was worse.

Elsie knelt over her husband, sobbing. "Oh Ben, Ben, you can't leave me now." His blue lips, his gray face, eyes staring vacantly--he looked so terrible. "Oh God, what are we to do?" The children had followed and clustered around her, frightened and clutching to one another. Standing off to one side, Jeremiah and Tillie watched, their eyes glistening at the death of the man who had owned them for so many years.

After a minute, Elsie noticed the crumpled letter in his hand. She shook so badly she could not pry open his fingers. "Jeremiah," she called, "see if you can open his hand a little and get the letter loose. The writing looks like Richard's."

Gently Jeremiah pried the dead man's fist open, one finger at a time. He freed the letter and handed it to Elsie. She stared blankly for several seconds, shaking badly, and then began to read, her body unsteady, her face pale. After a few lines, she collapsed, fainting dead away onto the dry summer grass.

Rebecca was seventeen. Since Jacob's death and her mother's collapse at the news, she had taken on more and more responsibility. She and Tillie had become quiet allies to see that the work was done, that Elsie was not bothered with things that would upset her, and that Benjamin would think Elsie was improving and not know she was often protected by them.

Now Rebecca faced a much larger trial. Her father was dead, her mother unconscious, perhaps dying. Her three younger sisters and her younger brother were standing in a state of shock, and she knew that no one else could help. She knelt beside her mother and saw she was breathing. "Tillie," she said, "could you and Jeremiah carry Mama into the parlor, please? I need to look at this letter and tend to the children."

"Yes'm," Tillie said, "here, Mister, you wait till I get a blanket to lay her on." She returned with a beautifully stitched log cabin quilt, and the two Blacks gently lifted the woman onto it. They stretched it out and raised her off the ground, then carried her up the front porch steps and into the parlor where she was lowered onto a fainting couch.

In the yard, Rebecca knelt beside her father for a moment and then reached across and closed his eyelids and folded his arms. "There, Papa," she said, "you look more comfortable." Then she looked at her frightened, tearful siblings. "Now we'll read Richard's letter," she said. "Gather around and let's hold hands together. We must be brave.

Dear Papa,

I have the worse news. I wish I didn't have to be the one to tell you and Mama that Claiborne is dead. He was killed in May at a place called Spotsylvania Courthouse. We won the battle, but Grant is a butcher who sacrificed two men for every one of ours who was killed. But our boys are dead and Claib was one of them. It breaks my heart to lose him. He was so good hearted. His men loved him and he fought well wherever he was and never complained. All his men died with him. I pray they're in a happier place.

He was my best friend and I don't know what I'll do without him. I wish it was me and he could be spared. The war goes on and no one knows when or how it will end. I guess you know I also lost my commander, Jeb Stuart. So many dead, why won't Lincoln let us be?

Give my love and condolences to the children. I miss them all. Tell Mama it is God's will that Claiborne and Jacob were taken away. I am proud they died nobly, but I wish they were still here and we were all back together as a family with our land and our horses.

Your loving son,
Richard"

Betsy, the youngest, broke the silence. "Papa's dead. Claiborne's dead. Jacob's dead. Is Mama dead too?"

"No, honey," Rebecca said, "Mama fainted because she was shocked by Papa dying and then reading the letter about Claiborne."

Timmy choked back a sob. "What's going to happen to us, Rebecca? Mama can't take care of us."

"She can help, Tim. We all can help. Can we be brave, like you brothers?"

Timmy bit his lip. "I guess," he said. Her two older sisters each hugged Rebecca and then Timmy and Betsy joined them as all five crowded together.

"We'll all help you, Rebecca," Rachel said.

Jeremiah returned. "Miss Elsie's restin' in de parlor, Miss Rebecca. Tillie dere with her. You want I should fetch de funeral man."

"Yes, Jeremiah, take the mule. But first, can you carry Papa into the sitting room out of the sun?"

"Yessum, I kin do dat."

The tall African picked up Ben Horine easily and took his body into the house. Rebecca and the children followed. Then Rebecca went to the parlor and found her mother was still unconscious but breathing easily. "Tillie," she said, "If you don't mind, I'll stay with Mama. Would you get dinner on? We'll have to eat."

Tillie looked at the girl and smiled. "Sure, honey, I'll be glad to."

11

Five families attended Ben Horine's funeral--a few relatives and long time friends. None of the cabal members were willing to take the risk of appearing. The five children had to support their mother who had recovered somewhat but was still on the verge of another collapse.

Elsie remained in shock for several days after the funeral. The children cared for the garden. Tillie cooked the meals. Jeremiah tended the land and the animals. Rebecca studied her father's records, trying to make sense of his business affairs. She found a bankbook with considerable savings, some railroad bonds, the deed to the farm, and the certificates of ownership for Jeremiah and Tillie. He also had stashed away a nest egg of gold coins and greenbacks locked in a box hidden in the back of his chiffonier.

Once Elsie was sufficiently recovered, Rebecca and her mother summoned Jeremiah and Tillie to the parlor. The Africans walked in slowly and stood side by side, saying nothing, wondering what they had done.

"We've decided to give you your freedom," Elsie said.

"Yes," Rebecca added, "I have your slave papers and we'll have a lawyer draw up a writ of manumission that will let everyone know you are freedmen."

Jeremiah and Tillie stared at them, speechless.

"What's wrong?" Elsie asked. "I thought you'd be happy."

"Yes ma'am," Tillie explained, "we is, in a way, but we ain't sure. You see, Miss Elsie, we don't know how to be free."

"Yessum, Miss Elsie, Miss Rebecca," Jeremiah said, "we wants to be free, but we don't know what to do. Where kin we go? How we gwine live?"

"If you care to stay," Rebecca said, choosing her words carefully, "we'll hire you to do the work you've been doing. We'll let you live in the cabin, give you a garden plot, and pay you fifteen dollars a month for your work."

Jeremiah and Tillie had never had money. Fifteen dollars sounded like a fortune. "Yessum," Jeremiah responded, "we'd like dat. Thank you, Miss Elsie, Miss Rebecca." The Africans nodded and departed the room, holding hands.

Elsie scolded, "Fifteen dollars, that's too much."

"No, Mama," Rebecca said, "it's fair. No matter what happens in the war, the slaves will be freed. People will have to pay for good help, and Jeremiah and Tillie will find out soon enough that we treated them right, maybe better than most."

At the Sunday morning worship service in Frederick, Jeremiah compared notes with other freedmen. None of the farm workers were receiving more than ten dollars. "I reckon Miss Elsie and Miss Rebecca treat us good," Tillie said.

12

After Claib's death, Richard felt as though he had lost his soul. The war around Richmond was a nightmarish, bitter struggle which forced the cavalry into constant, numbing action. At Cold Harbor, the Union suffered incredible losses in a few minutes when Grant launched an ill-advised attack on entrenched Confederate lines. After such a bloody repulse, they expected the Federal advance to collapse. Instead, Grant brought up more men and kept up the pressure.

Lee sent Hampton to harass Union supply lines while Fitz Lee remained with the main force. Richard was disappointed that he was not with Hampton since the action likely would take the Confederates near his uncle's farm and Cathy. He had not seen her or heard from her for a month, and he longed for her sweet smile and strong, gentle voice. Yet he doubted the families knew the worse, and dreaded having to tell them, especially Lettie, that Claib was dead.

His battalion was assigned to screen the army's southern flank and gather information on enemy movements. On June 14, Richard was waiting for his scouts' report in a grove a few miles east of the rail line south of Richmond when one of his troopers galloped up. "Whole Yank army over yonder," he shouted.

Richard gathered his men and rushed east. Behind a hedgerow they observed the enemy, division strength, maybe a full corps, the vanguard of a Yank movement south toward Petersburg, well beyond Confederate lines. Grant was close to outflanking Lee's army.

Richard used his spyglass to determine as much as he could about the invaders. He wrote out a report for headquarters. "Shanks, take two men and get this to Marse Robert or Gordon or Ewell. Granny, find Fitz Lee and tell him what's goin' on. Ride like the blazes. If you see any infantry, tell 'em to get down here quick and help us slow down those bastards."

Then Richard led his troopers laterally ahead of the Union column, avoiding their screen, until he located a position on high ground overlooking the route of advance. He had two six pounders which he unlimbered and trained on the road in front of the enemy. When the lumbering Yank units appeared, the guns fired from several hundred yards. The shell bursts startled a company of horsemen leading the Federals, causing them to scatter. Infantry units also broke ranks and scrambled for cover. After two more rounds were fired, Union riders re-formed and rode off to the left to get around the Rebel position. Richard sent two companies of his men to head them off, while the rest stayed with him to continue the bombardment and to counter any forward infantry movement.

After several minutes of confusion, the Yanks regrouped, brought forward several Napoleons, and formed a skirmish line. Richard had his men continue firing, but when the first shells from the Yank twelve pounders exploded, he broke off the engagement. They hitched up their guns and raced to gather the men who were engaging the Union riders a half mile away. Both sides had dismounted and taken cover. As soon as Horine appeared, his troopers gathered their horses and their wounded and fled the field.

The Union column remained in place for several minutes after the firing had stopped. The Union commander, Baldy Smith, rode forward. "It ain't nothin' but a few Rebel

riders," he shouted. "Get movin' and make up for lost time."
The encounter cost the Federals close to an hour.

When Lee received Horine's report, he recognized the crisis and ordered every unit available to locate and stop the enemy column. He sent word to Beauregard, who had Butler trapped in the Bermuda Hundred northeast of Petersburg, to send troops to help cut off the Union advance.

Richard set up for another delaying action a few miles down the road from the first and was joined by Grannie with two companies sent by Fitz Lee, but the Federals came forward better prepared. Outriders, artillery, and battle-ready infantry led the advance. After several minutes exchanging gunfire, Richard was forced to disengage and move westward where he found a better position to harass the enemy's right flank. This had little effect on the invaders, but the gunfire was heard by Confederate infantry moving down the rail line from Richmond.

It was a near thing. Beauregard's troops and the handful of men sent south by Lee barely beat the Union force to Petersburg. A combination of Rebel audacity and Yank confusion saved destruction of Lee's southern flank. Along a two mile wide front the Rebs piled into position, firing and shifting to meet repeated but uncoordinated enemy attacks.

Nearly half of Horine's battalion went down, wounded or dead. When a Yank brigade charged toward the railroad line, Richard led a group of his own men plus assorted infantry and local militia to head them off. Increasing numbers of men were fed into the fight from both sides before the battle dwindled into darkness.

At twilight a Yank shell struck and killed Shanks Duval, wounded several others, and slashed across Richard's entire right side. He had major lacerations on his right arm and leg, plus a deep cut across his cheek and nose, and a nasty hole torn into his rib cage. No surgeon was available, so two of his remaining officers and Granny attended his wounds. The leg was the most serious, and it took some time to get a bleeder to stop spurting. A shirt from a dead comrade was torn into strips to make a tourniquet and bandages. His shredded face was terribly painful, and he pressed a blood soaked handkerchief against it, trying to slow the hemorrhage.

As night fell, they rolled him onto a stretcher, found a wagon, and sent him with several other wounded to the hospital in Richmond. His last words as the wagon rolled away: "Thanks, boys, you fought a good fight, saved the day. Take care of Prince. Look after him till I get back. And make sure Shanks gets a proper burial. I'll try to get word to his folks. God, how I will miss him."

13

The Richmond hospital was a madhouse with over 10,000 Confederate casualties from battles dating back to the Wilderness. Doctors, nurses and volunteers were overwhelmed as the stream of new patients continued. When Richard arrived, he was unconscious from pain and loss of blood. His wounds became infected, and the doctors had little to offer.

After three days, he was conscious and feverish and realized he was in grave danger. He asked each person he saw if he or she knew the Mason Wise family who lived north of Richmond. After repeated failures, a lady responded, "Of course, they're dear friends. Oh my goodness, you're Richard, aren't you? I've heard so much about you from Grace. They're so proud of you and your brother. How can I help?"

Two days later Mason Wise and a slave named Ezekiel appeared and carried Richard in a carriage to the Wise estate. There he was bathed, his dressings changed, and given a bed with clean sheets. His fever continued and he was delirious, but he did not get worse. On the third day, he lapsed into a deep sleep and did not awaken for a dozen hours.

When he awoke, he stared with numb silence at the lovely visage beside his bed. Catherine Livingstone had come as soon as she heard he was wounded, and she shared the vigil at his bedside with Aunt Gracie Wise and the Wise daughters.

Catherine realized he was conscious and staring at her. "It's me, Richard," she said, "Catherine, Cathy. We've been so worried. How are you?"

Richard took a deep breath. "You don't know how wonderful I feel to find you here. How did you know?"

"Mister Wise sent word. Nothing could keep me from your side when I heard you were hurt so bad. Oh, my darling." Her voice was choking. She was near tears. "Do you mind if I call you darling? I've been so afraid. We've never said, I've only seen you a few times, but I found myself caring for you so much." She paused, emotions churning. Had she been too forward? Had she said too much?

Richard closed his eyes to convince himself he wasn't dreaming. Tears welled up in the corners of his eyes. "Cathy," he said, "you're the most wonderful girl I've ever known. I think I've loved you ever since we met, and now you say you care for me. It's like a dream. Please say it's true, that it's not just because I'm hurt."

Cathy reached over and took his hand. "Richard, I never meant anything more in my whole life." She lifted his hand to her lips and kissed it gently. Now the tears were sliding down both their cheeks.

That was how Grace found them a few minutes later. She saw in a glance they were in love. She would not comment on their secret. "Well, well," she said, "our Rip Van Winkle has awoken. How are you, honey?"

"I haven't felt this good for a long time, Aunt Gracie. You all are sure good nurses."

"You better say that, hadn't he, Cathy?"

"Yes, he must. What can I do now, Miss Grace?"

"I expect our patient might like a bite to eat. How about it, Richard? Have a nice meal right here in your room with Cathy and me."

Richard smiled and looked at Cathy. "Wonderful, just wonderful. This must be heaven."

14

The romance between Cathy and Richard became an open secret in the Wise household. As Richard's strength returned, they sat together on the porch and took leisurely strolls in the gardens. Richard fretted over the thick scab across his nose and cheek, but Cathy kissed it and said it made him look more dashing. It took all his courage, but after a week, he told the Wises and Cathy about Claib's death and asked permission to be the one to tell Lettie. Cathy pondered over this for a day and then asked Richard to change his mind. "I know Lettie, she and Dad and I are very close. It would be better for me to tell her. Please understand." After they talked it over some more, he agreed. It would be cruel for the news to come from him when those closest to Lettie already knew.

Once she was sure Richard was well on the road to recovery, Cathy returned home and told her father that she and Richard had an understanding, but that of course they must wait until the war was over to marry. Richard told the Wises also, but they had already guessed. Then she told her father about Claib's death and together they took the news to Lettie and shared her heartbreak.

At the end of June, Mason Wise found Richard seated alone in the library. Cathy had been gone a week and Richard planned to visit her in a few days. "Got a surprise for you," Mason said.

Richard looked up, puzzled.

"C'mon, I'll show you."

Richard followed his uncle outside and around to the side of the house. There he stopped, thunderstruck, for in front of him, held by the slave Ezekiel, stood his great black stallion, Prince, the horse he feared he'd lost forever.

Horse and owner greeted each other enthusiastically. Prince nuzzled Richard, who grasped the animal's head, stroked his mane, and spoke to him quietly.

"He sho' glad to see you, Marse Richard," Ezekiel said.

"Thank you so much, Mason, you too, Ezekiel. How did you ever find him?"

"Your men, Richard. All I had to do was find your battalion, tell them you were alive and coming back, and they would have given me anything I asked."

Richard clung to his horse. "I owe my life to you and Aunt Grace," he said, "and Cathy is the most wonderful girl in the world, but I must get back to them. I'm almost strong enough."

"Don't rush it, Richard," Mason said, "you've been terribly sick."

"You rest, Marse Richard," Ezekiel said, "I take care of yo' horse."

Three days later he rode Prince to the Livingstone home. He had dinner with the family, and afterwards, Lettie asked how Claib had died. For a few uncomfortable minutes, he told what he knew of his brother's death. "Claib and his men were wiped out," he concluded. "Their sacrifice saved our army there at the Bloody Angle below Spotsylvania Courthouse. I'll never forget him. He was not just my brother, he was my best friend. His men loved him, and he never lost his courage, never doubted our cause. He cared for you so much, Lettie. Every time I saw him, he asked about you or told me about your letters." There were no dry eyes when Richard finished. Lettie hugged him and then fled to her room, asking to be left alone for a while. Cathy and Richard held hands and walked outside. It was the saddest thing imaginable. Claib and Lettie would have had the same happiness they shared, and it would never be.

Later he and Cathy said goodbye. "I know you must go," she said, "but please, please, my dear, don't get hurt again. I'll pray for you every day. Don't take risks. Don't lose our chance for happiness. Remember how much I love you."

"I will," he promised. "You'll always be on my mind. I will come back." They kissed one last time. "So help me God," he whispered.

Then he was gone, and Cathy stood watching long after he had disappeared.

The following morning the Wises also said their farewells. Grace and Mason and their three daughters watched and waved until horse and rider vanished over the knoll on the road back to Richmond and the war.

It was August when Richard returned to his battalion. He had been able to stay with the Wises because their area had been cleared of Yankees as a result of campaigns by Hampton and Early. Richard's father had been dead a month, but he had no word from home and knew nothing of this. His nose and cheek retained a thick red scar, but his arm and leg had healed nicely. His chest gave him the most trouble, since a shell fragment had torn cartilage, making breathing painful. But he could do a day's fighting, and the war had evolved into stalemate, with Lee, still undefeated in Virginia, firmly entrenched opposite Grant from Richmond to below Petersburg.

15

By the end of July, Grant and Lincoln had enough of Jubal Early's forays into the north. The Rebel army was loose again, and in the process, burned Chambersburg for failing to raise a levy of $500,000. Newspapers lambasted the administration. Grant was pinned down in the trenches at Petersburg, and Sherman was unable to dislodge Joe Johnston from Atlanta. Hunter, like Sigel before him, was unable to cope with Early and his troops.

Grant decided to place his top cavalry officer, Phil Sheridan, in charge of the Union forces opposing Early. Grant met with Hunter near Frederick and accepted his resignation. He then gave Sheridan his instructions--find

Early and crush him. The Rebels were believed to be moving toward Cumberland. Sheridan sent cavalry to meet the enemy and forced Early back across the Potomac near Hancock.

It took Sheridan over a month to consolidate and organize the scattered Union troops into an effective fighting unit. He brought Crook's division up from West Virginia, so Matthews and his regiment were thrust back into the center of action.

In September Sheridan moved south into the Shenandoah. Early made a stand at Opequon Creek and was beaten. Sheridan defeated the Rebs again two days later at Fisher's Hill. Early withdrew further down the valley, brought up additional troops, and prepared a counter-attack.

On October 19, while Sheridan was away, Early surprised and routed Union forces camped at Cedar Creek. Sheridan was returning from a headquarters meeting near Washington when he heard the news. Without hesitation, he galloped twenty miles toward the front, gathering troops as he rode. The retreating troops, energized by Sheridan's fury, and augmented by the units following their commander, including Matthews' Marylanders, reversed course, gathered momentum and smashed into Early's celebrating troops, sending them fleeing back to the camps where they had launched their earlier attack.

From that point, as winter approached, Sheridan advanced steadily, burning barns and destroying crops and animals along the way. The breadbasket of Lee's army was disappearing.

The home guard had one final battle in 1864. In mid-October Mosby got behind Union lines and destroyed a supply train near Harpers Ferry. The next day he crossed the Potomac and again struck toward Buckeystown.

Union scouts spotted the raiders and sounded the alarm. Cole's cavalry, now at its strongest, met the Virginians outside Adamstown, and a battalion of guard infantry arrived to support the troopers. Mosby rode into unexpected trouble, suffered several casualties, and had to flee from the superior

Maryland force. Liston's company returned with a captured Rebel battle flag. It was the guards' biggest victory.

A few miles away, four of Mosby's marauders broke away during the confused retreat and found shelter in an abandoned shack in the woods above Burkittsville.

16

A week after the battle, Frankie, Eddie and Bobbie were sacking wheat in the Fraley barn to take to the mill for grinding into flour. They had already loaded Zimmerman and Matthews grain and were finishing loading the Fraley sacks. The wagon was nearly full.

The three of them piled on the last filled burlap bags and rested. They talked quietly about the war and their last battle. Eddie demonstrated a hole where his jacket was nicked by a Reb shot. "Sure that ain't a moth hole," Bobby chided.

"It sure ain't. I felt that shot tug at my coat and I thought I was hit. Plum lucky, that's what."

"Guess we all were," Frankie said. A noise outside caused him to look up. "That sound like a horse to you?" he asked. The hound raised his head and growled. Then he got up, barked once, and trotted outside.

The three young men arose and peered out through spaces in the barn's siding. "Comin' in across the field from the mountain," Frankie said. "Can't make out who they are. Four of 'em. You know any of 'em?"

"Strangers to me," Eddie said.

"Me too," Bobby echoed.

Four grim faced men rode quietly across the west pasture toward the farmhouse. They stopped for a moment and looked around, but saw only the Fraley's two horses, a cow, and three heifers grazing. Smoke was pouring from the house's chimney, but there was no sign of anyone outside.

Mary Ann and Sissy were busy making apple sauce when they heard the kitchen door open. "Howdy," a rough looking man greeted them. He was small and wore gray cavalry britches, but his worn jacket and old felt hat were not military. His eyes darted around the room, while three more men crowded through the door behind him. They had tied their horses by the meat house.

Mary Ann knew it was trouble soon as they pushed their way in. Sissy was gaping at the group. They were dirty and smelly, beards and clothing neglected. All carried muskets.

"What do you men want?" Mary Ann asked. "The idea, busting in on us like this when we got work to do. Sissy, keep stirring that sauce."

"You two alone?"

"No, the menfolk is out working."

"We just rode in and we didn't see no menfolk."

"Can't help that. I don't keep track of 'em. They're in the home guard and might be anywhere. What do you want. You've already messed up my clean kitchen with your filthy boots."

"We need food, supplies, a few spare horses."

Up to that point, the shortest of the group had done the talking. Now a thick, evil eyed man interrupted. "We'll take whatever Yank money y'all got."

A third pushed his way forward and grabbed for Sissy. He had long greasy hair and a receding chin. "I like the looks of this here gal," he said.

"Gahdamn it, Bro," the little man swore, "we said no more of that shit."

The one called Bro glowered and didn't move. "C'mon Perky," evil eye said. "Let's git movin'." He grabbed Bro by the arm and pulled him back. "You too, asshole," he said.

17

"Never seen any of 'em before," Eddie said. "Those bastards look like they're up to no good." They watched as the strangers tied up their horses and advanced into the house.

"We gotta get down there," Frankie said. "They got Springfields, and Mama and Sissy are alone in the kitchen."

"Hold up, Frankie," Eddie said, grabbing his cousin's arm, "they look like some of Mosby's men. We gotta be armed too."

"I've got my musket in the wagon," Bobby said.

"Good," Frankie said. "I've got my Colt and Springfield and Pap's old shotgun is down at the stables. C'mon, let's go." They scrambled down a ladder into the stable's feeding area and loaded their weapons.

"Now what," Bobby asked Frankie.

"They've gone in the house. Bobby, get your wagon and drive it down the lane by the house and do it quick. Keep the horses between you and the house, and have your gun ready to fire. If you stop by the lilacs, they won't be able to see you and they won't know if you're alone, so just wait there. They'll have to come out and that'll give me and Eddie a chance to jump 'em. They're up to some kind of mischief and we gotta stop 'em before they do sumpin' to Mama and Sissy. Eddie, take the shotgun and pistol. I got my Springfield."

18

Mary Ann stood in front of Sissy as the intruders advanced toward her. "Give me that butcher knife, lady," the leader growled.

"Not till you promise not to hurt her," Mary Ann snapped.

"C'mon, dammit," the evil eyed man called Poke said, "quit messin' with these two. We'd be better off just to shoot 'em."

"Before we shoot 'em, I'm gonna have my way with this little gal," Bro said. "She looks ripe as a peach."

Perky and Poke stopped and stared out the kitchen window.

"Whatcha lookin' at?" the fourth gang member named Mousey asked.

"Wagon just rolled up out there," Perky said. "Where in hell is the driver?"

"Can't see nobody," Poke said. "Must be on the other side."

"Is it just one?" Bro asked.

"Wagon's hid behind them damn bushes, ain't no way to tell. Bro, you and Poke go out there and find out. Watch out for tricks."

The two men went out the kitchen door and scanned the surroundings. Their horses were still tied where they'd left them, so they edged around the side of the house, but they still could not see anyone by the wagon.

"Bro," the larger man said, "you go down through the yard and work around them bushes. I'm gonna sneak by that shack and work down the other side."

As Poke crept toward the wash house, Bobby jiggled the reins and his horses stirred, rattling their traces. Poke concentrated on the noise as he worked his way past the wash house door. Frankie threw open the door, smashed Poke's head with his rifle butt before he could react, and then closed the door before he was observed. From a clump of lilacs bordering the yard, Bro heard a thump and checked on his partner. He saw Poke lying on the ground fifty feet away, and since he did not respond to repeated calls, Bro retraced his steps back to the corner of the house, not realizing Eddie had made his way to a spot around the corner. Bro decided to return to the kitchen, sensing it was dangerous to check on Poke, but when he turned the corner he was flattened by a hard smash from the butt of Eddie's shotgun.

Within the house Perky and Mousey were growing restless. "What're them two assholes doin'?" Perky demanded. "Keep these two covered, so I can check." He walked to the window and spotted Poke flat on the ground by an outbuilding, but he couldn't see Bro. He thought he could see a pair of legs standing beyond the wagon.

"Sumpin's done happened to Poke," he said, "and I can't see Bro."

"Whatcha mean, sumpin's happened to Poke?"

"Look for yourself. He's out there flat on his ass." He turned to Mary Ann and Sissy. "C'mon, you two, we're takin' you outside with us."

After smashing Bro, Eddie had rejoined Frankie in the wash house. They debated whether to rush the house when they spotted the two men pushing Mary Ann and Sissy ahead of them. Bobbie scrambled into the wagon when he heard the kitchen door slam. In their haste, the intruders had not noticed that Mary Ann had tucked her knife under her apron. "You stay here and wait your chance," Frankie whispered to Eddie inside the wash house. "I'll go out the other side where I can cover Bobby."

Perky stopped at the corner of the house and tried to raise Bro, who remained unconscious. "Have to find out who done this," he muttered. "Got ol' dumbass Poke from the door of that shack, I wager, but I can't figger how they got Bro. Well, shit, we gotta finish this."

Perky pushed the females forward and shouted, "I dunno where you are, but you better get your ass out here, or what we do to these two ain't gonna be purty." He waited. Nothing stirred. "You by the wagon, I seen your legs. C'mon out." He squatted to check and the legs were gone. "Gahdamn it, where are they?"

"Let's shoot these bitches and get the hell outta here," Mousey said. "This place is spookin' me."

"Somebody's aroun' here someplace, gahdamn it, and I ain't givin' these two up till I find 'em. Let's take a look at that wagon."

As their feet crunched on the dry grass, Bobby hunkered down lower among the sacks of grain. He had his musket ready. They were getting closer, but where were Frankie and Eddie?

Suddenly Frankie leaped into the open from behind the wash house and yelled, "Duck, Mama." Both of the intruders turned away from the wagon toward Frankie's voice. At the same moment, Mary Ann pulled away and grabbed her knife, jabbing it into Perkys' thigh. Sissy dove to the ground as

Mousey raised his musket to fire at Frankie, but Bobby was quicker. He rose from the wagon and shot Mousey through the head. The sudden explosion and the stabbing pain stunned Perky for a moment. He knocked Mary Ann away and turned to shoot Bobby, but he also was too slow. Both Frankie and Eddie fired, killing him instantly.

Frankie raced across the yard to check the other two. Poke was dead, his skull caved in. Bro was alive but still unconscious, so they tied him up and left him beside the house.

Then Frankie joined his family. Mary Ann was holding Sissy, and both were sobbing. "They, they were goin' to kill us, Frankie," Mary Ann stammered. "They were going to do awful things to Sissy. Where do such beasts come from?"

"Are they all dead?" Sissy asked. Her face and dress were speckled with blood.

"All but one, and he's tied up." Frankie hugged them both for a time while Eddie and Bobby stood nearby. They were all shaking from the terror they had escaped.

"Bobby and Eddie, I don't know how we can ever thank you," Frankie said. "You saved our lives."

"It was you who figgered out what to do," Bobby said.

"You're my family too," Eddie said. "I'd never forgive myself if anything bad had happened to you."

They stood a while longer trying to calm themselves. "Mama," Frankie said after a while, "take Sissy into the house and let her get cleaned up. She's got blood all over her, and she's had an awful fright. I reckon we all have. Eddie, could you take one of our horses and ride over and ask your mom to come over and stay a spell. Bobby and me will have to tie these four on their horses and take 'em to brigade headquarters and see what's to be done with 'em."

The shock of the killings stayed with the Fraleys for months. Frankie was unable to sleep, and Sissy had nightmares. Mary Ann read her Bible and quoted scripture to them.

It turned out the marauders were Reb deserters and not part of Mosby's regular troops. The sole survivor confessed they had raped and killed a woman near Burkittsville two days before their foray to the Fraley farm.

After a brief military trial, he was hung without fanfare.

Mary Ann, Sissy and the three young guardsmen became local celebrities, but none of them had much stomach for heroism. Desperate, close up killing was too ghastly to feel good about.

CHAPTER X. 1865

As 1864 drew to a close, the war seemed to have reached a stalemate, and the Confederates focused on the Union's November election. Hood had replaced Johnston in Georgia and launched an offensive against Sherman. If that succeeded, and Grant and Sheridan could be held at bay, then Lincoln would lose the election, the Democratic peace party would take power, and the South would be saved.

It didn't happen. Sherman smashed Hood's forces and captured Atlanta. Sheridan continued to press up the Shenandoah, destroying crops and burning barns as he advanced, and Grant held an iron grip on Lee in Virginia. Lincoln's popularity soared, and he was re-elected handily.

Winter approached with the grim realization for Richard that the situation was desperate. He was a colonel with barely half a battalion of ill clad, half starved troopers. They rode the lines and did their duty, but had to spend much of their time foraging for their horses. Farmers resisted giving up what remained of their crops for worthless scrip. Everyone, soldier and civilian, was hungry and desperate.

In February, Lee sent Hampton with part of the cavalry south toward Joe Johnston's ragged army, hastily assembled to make a stand against Sherman in the Carolinas. Horine's battalion remained with Fitz Lee to guard the rail lines and cover the over extended Confederate flanks as Spring approached and the armies prepared for action.

At Waynesboro in March, Sheridan destroyed the last remnants of Early's once stalwart army and rejoined Grant for the final push against Lee. Matthews and his regiment, including his company of Marylanders, were back with the Army of the Potomac for the first time since Gettysburg.

After a futile attack by Lee's men in late March, the Union army took the offensive and broke through the Rebel lines in early April. As Lee's defenses collapsed, A. P. Hill was killed and the Union assault became unstoppable. Richmond was lost. The last Confederate train departed the capitol with Jeff Davis and what remained of the government, heading southwest, hoping Lee and Johnston could join together and continue the war.

Sheridan's cavalry and infantry units overran Confederate positions throughout the day. Horine's men suffered more casualties, protecting the flanks of Lee's desperate, retreating army.

That evening Richard gathered his troopers and realized he was back to company size, half Marylanders. They were gaunt men, weary and homesick, some without mounts, the rest with horses staggering from exertion and inadequate rations. Still they persevered. Perhaps Marse Robert could come up with one more miracle.

2

On the Fraley farm, the Spring of 1865 was the earliest and kindest in years. In late March daffodils flooded the meadows with yellow, and a week later, bluebells began to paint the hillside above the stream. Robins and bluebirds arrived early, and the woods and fence rows burst with activity as every variety of plant and animal responded to the mild weather punctuated by rain showers.

Frankie caught up on his plowing. The earth turned over easily, with just the proper amount of moisture. They had acquired a young bull and two heifers to add to their herd, and the animals were content, with plenty of pasture and none of the usual problems of strays and broken fences.

Mary Ann's hens were thriving, with several nests each hatching out a dozen or more chicks. Frankie had trapped a troublesome raccoon and two skunks, and the hound had killed a possum. Two of last year's heifers were due to calve any day.

Frankie had a girlfriend, Margaret Ann Hargett, sister of a Maryland soldier wounded at Second Bull Run. Bobby Matthews was a regular visitor. He was sweet on Sissy, who had turned a pretty seventeen.

They've grown, Mary Ann thought, soon be married. The war was fading away in her mind. Early's army was destroyed. Sherman was in the Carolinas. Lucy Matthews told her in church the previous Sunday that Hiram and his men were with Grant.

On April 10, they learned that Lee had surrendered at a place west of Richmond called Appomattox Courthouse. The sexton rang the church bell, and people congregated at the church and around Holter's store to share the news and wonder that it was really over. Frankie and his friends went to Frederick where the guard celebrated and the church bells chimed for hours.

3

A day earlier Richard led a limping Prince along a dusty road thirty miles west of Richmond. He had still fewer men now, for a dozen had been unable to keep up without mounts, and they probably had deserted or been captured. Those remaining felt desolate, for to Richard and his men they seemed to be the only Confederate cavalry left in Virginia.

To the east, guns were booming again. One of his men reported, "Pickett's ahead. Longstreet and Gordon a ways beyond." A few of us left, Richard thought. Ewell and his Richmond defenders already had been trapped and forced to surrender.

They limped along another mile, leading their horses. Richard found Pickett sitting by an ash tree. He waited for the general to acknowledge him, but Pickett remained silent.

"Sir," Richard said.

"I see you, Colonel, ain't got nothin' to say. Marse Robert relieved me a few days ago. I'm on parole because I stopped for a fish fry."

Richard sat down. He'd heard Pickett was still bitter over Gettysburg. The general shifted his position and removed his hat. "Longstreet's with Lee now," he said, "trying to decide if it's time to surrender."

"Has it come to that?"

"This army's done for. Look at us, nothin' but half starved scarecrows, Grant and Meade all around us, Sheridan up ahead. We got nowhere to go, except to hell or surrender."

"We can join Johnston, get to the mountains. We can still fight."

Pickett looked away for a moment and then turned back. "Colonel," he said, "we lost our chance at Gettysburg. I had the best damn division in this army, or any army for that matter, and that old man threw them away in a mad charge up a hill against an entrenched enemy twice our size." He picked up a twig and tossed it away. "And everyone thinks he's a great hero. We're fought out. We got nothin' left. It's time to go home."

Richard was stunned by Pickett's bitterness. He worked his way back toward his men, tears streaking his cheeks. Everyone was awaiting news, but he needed to avoid human contact, so he led Prince to a quiet spot by a small roadside cemetery where he could rest and come to grips with what was occurring. He watched the horse graze, and after some time, he arose and listened intently. For the first time in years it seemed, the gunfire had stopped. He could hear birds singing in the quiet.

When he returned to his men, they knew. They clustered around him, seeking reassurance. "You know as much as I do," he said. "We're surrounded, and I reckon Marse Robert is asking terms."

"They'll treat us like dirt," Granny Coleman said.

"We'll have to wait and see," Richard said.

They curried their horses and tended the animals' saddle sores. "It don't mean nothin'," they told each other. "Damn Yanks will take 'em anyhow."

They learned later that Lee would meet with Grant in the morning for final arrangements, so they slept restlessly. The next day, they still waited, then slowly formed their lines, anticipating Lee's return. Richard stood at the head of the line, brushing his hand along Prince's mane and praying they would be able to stay together. "You're the last one, boy," he said, "the last of Papa's horses."

In the distance they observed what appeared to be Union officers saluting Lee. They heard Yank soldiers start to cheer but then the cheering died down. Suddenly there was Lee himself, approaching in dress uniform, riding slowly by his men. Troops crowded forward to touch him, to stroke Traveler, jostling one another for a last contact.

Battle weary veterans wept. Had he ordered it, most would have followed Lee to their death in one final cataclysm, but he said, "Enough, we shall die no more. The war is done." Over and over he repeated to his men, "My fault, you are the best soldiers any man ever had."

Richard stood quietly by Prince and came to attention as Lee approached. His salute was one of hundreds that Lee returned. He could hardly bear the moment, images clouded his mind, Claib and Jacob proudly wearing their new uniforms, Stuart waving his plumed hat, so many glorious victories, and yet they lost. All the valor, the sacrifice, so many dead, for naught. He knew his grief could never end.

The terms of their parole stunned the Confederates. They could keep their horses. Officers could keep their sidearms. The Yanks would furnish rations to replenish their knapsacks, and they could go home. The best news was that Lee also was paroled and free to go. He would not be imprisoned.

4

In a field near the river, Matthews stood with his regiment and watched the tattered remnants of Lee's once great army stack their weapons. Supply wagons were being rolled to the Reb camps to hand out rations. Lee had passed his last review the day before, and Gordon and Chamberlain were managing the formal surrender. Grant and Meade had departed, but Sheridan had ridden by and chatted briefly.

Matthews, Fisher and Angleberger strolled up the road and leaned on a rail fence watching a line of Rebs getting their rations. "Where you men from?" Matthews asked.

Most of the Rebs looked at him blankly. A gray bearded sergeant volunteered, "No'th Carolina mostly. Some of these boys is from Virginny. How 'bout y'all?"

"We're Marylanders, but some of my boys is from West Virginia. You boys been in all the big fights?"

"Bout all of 'em," the sergeant replied, "missed the First Manassas, weren't signed up yet, missed Freddy'burg, you Yanks shot me up some over at Sharpsburg. Was y'all in 'em?"

"Mostly, Second Bull Run, Antietam, Fredericksburg, Gettysburg. Then we fought some over in West Virginia and against ol' Jube and his boys outside Washington and in the Valley."

"Wounded?"

"Just once that was bad, nipped a few other times."

"Y'all hit me twice." He collected his grub in a tattered knapsack and filled his canteen. He waited for his comrades and then started to move away, but he hesitated a moment and spat. He looked back at the Marylanders and shrugged. "Well, Yank, thanks for the vittles. We beat y'all plenty of times, but I reckon it's the last 'un that counts."

"Good luck to you, Johnny. You goin' back to farmin'?"

"Yup. You too?"

"Yeah, can't wait to get home and plant the corn."

"I allus growed cotton, but I dunno if it'll sell now, the way things are. Mebbe I better grow me some corn, sumpin'

273

me and my family can eat." He shouldered his sack and strolled rapidly down the road to catch his comrades.

They watched as more Rebs drew their rations and moved on. They were a tired, ragged, shoeless bunch, but they stood straight and refused to act defeated.

"It's a helluva thing, Hi," Fisher said.

"What is?"

"Them Rebs, if we'd been neighbors, they'd been friends. They ain't much different from us."

They walked back to where the division was gathered, making preparations to move. Crooks was seated at a folding table working on a report. "What next?" Matthews asked.

"Depends on whether Johnston keeps fighting down in Carolina or gives it up. If he surrenders, we'll be heading for Washington and a big parade."

5

In a tavern near Upper Marlboro, Kilgour, Merryman, and Johns met with John Wilkes Booth and a Baltimore policeman name Rhodes. "It's all settled then," Johns said, "you have the money you need and you and your group will assassinate them all. Rhodes will contact you as soon as we know where he's going, and I'll make sure the guards are not a problem."

The four men arose and shook hands. Booth, highly excited and barely rational, made his way to the door and departed.

"Can we trust him?" Kilgour asked.

Johns smiled. "Oh yes, he'll kill Lincoln," he said. "He's just sane enough to do the job, but I don't know anything about the others."

"What about afterward?" Merryman said. "Doesn't he pose a danger for us?"

"Yes, he might, but I'll arrange to see he's not taken alive."

6

One by one, the cavalry departed. Fitz Lee watched and saluted the men as they rode out. Richard shook hands with each of his troopers. A few were headed south, one as far as Texas, others had only a short ride to ruined farms and burned out homes in Virginia. Richard and a dozen veterans would begin their ride home to Maryland the next day. Granny Coleman and a few others had already left.

Richard stroked Prince's flank after a cold but ample meal of Yank rations. The nearby pasture still had some decent graze and he had foraged a handful of carrots. "We made it, ol' boy," he said to the horse. "You and I are survivors. Pa will be pleased to have you back, maybe start a new herd." The black stallion swished his tail while he chomped on a carrot. His saddle sores and two battle lacerations still rankled but were mending.

The next day the Marylanders began their odyssey. From Appomattox they followed back roads to the northeast. The going was slow since they wanted to avoid Yank units and the inevitable problems of such encounters. Union combat troops were decent, but not all the rear echelons had gotten word of Grant's surrender terms and subjected homebound Rebs to considerable harassment.

The second morning Richard approached Mason Wise's farm, where he planned to see his relatives and then visit Cathy before going home for a few weeks. It had been nine dismal months since he left to return to the war. His spirits rose when he spotted the house, but as he drew near, his heart sank. The lawns and gardens were ruined, looking like a barnyard. The tall pecan trees had been cut down and some of the outbuildings were gone.

"Yanks sure been here," a trooper said.

"What a mess," Richard said. "This was a beautiful place." He dismounted and went to the front door. He saw someone peek from a window, but whoever it was ducked away. He knocked but there was no answer. He knocked louder.

"Go away," a frightened voice said.

"It's Richard Horine," he called. "I came to see my Aunt Grace and Uncle Mason Wise."

The door opened a crack. "Richard?"

"Aunt Gracie?"

"Richard, oh my poor boy, you're alive. I thought all you boys were dead with your poor father." The frail woman, looking years older, stepped outside, blinking in the morning sun.

Richard stood frozen. "Papa's dead?" he said.

"Oh dear, you didn't know. How could you? I'm so sorry. He died months ago. I heard from your sister, Rebecca, that he was dead, along with our dear, sweet Claiborne and Jacob. So many have been killed, I decided you must be gone too, what with all the killing and Lee having to surrender." She began to sob. "Grant and his butchers have killed everything." She fell into Richard's arms.

"What happened here?" he asked.

"They used our place as their headquarters for months after you left, made the front rooms into a hospital. When they came, Mason tried to get word to Hampton, but they shot him."

"The Yanks shot Uncle Mace?"

"Right out there by the end of the lane. He was trying to pass over to our lines in the middle of the night. I begged him not to go, but there was no stopping Mace once he made up his mind to do a thing. The boy that was on guard shot him right through the head."

"Papa and Uncle Mace both gone, and they weren't even in the war."

"We were all in the war, Richard."

For a moment she stared at her nephew. "Cathy's gone too, Richard. Lord knows where. Sheridan burned down the Livingstone house and they tried to live in one of the slave huts, but both girls came down with the fever. Letitia died and I helped bury her, poor thing. I don't think she ever got over Claiborne being killed. Cathy almost died too, but she fought it off. She said she'd promised she'd wait for you, and she refused to die. I wanted them to come live with us, but the Yanks had shot Mace, and they were using up all our space, and all our darkies ran off, and..." She broke down, weeping

Richard held her tightly until she recovered. At his signal, his men took the horses and went to the barn to seek water and pasture.

"I'm sorry, honey," she said, "I'm such a mess, and you, poor boy, you look so tired and thin, and you didn't even know your father was dead. Poor Benjamin, he had such dreams for the South." She sobbed quietly for a minute and then collected herself. "The Livingstones have family in Nashville, so I think that's where they must have gone. Neither Cathy nor her dad were well, so I don't know how they managed, but she was waiting for you, still is, far as I know."

The three Wise daughters had heard their mother's voice and ventured down the stairs to investigate. They squealed with delight when they recognized Richard. They embraced their idol and wept to see him alive. The troopers returned and shared their rations with the family, whose only food was from the garden and the woods. All their livestock had been slaughtered by the armies.

"I wish I could stay and help," Richard said.

"No, you must go on. Your mother needs you, what with five children to raise and a farm without a man. We'll manage somehow, now that the war is over. I still have friends. I just hope and pray the Yanks will go back north and leave us alone."

"I'll go on home, Aunt Gracie, but I won't stay. Once things are settled with Mama and the children, I have to come back. You understand, don't you? I must find Cathy. I cannot face life until I find her or know she's lost forever. I don't know how long it'll take, but I'll be back, count on it."

Grace Wise started to question her nephew, but when she looked into his eyes, she saw absolute determination. "Yes, Richard," she said, "I do understand."

Next morning found the Marylanders back on the road. Richard rode to the Spotsylvania battleground and sought the place where Claib had died. He urged his companions to go ahead without him, and two others departed. It took an hour to locate the area and find the marker placed nearly a year before. A poignant sign said simply: "final Resting Place of 500 men of Virginia Regiments CSA 1864 RIP." Richard knelt beside the marker and said a silent prayer while he shed more tears. "Goodbye, Claib," he whispered, "God be with you."

They bypassed Fredericksburg and went cross country to the Manassas battlefield. Richard rode to the knoll where he had laid Jacob to rest. The markers had still been there in the second battle in 1862, but now there was no sign or marker for Jacob or any of the dozens who were buried on the hillside. His inquiry at a nearby house was met by shrugs. Northern speculators had bought the battlefield property and planned to charge admission. Angry and frustrated, Richard gave up the search. The men who remained with him were equally disturbed. All had friends buried there from the battles.

They rode on, taking a familiar route, north toward Leesburg, ford the Potomac, bypass Poolesville, and keep to the high ground. They slept off the road during the day and traveled at night, following roads and trails lit by moonlight.

When they crossed the river, the surroundings changed. Despite three major campaigns and repetitive raids, Maryland was spared the devastation that afflicted Virginia. A few miles after the crossing, they came to a point where they would go separate ways. After another emotional farewell, Richard headed upriver to Shanks Duval's family farm near Petersville.

Shanks' father met Richard by a rundown barn. "We heard he was gone from the Coleman boy when he come by a few days ago," the gaunt farmer said. "Reckon you and Granny is the only Rebs that come back to these here parts."

"He was a brave soldier and a good friend," Richard said. "Lost him and my two brothers, and General Stuart, and my father died while I was gone. I wanted you to know what a fine cavalryman he was and how much I valued him as a companion."

"Much obliged to you, I reckon. I never had much use for the war. Never had no slaves, didn't care much one way or the other about the Union. We've always been dirt farmers, me and my family. It seemed such a dang waste to us, killin' all them boys."

Richard saluted, the Duvals nodded, and watched him till he was out of sight. The rest of his companions were gone, to Bladensburg, Westminister, and Annapolis, so he turned east toward the Ballenger Creek and home.

Richard's arrival at the farm was marked by Timmy and Betsy, now 12 and 10, who were picking berries in the meadow when the horseman appeared. "It's Richard," Timmy shouted as he dropped his bucket and ran toward him. "He's riding Prince." He still remembered the handsome black stallion.

Betsy stood entranced for a moment, but then she too ran to the gray figure. The Horine's new puppy bounced along with the children, yapping excitedly.

Richard leaped to the ground and hugged them both. "Papa died last summer," Timmy reported, "but we've all pitched in and helped with the work. Jeremiah and Tillie are free, but they still work for us. This is our new puppy. His name is Rascal."

"It so good to see you and you've grown so big," Richard said. He glanced around and saw the farm was in good condition. "How's Mama?" he asked.

"She's good, but Rebecca helps her a lot," Timmy replied. "What happened to your face?"

"Mama still cries a lot," Betsy added. "She thinks you're dead too."

"Get your berries and I'll ride you home," Richard said. "I have a scar on my face because I was cut pretty bad by a Yankee shell."

"Wow," Timmy said with a grimace, "it must have hurt awful."

At the barnyard gate, Timmy and Betsy leaped down and ran to the house, shouting their news. In moments they all appeared--Jennifer, now 15, Grace, 13, Rebecca, at 18 a mature, attractive stranger, and finally, their mother, Elsie, to welcome home her one adult male survivor of the war.

They stood together for a long time, saying little, simply holding one another. "I saw Aunt Grace," Richard said to his mother. "She told me Papa was gone. Uncle Mace too, shot by the Yanks on his own farm."

"Dear God, so many gone, Richard," Elsie said. "Only you left. It was your father's war, never mine. I didn't want you to go, but I was never asked. First Jacob, then Claiborne, then Benjamin. The Lord's will. I couldn't have survived without the other children. Rebecca has had to be a woman before her time. And we have no friends--all because of this awful war."

"It's over now, Mama, and Richard's back," Rebecca said. "We're so happy to have you home, and we know from Aunt Grace's letter how bad you were hurt. Tillie is fixing us something to eat, and you look famished."

"Sister," Richard said, "you're wonderful."

They walked to the house together once Richard had removed Prince's saddle, led him into an empty stable, and fed him some grain. At the door, Jeremiah and Tillie greeted him. "Welcome home, Mistah Richard," Jeremiah said.

"Thank you, Jeremiah. It's good to be home. I'm glad you're free."

The Africans relaxed, relieved that Richard accepted their new status. "C'mon in," Tillie called. "We got chicken, potatoes, fresh peas, snap beans, biscuits, and some nice cherry pies Miss Rebecca baked."

After the meal, Richard asked for his old clothes. He

looked into a mirror at his face, grimacing at the scars and the unruly beard, the sallow cheeks and weary eyes. He removed his uniform and bathed his thin body with the bowl of hot water his mother brought him. Then he used a straight edge razor and soap to shave and trim his mustache, and finally, he put on his farm work clothes, items from a forgotten past. They fit loosely, but felt soft and comfortable.

He folded the soiled uniform for laundering and storage. Well, he thought, as he glanced in the mirror again, the Maryland cavalry unit of the Army of Northern Virginia is no more.

7

Five days after Lee surrendered, John Wilkes Booth assassinated Abraham Lincoln. Others in his band failed in their efforts to slay Vice President Johnson and Secretary of State Seward.

Booth escaped over a preplanned route into southern Maryland. Eleven days later, the assassin was cornered in a barn in Virginia, across the Potomac from Maryland. There he was shot and killed by a Federal soldier named Boston Corbett.

At the end of the war, only five of the original Maryland plotters were alive. Turner was killed in the war. Horine was dead. Varley had succumbed to a variety of ailments. Kilgour was a despondent recluse. Merryman, Brown, Johns, and Hatcher were stunned that the death of Lincoln did nothing to change the war's outcome. The rebellion was finished soon after Lee surrendered, and slavery was ended. They returned to their homes and occupations and never met again as a group.

8

The government organized the greatest parade in the nation's history, a full two days to honor the victorious armies. Sam Zimmerman provided two carriages to travel to the event, carrying his family, the three Fraleys, and the

Matthews family. Oscar Fisher carried his family plus Ed Holter and Squire Fulmer. They were part of a long procession from the Mt. Nebo area. They brought picnic baskets and made arrangements to stay overnight at an inn near Rockville.

The first day the Army of the Potomac marched, Meade riding to the reviewing stand where the President, Grant, Stanton and the rest of the cabinet and dignitaries were seated. This was the final hoorah for the men who fought Lee and his army for four agonizing and frustrating years and finally won. They marched in perfect formation, bands playing martial music, drums beating lustily. Artillery rumbled by and regimental flags fluttered in the breeze. Thousands of black soldiers marched with the army, veterans of the past year's bloody battles.

The Marylanders marched with Crooks' division, saluting their friends and families as they marched up the avenue, a moment to be treasured.

The second day belonged to the westerners, Sherman's rugged, victorious troops. They had captured the heartland of the south from Vicksburg to Chattanooga, from Atlanta to the sea. Their formations were unexpectedly orderly, and their good behavior surprised both Grant and Sherman. For hours these veterans streamed by, then it was over, the crowds dissolving.

Sam and his passengers walked to the carriages. "It was all so grand," Mary Ann said. "It made me think of Johnny, but I wouldn't have missed it for the world."

Afterwards Crooks led his division back to their camp outside the city. They would soon begin the mustering out process. The next day Hiram walked among his men, giving them directions and answering questions. Pay was collected. Belongings packed. Tents were struck and weapons stacked. Train schedules were checked.

The men stared at one another. It was time to go, and they hardly knew what to say. They knew they were survivors of something colossal, something bigger than simply their victory or the avoidance of death. They had been together so long, and who would ever know what it had been like, how they had felt, what they had done?

Matthews made the rounds. "I'll never forget you," he told them. "You're the best soldiers in the world." His voice choked, he could say no more, so he shook hands with every man he could find.

The men murmured their thanks, many with glistening eyes. "God bless you, Colonel," some said. Others said simply, "You brought us through."

To his Marylanders, his old company, now led by Fisher, he said, "Nothing in the war ever made me so happy as having you men under my command. With you I never had anything but bravery and faithfulness to duty. Our dead comrades can rest easy because of what you did in their name."

Later, Hiram mounted his chestnut mare, Maude, took off his broad brimmed blue hat and waved it above his head. "And now," he shouted, "by the grace of God, we're going home."

The company erupted with cheers.

9

On a hot, sunny day in early June, 1865, two lone horsemen approached one another on the Jefferson Pike. One, clad in baggy work clothes, had worn the gray of the fallen Confederacy. His mustache was trimmed and he had regained some of his weight from generous farm meals, but a thick scar remained across his nose and cheek, and his eyes still reflected the bitterness of defeat and loss. He rode a handsome black stallion named Prince, last of the Horine cavalry horses.

The other was dressed as a farmer, but his trousers were government issue blue. His wounds still bothered him, but he reckoned that would pass. He rode his mare, Maude, who had missed the first three years of the war, but had been with him since he returned to duty after being wounded in 1864.

The two stopped and eyed each other cautiously. The older man, Hiram Matthews, spoke first. "You're Richard Horine, aren't you? Changed some since we were in the militia."

"Hello, Hiram. Yes, I got home a few weeks ago."

"I heard about your brothers and your father. I'm sorry."

"It's the way war works, I reckon. We lost."

"Lot of boys from around here dead on our side too. Their families don't feel like they won much."

"I know. John Fraley and me were good friends. I hear he got killed at Sharpsburg."

"Yeah, John got shot down at the lower bridge. We call it Antietam."

"Were you at Gettysburg?"

"Yep. Some of your Rebs nipped me there too."

"We should have whipped you there."

Hiram leaned forward, ready to argue, but thought better of it and leaned back. "It was a near thing," he said. "You had fine generals."

"So many of them killed, Stuart, Hill, Jackson."

"I know. We lost our share, Sedgwick, Reynolds, Reno. Those were the ones I remember, but there were others, and all the thousands of ordinary folks like us shot down." He sighed. "What are your plans? Going back to raising horses?"

"No. I'm going west. I can't stay around here."

"Doesn't your mother need you to help run the farm?"

"She wants me to stay, but I can't, not after all that's happened--two brothers dead, our barn burnt, horses killed, Papa dying because of it." He looked away for a moment, then changed the subject. "Mama needs to sell some of the land. It's too much for her with only Jeremiah to do the work and having to pay him now that he's free. Do you know anyone who might be interested?"

"I'd like to make an offer on the forty acre piece back by the little woods. She set a price?"

"I'll talk with her, and she and my sister will come up with something. My sister handles most of the business. She's real grown up." Richard stared at Matthews, dozens of questions flashing across his mind, but he let it go. They were talking almost as if the war had never happened. "Much obliged," he said. "I still remember my time in the militia," he grinned slightly, "when we were on the same side." He tightened up on Prince's reins. "So long, I don't expect to be around here much longer."

Hiram watched him go, riding that magnificent black horse, a colonel in Stuart's command, once the most famous cavalry in the world, but now another lost soul from the lost cause of the South. In a way, it was almost as if it had never happened. Except there were his scars and the memories and the men lost, and there was the harsh scar across Horine's face and nose, and his cold eyes speaking a lingering anger at defeat.

He'd been home only a few weeks, but Matthews was happy, using back pay for new livestock and land. So was Al Fisher, taking over for his father, and already calling on Mary Elizabeth Stone. Pete Angleberger had joined his father in the carpenter trade.

The problem, they were learning, was dealing with the memories of the hell the war had been. The fear almost left during the day, but at night it sometimes became unbearable. The dreams came and they were back amidst the horror that should be over, but wasn't, not in their minds. Matthews knew everything had changed because of the war, yet so much seemed the same, just, he told himself, don't ask me to explain it. His spirits would sag and his body would ache, but then he'd see Lucy and she'd give him a smile and a kiss, and he knew he'd never really been away.

10

Rebecca turned when she heard her brother coming up the lane, back from his visit to the Kings. She was standing by the barn, watching Jeremiah, with the help of a hired colored man and her little brother, Timmy, finish putting the last wooden shingles on the roof. It was nearly three years since the burning, and now the new barn was nearly complete.

Richard dismounted Prince and walked over beside her. "It looks good, Sis. Too bad we don't have more horses to put in it."

"We will, I know we will, it'd be so much easier if you'd stay."

"I can't stay here, Rebecca, you know that. I hate these people, and they hate me. They are traitors to the South, and they killed our father because he tried to help our cause. I can't forget that, and I can't forget Claib and Jacob."

"They don't all hate us."

"I suppose you're right. I ran into Matthews on the road, and he was decent enough for a Yank officer. He might be interested in some of our land if you'll give him a price. But that doesn't take away four years of fighting. Besides, there's the way Mama feels. She still blames me and Papa for losing Jacob and Claib. I must get away, find someplace to make a new start."

Jeremiah had climbed down the ladder and listened to the conversation. He liked Richard well enough, but he wondered what would have happened if his army had won. He'd probably still be a slave, so he wouldn't fret if Richard left.

Jeremiah's children would go to school in September, but it would be to a colored school in Frederick, not the nearby one room schoolhouse across from Holter's store. "It don't seem right," Tillie said, "them havin' to walk all that way while white chillun goes a short way."

"Tain't right," Jeremiah had agreed, "but what we gwine do. It's a start, I reckon."

The Horines were aware of the Africans' concern, but could not help. They could no longer afford private education, so Timmy and Betsy would have to go to the nearby public school, and the older girls would receive nothing further.

"You go ahead and tend the animals," Rebecca said to Jeremiah. "I'll stay and make sure Timmy and the hired man clean up. Where will you go?" she asked Richard.

"As far from the war as I can get. King says California might be a good spot."

"Mama will get over the hurt of Jacob and Claiborne, and stop blaming you. She's already told me she's sorry for some of the things she said."

"I wish that were true, but I don't think she'll ever feel the same about me. Too much has happened, too many things have been said."

Richard never told his family how deeply he felt about Cathy. They knew something about the relationship from Grace Wise's letter when he was wounded, but he ducked their inquiries when he got home, explaining simply that she had vanished and he had not heard from her. In his mind, he vowed to find her. He would return to Virginia, to Aunt Gracie and her daughters, back to the Livingstone's destroyed home. Someone would know where she went, and he would follow wherever it took him, to Nashville, to the end of the earth if necessary, for nothing had any meaning without her.

Two days later he packed his saddle bags with a few clothes, his revolvers, a canteen and a supply of food. He accepted his share of his father's inheritance, after Rebecca' repeated insistence. He saddled Prince and was ready.

Elsie hugged him. "I shouldn't have blamed you so much," she said. "You and your father was so strong and I was so weak. God be with you, Richard. All my boys gone but Timmy." She burst into tears. Richard hugged and kissed his mother, his four sisters, and his brother, each in turn.

Then he was on Prince and riding toward the pike. They stood with tear-streaked eyes and watched him disappear to the west. "My poor lost boy," Elsie said. "I don't suppose

I'll every see him again. Oh, that hateful war." Rebecca took Elsie's hand and the six of them returned to their house.

11

At the store Peck Handley and Squire Fulmer rose to their feet when Hiram Matthews entered. Ed Holter rushed to meet him. "Good to see you, Hiram, you look fit in them farm clothes."

"Yeah, home a week, and it seems almost like I never been gone." His son, Bobby, followed him inside. "Those cows secure?" he asked.

"Tied tight."

"Bought us two more cows, got 'em tied to the wagon," Hiram explained. "Need some nails, and Lucy wants some flour."

"Your wound all healed?" Peck asked.

"Which one?" Matthews asked, chuckling. "Got hit four times, but only the one over in West Virginia did real damage. It's fine, but the nick I got at Gettysburg still acts up, splitting open and bleeding."

"Where'd they getcha at Gettysburg?" the Squire asked.

Hiram pulled open his shirt, revealing a red gash. "Right across the dang belly. Shoulda been skinnier." They all laughed.

"Horine is gone," Holter said.

"Gone. Gone where?" Peck wanted to know.

"West, that's all I know," Holter replied. "His sister was in here yesterday and that's all she said."

"I'm glad he's gone," Peck said. "They got what was comin' to 'em, damn traitors."

Hiram sat and removed his hat. "I reckon they felt they were right, Peck, same as you and me. They sure fought us hard. I think Grant did a good thing in lettin' the Rebs off easy. We can all get on with our lives."

"But think of all you suffered, Hi," Peck said, "all them boys gone or shot up like my boy. Then, dammit, some bastard Reb up and kills Lincoln--killed ol' Abe just when it was about over and done."

"Hatin' ain't gonna bring them back, Peck, or grow a new leg on your son. At first, we was shocked at what Grant did, but then we saw the Rebs and talked to 'em and thought about it, and we reckon Grant did the best thing, let 'em go, let's get on with livin'. What good would more revenge do?"

They sat quietly for a while till Matthews arose and stretched. "Peck, I'm like you though when it comes to ol' Abe. I cried when I heard he was shot. Only seen him that one time, there when we fought Jube Early outside Washington, but I liked him. All the boys felt like he believed in 'em. He was plain folks, like us." Holter, Handley, and the Squire all nodded in agreement. "C'mon, Bobby," Matthews said, as he picked up his supplies and paid Holter, "we gotta get them critters home."

"So long, Hi," Peck said. "Mebbe you're right. Mebbe we gotta learn how to get on with the Rebs. They lost."

"That's right," Matthews said. "You never seen a place so ruined as Virginia. They'll be forever tryin' to get those farms back to workin' again. We can afford to let 'em be."

Outside the store Matthews was surprised to see the Horine's colored man. "What are you doin' here?" he asked.

Jeremiah recognized the former Yank officer and lowered his head. "Buy sumpin' at the store, suh," he replied. Matthews shook his head and moved on.

Ed Holter came out of the store and called to the African. "You, Jeremiah, you here to buy for Miss Elsie?"

"No suh, for my ownself."

"Not here, boy. Go to the colored store in Frederick."

Jeremiah stared, bewildered. "I'se got good money, suh."

"Don't want your money. This here's a white folks' store. You go to Frederick."

The African turned away, stunned and angry.

Holter returned inside. "Imagine the Horine's nigger wantin' to buy here."

Peck Handley chuckled. "You set him straight, Holter," he said. "That boy's gotta learn his place."

The Squire agreed. "Just because they're free, they think they're as good as white people. You ever hear anything so crazy."

At home, Jeremiah paced up and down angrily. "What Marse Abraham set us free for? White people still treat us like trash. Gotta go to Frederick for school, for church, even for what we buy. It ain't right."

Tillie peeled potatoes, trying not to cry. "Have to do ever'thin' with our own people, I reckon, but it ain't fair. We talk to Miss Elsie and Miss Rebecca, mebbe dey help."

"Won't do no good. Dey's Rebs. Ah thought white folks on the Yank side would treat us right after dey won de war and Marse Abraham set us free, but dey ain't no diffrunt from de Rebs, treat us like dirt." Jeremiah and Tillie sat and stared as the sad reality of their situation pressed in upon them.

12

Two weeks later, Mary Ann stood by the barnyard gate and watched as Frankie lugged two pails of fresh milk toward her. "Got enough so we can churn some butter?" she asked.

"More'n enough. Those new heifers are doin' good. How about the chickens?"

"The pullets is beginnin' to lay. Their eggs are small, but they're good. You ready to eat? Sissy should have supper about done."

The war was over, Lincoln was dead, and the men who had lived through it were home. The home guard was disbanded. Hiram Matthews was hard at work on his neglected farm. Al Fisher had taken over for his aging father and there was talk that he and Mary Elizabeth would marry. Richard Horine had come home but then departed, perhaps for good.

Sissy still had nightmares occasionally about their encounter with the four marauders, but they weren't quite so bad as the weeks rolled by.

Johnny was gone nearly three years, and at Easter they covered his grave with daffodils and bluebells gathered from the meadow. In the evening, Mary Ann sometimes would sit rocking alone on the porch and remember him. Most nights a pair of whippoorwills would zoom across the darkening sky, and their calls always brought moisture to her eyes for they seemed to be singing his song of yearning, of a low valley and a soft wind blowing memories of the past.

A rider trotted up the farm lane. "Looks like Bobby," Frankie said. "Little early to come courtin'." Buster the hound, dozing on the porch, looked up but didn't bother to bark. He was feeling his age, and he knew the rider.

"You're early, Bobby," Mary Ann said. "We still ain't et."

"Well, yes'm," he explained, "I reckon so, but Sunday, ma'am, well, Sissy said I should come over for supper, what with Pa being home and workin' me pretty hard, I don't get that much time to see her, so I thought, well, I hope you don't mind."

Mary Ann smiled. "No, Bobby, we don't mind at all."

THE END